ARROW
OF THE
ALMIGHTY

BOOKS BY GILBERT MORRIS

THE HOUSE OF WINSLOW SERIES

1. *The Honorable Imposter*
2. *The Captive Bride*
3. *The Indentured Heart*
4. *The Gentle Rebel*
5. *The Saintly Buccaneer*
6. *The Holy Warrior*
7. *The Reluctant Bridegroom*
8. *The Last Confederate*
9. *The Dixie Widow*
10. *The Wounded Yankee*
11. *The Union Belle*
12. *The Final Adversary*
13. *The Crossed Sabres*
14. *The Valiant Gunman*
15. *The Gallant Outlaw*
16. *The Jeweled Spur*
17. *The Yukon Queen*
18. *The Rough Rider*
19. *The Iron Lady*
20. *The Silver Star*

THE LIBERTY BELL

1. *Sound the Trumpet*
2. *Song in a Strange Land*
3. *Tread Upon the Lion*
4. *Arrow of the Almighty*

CHENEY DUVALL, M.D.
(with Lynn Morris)

1. *The Stars for a Light*
2. *Shadow of the Mountains*
3. *A City Not Forsaken*
4. *Toward the Sunrising*
5. *Secret Place of Thunder*
6. *In the Twilight, in the Evening*

THE SPIRIT OF APPALACHIA
(with Aaron McCarver)

1. *Over the Misty Mountains*
2. *Beyond the Quiet Hills*

TIME NAVIGATORS
(For Young Teens)

1. *Dangerous Voyage*
2. *Vanishing Clues*
3. *Race Against Time*

9704

ARROW
OF THE
ALMIGHTY

GILBERT
MORRIS

BETHANY HOUSE PUBLISHERS
MINNEAPOLIS, MINNESOTA 55438

Published by Bethany House Publishers
A Ministry of Bethany Fellowship, Inc.
11300 Hampshire Avenue South
Minneapolis, Minnesota 55438

Printed in the United States of America.

Library of Congress Cataloging-in-Publication Data

Morris, Gilbert.
    Arrow of the almighty / Gilbert Morris.
       p.   cm. — (The liberty bell ; bk. 4)
    ISBN 1–55661–568–X
    I. Title. II. Series: Morris, Gilbert. Liberty Bell ; bk. 4.
PS3563.O8742A89   1997
813'.54—dc21   97–21200
                                                    CIP

To Herman Sandford

Ever since the antediluvian days when I first set foot on the campus of Ouachita Baptist College, you and I were always The Odd Couple—so different in so many ways. I can recall some torrid arguments we had—but I remember quite vividly how you stood at my side when I most needed a friend.

As Bob Hope put it—thanks for the memory, Herman!

GILBERT MORRIS spent ten years as a pastor before becoming Professor of English at Ouachita Baptist University in Arkansas and earning a Ph.D. at the University of Arkansas. During the summers of 1984 and 1985, he did postgraduate work at the University of London. A prolific writer, he has had over 25 scholarly articles and 200 poems published in various periodicals, and over the past years has had more than 70 novels published. His family includes three grown children, and he and his wife live in Texas.

CONTENTS

PART FOUR
The Gathering of Eagles
Lafayette Joins Washington, Spring 1777

THE LIBERTY BELL

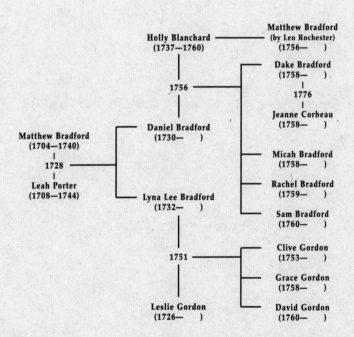

Matthew Bradford (1704—1740)
 1728
Leah Porter (1708—1744)

Daniel Bradford (1730—)

Holly Blanchard (1737—1760)
 1756

Matthew Bradford (by Leo Rochester) (1756—)

Dake Bradford (1758—)
 1776
Jeanne Corbeau (1758—)

Lyna Lee Bradford (1732—)

Micah Bradford (1758—)

Rachel Bradford (1759—)

Sam Bradford (1760—)

 1751

Leslie Gordon (1726—)

Clive Gordon (1753—)

Grace Gordon (1758—)

David Gordon (1760—)

PART ONE

THE DARKEST HOUR

Retreat From New York, November 1776

1

A Dress for Sarah

"SARAH, AREN'T YOU READY YET?"

The sound of her mother's voice caused Sarah Dennison to pull her shoulders together in a defensive motion. She was a petite young woman of twenty, but there was something much younger in her face—a vulnerability that contrasted almost violently with her mother's features. Sarah had been sitting on a carved walnut couch upholstered in a crimson silk damask, but now she rose nervously and twisted her fingers together, saying quickly, "I'm sorry, Mother."

Helen Dennison was a tall blond woman with cold blue eyes. She displayed an almost military attitude in all she did, and her back was stiff with displeasure as she looked down at her daughter. Shaking her head in exasperation, she said in an irritating voice, "I don't know what's wrong with you, Sarah! You haven't even started to get ready for the ball. Your hair's not even fixed properly. Where is Lucy?"

"I don't know, Mother."

"What good is a maid if you won't use her? That's what servants are for!"

"I . . . thought I could do it myself."

Helen Dennison snorted in derision. "Do it yourself! A daughter of mine doing her own hair!" Throwing up her hands in a gesture of despair, she stepped closer to her daughter, who looked at her with apprehension. Mrs. Dennison was six inches taller than Sarah and towered over her. For a moment she stood looking at her daughter, then shook her head with habitual distaste. It was a gesture she used when things did not go her way—which was not often, for Helen and her husband, Thomas, had enough money and a high enough position in Boston's society to ensure that their wishes were carried out more often than not.

Sarah stood helplessly watching as her mother walked to the door and called down the hall stridently, "Lucy, get yourself in here!"

13

A small maid with carrot red hair and an upturned nose scooted into the room breathlessly. "I'm sorry, Mrs. Dennison—"

"Never mind that! You're never where I need you! Now, fix Sarah's hair—and see you do it right, or it will be the worse for you!" Whirling toward the door, she left the room, and the sound of her footsteps echoed as she made her way down the large oak stairs.

Sarah sat quietly as Lucy quickly began to do her hair, only half listening to the maid's chatter. Sarah's hair was her best feature, golden blond, thick, and glossy with just a touch of red and just enough curl to make it cascade around her shoulders in a very attractive manner. The rest of her features were not particularly beautiful, but her complexion was exceptional—soft and flawless. She had an oval face, dark blue eyes, rather well shaped, and a small nose with a slight upturn, and a dimple on her right cheek when she smiled—which was not what she was doing now.

"My, you're going to have a fine time at the ball!" Lucy nodded vigorously, brushing Sarah's hair back from her face, pinning it in place, and then forming large cascading curls so that they fell down the middle of her back, intertwining pieces of white ribbon as she did so.

"No, I'm not!"

"Why do you say that, Miss Sarah? Of course you'll have a good time! There'll be music and dancing, bright lights, and plenty of officers in their dashing uniforms. Don't talk foolish." The small maid punched and poked at Sarah's hair, much as if she were fussing over a doll. Lucy was still chattering away in her pleasant Irish brogue when the door flew open and Mrs. Dennison entered. "I just finished, Mrs. Dennison," Lucy said, stepping away from the dressing table as her mistress approached. "Don't she look pretty now?"

Helen Dennison examined Sarah as one might examine a horse one was considering purchasing. "The hair looks very nice," she said. "Now, hurry and get your dress on, Sarah."

Lucy whirled and moved to the large oak chifferobe standing in the corner. Opening the door, she pulled out a dress and held it up. "Ain't this elegant!" she breathed as she came over and laid the dress on the bed. Lucy picked up a white linen chemise and slipped the loose-fitting garment over Sarah's head, then she helped Sarah don a pair of white silk pantalettes edged with pink lace and tied with white ribbon at the waist and just below the knees. Next came a white silk corset with whalebone stiffening, which Lucy pulled as tight as Sarah would let her, and then a pair of white silk stockings that attached to the pantalettes.

Dashing back to the chifferobe, Lucy picked out three tiered panniers, held each one for Sarah to step into, then tied each one around

Sarah's tiny waist. The final step in dressing Sarah was the elegant ball gown made of plum-colored silk with a square neckline edged in a light pink ruched detail. The bodice was tight fitting, front and back, and the sleeves ended just below the elbows in a tiered ruffle of plum and light pink. The plum-colored overskirt was held up at the sides and in the back with light pink bows, and the petticoat was made of an opalescent pink and plum fabric that shimmered in the light.

"Now, that is fine!" Lucy beamed.

"You may go now, Lucy," Helen Dennison said.

"Yes, ma'am." Lucy scooted out of the room like a startled rabbit, shutting the door nervously behind her. She had a healthy fear of Mrs. Dennison, who was not noted for her good temper or gentle manners. Most of the servants in the Dennison household felt the same way— and to be truthful, Sarah was only slightly less terrified of the master and the mistress than the servants themselves.

"There, that will do very well," Mrs. Dennison said, her mouth drawn tight but an expression of approval in her eyes. Then she added, "You'll never be able to wear clothes as well as Mary or Belinda. They had impeccable taste, and whatever they put on suited them."

"Yes, Mother."

As her mother straightened the material of the dress, Sarah wondered, *Am I going to have to hear another lecture about how wonderful my sisters are?* A slight flush touched her cheek at this rather uncharitable thought, but in truth she had endured many lectures about her two sisters. Mary, her older sister, and Belinda, two years younger than she, were both beautiful and accomplished. Sarah often thought they came from the womb knowing what to wear, how to look beautiful, and how to primly perform all the proper things required of a lady. For as long as Sarah could remember, she had heard statements from her mother such as, "Sarah, why can't you do your needlework as neatly as Belinda?" or, "If you would just put forth a little effort, you might learn something from the way Mary treats her eligible suitors when they come calling."

Such comments had cut deeply when Sarah was a child, and did so even now that she was a woman of twenty, the only unmarried daughter left in the Dennison household. She had learned, at least outwardly, to let the remarks pass by. Inwardly, however, she was still deeply insecure, and one mention of either of her sisters was enough to cause a cloud of despair to fall on her. But she knew better than to argue with her mother. No one *ever* won an argument with Mrs. Helen Dennison.

"Well, you're all ready. Mr. Potter will arrive shortly, and I want you to be especially nice to him. Understand?"

Sarah said the only thing possible. "I'll try my best, Mother."

"I don't know why you're so resistant to Mr. Potter. He's quite a catch."

Sarah almost said, "I don't want to catch a man," but she knew such a statement would only inflame her mother and drive her into another long speech about how a woman must entice a man. She had heard many lectures on the art of feminine wiles, not only from her mother but from her sisters as well. Belinda, her younger sister, had warned her constantly, "You've got to make men *want* you but not *have* you." Belinda had learned her lesson well and now was married to Byron Jennings, a wealthy Philadelphia merchant. Mary had done even better by marrying Claude Atkins, who owned large estates in England, where they now lived, rubbing elbows with English royalty.

"What's wrong with Mr. Potter?" her mother demanded.

Sarah flinched at her mother's persistent inquiry and dropped her eyes. "He's not—" she began, but then futility swept over her as she realized she could not possibly explain to her mother how Silas Potter, for all of his wealth, was not a man she would care to marry. Potter was thirty-five, tall and fat, with a demanding and pretentious personality. He had inherited a shipping business from his father and had invested in plantation lands in the Carolinas. If money were the only criterion, he was indeed a catch.

But in Sarah's opinion, he was a boorish oaf who drank excessively and, if the rumors were true, had been a womanizer for years. His first wife had died in childbirth, and now Potter, Sarah knew, was looking around for someone to raise his infant son and to manage his house. He was also looking for a woman of means who would bring a sizable dowry and inheritance into his hands. Sarah had known him long enough to understand that he would not make a good husband, but she could not explain this to her mother, who was blinded by his wealth.

The door opened and Lucy poked her head inside. "Mr. Potter has arrived."

"All right. Tell him we'll be right down," Mrs. Dennison said.

Sarah's heart began to beat faster, and she vainly wished she could run away and hide, but there was no hiding from her mother, or from Mr. Potter. Meekly she followed her mother out of the room and down the winding stairs. When they reached the bottom, she was greeted boisterously by Mr. Potter, who reached out, took her hand, and squeezed it, drawing her closer than she cared for.

"Why, you look very lovely, Miss Dennison."

"She does, doesn't she?" Mrs. Dennison beamed at Potter and then smiled roguishly. "You'll have to keep your rivals away, I'm afraid."

"Ho! I'm not afraid of that!" Potter laughed. He had a large, round, beefy face with large teeth that offended Sarah. He was wearing an expensively cut suit of brown velvet woven in a lattice design with black floral sprigs. The coat fell below his knees and had brass buttons on the sleeves and down the front. The waistcoat was buttoned to the neck, and the breeches were tight fitting and fastened below the knees with brass buttons. He had on a white linen shirt, white silk stockings, and black leather shoes with a silver buckle, but the fashionable clothes did very little to make him any more attractive. He still looked, for all the world, like a butcher putting on airs.

"Well, shall we go?"

"Yes . . ." Sarah said hesitantly, then walked outside the house.

Potter helped her up into the waiting carriage, and as soon as she was seated, he leaped in beside her. He moved closer, and she was trapped in a corner, unable to escape his attentions. As the carriage started up, he reached over and put his arm around her in a familiar gesture. "Now," he smiled, his large teeth gleaming in the lamplight that filtered through the window, "you and I'll have a fine time tonight. I'll dance every dance with you. Don't dance with anyone else, or I may have to call the fellow out."

Sarah could only try to smile and brace herself for an evening of pure misery.

When the carriage pulled up in front of the Horton mansion where the ball was being held, Potter leaped out at once, then reached back to assist Sarah as she stepped to the ground. He held her arm tightly, as if he were afraid she would fall, all the way up the massive steps. When they entered the house, they gave their coats to a pair of black servants wearing white wigs and bright blue livery. Potter leaned over and whispered hoarsely, "I never could stand the Hortons, but they do know how to put on a ball."

Moving into the ballroom, Sarah looked around quickly, noting the gleam of fashionable dresses in reds and blues and yellows, counterpointed by the uniformed officers. Most of the American army was fighting its way on a desperate retreat in New Jersey, but some of the staff were here in their buff uniforms with gleaming epaulets and brightly shining brass buttons.

"Come along! I love to dance!" Potter exclaimed as he grabbed her arm forcibly.

He might have loved to dance, but he was an abominable dancer, as Sarah soon discovered. Within five minutes, her toes were aching from being trodden on by Potter's massive, clumsy feet. She longed to excuse herself and sit and watch, which was what she usually did at dances, but Potter was insistent.

"No, Lieutenant, I'm sorry. Miss Dennison is taken." Potter laughed at the elderly lieutenant who had come to request a dance, then shook his head as he pulled Sarah toward the refreshment table. "We don't want any of those fellows, do we? You know, I can't imagine being a soldier."

"Don't you admire our men who are fighting to save our country?"

Potter shrugged his beefy shoulders. "It's a hopeless cause, my dear. Surely you know that."

"No, I don't know that." Sarah looked up and said more boldly than was her custom, "I have the greatest respect and admiration for General Washington and the loyal men under his command."

"Well, he won't have the command for long, Sarah." He looked intently at her and said, "I think I may call you by your first name now. After all, we're that close, aren't we?"

Sarah wanted to say no, but her timidity got the better of her. Instead, she said, "I'm afraid we disagree on this matter."

"Oh, I never talk politics with a woman. They're too pretty and tender for such things as blood and battle. Come now. The music's starting again."

For the next hour, Sarah endured the misery she had expected. The dances proceeded one after another, and several times she was approached by men who would have danced with her, but each time Potter blocked them rather rudely. The only comfort Sarah Dennison had to hang on to was that the dance, like all other things on earth, would eventually come to an end. During one brief respite between dances, she remembered a favorite reminder she liked to note in her journal whenever unpleasant things happened: "It will pass!" And so, trying to keep her rather small feet out from under the massive boots of Silas Potter, she murmured to herself, "Be still, Sarah. It will pass—!"

🔔   🔔   🔔

Micah Bradford paused outside of the home where he had grown up and stared at it with a slight smile. He knew every brick of this place, every square inch, and almost every tile on the roof. After the bitter battles around New York, it looked better to him than it ever had. "You're a fine old house," he murmured as he stood there taking it in, savoring the moment before he entered. The house was a large two-story Georgian-style home with four twelve-over-twelve windows on the first floor and two on the second story. It was made of a fine pinkish red brick with white mortar, and the windows and doors were trimmed in a dark green. The hipped roof had black tiles covering it, and there was a white balustrade across the top deck. Red brick chimneys rose high at each end of the house, and the front door had white pilasters flanking it with pedimented dormers and modillion blocks at the eaves.

The cold November wind bit at Micah's cheeks, and he thought of his twin, Dake, who was still in New Jersey, holding off the British forces for General Howe, along with the thin, starving lines of the Continental Army. Micah was a tall young man, a trifle over six feet, and weighed one hundred eighty pounds as a rule, although now the poor rations had brought him down to one hundred seventy. He had straw-colored hair that escaped the tricorn hat he wore, and a pair of steady hazel eyes that were deep and well-set in their sockets. His nose was strong and straight, his mouth wide and firm. He had rather high cheekbones and a prominent chin. There was a masculine look about him, but also something of a dreamer in his expression and in his eyes, unlike his brother Dake, who was rather wild and boisterous. Micah Bradford had a gentle side, very much like his mother had been before she died.

Abruptly the door burst open, and a woman came hurtling out, crying, "Micah—!"

Lifting his arms quickly, Micah caught his sister, Rachel, and lifted her off the walk. At the age of seventeen, one year younger than Micah and Dake, Rachel had red hair, green eyes, and a beautiful heart-shaped face. She was strong for a woman and taller than most, and she hugged her brother fiercely for a moment. When he put her down, she reached up and tugged at his tattered coat. "Is this the only coat you have?" she scolded. "You'll freeze to death. Come on in the house by the fire and warm yourself."

"Better than most of our fellows have. Some of them don't have anything but a blanket," Micah said. He kept his arm around Rachel, and the two quickly entered the house.

"Father. . . ! Sam. . . ! Jeanne! Micah's home!" Rachel began to call at once.

A young woman appeared with very curly hair framing her oval face, Dake's wife. She came forward at once, and Micah grinned as he took her kiss. "Hello, Jeanne." He kissed her again, saying, "Dake sent you that one."

"Couldn't he come?" Jeanne Corbeau and Dake Bradford had not been married long, and the loneliness showed in her large violet eyes as she stood before her tall brother-in-law.

"I wish he could've come instead of me. I told the general he could carry dispatches as well as I could."

"What's this? The soldier's home!"

Daniel Bradford came quickly down the hall. At forty-six he was still a strong and active man, an inch over six feet, with a smoothly muscled upper body. He had wheat-colored hair and eyebrows, and the same hazel eyes as his son. The two men stared at each other for a moment, then Daniel laughed and threw his arms around his son. "Welcome home, Micah."

"Father, it's good to be here." Micah felt the strength of his father's body as he stepped back, saying, "You're looking well."

"No reason why I shouldn't," Daniel said, shrugging his shoulders. "You're the one who's having the hard time."

The sudden pounding of footsteps startled Micah, and he turned to see his sixteen-year-old brother Sam propelled out of the kitchen as if shot from a cannon.

"Hey, brother!" Sam cried and reached out and struck Micah a hard blow on the arm, then grabbed him and began to wrestle him around. Samuel Bradford had auburn hair, electric blue eyes, and was handsome enough that girls turned their heads whenever he walked by. Now he stepped back and shook his head. "Why didn't Dake come?"

Micah stood smiling at his younger brother, of whom he was inordinately fond. "I was just saying, Sam, I told General Washington that Dake should be the one to bring the dispatches, but since I had served under Sam Adams and already knew many of the men in Philadelphia, he insisted I would be the best choice."

"How is Dake?" Sam asked. "Has he shot any lobsterbacks?"

The question was light and carefree, but it brought a frown to Micah's face. He did not answer for a moment, then said slowly, "There's been quite a few men go down on both sides."

"Come on in. You must be starved," Rachel said quickly. "We were just sitting down to eat."

"You always did know enough to come when the food was on the table, Micah," the irrepressible Sam said. He poked his brother in the ribs and said, "You've lost some weight. You need some of Rachel's cooking to put it back on."

"Unfortunately, I won't be here that long," Micah murmured as they walked toward the dining room and seated themselves. "General Washington had important dispatches for Congress in Philadelphia," Micah explained. "General Knox also had some for the forces here in Boston, so they made a dispatcher out of me."

"We've already blessed this food once," Daniel said, "but I think another one would be in order." He bowed his head, and the others followed suit as he prayed simply, "Thank you, God, for bringing Micah home. We pray for Dake, and we pray for all the young men who are fighting for our country. We ask it in the name of Jesus." Looking up, he said, "Been quite a few prayers said for you and Dake around this house."

Micah grinned as Rachel began to pile his plate high with food—potatoes, beef, and a huge chunk of fresh-baked bread on which he spread a thick dollop of yellow butter. "We've needed all of those prayers, Father," he said. "Things haven't fared well for the troops."

"Tell us about it," Sam insisted. "Tell us about the fight at New York."

"It's not a pleasant story," Micah said, shaking his head sadly. "We never should have tried to hold New York. General Greene wanted to burn it to the ground so the British wouldn't get it."

"What went wrong with the battle?" Rachel asked. She filled Sam's glass with fresh milk, for he had drained the first one almost in one draught. "Did the British have more men?"

"More men, more guns—and most of all, they had the good positions. New York's on an island, you know. They easily pulled their warships in and surrounded us. The army was lucky to get away. It was only the general who got us out of that tight spot." Micah went on to describe how General Washington had commandeered every boat on the river and had engaged a regiment of Maine fishermen from Marblehead to remove the Continental Army to safety under the very noses of the British.

"What happened after you left New York?" Sam asked, shoving a huge morsel of corn bread into his mouth. "Were there any more fights?"

"It's been a fight ever since we retreated. We lost both Fort Washington and Fort Lee. A lot of good men died, and we lost lots of supplies in Fort Lee that we couldn't afford to lose."

Daniel Bradford leaned back and toyed with his food. He had spent countless hours praying for these two sons of his in the army, at the same time fending off Sam, who was determined to join them. He saw the weariness etched on Micah's face and knew it had been even harder than his son was admitting. "What will happen next?" Daniel asked quietly.

Looking up at his father, Micah said, "I think we'll retreat, and the British will follow until they get tired. Hopefully they'll give up and go back to New York to wait for spring. Then they'll come out and try to finish us off."

"Do you think the army will stay together?" Rachel asked. "We hear stories about men deserting."

"A lot of them have," Micah admitted. "I don't think we have more than four or five thousand men under arms right now, but His Excel-

lency will save us. There's nobody like that man," he said, his face glowing, his eyes gleaming with admiration. "Nobody could've gotten us
out of New York except General Washington."

The talk ran around the table, and finally it was Rachel who said,
"You're going to a ball tonight."

"A ball?" Micah stared at her. "What do you mean going to a ball?"

"The Hortons are having a ball, and I'm going, and so are you."

Micah began to protest, but Rachel cut him off and said, "If you're
only going to be here a short time, we're going to do everything we can
together, and tonight it's a ball at the Hortons'."

Micah groaned. "All I want to do is eat, go to bed, and sleep."

"You can sleep after the ball," Rachel said firmly. "Now, you go
shave and get cleaned up. Then put on that nice blue suit that looks so
good on you."

As the family left the dining room Micah was alone with his father
for a moment. "How are things here, Father?" he asked. "How is Matthew?"

A cloud seemed to darken Daniel Bradford's eyes. Matthew Bradford was his oldest son, not by blood, for he had married Matthew's
mother when she was carrying Leo Rochester's child. Daniel had raised
the boy as his own, treating him no differently from his other sons, and
had been shocked and apprehensive when Leo Rochester had discovered that Matthew was *his* son, not Daniel's. From that time on, the nobleman had made every attempt to convince Matthew to leave the Bradford house and change his name to Rochester. Leo had not succeeded
completely when he died suddenly of a heart attack, leaving his wife,
Marian, alone.

"Matthew is sometimes in England, sometimes in France. We've had
three letters since he left."

"Why did he leave so abruptly, Father?" Micah asked, studying his
father's face. "I thought he was seeing Abigail Howland."

"Something happened, Micah, but I don't know what. Abigail won't
say, and neither will Matthew."

"They've broken up, then?"

"It looks that way."

Micah was a thoughtful young man. As usual, he took time to think
the matter over, then finally asked directly, "Will he take Leo's name
and become Sir Matthew Rochester?"

"I don't know, Micah. I don't think he knows himself. He's very confused and very angry. Something to do with Abigail, I think, but he refuses to talk about it—at least to me. Well," he said abruptly, "we'll have
plenty of time to talk later. You'd better get ready for the ball now."

"It . . . it seems a little bit wrong. Here I am going to a ball when the men back at the camp are half starved and freezing to death. But I'll be back with them soon." Then he added, "Dake sends his love. He sure wanted to come. Maybe he can when the army gets into winter quarters. Well, I'll put on that fancy suit and go make an appearance, anyhow." A sour expression came to his face and he muttered as he left the room, "I never did like balls."

𝕋   𝕋   𝕋

The music was lively enough to interest Micah, but he would have much preferred to simply stand along the wall and watch. Rachel, however, had not come to stand still and idly watch others enjoy the festivities.

"There are too many young women who need a partner," she prompted. "Now, let's see you charm some of these Boston belles. Most of them are looking for husbands, and you're a prime candidate, Micah." She reached up and touched his chest, with admiration in her eyes. "You are a handsome thing," she said, "and that suit sets you off very well." It was made of a dark blue luxuriant velvet, with the small spotted design of the material adding to its richness. A white linen shirt peeked out at the neck of his buttoned waistcoat, and white ruffles flowed from beneath the turned-up cuffs of his long coat. His breeches were tight fitting and ended below the knees, with white silk stockings that showed off his lean, muscular legs.

"It's the first time I've had on dry, clean clothes in so long I'd forgotten what it was like," Micah grinned. He admired Rachel, who was wearing a beautiful dress of kelly green silk and had a petticoat on with tiers of white lace decorated with small green bows. She had been escorted by a young captain who was obviously much taken with her. She, however, had laughed when Micah had asked about her intentions, saying, "Oh, soldiers like any girl. He's not serious about me."

The music started again, and Rachel said, "Oh, look. There's Sarah Dennison all by herself. Come, you've met her, haven't you?"

"I don't think so," Micah said, glancing across the ballroom at the young woman.

"I thought you knew them. But surely you remember her sister Belinda? You danced with her several times at the ball at the Penningtons'."

"Why, yes! I do remember. She married some merchant from Philadelphia, didn't she?"

"That's right. Come along now."

Sarah was standing alone, dreading the return of Potter. Her feet felt mashed beyond endurance, and when she looked up and saw the couple approaching, she glanced around, assuring herself that Potter was not in sight. He had already insulted several men, and all Sarah wanted was to go home.

"Sarah, I don't know if you've met my brother Micah. Micah, may I introduce you to Sarah Dennison?"

"I'm happy to make your acquaintance, Miss Dennison. I remember your sister Belinda well."

Sarah curtsied slightly and murmured something suitable. She had not known the Bradfords well, although most people in Boston knew of them. They were working people, however, and her own parents would never have admitted them to her house as guests.

"May I have this dance, Miss Dennison?"

Nervously, Sarah cast her eyes around the room and then said with relief, "Yes, of course."

As they moved out onto the dance floor, Rachel watched until she was claimed by her officer. She was satisfied with herself, for Micah had always been a particular favorite of hers among her brothers.

"A beautiful home," Micah observed as they moved through the figures of the dance. He found the young woman extremely light on her feet, and as he studied her face he decided she was much more attractive than he had thought at first glance. Her complexion was the most beautiful he'd ever seen. He had heard the expression "Peaches and cream," and Sarah Dennison's skin was smooth and beautifully colored. She seemed shy, and as they glided around the floor, he tried to think of ways to draw her out. After asking several questions that elicited only one-word responses from the young woman, he finally happened upon a topic that did engage her attention. He had mentioned a poem by Thomas Gray, and it was as if a light had gone on in Sarah Dennison's eyes.

"Oh, do you like Gray?" she asked, excitement stirring her face. "He's my favorite poet!"

"I like him very well indeed. There is such power in his lines."

"Have you read his poem 'Elegy Written in a Country Church Yard'?"

"Yes, I have. It's a moving piece, isn't it?"

"I think I know it all by heart."

"You do? Well, that does show your devotion."

The talk went on for some time, and Micah was aware that when Sarah Dennison was animated, she appeared quite pretty.

Her hand was warm in his, and when she looked up at him, he found himself pleased with her company. He was not a ladies' man, this Micah

Bradford. Actually, Dake had that reputation before he married, and Sam was beginning to.

The conversation took another turn when he mentioned George Whitefield and found that the famous British preacher interested Sarah even more than poetry.

"Oh, I heard him preach once in Philadelphia!" she said warmly. "He's a marvelous preacher! He's able to stir thousands just with the sound of his voice."

"He is a fine preacher. I've had the privilege of hearing him twice. He seems to be shaking up this country as he shook England. It's interesting, isn't it, how God can use one man to awaken a whole country to its spiritual condition?"

He had hit on a subject that Sarah could speak about with enthusiasm. She alone of her family was devout. Her sisters had cared little for any sort of religion, and her parents were Episcopalian, but only nominally so. Sarah Dennison, however, revealed her sincere love for God as she spoke warmly of the gospel that George Whitefield had preached all over the Colonies. "It's marvelous to see that the gospel is so powerful it can save anyone."

Micah found himself fascinated, for most young women were not particularly excited about fiery evangelists such as George Whitefield. He started to reply when suddenly a large hand closed on his arm and he felt himself pulled around roughly.

"I believe this is my dance!"

Sarah blinked with something close to fear, for Silas Potter had strode across the floor, bumping into another couple and grabbing on to Micah's arm quite forcefully.

"Please, Mr. Potter, let me finish the dance with Mr. Bradford."

"Bradford, is it? Don't believe I know you."

"Nor I you," Micah said coolly. He resented Potter's hand on his arm. He recognized instantly that Potter was one of those massive men who took pride in their strength, and he knew that the fingers of the big man were digging in more than necessary. "If you will remove your hand from my arm," he said, "Miss Dennison and I will finish the dance."

Silas Potter was a man who could not bear to be crossed. His large beefy face flushed brick red, and he said loudly, "I told you, Bradford, this is my dance. Now, you will kindly leave us. . . ."

"If you do not remove your hand from my arm, I will remove *you* from this floor, sir!" Micah said in a restrained voice but with a steadiness in his hazel eyes that burned with a hidden fire. He was a peaceful young man ordinarily, but something about Potter irritated him. Micah could not understand what authority this man had over Sarah Dennison, and he stood his ground.

"Please, Mr. Bradford," Sarah whispered. "Perhaps it would be best."

Micah turned to her, wrenching his arm away from Potter's grasp. "I'm sorry, Miss Dennison. I've enjoyed the dance very much."

"Yes, so have I. But—"

"Come along, Sarah," Potter interrupted.

Micah watched as the big man pulled Sarah around as if she were a small child and began dancing. Anger blazed up in him, and for one moment he thought of calling the man out, but he knew such a challenge would not do.

Micah moved to the side of the room, and suddenly a wave of weariness fell on him. He stood there long enough for Rachel to come to him, and he saw the concern in her eyes.

"What happened with Sarah and that big man?"

"Who is he?"

"All I know is, his name's Silas Potter. A very wealthy man, I understand."

"He forgot to take lessons in being a gentleman." Micah was still angry, and it showed in the way he moved his shoulders restlessly and in the stubborn set of his mouth. "I should have called the fellow out."

"No, you shouldn't have done that." Rachel studied her brother's face and said, "I think you're tired. Come, we'll go home."

"Your officer won't like that."

Rachel did not answer him. She cast one look back at Sarah, who was being propelled around the room clumsily by Potter, and shook her head. "He is a boor, isn't he?"

"Yes, he is. I don't think Belinda would have put up with the likes of him."

"Sarah's different from her sisters," Rachel said. "She must feel like an old maid—and having two sophisticated and beautiful sisters to compete with must have been difficult. Not that Sarah is unattractive, mind you, but she is terribly shy around men. I've heard that her parents are looking for a rich husband."

"I don't know how much money Potter has, but certainly not enough to make it worth marrying him," Micah said with a grimace.

Rachel took Micah's arm and squeezed it. She smiled at her brother and said, "Come along. We'll get our coats. I've had enough dancing for one night."

"So have I."

While they waited for a servant to retrieve their coats, Micah watched Sarah Dennison and Silas Potter on the dance floor. He had enjoyed his brief time with her more than he had with any other young woman he could remember. There was a liveliness in her—when she was not subdued by Potter—that he admired. Casting one last look, he shrugged his shoulders and muttered under his breath, "She deserves better than that fellow!"

2

An Expected Announcement

A RAY OF YELLOW SUNLIGHT struck Micah's face, causing him to stir restlessly. He turned over and burrowed into the featherbed, savoring the warmth of the comforters piled high over him. On his army marches he had been fortunate to find a dry spot on the ground. More than once he had awakened to find himself half buried by the snow that drifted down while he slept an exhausted sleep.

Now a smile curved the edges of his lips as he drowsily lay in the warmth of the soft bed and, with regrets, thought of Dake, who was certainly not faring so well. From outside he heard the cry of a man urging his horses on, but it seemed distant. The sound of rattling dishes came to him from downstairs, and he considered getting up to eat breakfast. Just the thought of one of Rachel's breakfasts brought a sharp stab of hunger. Throwing the covers back, he put his feet out on the knitted rug that Rachel had made for him to take the cold out of the hardwood floors. Shivering in the chilly air, he swiftly pulled on his clothes and resolved to find a better coat for himself and one for Dake. He looked at his socks, which had no toes in them, threw them aside, and rummaged through the chest at the foot of his bed until he came up with a pair that were warm enough—a scarlet color so bright they almost hurt his eyes.

"Well, my feet sure won't go to sleep in these," he muttered as he pulled them on. Picking up his knee-length boots, he studied the soles and saw they were growing thin. "Won't have time to get them fixed. They will have to do," he muttered as he pulled them on. Straightening up, he stepped over to the enamel washbasin and found the water frozen.

Leaving his bedroom, he noticed the house was strangely quiet. When he entered the kitchen, he saw Jeanne and Rachel sitting in front of the fireplace. It was a cheerful kitchen with bright yellow walls, hardwood floors covered with yellow oilcloth, and four small windows covered with white muslin curtains tied back with green ribbons to let in the morning sunlight. He smiled and went over and pulled Rachel's hair. "What does a man have to do to get breakfast?"

Rachel leaped to her feet and grabbed a handful of Micah's thick hair and jerked it until he winced. "You have to get up before noon," she said. "Now, you sit down there, and I'll have it ready for you in a moment."

Micah grinned, sat down, and began talking with Jeanne, who listened eagerly. She wanted to know every small detail that had anything to do with her husband.

Finally, Micah threw up his hands in despair. "I'm a headline man," he said. "I'm not much for fine print."

Jeanne shook her head, her black curls dancing around her face. "The fine print is what women want," she insisted firmly. "Now, tell me more about Dake. Has he lost weight?"

"I reckon he has, like all of us, since we're going to be eating shoe leather pretty soon." He paused, then said thoughtfully, "Except some of the men don't even have shoes. They wrap blankets around their feet and tie them on with strips of rawhide."

"Why is that?" Jeanne demanded with indignation. "If they're going to fight for our country, the least Congress could do is supply them with decent shoes."

Micah leaned back, and Rachel came over and set a heaping plate of battered eggs before him. On another plate she had piled fresh-baked biscuits and thick slices of fried bacon. He stared at the food and shook his head. "I haven't had a breakfast like this in a long time. I wish all the men of our unit could enjoy this good cooking."

"It's not fair," Rachel insisted.

"Life isn't fair," Micah grinned. "We'd all have rich daddies if it were." Then he grew more serious and held a biscuit for a moment and seemed to be studying it. It was flaky, and he had cut it and put butter on the inside so that it came dripping out. He held it over the plate, licked the edges of it, and then shook his head. "Congress doesn't seem to understand we're fighting a war with men, and you can't keep men together if they're starving. There've been thousands of our fellows, good men most of them, who just couldn't take it." He thought about the starving scarecrow army out there trying to hold up against the finest infantry in the world that had journeyed all the way from England

30

to subdue the Colonies. For a moment his face clouded, but then he brightened up and said, "We'll get away from them, and come spring we'll have another try at it."

Jeanne leaned forward. She was wearing a honey-colored dress made out of a light woolen material. A kerchief of white muslin had been wrapped around her shoulders and tucked into the bodice, adding a delicate touch to the otherwise plain garment, and she looked especially pretty. "You don't think there'll be any fighting until spring?"

"I doubt it. We don't have muskets and powder enough to fight with. All we can do is hide and shoot, turn around and bite 'em, and then run like the devil."

Jeanne drew a deep sigh of relief. "That's good," she said in her charming French accent. Her father, a Frenchman, had recently died, and for a time there had been a spirited contest between Dake and his cousin Clive Gordon over who would marry the beautiful young woman. Dake had eventually won, and Clive had resigned himself to losing Jeanne, especially after meeting another young woman named Katherine Yancy.

"Hey, save some of those biscuits for me!"

Sam entered the back door carrying a load of wood, which he dropped beside the stove with a resounding crash. He was wearing dark blue britches stuffed into a pair of heavy boots, and a green woolen coat, which he pulled off and threw on the floor.

"Pick up that coat, Sam!" Rachel demanded.

"Aw, that's what I got you for," Sam grinned brazenly. But seeing the warning light in her eyes and the tightening of her lips, he stooped over, picked it up, and hung it on a peg driven into the side of the wall. "Let me have some of those, you hog!" he said to Micah, who was reaching for another biscuit.

"You've already had breakfast once," Rachel said.

"Well, if once is good, twice is better." Sam pitched in, and between bites he declared that this could be his lunch that would hold him until his midafternoon break. As he ate, he began describing his latest invention.

"It's going to make me rich and famous, Micah," he boasted, waving a spoonful of yellow battered eggs around. Stuffing them into his mouth, he swallowed them without chewing and went on to say, "You're going to see the day when you'll be saying proudly, 'My brother is Samuel Bradford, the famous inventor!' "

All three of his listeners looked amused, and it was Micah who asked, "Is this number ninety-seven or ninety-eight of your inventions that is going to make you rich and famous? I lose count sometimes, there're so many of them."

"Go on and laugh," Sam said airily. "You'll see. Hurry up and finish your breakfast, and I'll show you."

Micah winked at Rachel. "I'm glad you've got one brother who's going to be rich and famous. I don't think the rest of us have much of a chance."

"Oh, you know Sam," Rachel laughed. With only one year difference between them, she and Sam had grown up together, and she felt a certain protectiveness toward him. Now she smiled as she touched her hair lightly, saying thoughtfully, "You know, Micah, he might have something this time."

"Really? What is it?"

"Let him show you."

Sam soon came back bearing four wooden churns that he set in a row in front of them. Talking all the while, he then poured milk into each one. "Now you'll see something. Stay right there, Micah." He darted outside and came back with a metal frame that he placed over the churns. Sam quickly assembled the arms that hung down from the framework, then he looked up triumphantly and said, "Now watch this." He sat down at the end of the contraption and began pulling at it. "It's a multiple churn," he announced proudly. "Look at that. All their lives people have sat before one churn, then they get another one out. But that's all going to change now."

Micah was amused—but somewhat impressed with the invention. He leaned closer and saw that short arms with wooden paddles extending down from the upper arm were indeed moving up and down in their respective churn. He shook his head and whistled low. "Well, I hate to admit it, but this contraption might work. At least you're not going to blow us up with some of your fancy cannons," he said, referring to an unfortunate invention that had turned out rather disastrously.

They sat there for a while taking turns with Sam's invention, and finally a knock sounded from the front door.

"I'll get it," Rachel said. She left the room but soon returned with a young man.

"Jubal," Sam piped up. A smile creased his lips, and he waved his left hand while his right kept pumping. "This is my brother Micah. Micah, this is my friend Jubal Morrison."

"I'm happy to meet you, sir," Morrison said, taking the hand that Micah offered. He was as tall as Micah, with rusty red hair and large blue-gray eyes set in a squarish face. A scar beside his left eye drew that side slightly down into a permanent squint, and his grip was strong and hard.

"I've heard a great deal about you, Mr. Bradford."

"Micah is fine."

"Well, Micah, then, and I'm Jubal."

"Unusual name."

"From the Bible, of course," Jubal Morrison shrugged. "Not a particularly heroic character, I suppose, but at least it's biblical." He moved over to watch Sam for a moment, and then shook his head. "When are you going to start marketing this thing?"

"Any day now. I'm planning to go to Philadelphia and get Mr. Franklin to help me."

"He's not in Philadelphia," Morrison said. "He's in France."

"France!" Jeanne exclaimed. "What's he doing in France?"

"He's gone over there to try to get the French to sell us supplies— or give them to us. What he really wants," Jubal Morrison said, "is to have them declare war on England. Then we'd get somewhere!"

"Sit down, Mr. Morrison," Jeanne said, moving a chair closer. "Would you like some tea?"

"Why, yes, I believe I would." Morrison sat down and at once began peppering Micah with questions about the army. He was intensely interested in all the skirmishes that had already taken place. Finally he drew a deep sigh and said, "I almost joined up myself at Bunker Hill."

"We could have used you. We still could," Micah nodded.

Jubal Morrison glanced over at Sam and winked. "We've got bigger plans, haven't we, Sam?"

"Oh no," Micah groaned. "You're not involved with Sam! What kind of a wild scheme has he dreamed up now?"

"It's not wild at all," Sam shot back indignantly. He stopped pumping, then looked down and said, "There—that's done. You women can take over now. I've done all the hard work." He turned back to the men, and his blue eyes sparkled as he said, "We're going to build a boat and become privateers."

"Privateers?" Micah studied Morrison more carefully. "Are you a sailor, sir?"

"Yes, I am, and I'm convinced this war will be won by naval forces."

Micah stared at the strong-looking features of the young man. "But we don't have a navy."

"We don't have now."

"And Britain's got a hundred ships of the line. We got a taste of their fire power in New York. They came up the river, opened their gun ports, and blew some of our poor fellows to bits. There was no defense at all."

"Ground troops can't stand against ships of the line and thirty-pound cannons," Morrison shrugged.

"How do you propose to get a ship that can stand up against a ship from Britain's navy?"

"Well, we don't have anything quite that ambitious." Jubal sipped the cup of tea that Jeanne had put in front of him and smiled at her. "That's very good, Miss Jeanne." Then he turned his attention to Micah. He held the cup in his hands, and it looked very small, for his hands were large and strong. "Actually, what we are going to do is build a small craft that can take merchantmen off the coast. That way you don't have to have a large crew and big guns. Merchantmen carry no arms, you see, Micah. And with the craft I propose to build, we can move right in. If they don't obey our hail, we can blast the ship out of the water."

Micah listened as the young man spoke, and finally when Morrison was through, he said, "Will it be expensive building a ship like that?"

"Well, they're not free. We need seasoned timber, a good crew, and some good guns, but it can all be done." He looked over at Micah and smiled. "I imagine the army could use some food and warm clothing?"

"You're right about that!"

"Well, one merchant ship could carry enough supplies in its holds to clothe the whole army." He winked at Sam and grinned. "It might not be the right color, but it would be warm."

Morrison stayed for only a few minutes, for he and Sam were planning on going down to the harbor to look at some ships. He shook Micah's hand firmly and said, "You whip the lobsterbacks by land, and Sam and I will do it by sea."

After the two had left, Micah asked Rachel, "What do you make of all that?"

"Jubal is a very enthusiastic young man. He makes it sound so plausible. He comes from a family with money, from New York. Still, I can't see how a small ship could do much good. Just one armed brig from the British navy would be all it would take to finish it off, but Sam's excited about it." She smiled and began cleaning the table. "He's always excited about something."

"If it will keep him out of the army, it will be a good thing," Micah said, then finished his breakfast and left.

After he was gone, Rachel said, "He's so different from Dake. I wonder if he'll ever change." She then gave a half-laugh and turned and said, "I don't want him to change, Jeanne. He's fine the way he is."

☙   ☙   ☙

Micah spent the day speaking with officers of the army station in

Boston. He delivered his dispatches and then was ordered to wait until the responses could be written.

It was an enjoyable day for him, and he walked down the streets of Boston, buying what supplies were available to take back to Dake and others in his company. He could not carry much since he was on horseback, but he did purchase some warm socks and determined to take a pack horse back with him to carry as much food as possible.

He returned to the house early and saw a carriage out in front that looked familiar. As he grew closer he recognized it as having the crest of Sir Leo Rochester. "I suppose Marian is here," he said half aloud.

As he moved to the door, he thought about the strained relationship that existed between his father and Marian Rochester. He was not the only one to know that they had been in love for years, but since Marian had had a husband, and Daniel Bradford would be the last man in the world to have any illicit dealings with a married woman, Micah could only guess at what had gone on in their lives. He had heard enough of the story from his father to know that the two had long had a mutual attraction going back before Marian married Leo. Daniel had married Holly Blanchard, the mother of Matthew, and she had borne the rest of the Bradford youngsters. *Still, something about the way he looks at her, and the way she looks at him,* Micah thought as he stepped inside the house. *I guess you never know your parents very well.*

He found Marian Rochester seated in the large parlor along with Jeanne and his father. He went over at once to bow and say, "You're looking very well, Marian."

"And you're looking hungry and thin, Micah."

Marian Rochester had been a Frazier before her marriage. She was tall with dark auburn hair and no gray despite her forty-four years. A heart-shaped face was framed by her hair, and she had intense, oddly colored green eyes. She was a strong-willed woman, and although her marriage to Sir Leo Rochester had been a disaster from the beginning, no one had ever heard her complain. Though she had endured much from Leo's abuse and unfaithfulness, she had never broken her own wedding vows. She had silently suffered and prayed for God's help through those difficult times.

"How long will you be able to stay, Micah?"

"Depends on the military command here. I have to wait until they have their dispatches ready to send back to the army."

He would have said more, but at that moment Rachel stepped inside and said, "As usual, you suddenly appear when the meal's on the table."

Sam popped in from behind Rachel and said, "Let's eat! I'm starved!"

35

The group moved into the dining room and was joined by Jeanne, and they all noticed that their father seated Marian at his right hand. They waited until he had asked the blessing, then Sam immediately launched into a description of the boat he was going to build. "It's got a funny name. It's called a *spider catcher*," Sam said.

"Don't talk with your mouth full, Sam," Daniel reproved him. "What in the world is a spider catcher?"

"Well, it's a boat with a cannon in the front of it."

"Does it have a sail?" Marian asked.

"Some of them do. But all of them are rowed by a crew—ten or twelve men, and one man to steer. When you get close, some of the men fire the gun. We're going to put a sail on ours, and it'll be about thirty feet long and about eight to ten tons burden. Of course, that's just the first one that Jubal and me are going to build. We're gonna build a whole fleet of them. Some of them will be big enough to take on even a sloop of the Royal Navy...."

Everyone around the table was highly entertained by Sam, whose excitement was unrivaled. He spoke for some time, and when the meal was finished, Daniel took a deep breath and stood to his feet. "I guess we know all about spider catchers now and how they're going to win the war." He looked at Sam, who seemed hurt. "I was just teasing, son." Then he shot a quick glance at Marian.

Rachel, who was sitting across from her, saw that Marian was looking agitated. A sudden thought came to her, and a smile touched her lips.

"I have an announcement to make," Daniel said. He was looking very handsome, wearing a new brown suit and a white shirt with frills on the front. He did not wear a wig as most men were doing, but his hair was clubbed back with a small leather thong. The light from the lamps flickered and threw his strong features into relief, and he said with some effort, "This will come . . . a little bit hard." He hesitated for a long time and then finally looked directly into the eyes of each of them. "I don't know any other way to say this, but Marian and I are going to get married."

Marian's face flushed, and she dropped her eyes for a moment but then quickly lifted them and shifted her gaze to the faces around the table. She had not known what to expect, for there had already been talk about her and Daniel Bradford, gossip about their relationship. Since Daniel operated the foundry owned jointly by her father and himself, she was often at their house, and it had been Sam who had asked directly once, "Are you in love with my father?"

Marian thought of that as she studied Sam's face, and a feeling of relief swept through her as she saw his lips turn up in a delighted grin and his eyes flash.

"I think that's great!" Sam said, leaping off his chair. He ran around and pulled Marian to her feet and kissed her heartily on the cheek. "Well, Ma, you can start patching my clothes and taking care of me as a son should be taken care of."

"Samuel Bradford!" Rachel chided, but she was laughing. She got up and moved around the table and embraced Marian, whom she had grown to love. "I'm so happy for you both," she whispered to her. "You're going to be very happy."

Tears burned in Marian Rochester's eyes as one by one they all came by and wished her well. When they had all taken their places again, she said in a subdued voice, "I don't know how to thank you. You make me feel so welcome."

"When is the wedding?" Sam demanded.

"Next month. The middle of December, I think."

"Will you come and live here, Marian?" Jeanne asked.

"No, my father is not well, and Daniel has agreed to come and stay with us. So you'll have this house all to yourselves."

"Good, I can be the boss," Sam said. "Micah and Dake are gone, so you women get your orders from me from now on!"

There was considerable protest from Rachel over this, but it was a happy time, and for the rest of the evening Daniel Bradford felt a sense of relief, for he had not realized how tense he had been at making the announcement to his family.

He drew near to Marian once and put his arm around her. "I feel better. I don't know what I would have done if they had raised a fuss, but they wouldn't do that. They all love you, my dear."

"And I love them. Since I have no children of my own, it will be good to have these, even though they're a little bit large—larger than babies."

"They're still babies, especially Sam," Daniel grinned. He held her for a moment and then reached forward and pulled her into his arms. As he kissed her tenderly, he savored the lilac scent of her hair and pulled her even closer.

Finally, Marian drew back, her face tinged with pink. "You mustn't do that. Someone will see us."

"They won't have any trouble seeing us after we get married, so why should it bother them now?"

The men went back to the parlor and talked with animation, Sam mostly discussing the spider catcher, and finally Micah said to his father, "I can't tell you how glad I am to see this happen."

"It's a little bit quick, I know. Leo hasn't been dead very long."

"Things happen in a war," Micah shrugged. "You two love each other."

"You've heard the talk about Marian and me?"

"Why, there's nothing to that. Anyone who knows you knows it's empty tongue-waggling."

Daniel smiled fully and said, "It'll be different for me, but Dake's married, and you will be someday, I'm sure."

Micah gave a tiny shrug of his shoulders to indicate his indifference and finally asked, "Do you know the Dennisons, Pa?"

"Thomas Dennison?"

"That's the one, I think. They have a daughter named Sarah."

"Yes, I know them slightly. We've done some work for them at the foundry. They're a very wealthy family. Why do you ask?"

"When I went to the Hortons' ball last night with Rachel, I met their daughter there."

"Oh?" Daniel observed, his eyebrows going up. "What was she like?" He listened as Micah explained how he had been taken by her knowledge of poetry.

"Is that all you did, talk poetry at a dance?"

A frown creased Micah's forehead, and he shook his head. "There was a fellow there named Silas Potter. He seemed to be extremely possessive of the young woman."

"I take it you didn't care for him?" Daniel said, arching his eyebrow.

"I thought he was a boor!" He smiled suddenly and said, "Did you ever meet a man, and the first time you came into his presence you wanted to hit him?"

Daniel thought quickly of Leo Rochester, whom he had detested thoroughly. He nodded, saying only, "Some people strike you that way. Christians just have to learn to get over it."

"Well, Potter tested my patience to the limit." Micah repeated the details of the incident to his father, and finally a rather wry humor turned up the corners of his mouth. "Ordinarily I'd let it go, but the fellow made me quite angry, so I'm going to get a little bit of my own on him."

"How's that, Micah?"

"I'm going to go calling on Miss Sarah Dennison. If he's there, I may throw him through a window or down the stairs."

"He's a pretty wealthy fellow, so I hear."

"Wealthy folks need to learn manners just like us poor ones do. Anyway"—Micah rose to his feet—"I'm going calling. Won't have much time for courting, but at least I'll put Potter in his place. Besides," he said thoughtfully, "that young woman interests me."

Daniel knew that Micah had been reserved in his relationships with women. "I never knew you to be so interested—so quickly, at least."

"Well, it's not just poetry. She's very fond of the preaching of George Whitefield. She seems a very devoted young lady."

"Might make a good minister's wife," Daniel said.

Micah was taken aback. "What do you mean by that, Pa?"

Daniel Bradford leaned forward and locked his hands together, strong hands from his years at a forge and at the foundry. He studied this tall young son of his, so unlike any of the other boys, and said quietly, "It wouldn't surprise me greatly if God spoke to you about becoming a minister—or perhaps He has already?"

Micah said nothing for a long time, and then he looked down and studied his feet for a moment. "Maybe, Pa. It's too soon to tell, and nothing's certain with this war on."

"Go see your young lady. If she likes George Whitefield, she must be all right." He watched as Micah left, then rose and went to his own bedroom. He lay down and thought of the long years he had suppressed his love for Marian. "Now I don't have to hide it any longer," he said aloud, and a quiet joy flowed through him as he thought of the woman who would soon be his wife.

🏛   🏛   🏛

"Miss Sarah—Miss Sarah!"

Looking up from the small but rather thick Bible she was reading, Sarah stared at the diminutive maid. "What is it, Lucy?"

"It's a young man come calling on you."

"It's not Mr. Potter, is it?"

"Oh no, Miss Sarah! This is a young man I ain't never seen before, and he is *fine* lookin'!"

"Did he give his name?"

"Yes, ma'am. He said his name is Micah Bradford."

Instantly a flush colored Sarah's cheeks. She put the Bible down on the rosewood table as she stood but then hesitated. "Are you sure he's come to see me?"

"Yes, ma'am. He asked for you by name, especial."

"And you're sure his name is Micah Bradford?"

Lucy sniffed. "You think I ain't got no sense at all? He said his name was Mr. Micah Bradford, and he wants to see Miss Sarah Dennison. Now, will you get yourself downstairs—wait a minute! You ain't goin' down with your hair lookin' like that and wearin' that old dress, are you?"

Sarah refused to change dresses, but she did allow Lucy to fix her

39

hair, then pushed her back when the maid would have added rice powder. "I don't need any of that."

"You sure don't," Lucy grinned. "You're all flushed up like a morning sunrise. My, a young man come callin' so early!" She winked, then said impudently, "He sure looks better than that old Mr. Potter, don't he, now?"

"Lucy, don't talk so!" Sarah said, yet curious as to why a young man she hardly knew had come to see her.

"Yes, ma'am." Lucy waited until her mistress had left the room, and then she said under her breath, "Well, I guess I got eyes, ain't I? That old Potter looks like a stuffed-up fat steer goin' to market." She came to the door and tiptoed down to where she could peer around the stairs where Sarah was greeting the visitor.

Micah had put on his uniform for his visit with Sarah. It was worn, but he filled out the buff uniform well despite his thinness. "I apologize for calling this early, Miss Dennison."

"Oh, that's quite all right, Mr. Bradford." Sarah hesitated and then blurted out, "Are you sure it wasn't my father that you came to see?"

"Your father? No." Micah grinned brashly, something unusual for him. "It wasn't your father I danced with last night."

Despite herself, Sarah giggled, something she rarely did. "Well, come into the small parlor. My parents aren't at home right now."

Micah said under his breath, "Good!" and followed her into the ornately furnished, high-ceilinged parlor.

A brass bird cage hung beside one of the floor-length windows, and a mockingbird chattered at them as they walked through the door. A brass chandelier hung from the high ceiling. The walls were papered in a striped design and flocked in red, green, and white above a chair rail, and the lower half of the wall was painted a deep forest green. The furniture was all very large, carved from the best mahogany and walnut and covered with only the finest materials. A walnut cabinet displayed an array of silver trays, soup tureens, plates, and candlesticks, each one more ornate than the next.

"Will you sit down there, Mr. Bradford?"

"After you." Bradford waited until Sarah sat down, then seated himself rather carefully on the small, fragile-looking chair. "I might break this," he said.

"Oh, it's very well built. By Chippendale."

"It is?" He looked at it carefully, then shook his head. "It still looks fragile. I believe I could make a stronger one."

"I'm sure you could," she said, a demure smile turning her mouth upward.

Now that he was in the house and facing the young woman, Micah had almost no idea what to say. He had come on an impulse, out of a sense of outraged dignity, but he suddenly realized that at this hour Potter would not be present to see his victory. Carefully he said, "I'm glad I didn't have any more trouble than I did with your friend Mr. Potter."

Sarah blinked and tried to think of something to say, but for the moment nothing came. Finally she said quietly, "I apologize for Mr. Potter. He's—" She could not go on and finally shook her head slightly. "I'm glad, too, that you didn't have any more trouble with him."

"Is he a longtime friend of yours?"

"Oh no, but he's known my parents a long time."

"I understand he's quite wealthy."

"I believe so."

Looking around the room, Micah took in the wealth that surrounded this young woman and her family. He noted the expensive Oriental vases, the gilt-framed paintings on the wall, the statues on special bases, and the rich rugs. "As I told you, I knew your sister Belinda. I trust she's well."

"Very well indeed. She lives in Philadelphia with her husband, Mr. Jennings."

For a while the conversation seemed to lag, and finally Sarah said in desperation, "Allow me to tell you, Mr. Bradford, how much I respect you for serving with our army." Her cheeks glowed as she added, "No praise is too high for you and those like you who are risking their lives to fight for our freedom."

"You believe in the cause, then?" Micah said, surprised by her interest.

"Why—certainly I do." The question seemed to surprise her, and she asked, "You didn't think we were Tories, I trust."

"Oh, certainly not, although there's plenty of them here in Boston. They're just not flying their flags right now. Do you know what they did in New York as soon as the battle started?"

"I have no idea."

"Those who were opposed to the revolution nailed pieces of red flannel to their doors to show the British they were Tories and sympathizers with England." His face grew stern, and he said, "They were two-faced hypocrites! While we were there, they were all for General Washington and the Continental Army. As soon as things turned against us, they showed their true colors."

"Perhaps it's always that way," Sarah offered. She had a gentle spirit about her, and for a time encouraged Micah as he spoke of the hardships of the war. He spoke well, Micah did, and made the scenes of battle come alive for her. Unaware of what she was doing, Sarah leaned forward and clasped her hands with her lips slightly open, her eyes wide with interest. She was unconscious of the fact that she made a rather fetching picture sitting there. Though she was not as beautiful as her sisters, Mary and Belinda, she had an engaging manner and pleasant appearance that Micah could not miss.

"I'll pray for you," she said finally in a soft voice, and there was something appealing in her gaze and in her entire demeanor.

"That's very kind of you, Miss Dennison." He hesitated, then said, "Do you attend church here?"

"My parents attend the Episcopal church, but I attend the Baptist church quite often."

"Oh yes. The minister's a very fine preacher."

"Indeed he is."

"Not as eloquent as Mr. Whitefield, perhaps," Micah offered.

"Very few are as gifted as Mr. Whitefield," Sarah said. "What is your own persuasion, sir?"

"We attend the Methodist church."

"Oh, I heard Reverend Carrington speak. He is indeed a fine minister."

"You have an unusual interest in churches and ministers."

"Yes, well, not as much as I should."

"I suspect you're a student of the Bible."

"No, not really," Sarah protested, "although I do love the Word of God."

This pleased Micah tremendously. Leaning forward, he said, "I find that most appealing and quite gratifying, Miss Dennison. In the midst of a struggle such as ours, people need to learn to look to God—"

The two were startled when the door suddenly opened, and Sarah came to her feet as her parents stepped inside, their eyes fixed upon Bradford.

"Oh, Mother—Father! This is Mr. Micah Bradford. Perhaps you may remember him. His father is Daniel Bradford."

"How do you do, sir?" Mr. Thomas Dennison said in a clipped voice. He was short and overweight, with rather small eyes and thinning brown hair. Perhaps the fact that he was several inches shorter than his wife caused him to stand absolutely straight and rigid. His tone was not warm, and he stood staring at Bradford as if he were an intruder.

Mrs. Dennison said rather coldly, "How do you do, sir? You came to call upon us?"

"I met your daughter last night at the ball, and I came to give my respects to her—and to you, of course."

"Very thoughtful of you," Mrs. Dennison said.

A silence fell over the room, and both Micah and Sarah felt the discomfort that her parents had brought into the room.

"Well, I must be going," Micah said. "I'm leaving for the army very soon."

Sarah extended her hand to Micah and curtsied. "Thank you for calling, Mr. Bradford."

"You're welcome indeed, Miss Dennison. Good day, Mrs. Dennison—Mr. Dennison."

As soon as Micah was out of the room, Helen Dennison came to stand before her daughter. "What was he doing here? Did you ask him to call?"

"Why, no—"

"Rather impertinent, I'd say."

"It certainly was," Thomas agreed. "Why, he's nothing but a workingman! That sort of thing is to be discouraged, Sarah. I'm surprised at you."

Sarah stood silently and listened to the inevitable lecture, and finally she was ready for the ending when her mother said, "Well, your father and I have something to talk to you about."

Instantly a wave of fear swept through Sarah. Never had her mother said this when it did not mean trouble and a feeling of humiliation for her. "What is it, Mother?"

"Your father and I feel that you need to be . . . encouraged."

"Encouraged to do what?"

"Why, it must be obvious. You have a suitable man coming to call on you. He's already given broad hints that he cares for you. We think it's time for you to respond."

"Mr. Potter?"

"Why, of course, Sarah! You don't see any other men coming here to court you, do you?"

Sarah shook her head. "No, I . . . I don't."

"Very well, then." Mrs. Dennison felt a moment's pang for this daughter of hers, so unlike the rest of the family. Such an emotion did not come often to her, and when she went over and put her hand gently on Sarah's shoulders, the girl looked up, her eyes filled with surprise. "You must marry, Sarah," Helen said quietly. "You're not going to get a prince charming riding up on a white horse. You need a good home and security. You need to be mistress of your own house. Silas Potter offers all that."

"But I don't love him, Mother."

This statement seemed to displease Helen Dennison. "You've been reading too many novels! I suggest you stop it at once!"

"Indeed! I think you are too romantic, Sarah!" Thomas Dennison had little enough say in his own house. He had had absolutely nothing to do with the marriages of his other two daughters. They had both been dutifully managed by his wife. He did, however, have some sense of fondness for this child of his and said with uncharacteristic gentleness, "I think your mother may be right. Mr. Potter may be lacking in the finer qualities of manners, but he'll give you a good home."

"No, he'll give me a good house. That's not the same thing as a home."

Thomas and Helen Dennison stared at Sarah as if she had uttered some sort of heresy. Then, the moment of gentleness over, Helen said firmly, "He's going to make you an offer, and you're going to accept it. Come now, Thomas."

The two left the room, and Sarah stood there filled with anguish. The thought of marrying Silas Potter was a torment, and her eyes glistened with tears, but she blinked them back and, moving to the window, stared blindly through the thick glass. Thoughts about Micah Bradford came to her, and she said aloud, "I wonder why he came here?"

3

A Midnight Visit

THE ALMOST EMPTY STREETS of Boston seemed shabby and worn to Micah as he strolled along peering into the shop windows. The buildings themselves showed the scars left by the British army, who had taken over Boston, commandeered the finest houses for their officers, and roamed the streets on their off-duty hours, doing considerable damage. When driven out by George Washington and his Continental Army, the British had burned as much of the city as they could. With the freezing weather no one could rebuild or even do necessary repairs.

Micah saw a pair of boots in the window and turned to go inside the shop. As he entered, he almost ran into a young woman who was leaving the shop. He whipped off his hat and started to apologize, but then said in a startled tone, "Why, Abigail!"

Abigail Howland stepped back and looked up at Micah. She was a full-figured woman of nineteen with hazel eyes, much the same color as Micah's. She was wearing a rather sedate dress, Micah thought, remembering the flamboyant outfits he had once seen her in.

"I didn't know you were home," Abigail said.

"I came in with dispatches from headquarters. I'll be riding out, probably tomorrow. How are you, Abigail?"

"Very well. My mother and I are staying with my aunt."

"I heard her home got burned in New York. I was sorry to hear it."

Abigail nodded. "It was a fine home, and most of her things were in it. Still, she did have this place here, and she was kind enough to take us in."

"How is your mother? Better, I trust?"

"No, I'm afraid not. She's in very poor health." Abigail hesitated, then said, "How is Dake?" She listened as Micah repeated some of what he had told the family.

He studied her face carefully, trying to find something in it that he

45

had missed. He knew Abigail Howland had been a rather wild young woman. He had it on good authority that she had been involved with one of the Winslow clan, Paul Winslow, and perhaps with Paul's cousin Nathan. He knew also that his brother Matthew had been in love with her at one time. Micah longed to ask about it but felt that would be out of place.

"May I take you somewhere?" he offered.

"Didn't you come into the shop to buy something, Micah?"

"Oh, nothing important."

"Then you may walk me down to the hardware store."

"Hardware? Why are you going to a hardware store?"

Abigail fished in the small bag she was carrying. "This is something that broke at our house. Part of the hinge, I think."

Micah took it and said, "You don't have to go to the hardware store, Abigail. I can make this for you down at the foundry."

"Oh, that's too much trouble," Abigail protested.

But Micah prevailed and said, "Would you care to go with me? Have you ever seen a full-fledged blacksmith?"

"That would be very nice. I haven't seen your father in a long time."

The two made their way out, and Micah waved a carriage over, and soon the two were on their way to the foundry. As they moved along, he listened as Abigail told about the destruction of New York.

"It was really a terrible thing to see all those lovely old homes burning," she said wistfully.

"Wars do bad things to people," Micah said quietly.

All the way to the foundry, he kept expecting her to mention Matthew, but she did not. After he had mended the hinge, he took her to her house, where he installed it. After giving his greeting to her mother and to her aunt, he then left.

🔔   🔔   🔔

The next morning was Sunday, and when Micah got up he found Rachel, Jeanne, his father, and Sam ready to go to church.

"I hope I hear a good sermon," Micah said.

"You need it. I know how wicked all you soldiers are," Sam jeered, jabbing his brother with his elbow.

Micah grunted and said, "Can't you walk without running into me, Sam? And don't start telling me about the spider catcher again. I've heard enough about ships to last me a lifetime!"

They arrived at the Methodist church, a rather austere building of gray brick with a towering steeple, and moved inside. Almost at once,

Micah saw Sarah Dennison sitting alone on a pew toward the back of the room.

"Excuse me," he said, eyeing his family firmly. "I'll go speak to Miss Dennison."

"So that's the girl he was so interested in," Daniel Bradford mused. "Pretty little thing."

"Not nearly as beautiful as her sisters, and I expect that's been a hardship," Rachel said. "It must be hard to have two terribly beautiful sisters who do absolutely nothing wrong. I think I'd have murdered both of them!"

"Don't say that, Rachel!" Jeanne protested, but she could not help giggling. "You wouldn't have done that."

"No, but I'd have wanted to. Come along. I see Micah's not going to be sitting with us."

Indeed, Micah had taken his seat so quietly, and so possessively, that Sarah Dennison was startled at first. She felt the pressure of his arm against hers, and when she looked up and met his eyes, she gasped, "Oh—it's you!"

"Yes, it's me all right," Micah whispered cheerfully. "I'm glad to see you here. Your family didn't come with you?"

Hesitating for a moment, Sarah shook her head. "No. They don't attend church very often."

The two of them sat there whispering until the service started. Micah joined in the singing lustily and noted with delight that though Sarah Dennison was not the most beautiful woman in Boston, she surely had one of the best voices, a high, clear soprano, sweet and pure. When the song was over, he whispered, "You sing very well."

The compliment seemed to startle Sarah. Her cheeks flushed, and she could not answer for a moment. She finally whispered, "Thank you."

Micah sat there enjoying the service. The only services he had been able to attend the last few months had been the few the chaplains had managed to give just off the battlefield. Here the quietness of the room, the soaring ceiling, the music that swelled from the great organ, all seemed right to him.

"I've missed this," he said. "I love this church."

"It is beautiful, isn't it?"

"Look, it's time for the sermon. I hope it's a good one."

Reverend Asa Carrington was a man of fifty with very black hair and eyes so dark they seemed to be fathomless. He was not tall but was strongly built, and he had a voice like a bell. He began by reading the third chapter of John, and as he did so, Micah glanced at his companion and saw that although her Bible was closed, her lips were repeating the words of the Scripture. *She knows it by heart!* he thought in surprise. Since the pastor read the whole chapter, he was rather amazed to see that she knew it all.

The sermon was powerful, crisp, and clear, urging men and women, all sinners, to come to Jesus. It was a simple message, and when it was over, Micah said, "That was wonderful. I've missed hearing the Word preached like that."

The congregation was standing now, and he said, "Allow me to see you home."

"Oh, I really don't think that's—" But Sarah was dealing with a man with a firm will. He hurried her out the door, avoiding his family, especially Sam, and soon they were walking down the street. It was cold, but the sun was shining, giving its pale yellow light and a little warmth.

They talked of the sermon, and Micah was not surprised to find that the young woman beside him had it sorted out and was now going over it point by point.

"You ought to be a preacher yourself," he smiled. She turned to look up at him, and there was a pleasant expression on her face. When she was not around her parents, he noted, her features were smooth and composed. But as soon as they reached the front door, which was opened by Mr. Dennison, he saw Sarah's face grow tight.

Mr. Dennison stared at the young man and said, "Sir, I must ask you not to call at this house again."

"Papa!" Sarah protested, but her father was already speaking.

"My daughter is practically engaged. We would appreciate it if you would pay your attentions elsewhere." He reached out and pulled Sarah forcibly inside the house. All Micah got was a glimpse of her face as it filled with pain and humiliation.

"Well, that's what you say, Mr. Thomas Dennison, " Micah muttered, staring at the door. "But I'll have to hear it from the young woman's lips herself."

✠ ✠ ✠

There was, perhaps, less romance in Micah Bradford than in most young men of his age. He had always been serious, loving books and quiet things rather than the world of adventure and action. That seemed to have fallen to his brother Dake. Micah had not been especially fond of romances, although he had read his share of the classics. He considered most romances worthless, nothing but a waste of time.

Some thought of this came to Micah that evening as he cautiously approached the home of the Dennisons. He felt somewhat like a fool, but he had grace enough to smile at his own audacity.

"If I get caught trying to see Sarah again, her father may have me thrown into jail."

Dusk had fallen early, and now the skies were dark without a cloud. One day Boston might be filled with streetlights, but now there were only a few, and none close to the Dennison house. He had been standing outside waiting for the lights to go off, showing that the inhabitants were going to bed. As he stared at the house, he was aware that one light was still burning on the second floor. His patience was rewarded when the curtains parted, and he saw Sarah outlined against the yellow light of the lamp in her room. Her hair was down, and she stared out into the blackness for a long time.

A smile came to Micah's broad lips, and as the drapes closed, he silently moved closer to the house. Her room was on the second story, but fortunately, for his purpose, a long, low roof was built two feet beneath the window line, sheltering a walkway that led to a large garden in the back.

Groping his way awkwardly, Micah found a latticework that allowed him to climb to the roof. He swung up onto the cedar shingles and moved carefully along the edge of the roof, pressing his body against the sides of the building. When he reached the window he hesitated, and a thought came into his mind.

I don't suppose she'd have a gun? No, she wouldn't. Her father might, though.

As he stood there outside the window, he almost turned and climbed back down to the ground. It had seemed a sensible enough thing when he had first thought of it, for he knew he had to speak once more to Sarah. Something about the young woman attracted him in a way that no other young woman had. Nevertheless, she was not the kind of person who could calmly take a man knocking at her window.

Taking a deep breath, Micah leaned forward and tapped on the glass windowpane four times. *Tap, tap, tap, tap.* He thought he could hear her voice as she hummed to herself, but the voice broke off at once. He tapped again and called out cautiously, "Sarah—?"

Inside her room, Sarah had frozen at the sound of the tapping. She had exceptionally good hearing and knew this was no bird or night animal. Fear swept over her. Since the British had left there had been little in the way of vandalism, but there were still rough people around, and she thought at once of a burglar.

Then she heard a voice whispering her name, and she knew the voice. "Micah?" she whispered back, then moved forward and lifted the window. His face appeared at once.

"I was just passing by the neighborhood and decided to call," he said with a straight face.

Despite the apprehension that filled her, Sarah could not help smiling. "You must be insane."

"I don't know. You may be right. I've never done anything quite like this before. May I come in?"

"No, you can't."

"Well, then we'll have to talk like this. However, I find it a little bit inconvenient."

Sarah was wearing a heavy blue robe over her nightgown. Her long hair looked rich and abundant by the light of the lamp on her dressing table. Even though the heavy robe covered her modestly, she felt somehow odd, for she had never been caught in her nightclothes by a man before. "What do you want, Micah?" she asked, unaware that she had called him by his first name.

"I want to talk to you."

"You can't. If my father hears you, he'll shoot you."

"I've thought about you, Sarah. Let your father blaze away. I guess I've been shot at so many times these last few months, I've gotten used to it."

Though Sarah was shocked by Micah's unusual visit, she was also fascinated. She had never had a thing like this happen to her, and now she studied the young man carefully. He looked cheerful enough, but there was, as always, a rather serious look in his hazel eyes.

"Really, Micah, you must go," she whispered.

"I will . . . if you'll tell me one thing."

"What's that?"

"Are you really going to marry that fellow Potter?"

The question came like a blow to Sarah, or rather like a wound from a large knife right in her heart. She had done nothing but grieve ever since her parents had told her that her marriage to Silas Potter was already decided. Now that Micah was standing there, she could think of nothing to say. Finally she whispered, "Why do you want to know?"

"Because I think you'd be making a mistake. You'll not like that man. He'd make you unhappy."

"You can't know that. You don't even know him. And you don't know me either."

"Yes I do!" Micah said. He stooped down suddenly, and his face was on the same level as hers. He could've reached out and touched her, and he had a sudden impulse to run his hand over the abundant wealth of her golden hair. He restrained himself and said, "You're too fine for him. He's nothing but one of those roughs. I don't care how much money he has."

"I've got to marry somebody."

"Just because your mother and father say so?"

"No, it's all that there is for a woman to do." Sarah felt the repressed rage that occasionally rose in her over the plight of women. "What else can I do? Stay with my parents until they die and then live in this house all alone? A woman wants a home—a family, children."

Micah Bradford studied the young woman's face. She seemed almost childlike, so childlike he did what he had been wanting to do. He reached out, touched her hair, and said, "You have beautiful hair, Sarah."

His compliment brought a sharp reaction to Sarah. He seemed to be ignoring everything she had said, and the touch of his hand was shocking. She knew she should pull away, yet she could not move as he continued to stroke her tresses for a moment. When he pulled back his hand, she almost regretted it. "You must go," she said again earnestly, nervous that her parents would catch them in this indiscretion.

"Just tell me you won't marry Potter."

Sarah suddenly did something she had never done before. Without warning, tears rose in her eyes, and her shoulders began to shake.

Micah was shocked. He knew she was a fragile young woman and unable to stand up against her parents' unreasonable demands, but the sight of her standing there with tears running down her face moved him as nothing ever had in his life. Impulsively he climbed through the window and put his arms around her. "Don't cry," he whispered. "Please don't cry."

Sarah leaned against his broad chest, and the tears came quick and fast. Her body shook, and she felt his strong hands on her back, holding her as a parent would hold a distressed child. Indeed, she felt like a child as he held her. For a long time she had longed for someone to reach out to, someone who would understand, and then suddenly out of nowhere had appeared this concerned young man—this tall, handsome young man.

Micah waited until he felt her sobs slowly subside. Finally, she straightened up and touched the tears on her cheeks. "I'm sorry," she whispered. "I've never done that before."

Micah Bradford leaned forward and kissed her on the cheek. "It's all right," he said. He saw the fear that lurked in her eyes, but it was not a fear of him, of a strange man in her bedroom. Suddenly he understood that it was the fear of life that troubled this young woman. He had seen that same fear in her eyes as she had faced her parents, or tried to, and now he realized that she was afraid of many things.

He took one hand and held it for a moment and looked down on it, then he enfolded his other around it and said quietly, "You must have courage, Sarah. You're a woman of God. He's not going to fail you. He's never failed anyone."

Sarah could not answer, her throat was so full. The weeping had drained her of all energy, and she could only whisper, "Please go."

"All right." He climbed back out the window and turned to say, "I'll be leaving tomorrow, I think, but you'll be in my prayers every day, Sarah."

And then he was gone. She heard his footsteps scrabble on the top of the shingle roof, and finally she moved forward and saw his shadowy form disappear into the blackness. For a long time she stood there staring. She had never felt so weak or so defenseless. Tentatively she reached up and touched the cheek he had kissed. It seemed to glow under her touch, and she knew she would think about this for a long time to come.

4

KETURAH

A RAW, GUSTY BREEZE SWEPT across the barren plains of New Jersey, numbing the cheeks of the young woman who plodded wearily through the thick snow in drifts over her knees. The November sky resembled a dull gray blanket that admitted only a sickly gleam from a pale sun that seemed to be hiding from the world.

Actually, it would have been difficult for an observer more than ten feet away to identify the struggling figure as a young woman. She was bundled in a man's garb with full baggy trousers, a bulky coat with a ragged collar pulled up around her ears, and a pair of boxy shoes with rawhide thongs holding on the soles. Only the strands of curly dark brown hair that slipped out from beneath a floppy worn hat, and the startling light blue eyes under arched black brows revealed her sex. That and the thick dark lashes that curved upward—but they, of course, were invisible except when viewed closely.

Keturah Burns stumbled over a branch buried in a drift and fell full length in the snow. She uttered a muffled cry. For a moment she lay still, so exhausted she could not move. She had been up since dawn with nothing to eat except a fragment of cold potato she had baked in her small fire the evening before, and now the strength had drained out of her. As she lay there a sensation simply to lower her head, curl up, and let the cold do its worst overcame her. To do so, however, would be a fatal step, and her lips drew into a tight line as the spirit rose up in the young woman. Pushing herself up, she struggled to her feet. With a futile gesture she brushed the snow from the front of her coat, then looked up to the horizon that stretched out before her. It was a dismal sight, for the land seemed frozen in an iron grip, and neither bird nor beast was evident across the barren landscape.

"Got to keep movin' . . ." Keturah muttered through lips so numb that the words were garbled. Beating her arms across her chest, she heaved a lumpy cotton sack over her shoulder and continued her way across the wet snow. Her feet sank in at each step. It became a terrible chore simply to lift one foot and place it ahead of the other. Her breath came in ragged, rapid gasps, and twenty minutes later she was totally exhausted.

Looking around for a place to sit and rest, Keturah heard a voice saying, "Halt!" Immediately she stopped and whirled around. From a copse of dead bushes, dried and brittle, a soldier appeared. His uniform was negligible, for George Washington's Continental Army had no uniforms to speak of. A hunting shirt comprised the top of his garments, while a pair of rawhide pants sheathed his thick legs. Crude rawhide boots were tied around his calves with thongs, and he wore a fur cap pulled down over his ears. Moving closer, he held his musket pointed toward her and said, "Who are you?"

"My name's Keturah Burns."

Immediately the soldier halted and half lowered the musket. "A woman?" he asked incredulously. Lowering the musket to a rest, he examined her. "What're you doin' here?"

"I'm looking for the camp."

Her announcement silenced the soldier, who studied her suspiciously. He was a burly man, thick in body with a barrel chest. His face was broad and brown and weathered, and the long greasy pigtail that fell down his back was wound into a braid and tied with a leather thong. He had oddly colored eyes, a muddy yellow, and there was a cruel set to his rather loose lips. A grin came to those lips as he laid the rifle down and moved toward her, saying, "Well now, I didn't 'spect to find no woman out here."

Instantly Keturah grew defensive. She had lived in the camps with her mother long enough to know that a woman was fair game for most soldiers. Frantically she looked around and saw that though there was a road, of sorts, from where the soldier had emerged, there was no sign of a building, a man, or anyone who might offer help. Her wide eyes narrowed, and her hand darted into the coat. Pulling a knife, she held it and pointed it at the man. "Stay away from me!" she said tightly, not taking her eyes off of him.

"Wal now!" The loose lips grinned even more broadly, and a pleased light appeared in the murky yellow eyes. "Now, I like thet. I like a gal with spirit! One who puts up a fight. Back in Virginia, where I come from, I wouldn't cross a creek to get to a gal who wouldn't put up a little struggle. You and me—we're gonna get along fine!"

Keturah did not answer. A wave of fear overwhelmed her, for since the death of her mother two weeks earlier, she had no protection at all.

Her mother had been a mere camp follower, but she had protected Keturah as much as she could from the rough advances of the soldiers. Now, however, Keturah was completely alone and wished desperately she had gone the other way, away from the camp.

"Stay away from me! I'll cut you!" she threatened.

With a loud laugh, the thick-bodied soldier stepped forward. He found the whole thing amusing and as he approached said, "Now, what are you going to do with that little jackknife, missy?" He was only a few feet away. When he put his hand out, Keturah slashed at it, but the big man had quicker reflexes than she had thought. Withdrawing the hand, he let the blade pass by harmlessly, and then moving like a striking snake, his hand shot forward and he grasped her wrist.

"Now, you just drop that knife, and we'll get along just fine."

Keturah's arm was grasped in an agonizing grip, causing pain to shoot up her arm. Slowly the soldier twisted her, laughing into her face. Involuntarily her hand opened, and the knife fell to the frozen snow.

"Now thet's out of the way. . . ." With an easy gesture the soldier grabbed her by the shoulders and pulled her around. "Why don't you give me a little kiss."

Silently Keturah tried to fight, but his strength was frightening. There was a feral quality in the soldier's features, and she knew with a sense of total despair that this time she was helpless. At other times she had been able to scream, to fight off the advances of men, but now there was no one to help. She felt herself enfolded to the man's chest, his arms pulling her close, and though she tried to kick and butt at him with her head, he only laughed.

"Now, that's what I like to see! Let's have a little more of that fight!"

Keturah felt his hand suddenly shift. He jerked her hat off and then caught her by the hair and held her head tilted back. His face seemed enlarged, swollen, as it came closer, and then she felt his large lips fall on hers. Desperately she tried to turn her head, but she could not avoid the kiss. He held her as if in a vise, his hand holding her back, pinioning her arms, and her head held tightly with the other.

"Well now. Ain't you a sweet one?" The soldier looked around. "Ain't no sergeants or officers likely to come along for another hour. Come on, sweetheart—"

Keturah was a child in his grasp, but she fought stubbornly with all the strength she could muster, kicking and trying to get a hand free to claw at his face. He only laughed and encouraged her. Finally he dragged her out toward the road where she saw he had a blanket beside the shelter of a tree.

As he dragged her toward the tree, Keturah could stand it no longer.

She began to scream, her voice splitting the stillness of the frozen air.

"Go on, scream! There ain't nobody to hear you!"

Rage and humiliation filled Keturah as she continued to struggle. Freeing one hand, she scratched at his face. Her fingernails caught him across the bearded cheek, and she saw ridges form, and the soldier cursed.

Suddenly he doubled his fist and struck her a blow in the temple. Keturah felt the world suddenly explode into an exhibition of fireworks. Red and green and yellow lights flashed before her eyes as she fought desperately to avoid slipping into unconsciousness. She felt his hands pulling at her, and once again she lifted her voice in a scream, but there was no hope in her. Who would come out in these barren woods along this forsaken road?

As her coat was ripped from her, desperately she turned, still half conscious, and raising her legs, she kicked with the last of her strength.

Her feet caught the soldier in the pit of the stomach and drove him back momentarily. His face grew angry then, and as she struggled to her feet, he said, "That's enough of this!" and deliberately aimed a blow at Keturah's face. It caught her in the forehead, and instantly she fell to the ground and lay still.

"Wal, that takes care of your fightin'!" the soldier said, breathing hard. He leaned over and started to touch the girl when suddenly a voice behind him caused him to jerk his head around.

"Let that girl alone!"

Whirling around, the soldier's eyes narrowed. He saw a tall soldier with straw-colored hair and hazel eyes who had come up behind him. He had stepped off a tall bay stallion, whose approach had been muffled by the snow in the road.

Keturah's attacker studied him carefully. "Get on! I'm doin' right well without your help!"

"You'll be the one that will get on!" Micah Bradford said deliberately, stepping closer to the burly soldier.

Micah had been riding down the road at a slow walk. Cold and muffled up to the ears, he had been thinking of his visit to Boston. Some of his thoughts had been of Sarah Dennison—indeed, a great many of them—but he had been drawn from them by a cry for help. Moving the horse forward, he had seen a huge soldier knock a young girl to the ground and then begin to tear at her clothing. Slipping off of his horse, he had advanced and now stood only a few feet away, keeping his eyes carefully on the soldier. He knew many of the troops were rough fellows. As he stood there measuring the thickness of the man's body, he had no desire to see it come to a matter of fists.

"Get on with you!" the burly soldier sneered. The man he saw before him was tall, but rather thin, and had a citified look. "This ain't none of your business!"

"If you leave now, you won't be harmed," Micah said coolly. "If not, I can't answer for it. Now get out of here!"

Anger flickered in the oddly tinted eyes, turning them almost amber. He moved forward, his hands held out, saying, "All right, sonny! I'm gonna bust your teeth out so that you whistle through the snags!"

There was no doubt he was a veteran of many crude brawls, and Micah knew he would have little chance in such a fight. Quickly he pulled his coat open and drew a pistol from the holster. It was primed and loaded, and as he pulled the trigger back to half cocked and aimed it directly in the man's face, he said, "This isn't a good day to die, soldier."

Staring into the bore of the pistol held in a hand so steady it seemed to be embedded in rock, the soldier halted abruptly, as if he had run into a stone wall. "Wait—" he said quickly and took a step backward. "Watch out with that thing!"

"I said be on your way!" Micah ordered.

"But I'm on watch here. If I leave my post, they'll hang me!"

"They may hang you later, but I'll kill you *now* if you don't leave. Take your choice." Micah's eyes were cold, and a raging anger began to bubble in him as he thought of the man's actions. He saw the yellowish eyes waver, then he lifted the pistol and his finger tightened on the trigger.

"Wait! I'm goin'. . . !"

Awkwardly, the huge soldier whirled and lumbered down the frozen road, leaving his musket and blanket. As he moved, he bellowed, "Who needs this blasted army, anyhow? I'm goin' back to Virginia!" He headed in the direction away from the camp and became another of the many deserters of the Continental Army.

Micah waited until the man was well on his way, then slipped the pistol back into the leather holster. He moved to stand over the young woman, then knelt beside her. Reaching out, he lifted her head and asked, "Are you all right, miss?" He got no response, however, for she was unconscious. "She's going to freeze in this weather." Gently lowering her head back to the ground, he walked over to his horse, which avoided him for a moment. In his haste he had forgotten to tie him up, but he encouraged the bay until he was finally able to catch the reins. He tied the animal firmly to a sapling, then fumbled in the saddlebag with numbed fingers. The pack horse he had been leading did not wander far, and Micah gave him only a glance. "He won't run off. It's too cold," he muttered through stiff lips. Retrieving a bottle of brandy he had brought along for medicinal purposes, Micah hurried back to the girl. She was stirring, he saw, and quickly he moved to help her.

Kneeling down beside her, he reached out and pulled her to a sitting position, and instantly her eyes flew open—and she struck him in the mouth with her fist.

The blow drove the inside of Micah's lips against his teeth and he tasted blood. Instantly he released the girl, crying, "Wait a minute . . . I'm not the one who hurt you!"

Keturah had recovered to find a man holding her and struck out with a quick reflex. She was unaware of the encounter that had taken place between Micah and her attacker. All she knew was that a man was still pawing at her. Rising to her knees, her hand landed on a thick piece of oak, not rotten, but hard and firm. Without hesitation, she whirled around, grasping it with both hands, and swung it in a short, vicious arc that made the wood whistle through the air. It struck the man on the side of the head just over the ear with a solid *thunk*, and Keturah saw him drop to the ground, facedown, knocked unconscious by the solid blow.

Standing there, Keturah tried to regain a sense of what had happened. She dropped the stick and stood looking down at the man, but something about him bothered her. Hearing the whicker of a horse, she glanced across to the line of trees and saw a fine horse tied up and a pack horse standing close beside him. Confused, she shook her head and tried to remember if there had been any such thing before, but she knew there had not been.

Dropping to her knees, she reached over and rolled the limp body of the unconscious man over. Snow covered the side of his face, and she reached out and brushed it away. His hat had fallen, and she saw that, unlike the other man's hair, which had been dirty brown, this man had pale yellow hair. His face was not the same either, and Keturah knelt beside him in confusion. She was a quick young woman, and glancing down the road, she saw the figure of a heavyset man almost out of sight, and she put the situation together.

"Why, he run that other soldier off." She felt horrified at what she'd done and said, "And I smacked him, maybe kilt him with that stick!" Reaching down, she pulled the man's head free and whispered, "Are you all right?" He did not speak, but she saw a slight fluttering of his eyes, so she sat there for a moment holding him. After a few moments, she saw his eyes open and looked into a pair of clear hazel eyes, such as she had rarely seen. She repeated her question. "Are you all right? You ain't dead?"

Pain shot through Micah's head, and the world seemed to be swimming. He had not even seen the stick that had struck him, and now as he awoke, looking into the face of the young woman, he could not speak for a moment. He took in the thick dark lashes, the slightly upturned nose, and the clear eyes. The girl had an olive complexion and a definite cleft in the center of her chin. Her face was dirty and her hair also. He guessed her age to be around fourteen.

"What did you hit me with?" he asked thickly.

Keturah flushed and said, "I thought you was the feller that was comin' at me. I reckon I'm right sorry, mister."

Micah became aware of the girl's arm around him, and she was holding him in a half-sitting position. He glanced at her and saw her face redden, and alarm leaped into her eyes. She released him, and with a grunt he sat up and gingerly felt the side of his head. Slowly he climbed to his feet, ignoring the shooting pain that ran through his skull, then stood looking down at the young girl. She had retreated a couple of paces, and there was a defensive air about her. *No wonder*, he thought. *After a thing like this, she's going to be pretty suspicious of any strange man.* "Are you all right?" he asked.

Taking his meaning at once, the girl nodded. "He didn't get at me, but he would've if you hadn't come along."

"Well, I'm glad I came along, then." Micah looked over to the horses and asked, "Where you headed? Is your home around here?"

"No, I was headed for the soldiers' camp."

Micah studied her carefully. He was well aware that there were camp prostitutes who followed the movement of the army. For a moment he thought this young woman might be one of them, but there was none of the hardness about her that he had observed in such women. He stood there wondering how to ask what business she had at a camp, when she answered it without being asked.

"My ma, she followed the soldiers," Keturah said. The very statement brought a flush to her clear olive complexion, and she now reached up and rubbed her cheek in embarrassment. She had been accustomed to the fact that her mother was a camp follower, yet now, looking at this tall young man, it was hard to put it into words. "She died two weeks ago. I didn't have no place else to go. I stayed back and ate all the food we had, and now I don't know no place to go except to the camp."

Micah's mind worked quickly. "Well," he said slowly, "I'm headed toward the encampment. You can come along if you'd like."

Relief leaped into the young woman's eyes. "My name's Keturah Burns," she said. "What's yours?"

"Micah Bradford."

"I'd be obliged for your company." A look of gratitude filled her eyes then, and she said, "If you hadn't come, that feller he would have—I didn't have no chance with him."

"Well, there'll be no more of that. Come along. You can ride the pack horse. I'll have to rearrange the load a little bit."

Ten minutes later Keturah was mounted on the brown mare. She had ridden a horse only a few times, but she was so weary that it was a delicious relief to cover the distance on the mare's legs instead of her own. Her rescuer rode at her side saying very little, and finally he turned to her and asked, "How old are you, Keturah?"

"Just turned sixteen a month ago."

She was a small girl, and for some reason Micah had thought she was much younger. Now he kept his eyes on the road ahead and said as he saw a horseman coming toward them, "I expect that will be one of the guards."

"Will he let us in the camp?"

"Yes, I think he will." He shifted in his saddle and turned to ask, "What will you do in camp, Keturah?"

The girl seemed puzzled by his questions. "Don't rightly know," she admitted. "I just had to get someplace where I could get warm and get somethin' to eat."

To Micah, who had led a fairly safe and secure life, there was something appalling about the simplicity of the girl's reply. For a young woman to go to a camp full of men, many of them no better than the one she had met, alone and without protection, was unthinkable. He studied her face for a moment, trying to think what it must be like to be so alone in the world, but he had no time to say more, for the horseman, a short lieutenant wearing a buff coat and a tricorn hat, had stopped in front of him, pistol drawn and aimed at Micah.

"What's your business?"

"Private Micah Bradford on special dispatch mission for General Washington. I have papers from Boston and Philadelphia, Lieutenant."

The officer lowered his pistol and put his eyes suspiciously on Keturah. "Who's this woman?"

"I found her back along the road, Lieutenant. She had had trouble with one of our men. I came along just in time to keep him from—harming her."

"What's your name, and what are you doing here, girl?"

"My name's Keturah Burns. I—"

Keturah could not go on, and Micah said quickly, "Her mother died a couple of weeks ago." He tried to find some better way to put it but could not. "She was attached to the camp."

Instantly the short lieutenant apprehended his meaning. His eyes went quickly to the girl, and he shook his head. "We can't have civilians running around in the camp."

"I'll be responsible for her, sir," Micah said quickly. "Just give me a chance to deliver my papers to His Excellency, then I'll see if something can be done."

Scowling, the lieutenant shrugged. "All right, it's your business. Come along."

Micah saw that the girl was frightened and said, "Don't worry. We'll find something."

Keturah rode alongside Micah, noting that most of the soldiers had no shelter at all. They were gathered around fires cooking, for the most part, and they looked almost like scarecrows. She was accustomed to this, however, and finally when they approached a line of tents where several officers were outside standing at a table, she grew fearful again.

Sensing the girl's apprehension, Micah said, "Keturah, you wait here, and after I see the general, we'll find some place to send you."

"Ain't no place to send me," Keturah said simply.

Micah stared at the young woman and shook his head. "Just wait here." Stepping off of his horse, he saw Keturah slip to the ground and said, "Here, you can hold the horses." Moving to his saddlebag, he extracted an oilskin packet, then followed the stubby lieutenant down to the group of men.

"Sir, dispatches from Boston."

General George Washington, standing between two other officers, his face craggy and rather homely, lit up at once as he said, "Well, Private Bradford, you made good time, I see."

"I would have made better, Your Excellency," Micah said, stepping forward, "but the officers in Boston took some time to form their answers."

Washington took the oilskin bag and said, "Did you go to Philadelphia?"

"Yes, sir, I did."

"And what was the situation there? Did you see Sam Adams?"

For a time Micah stood there answering the questions that Washington fired at him, and then finally the general said, "You make a fine courier."

"Well, sir, I still wish my brother Dake could have gone. He would have gotten to see his wife."

"Dake's in for the duration of the war," Washington observed. "Your time will be up soon." He looked at the bulky man who was standing beside him. "We have to get all the use we can out of him, Colonel Knox."

Henry Knox, the burly ex-bookseller from Boston, chuckled. He was a romantic man at heart and turned his eyes to the figure standing beside Micah's horse. "Do my eyes deceive me, or is that a young woman, Private Bradford?"

Micah felt the eyes of Washington and the other officers fasten on him after glancing at the girl. Stumbling over his words, he explained how he had found the young woman, and finally turned to the commander. "She has no place at all to go. Her mother was not a good woman, but I feel some obligation to her."

Knox chuckled. "There's an old Persian legend, that if you save somebody's life, you are obligated to them forever."

"Nothing like that, Colonel," Micah protested. This was intolerable! He knew the men were laughing at him openly and said hurriedly, "I'd be glad to turn her over to you, Colonel Knox."

"No, not me. She's your responsibility."

Washington studied the young man and said, "Do what you can for her. It's a hard time for a young woman in a place like this. Does she seem decent to you?"

"Oh yes, sir! I think so. She's very young."

"Some of them are young." The speaker was a slender, sour-faced man, General Charles Lee. He glanced at the woman and sniffed, "Let her go her own way. She will anyway."

Micah had never cared for General Lee, and he was glad when Washington said, "Well, we must do what we can, General." Turning to Micah, he said, "See if you can find some place for her." He hesitated, then said, "We'll be moving on almost at once. I imagine that's part of the information in these dispatches."

Colonel Knox nodded, saying, "We've got to get away from the British. If they catch us here, we're doomed."

"Yes, but we'll fight a delaying action as best we can."

"The whole army will have deserted if this goes on," Lee protested.

"We will fight with what we have, and the men will stay." There was an assurance in Washington, a rocklike conviction that all would be well somehow. He had this air about him that made men believe in him. They might lose battles, they might freeze and go hungry—but still Washington was the man who held the army together. Without him, the revolution would be over, and the Colonies would fall under the tyranny of the Crown once again.

Saluting, Micah took his leave and went back to where Keturah was standing. "Come along," he said. "I've got to find my brother Dake, and then we'll see what we can do. At least we've got food here."

"Was that the general?"

"Yes, that was General Washington."

"I heard about him, but I ain't never seen him. He's a powerful big man."

"Big in every way," Micah said. "Inside and out." He started to help Keturah back on the pack horse but then changed his mind. "We might as well walk. I think we'll find our unit somewhere over there."

Ten minutes later the two arrived before a line of cooking fires, and a familiar voice rose above the hubbub of talk: "Hey, Micah, over here!"

Turning quickly, Micah saw Dake come out from a small group of men. His twin brother had the same straw-colored hair and the same hazel eyes as Micah. Only a scar on his left eyebrow differentiated the two, but no one would ever mistake them no matter how much alike they looked. Whereas Micah was slow and gentle and spoke with a drawl, Dake was quick and impulsive. His eyes flashed, and he made up his mind instantly. The two had great affection for each other, however, as different as they were, and Dake came at once to strike Micah in the chest lightly and grin. "Why, you! How was your vacation?"

"Wish you could have been there, Dake." Reaching into his coat, he pulled out a small packet. "Letters from everybody." He smiled as Dake grabbed the package and said, "Yes, most of them are from Jeanne. I got so sick of talking about you, I wanted to run away."

"How is she?"

"Pretty as ever and misses you."

"Not as much as I miss her." Dake suddenly turned and looked at the young woman who stood beside the pack horse. He examined her silently, then turned back with a question in his eyes.

"Oh, this is Miss Keturah Burns, Dake—my brother Dake Bradford. I found Keturah back on the road. She lost her mother and I brought her along."

Dake's eyebrows rose, and Micah knew he wanted to ask, "Why did you bring her here?" but he only said, "I'm glad to know you, Miss Burns."

Micah knew he would have to explain more thoroughly, but for now he said, "Well, I got a pack horse full of food and some warm clothing. It won't do for everybody, but at least it will help."

"Something to eat?" Dake's expression changed. "We're about ready to eat branches off the trees! Come along. We'll celebrate the prodigal's return."

⚜   ⚜   ⚜

"But what are you going to *do* with her, Micah?"

Dake and Micah were sitting over a campfire eating bits of meat that they toasted on sticks. From time to time their covert glances went toward the young woman, who was rolled up in a blanket as close to the fire as she dared. She had evidently been exhausted, for after eating like a starved wolf, Micah had offered her some blankets. She had taken them with a grateful look, rolled up in them, and had fallen fast asleep from exhaustion and the ordeal she had gone through.

"I don't have any idea," Micah said.

"Is she a camp follower?"

Micah pulled a piece of the scorched meat from the stick and put it into his mouth. Chewing on it thoughtfully, he shook his head. "No, she's not, but her mother was. She told me that herself."

Dake also put a piece of the meat in his mouth. "This is delicious," he said. "I wish we had enough for the whole army." His eyes went back to the girl, then he looked at his brother. "Only you would do a thing like this—bring a daughter of a camp follower into an army camp."

"No, you would have done it too, Dake."

Dake started to argue but then began to laugh. "I guess I would, Micah," he said. "Now we just have to decide what to do with her."

"What's the army planning to do about the British? I don't see anything for it but to run."

"That's all there is to do. We'd better hope that General Howe gives up. With the cold winter and the poor condition of the men, we're not fit for a battle. All we're fit for is running. I don't see why those lobsterbacks haven't swallowed us up already."

"Howe's a cautious man," Micah said. The two brothers talked for some time about the poor position of the army and then were silent for a while.

"If we can just get away from him this time," Dake said finally, "the general will pull us together, and we can fight again." His eyes went back to the sleeping girl. "Jeanne would have the hide off me if she found out I was taking care of a young woman, but you don't have a wife, so I guess she's your chore."

Micah felt a wave of despair. He had had no choice but to help the girl, but to keep on helping her—well, that was something else again. The fire flickered, the yellow flames reaching up, and he was close enough to see the face of Keturah Burns as she lay on her back. The impossibly long eyelashes curled upward, and her lips were calm and relaxed. There was an innocence about the girl that convinced him she had somehow kept herself pure in spite of the life her mother had led.

Finally he tossed his stick into the fire and shrugged his shoulders.

"I don't know what to do, but I can't just turn her loose." He stared into the fire, his mind working slowly, for he was tired himself. Finally he said, "Well, I've got to get some sleep. I'll think on it tomorrow. Something will turn up."

"Sure it will," Dake said. He grinned broadly and slapped his brother across the shoulder. "Glad to see you back, Micah."

"They miss you at home, Dake."

The two brothers sat silently staring into the fire, then they rolled into their blankets. As Micah drifted off to sleep, his last thought was, *How can I possibly take care of a young woman in the middle of an army camp. . . ?*

5

RETREAT TO THE SOUTH

THE TALL MAN TOSSED AND TURNED on his bed. He was dreaming of his home at Mount Vernon, far away in Virginia. During his waking hours, that blessed place seemed as far distant as if it were across the sea. Often he would be struck with homesickness almost as severe as the illnesses that plagued his troops.

George Washington's dream was extremely clear and sharp. He was standing on the massive portico surveying his land—the green trees and rolling hills, the lawn he had planted and lovingly tended, the peaceful Potomac meandering past his beloved estate. The terrors of war could not be heard in this quiet place—the death, the stench, the cries of wounded men were not a part of this world. He could almost smell the scent of Virginia's spring and feel the strong muscles of his horse as he rode over the fields still wet with dew. The dream changed then, and he saw himself chasing a fox once again, moving smoothly with the powerful motion of his horse and delighting in the life that teemed all around him on the plantation.

From somewhere far off the sound of men's voices interrupted the dream. The sleeper stirred, came half out of his sleep, then sank back into an exhausted comalike state. The dream returned then, and he found himself having breakfast with his wife, going over the accounts with her. It had been a life he loved, simply being a gentleman farmer. Talking to his neighbors about livestock was more exciting to him than any battle. He had loved the life, and tearing himself away from it had been like an amputation. He could have done as well without an arm as to do without his beloved Mount Vernon. Now the sound of men's voices grew louder, and Washington stirred on his cot. He sat up, a tall, lanky, rawboned man, broad at the shoulders, broad at the hip with the full, strong legs of a born horseman. He had not taken off his uniform, and now stepping over to the small portable table, he washed his face in the freezing water, splashing and bubbling noisily as the cold brought him fully awake. Drying off on a handkerchief and settling his hat on his head, he pulled his coat around him and stepped outside.

General Knox was speaking with Captain Hamilton, and the two stopped immediately when Washington appeared. The deep respect and admiration they held for their commander bordered on idolatry, for each of them felt that this man, if he wanted to, could stop the sun from coming up.

"Did you take a count, Captain Hamilton?"

Hamilton dropped his head. Washington had ordered for the troops to be counted, and now the man was embarrassed. Hamilton was a small, handsome man with reddish hair and incredibly deep violet eyes. "Sir, there have been so many desertions."

"I have eyes. What's the count?"

"Well, sir, it's not individual desertions, but whole regiments are walking off."

Washington stared at the two men and said finally, "Gentlemen, we must face the truth. However few men we have, I need to know it."

Hamilton licked his lips, then nodded. "Yes, Your Excellency. The count that I have is three thousand and thirty-six."

Washington considered the man's words, then without any change in his expression he said, "Thank you, Captain."

Knox watched his commanding officer turn and walk back to his tent, his head held high and eyes forward, but with the weight of his responsibilities evident in his posture. "Where does he find the courage to go on?" Knox asked, as much to himself as to Hamilton. "I don't think he'd change if the heavens were falling."

Hamilton did not move. There were tears in his eyes, and he said quietly, almost in a whisper, "I think they have fallen—at least for him, Henry. When we lost Fort Lee and Fort Washington, and then lost again at White Plains, it was like tearing his flesh from his bones, but he'll go on. He doesn't know anything else but to go on."

🔔   🔔   🔔

Dake glanced across at Micah and grinned. "Not quite as glamorous as being a courier for His Excellency, is it?"

"I'm not complaining."

Sloshing along beside the two men, who moved in a ragged column down a serpentine road, Keturah said nothing. She was content, having had a good breakfast out of the supplies that Micah had brought back with him. Keturah had a warm coat, and at least for the day she was safe. Facing one day at a time had become a way of life for her. Tomorrow might be bad, the day after might be terrible, but if today one had a full stomach and safety—that was enough.

The rain fell in a drizzle as they plodded on toward Newark. Sometimes it pelted them like icy water poured out of a giant boot. A strong, cold stream had turned the road to mud. Now as they moved along, there was no sound except the constant sucking of their boots and shoes as they squished in the mud. Many of the men hunched over to keep the icy rain out of their faces. They looked like scarecrows dragging themselves along by their last shred of willpower.

Looking ahead, Dake saw Washington himself at the head of the column with Reed and Putnam. All three of them were soaking wet, and Dake said, "Putnam ought to be out of this. He's an old man, and he's got rheumatism."

"Old Put will never quit," Micah shrugged. "Stubbornest man in the Continental Army."

Closer down the line, the rest of Washington's staff straggled. Nathaniel Greene trudged along, the Quaker who had given up his faith and his vow never to kill to become a fighting machine. Knox, the portly bookseller turned artillery man, self-taught out of books, accompanied him. Behind them, Alexander Hamilton and a small fragment of artillery made a pitiful display. Most of their guns had been left at Fort Lee when they had been forced to retreat quickly.

As they moved along, Micah asked, "Where will we camp?"

"I don't know," Dake answered. "Maybe Newark."

"Then retreat some more?"

"I reckon that's what we'll have to do, Micah. Retreat's all we got left."

Up ahead in the column, strangely enough, Washington and Greene were speaking about the same subject.

"We can't retreat forever," Greene said. "We'll have to stop and fight sooner or later."

"Not now, Nathaniel."

Greene was still stung over the defeats at Fort Lee and Fort Washington. He had insisted these two forts could be defended, and Washington had listened to his stubborn pleas. As a result, an enormous store of precious guns and supplies had fallen to the British, as well as hundreds of prisoners. Greene had nearly lost his mind, and it had been Washington who had gone to him and said, "We must not dwell on the past, Nathaniel. Tomorrow we will fight again."

Now as they moved on, sloshing through the rain, Greene turned around and looked back over the ragged line of men. "We don't have many left," he said.

"No, we don't," Washington said.

"Do you think there are enough?" He asked the question and then felt foolish, for obviously their ranks had been depleted to a skeleton army. "Sorry, Your Excellency, I shouldn't have said that."

Washington turned his craggy face on this soldier he admired so greatly. Nathaniel Greene had made a devastating mistake for the Continental Army at Fort Lee, but Washington knew he had good leadership qualities and possessed a fierce white-hot streak of loyalty toward the fledgling country.

"No, there are not enough, but there will be," Washington assured him.

The calm confidence Washington exuded seemed to soothe Nathaniel Greene. He did not know it, but Washington himself spent countless hours agonizing over the pathetic condition of the troops. He had learned, however, not to let the difficult circumstances show in his face. Toward his officers and troops he manifested a calm exterior—never ruffled—but inside there were times when he was as deeply troubled as Nathaniel Greene, or any other of the soldiers that so looked up to him.

"How far will we retreat, sir?"

"As far as we have to."

"But we have to fight sometime. We can't always retreat."

"You know, Nathaniel, I think we almost could. Almost forever. Look at all that land out there. The British wouldn't follow us there."

Suddenly Nathaniel Greene had the thought, *If the British pursue us, this man will lead us across the Alleghenies and to the ocean that lies far across the untamed land. He'll never quit!* He thought about the vast, unexplored territory that lay beyond the Allegheny Mountains. So far the Colonies were entrenched on one small strip of land across the eastern seaboard, but Greene had seen the maps and had talked with men who had journeyed west, and he knew the Colonies were only a small part of this expansive continent that waited to be claimed.

⚜   ⚜   ⚜

The rain soon turned to large flakes of snow as they marched onward toward New Brunswick. It had been summer when the battle was fought in New York, and now it was almost the end of November—yet most of the men wore the same tattered clothing.

Finally they made camp, and after they'd eaten and were sitting close to the fire, Dake looked down and saw his dirty toes poking through his shoe and shook his head. "I wish you could have brought some boots from home."

Micah glanced over at his brother. He was sitting on a log, toasting a piece of cheese. "I wish I could have, too," he said. "I thought about socks and coats, but I didn't have time or money to buy new boots." He looked down the line where campfires winked in the semidarkness, looking like malevolent eyes. He shuddered and drew his coat closer about him. Glancing over, he asked, "Are you warm enough, Keturah?"

"Yes. The fire's good."

Keturah was sitting so close that a flying spark landed on her knee. Quickly she brushed it off, then looked up and gave Micah a brief smile. "This coat is real warm, and this sweater that you brought from your sister, why, it's just the warmest thing I've ever had."

"A bit colorful."

Keturah hugged her coat closer around her. "I like it. I always did like red." The sweater had belonged to Rachel and was indeed a crimson of the most shocking hue. Keturah had put it on at once, and as far as Micah knew, never had it off. She had taken off her cap now, for the snow had stopped, and her short, curly brown hair fell about her head in ringlets on the collar of the coat. She reached up and ran her hand through it and shook it so that it shimmered in the amber light of the fire. Keturah sat cross-legged now and turned her eyes back, staring dreamily into the blaze. The yellow and red flames flickered, sending tiny sparks upward, swirling madly. She watched them until they rose high, and then they almost seemed to entangle themselves with the multitude of stars that twinkled in the velvet blackness overhead.

"Are you tired, Keturah?" Dake asked.

"Me? No, I'm fine. It's you fellers carrying all them heavy packs and guns that ought to be tired."

Micah thought about the young woman's plight. It had been a difficult thing to bring her on this trip. He had racked his brain trying to think of some way to get her away from the camp. He had even stopped at one cabin on the march and inquired if anyone would take a young woman, but it had been hopeless from the start. "What kind of a young woman are you intending to give away?" an old man had leered—which had ended the conversation.

Micah had given up then and simply done the best he could for Keturah. She had fared well enough and had stayed far away from the other women who tagged along with some of the soldiers. At times, at night, Micah could hear their raucous laughter. Some of them had gotten liquor from somewhere, and he had glanced at Keturah, but she was evidently used to this sort of thing and did not even look up.

Once he asked her, "Tell me about yourself," and she looked at him with surprise.

71

"Why, there ain't nothin' to tell."

"When you were a little girl, I mean. Your growing up. Your family."

"Never knew my pa," she said. "We had a house once, but we lost it, and for a while Ma was a washerwoman at a big house, but then we left there."

A sad look of regret had come into her eyes at that point, and Micah suspected it was at that time in her life when Keturah's mother had fallen into a life of ill-repute.

"Then the war come, and we went to be with the soldiers. That's all there is, I reckon."

It seemed a bitter and poor excuse for a life. Micah thought about the richness of his own life—his family, his friends, plenty to eat, plenty to wear—and looking over at this small young woman, he felt a wave of pity. "Things will be better someday, Keturah."

"Don't know about that."

"Why, of course they will," Micah said. "You've got to think good things, and good things will happen."

Keturah looked up at him and touched the dimple in her chin. It was a habitual gesture with her. She had told him once that she hated it and wished she could cut it out or fill it up with something. Micah thought it was rather attractive and noticed that she touched it whenever she was thinking. "I don't know why it would be any better," she said. "Things mostly don't get better."

"Sometimes they do."

"For you maybe."

"For you too, Keturah."

"They ain't never got better yet. Mostly they just get worse." She looked up quickly and said, "Don't mean to be complainin'. I'm beholden to you for what you've done for me, Mr. Micah."

"I haven't done anything much yet, but I hope to."

Keturah turned to face Micah. Dake had nodded off to sleep, his chin resting on his chest. The soldiers were so exhausted they dozed whenever they could. Some of them even slept on horseback. "Tell me about you. What's your family like?" Keturah asked.

It seemed to give Micah some relief to talk about his home, so he sat there soaking up the warmth of the fire, talking about his brothers and sister. To his surprise, he even found himself talking about Sarah Dennison. He broke off suddenly and laughed with embarrassment. "Well, I've become quite a talker."

"I like it," Keturah said simply. "It must be great. You and Dake have family, and a pretty sister, and your pa is a good man."

"Yes, I have a fine family."

"What about this Sarah Dennison?"

"What about her?"

"Is she your woman?"

Micah's face seemed to burn at the bluntness of the question. "No, she's not my woman!" he exclaimed. "Just a lady I know."

"Are you partial to her?"

"Why . . . I don't know." Micah looked over at the young woman and saw her smiling strangely. "Why do you ask? What are you smiling about?"

"Your voice got kind of funny when you talked about her. I think you're sweet on her."

"Oh, don't be silly, Keturah!"

Keturah did not answer, but from then on she was very curious about Micah's relationship with Sarah Dennison. Time and again she would ask him questions about her. What did she look like? What kind of clothes did she wear? What color were her eyes?

Dake soon picked up on all this, and as the days passed and they trudged along, he said, "You'd better watch out and not let Keturah get close to that new lady friend of yours, Micah."

"What are you talking about?"

"I mean, she's jealous already."

"Don't be a fool, Dake!" Micah snapped with irritation. "She's just a child!"

"Who is? Keturah or Sarah?"

"You know what I mean!"

"And you know what *I* mean. She's just a young girl, but she's had a poor life. It looks to me, Micah," Dake observed, "that she's getting possessive of you. Better watch yourself."

Again Micah gave his brother a disgusted look. "Don't be foolish! We'll find a home for her, and that's all there'll be to it."

Micah seriously pondered his words to Keturah—"Things can get better"—for as their long march continued through New Jersey, things did *not* get better. The shoes of the soldiers shredded off until they were paper thin or gone completely, and since manufactured wool had been forbidden in America, most of them wore linen shirts and homespun breeches, which were neither warm nor comfortable. Their clothing had deteriorated since early fall, and now when they needed them the most, they were reduced to rags.

The weather grew constantly worse. It was a damp, bone-penetrating winter, cold, wet, and nasty. As the soldiers trudged along the Jersey roads they began to leave their bloody footprints in the snow, a suffering that neither Micah nor Dake would ever forget.

Though the weather was terrible, the morale of the men was even worse. Washington knew no better than anyone else what to do about it. When they finally arrived at New Brunswick, two whole brigades of Pennsylvania Riflemen approached the officers, saying, "We're going back home."

"You can't go home," they were ordered. "That's deserting."

"We're going anyway," the men said, their eyes like flint.

Washington was shaken out of his sleep by Nathaniel Greene. "Sir, two whole brigades, the Pennsylvania men—"

"What about them?"

"They're deserting. They're just walking away!"

Instantly General Washington dashed out of his tent and marched with Greene down to where the Pennsylvania men were preparing to leave.

"General Knox, load your cannon with grape."

Knox stared at the general but then turned at once and obeyed. It was one of the few cannons they had left, a small six-pounder. It could not do much damage in war, but loaded with grape shot it could tear a line of men to shreds.

Knox loaded the cannon, then said uncertainly, "Ready, sir."

Washington called out, "If you men return to your duty, there will be no more said."

"We're going home, General."

Only one of the men spoke, a tall, rawboned man with black hair and a determined look on his face.

The Pennsylvania men started marching. General Knox gave an agonizing stare at them. His hand was on the quick match that would touch the powder and blow the men in front of him to shreds. He turned his eyes on General Washington, whose features did not move. Knox looked back toward the marching soldiers, who did not hesitate for a moment. Desperation and resignation were etched on their faces.

On and on the men marched past the mouth of Knox's cannon. Finally they were all gone, and Knox went over to stand in front of General Washington. "Should I have fired, sir? What should I have done? What would you have done?"

Washington shook his head. He had been sickened by the sight of so many men deserting his tiny army, and now he said, "You did the right thing, Henry." He turned and walked slowly away, and as he did Knox's heart seemed to shrivel, for he had never seen such despair cloud a man's face.

Washington went directly to his tent. His aide was there, and he turned to him, saying, "Did you see what happened, Reed?"

"Yes, sir."

"I don't think we can go on much longer."

Washington sat down and said, "I will write again to General Lee. He has not moved at my orders. I cannot understand why."

Reed said nothing, but he watched as Washington labored at writing the letter. The general's hands were too large for a quill. They felt more at home with a farming implement or a musket. Nevertheless, he continued pushing the quill, which made a faint screech across the parchment as he penned the missive.

That same day a letter came from Lee, addressed to the Adjutant General, Joseph Reed. The dispatch rider handed it to a captain, who brought it at once to General Washington, saying, "This just arrived for the Adjutant General, sir."

"Thank you."

Washington recognized the handwriting to be that of General Lee. Since Reed had been taking care of most of his correspondence, he had no compunction about opening it. As his eyes ran over the page, they opened wide with shock. The letter was full of blatant treason, betrayal, and the falling away of a man he had trusted implicitly. Charles Lee had come from England with a sterling military reputation. In his personal manners he was an abominable man, unattractive in his looks, and yet Washington had deferred to him because he was a highly skilled professional soldier. Washington stared at the signature, *Charles Lee*, and an overwhelming sense of grief weighed down on him. Though he was a good judge of character, he had made a mistake concerning Lee, for he had trusted this man. Now he put the letter down on his desk and wrote a note to Reed, explaining how he had opened it, as he had done with other letters. He sighed and put aside the hope and dream of having a close friend—and moved on to the next crisis.

🜚   🜚   🜚

In every war and revolution, destiny sometimes turns on the deeds of one man—not often, but occasionally. Such a man was Thomas Paine, a small, unobtrusive Englishman who had sailed across the ocean to take part in the great experiment in liberty. He had failed at everything in England, and now it was to be expected that he would repeat his failures in this country as well.

However, Paine soon became a spark of inspiration that ignited the spirits of the weary soldiers. He walked with them with a musket slung over his back, and he shared their food around their fires in the camps.

He became one of them in a way that a writer, far away in England, or even in Philadelphia, could not. He had joined their miseries, and he had answers to their questions about the value of the revolution.

As Paine walked down the muddy roads of Newark, he preached to the troops. It could be called nothing else. If he had been other than what he was, the soldiers would have laughed at him. If he had ridden alongside, dressed in a clean suit on a fine horse, they would have scoffed at his remarks, but he was as dirty and lousy as the worst of them, and he spoke a fervent language they had not heard for a long time—not since Concord and Lexington.

"Patriots! Americans! Hear what I have to say! Do not be discouraged, for our cause is right, and the right will always win! We have the banner of truth to hold up," Paine cried out. It sounded like foolish talk in light of the defeat the Continental Army had suffered, but somehow they listened. And the flame for liberty slowly caught ablaze again.

"Let me tell you, there's nothing more glorious in this world than this thing we call freedom. We must treasure it as a man treasures his own child. When another comes to threaten that child, we must rise up as one man and strike the culprit, and we will be victorious!"

Once he cried out, "I say there's a God Almighty, and that the God of justice, and liberty, and truth will not allow us to be destroyed by tyrants!"

One of the flea-bitten soldiers laughed aloud. "It looks to me like the good Lord done allowed a lot of that, Tom. Are we winnin' or losin' in this here war?"

"We're winning!"

A laugh went up, but the men crowded closer as Paine said, "Don't look at this moment. Great causes have always had their dark moments. We will win this war! We are winning it! We are a peaceful, humble people, and we bear arms only for our liberty!"

"Keep on preachin', Tom," a tall scarecrow of a soldier called out. He laughed, but somehow he was encouraged. Here was a man who believed what was happening was good. His was the reason most of the men had joined Washington's army, and now they had a spokesman.

Late that night Tom Paine sat down at a battered table, writing furiously. More and more men came, and he began to read out loud what he was writing, words that stirred the hearts of those gathered around.

"These are times that try men's souls. The summer soldier and the sunshine patriot will, in this crisis, shrink from the service of their country; but he that stands it now deserves the love and thanks of man and woman. Tyranny, like hell, is not easily conquered; yet we have this consolation with us, that the harder the conflict, the more glorious the triumph. . . . Heaven knows how to put a proper price upon its goods; and it would be strange indeed if so celestial an article as freedom should not be highly rated. . . ."

As Paine's words rang through the Colonies, men smiled but some wept. Tom Paine's fiery zeal and eloquent speeches soon became the cord that drew the revolution together. His words were printed into a pamphlet called *Common Sense*, and they fell on the Colonies like a welcome rain after a long drought. Every Colonist read them and was inspired, for here was a man who proclaimed, "We are right, and we shall win!"

6

"I'll Be Your Woman?"

ON A COLD, BITTER AFTERNOON, November 29, 1776, the ragged, starving army of George Washington reached the Delaware River. They had lost men along the way, some deserting out of disgust, others out of pure weakness. But now as they approached the river, Washington drew up and said with a sigh of relief, "At last we can do something."

Nathaniel Greene, standing close by, said, "What are your orders, General?"

Washington's gray eyes swept up and down the river, which was brown and roiling. "Gather every boat you can find for twenty miles up and down the river."

"We're going to cross, sir?"

"Yes, and if we take all the boats, the British can't follow us, can they, Nathaniel?"

A light leaped into Greene's eyes, and he slapped his thigh, saying with delight, "Exactly, sir! I'll see to it right away!"

As soon as Greene left, Washington turned to Alexander Hamilton, who was standing nearby. "We'll want to send messages, Captain, to Boston, and to the Congress in Philadelphia."

"Yes, sir."

Washington paused for a moment, then said, "Find Private Micah Bradford. Give him a good horse. He will be the courier."

"Yes, sir. I will take care of it."

Micah was standing on the river looking across with Keturah at his side when an officer rode up. Turning, he took his hat off and swept it to his right in the salute. "Captain Hamilton!"

"Private Bradford. I have orders for you." He glanced at the woman and said, "Private orders."

Keturah quickly turned and walked away, and as soon as she was

79

out of hearing distance, Hamilton leaned forward and said, "His Excellency commands that you serve as a courier. There will be messages to Philadelphia and to Boston the same as the last time."

"Yes, sir! But, sir, could I request again that my brother Dake go? He has a wife there in Boston he hasn't seen for a very long time. They haven't been married very long, and—"

"I can't deal with that, Private. His Excellency has given the order. You'll have to speak to him." He grinned then and said, "I don't think I would advise it, though."

Despite himself, Micah returned the grin. "No, sir. I think you're right."

"Get your things together, dress warmly, and I'll see that you get a good horse. Our men have eaten most of them, but I think we have one left that will carry you there and back."

As soon as Hamilton left, Micah began to walk toward Keturah. She met him halfway, and he said, "Keturah, I've got to go."

"Go? Where are you goin'?"

"I'm being sent on a special mission. You'll be all right here."

Her eyes were large as she pleaded softly, "Can't I go with you?" She had grown more attached to this tall soldier than she had ever grown to anyone. She had waited time and again for him to touch her, to try to kiss her, to try to take advantage of her, but he never had. Micah's conduct toward her seemed strange to Keturah and made her curious, for she had learned to fight off men. The kind manner in which he treated her had given her a sense of dependency on Micah Bradford that she had never experienced with anyone, not even with her mother. Now the thought of being alone in the camp frightened her, and she waited anxiously for his answer.

"I'm afraid not," Micah said, shaking his head with a gesture of finality. "I'll be traveling fast, and I only have the one horse, but you'll be all right. I'll ask Dake to take care of you."

"How long will you be gone?"

"Hard to say. Not any longer than I can help."

Keturah said, "All right. I'll wait for you."

"While I'm in Boston, I'll see if I can find some place for you to stay."

"I don't know anybody in Boston."

"Well," Micah shrugged, "you can't stay with the army forever." He tried to smile and said, "I'll have to hurry. Shall I bring you anything back?"

Keturah blinked with surprise. "You might bring me back a pair of heavy socks."

"I'll do that. My sister, Rachel, is always knitting socks. You like that red sweater," he grinned, "maybe I can get you some socks to match."

"Yes, and get me some warm underwear, too. Red, if you can find it."

Micah flushed, for it was exactly the sort of thing that no lady would say to a man.

Keturah saw his face and bit her lip. "I . . . I guess I said somethin' wrong."

"No, of course not."

"Yes I did! I can tell by lookin' at you. What was it?"

"Well, a lady doesn't usually talk about her undergarments to a gentleman."

"Why not? That's what I need, and you asked me what I wanted."

Micah felt awkward. He laughed and said, "I can't go into that now, but I'll do what I can."

Suddenly Keturah leaned over and put her hand on his chest very lightly. It was the first time she had touched a man of her own free will, ever. "Be careful," she whispered. "Don't let anythin' happen to you."

Micah reached up and covered her small hand with his own. "I'll be careful, but this isn't dangerous. You take care of yourself."

Keturah watched as he strode away purposefully, and an hour later she saw him ride out of camp. Mournfully she watched until he was out of sight, then she went back to where Dake was whittling on a stick of wood. He looked up and saw the expression on her face. "He'll be back."

Keturah glanced at him sharply. "What do you mean by that?"

"Why, you look like a calf that just lost her mama."

"Mr. Micah's not my mama, nor my daddy neither!" Keturah said defensively.

Dake looked down so she could not see his smile. "Didn't mean a thing by it, Keturah. Don't worry. He'll be back." He continued to whittle and looked up to see the young woman wander off.

She's got a bad case on that brother of mine. If she were a couple of years older, there might be some danger, but I guess he's safe enough. Micah never had any girlfriends much, and now he's got a fancy, educated lady in Boston, and Keturah. If those two ever met, that would be somethin' to see. Dake laughed aloud, threw the stick down, put the knife back in its sheath, and walked over to where Ezra Lee was boiling coffee. "How about some of that coffee, Ezra? Smells strong enough to float a horseshoe nail!"

♟   ♟   ♟

The trip to Philadelphia was arduous because of the deep snow, but the horse was a sturdy mount. As on his previous trip, as soon as Micah delivered the letters to John Adams, he left and received orders to go back to the general, then he went at once to make the long trip to Boston. Upon arriving, instead of going to his father's house, he went immediately to the Dennison home.

He mounted the steps and knocked on the door, his lips drawn into a determined line. "I expect they'll throw me out," he murmured. "But they'll have to do so."

He stood there nervously, and when the door opened, he was greeted by Sarah herself instead of by a maid.

"Why—Micah!"

"Hello, Sarah. May I come in?"

Sarah gave a harried look around and whispered, "No. That wouldn't be wise."

"Your father carrying a gun to shoot me with?"

"Don't joke about it." Sarah's face was drawn, and Micah knew instantly there was something terribly wrong.

"What is it, Sarah?"

"You haven't heard?"

"I just got back from the army. What's happening?"

Sarah was wearing a simple brown dress of a light woolen material with long sleeves and a full skirt. The neckline had a high collar and was decorated with a simple gold broach. She seemed to have lost weight, for there were hollows in her cheeks that he did not remember. "It's my parents," she whispered. "They're insisting that I marry Mr. Potter."

Micah had suspected as much. "You don't have to do that, Sarah."

She stared at him as if he had said something rather stupid. "Of course I do," she said. "They're my parents."

"You're a grown woman. That's answer enough."

"What would I do if I don't marry? I'm not fit for anything else."

Her answer struck hard against Micah Bradford. He well knew that there was little enough for a woman to do except to marry, so now he had no answer to make to this. But suddenly he reached out and took her hand and kissed it, then gently held it. "I know we haven't known each other long," he said quietly, "and I don't know what will happen to the two of us, but if you marry Potter or anyone else, I know what will happen. It will be all over between us."

Sarah was very much aware of the young man's strong hand on hers. She had thought about him every night and every day since he had left. She did not know if she was in love with him or not. She only knew that he was kind and strong and gentle, and that there was a smile in his eyes, and that she enjoyed being with him. Perhaps this was enough.

Perhaps this was love. In any case, time and again, when she would think of Micah's handsome face, and then the beefy face of Potter with his crude manners, her heart was devastated.

"You'll have to go," she whispered.

"Promise me you won't marry. Not until we talk."

Sarah looked at him with a startled expression. "Why, it won't be all that soon."

"Good. I'll have to return to the army, but I have a feeling that this winter the army won't be doing much. My enlistment will be up in a few weeks. I'll come back then."

"You're not going to sign up again with the army?"

"No, not until—" Micah started to say, "Not until I get you settled," but decided that did not sound exactly right. "Not for a while," he said. "Please, Sarah. Postpone this thing."

"I'm already doing that as much as I can. Are you all right, Micah? You haven't been hurt or anything?"

"No, I'm fine." He stood holding her hand, then suddenly lifted it to his lips and kissed it again. "I'll see you before I leave, if I can."

Turning, he left, and Sarah Dennison stood watching him as he walked away. She almost called out to him but didn't. She had been miserable ever since her parents had informed her she had to marry Silas Potter, but now somehow a glimmer of hope rose in her heart, and she closed the door and fled up the stairs to her room.

☥   ☥   ☥

Micah took only one day to visit with his father and fill him and Marian in on the news of the army. They had already heard of the fiery zeal of Thomas Paine. He also stopped by the house and talked with Rachel and Jeanne, telling them how their gifts had been so well received. As usual, he spent a long hour with Jeanne relating everything about Dake, until he finally excused himself to go to bed, for the long days of travel had left him exhausted.

Rachel stopped him as he rose, saying, "Is there anything you need to take back?"

"Well . . . there is, but I'll take care of it."

"Let me help you," Rachel said gently. "If it's something I can get."

"Well, I need—" Micah's face flushed, and Rachel stared at him curiously. "Oh, never mind, Rachel."

Coming close to him, Rachel put her hand on his arm. "I've never seen you so flustered. What's wrong?"

"Well, the truth is, on my way back, there was a young woman who was having trouble. . . ."

83

Rachel listened as Micah awkwardly related the story about Keturah, then said, "I think that was noble of you, Micah. Just the sort of thing you would do. Does she need some things?"

"I gave her your sweater, which she likes very much, and she wants some wool socks if you have them."

"Of course. Anything else?"

Then Micah's face did flush a royal red. "Well, she . . . she wanted some warm underwear."

Rachel broke out into laughter, and Micah stared at her with chagrin. "It's not funny, Rachel!"

"Oh, yes it is! Did she come right out and say that?"

"Well, actually, she asked me for some *red* underwear," Micah admitted, painfully embarrassed.

At this, Rachel collapsed into gales of laughter, which upset Micah even more. Angry with his sister, he snapped, "She's just a poor, unfortunate girl who doesn't know any proper manners! You don't have to laugh at her!"

"I wasn't laughing at *her*," Rachel apologized, patting his arm. "I was laughing at you. I bet you were astonished, weren't you?"

Suddenly Micah could not contain the smile that jumped to his lips. "I nearly fell over backward," he admitted sheepishly. "Imagine asking a man to bring you some red underwear!"

"Well, I don't think I have any red underwear, but we can at least find something that will keep her warm."

The next day, before Micah left, Rachel whispered, "Let me know how things work out for Keturah."

"Rachel, would you look around for a family for her to stay with? I think she would be a good worker, and we've got to help her."

"All right." Rachel pulled his head down, kissed him, and said, "You be careful now. Don't get yourself shot. . . ."

🔔   🔔   🔔

Keturah was stirring a stew over the fire when she heard Jake Simmons call out, "Hey, Keturah, there comes your feller."

Looking up, Keturah saw Micah striding across the snow. He held a package tucked under his arm, and when he got close, he waved his other arm and said, "Hello!"

Keturah waited until he had greeted the soldiers, then he came to her. "I'm right glad you're back," she said.

"Glad to be back. Are you all right?"

"Sure."

"I've got something for you." Micah handed her the package and she started to tear the string off of it. "Wait a minute! Don't open it here."

"Why not?"

"Why not? Because it's got your underwear in it!" he said quietly. "You don't want all these men seeing your underwear, do you?"

"Oh! I didn't think about that." She looked up at him with a smile and said, "You didn't forget."

"Well, of course I didn't. There's a note in there from Rachel, too. She got all your things together. Now go open it someplace private."

Keturah slipped away from him into the small tent that Dake and Micah had commandeered for her. Closing the front flap, she slipped out of her clothes and into the warm underwear and pulled on the socks, then dressed again, pulling on her boots. Stepping outside, she found Micah waiting. "Oh, these are just fine! I feel so warm!"

"Good."

"They aren't red, the underwear, but they're nice and warm."

"I'm sure they are," Micah said, wondering if he was ever going to stop this young woman from talking about her undergarments!

🏹   🏹   🏹

For the next two days, Washington's troops waited along the banks of the Delaware, until all the boats were gathered and it was time to slip across the river. There were a great many mistakes made, but one by one the boats crossed over. Micah went with Dake and Keturah in a small dory rowed by six soldiers. When they reached the other side, he jumped out first in order to help Keturah out of the boat. Keturah awkwardly took his hand and leaped for the shore. She landed lightly, and he kept hold of her hand until he led her up the bank. Releasing it, he said, "Well, we're safe for a while. The British can't cross without any boats."

"Where will the general set up camp?"

"Not far from here. Come along. We'll get with the rest of the unit."

For the remainder of the day the army milled around, finally settling in to what would be a long winter's camp. Dake commandeered the best spot, a little knoll that was high and dry, and said, "We'd better start gathering firewood before these other fellas get it all."

Soon they had a fire going and were cooking what little food they had with them. Keturah helped with the cooking, and when it grew late, she and Micah sat in front of the fire.

"Did you see that Sarah woman you talked about?" Keturah asked finally.

"Well . . . just for a minute."

"What does she look like?"

"I've already told you that, Keturah."

"Tell me again."

"She's very small, not as tall as you are, and she has blond hair and dark blue eyes."

"Is she pretty?"

"Some people wouldn't think so, but I find her very pretty," Micah said as he stared into the fire.

Keturah sat quietly for a long time, and then she asked, "And she's not your woman, Micah?"

"No, she's not my woman. I don't like the way you say that, Keturah. I will never *have* a woman. I may be married to one, but—"

"I don't know what you mean."

"Well," Micah said uncomfortably, "when men and women get married, they *belong* to each other in a way, but it's different from *owning* something." He went on awkwardly trying to explain his ideas of marriage, and Keturah listened quietly. She said no more that night, and for two days she kept to herself and said very little.

He was standing beside the river watching as it rolled along its broad banks when Keturah came up to him and said without preamble, "Micah, I been thinkin'."

He turned to her and smiled. "You think a lot, Keturah. You've been quiet lately. What have you been thinking now?"

"I'll be your woman, Micah."

Micah Bradford had received several shocks in his life, but nothing like this one. He could not answer for a moment and thought he had misunderstood her, but then after looking into her eager face, he knew he had not. He tried desperately to think of some reply, but the differences between himself and this young woman, who had known none of the comforts of life, were too great. The only world she knew was the rough world of the camp. When he looked down into her eyes, he saw they were soft, and her lips were vulnerable and gentle. He knew she was offering him the only thing she had—herself. She was totally ignorant of the fineness of marriage, and the dignity of a man and a woman joining themselves for life—having never seen it herself.

I've got to be careful or I'll hurt her terribly, he thought. Then he said gently, "That's very nice of you to offer me a thing like that, Keturah." He tried to think of something else to say but finally could only add, "I don't think it would be the best thing for you."

Keturah had caught the expression in Micah's eyes. "I said something wrong again, didn't I?"

"Keturah," Micah said, "you're so very young."

"I'm sixteen."

"I know—but that's very young. I want you to grow up and be a fine woman, and find a man who loves you and will take care of you. And one you will love."

"I reckon I love you enough."

"You don't even know me, Keturah. People need to know each other before they make a commitment to marry."

"How long have you known Sarah Dennison?"

The abrupt question took Micah by surprise, and he said defensively, "Well, actually, not too long."

Keturah listened and watched as Micah spoke haltingly, then looked at the ground and murmured, "You don't want me, do you?"

"It's too big a decision, Keturah. And as I say, you don't know me, and I don't know you."

Keturah nodded slowly. "Maybe we'll get to know each other better, and then I can be your woman."

Micah was at a loss for words. He wanted to run but knew that for the next few weeks he would be in close proximity to this young woman, and he thought, *Maybe I can teach her something in that time.* Somehow he doubted it, though, and he nodded slowly, saying, "We'll see what happens, Keturah."

Keturah Burns realized Micah Bradford was far above her station in life. Still, she had come to trust him, and in her own innocent way, to love him, although she did not know what that meant. Now she said quietly, "One of these days I'll be your woman, Micah Bradford!"

PART TWO

THE TIDE TURNS

The Battle of Trenton, December 1776

7

A WEDDING LONG DELAYED

THE BACK ROOM OF THE METHODIST CHURCH that Pastor Asa Carrington used for a study and a place to seek God suddenly seemed too small for Daniel Bradford. The pastor had stepped outside, and now Bradford paced the floor like a caged lion. Once he stopped, pulled a handkerchief from his inner coat pocket, and mopped his forehead. Replacing the handkerchief, he moved over to the window and stared outside at the snow that was falling in flakes as large as shillings. For a long time he stood there, gazing at the scene and watching the carriages and horsemen as they arrived in front of the church.

The door opened abruptly, and Reverend Carrington stepped inside. He was a short man, strongly built, with black hair and direct, dark eyes. Taking one look at the man in front of him, he smiled and a spark of humor flared in his eyes. "It never changes."

"What never changes, Pastor?"

"Bridegrooms at weddings." Carrington rolled back on his heels and put his hands behind his back, studying Bradford. The prospective groom was wearing an uncut black velvet suit with the coat buttoned to the neck, with a pleated back that fell just below his knees. A white linen shirt peeked out slightly above the high collar of the coat, and a white ruffle flowed out from under the turned-back cuffs. The rest of his suit consisted of a matching waistcoat, breeches that ended just below his knees, white silk stockings, and shiny black leather shoes. "You look good enough for your own funeral. If you drop dead, we won't have to do anything to you."

Bradford stared at the pastor, then his lips turned upward in a grin. "Well, that may happen, Reverend Carrington. I don't know what's the

91

matter with me. I wasn't this nervous when I was facing British bullets at Lexington."

"Bullets are one thing," Carrington smiled. "Weddings are another." Coming over to stand beside Bradford, he laid his hands on the taller man's shoulders. "As I say, it never changes. Bridegrooms the world over, I suppose, are nervous."

"I wonder why that is?"

"They're giving away their freedom."

Bradford stared at his pastor. "I don't put much value on my freedom. This is what I want to do."

"Of course. Still, most men, I suppose, have a bit of wildness in them. They want to do exactly what they want to do, and when a man marries, he must partly give up some of that independence."

"I don't see that, Pastor."

"I think you do. From this day forward, if you decide to go to Philadelphia, it'll be different. Now all you have to do is go out, get on your horse, and ride off. Tomorrow you'll have to say, 'Marian, would it be all right with you if I made a trip to Philadelphia?' and then you'll have to spend some time explaining why you need to go, and why she shouldn't go with you because it's too hard a trip, and all sorts of things."

The sound of organ music suddenly came to them, and Daniel started as if he had been struck by a bolt of lightning. Nervously he ran his hand across his wheat-colored hair and licked his lips. "Is it time?"

"Oh no. That's just to give people time to get settled down." Carrington laughed outright. "You look like a man on his way to be hanged."

"Well, I don't feel like that. I'm glad of this—it's what I want. I've loved Marian for a long time, and now we can marry and—"

"And live happily ever after?" Carrington inquired. He was well aware of the circumstances of Daniel Bradford's attachment to Marian Rochester. Talk had run around Boston about them, but Carrington had believed none of it. He knew Daniel Bradford too well to believe that he would have a clandestine affair with a married woman. Now as he studied the tall, strong form of Bradford, he found himself liking the man even more. "Not many men," he said, "would have waited as faithfully as you. Have you never been attracted to another woman since your wife died?" It was the closest the pastor had ever come to inquire into Daniel's private affairs, but he felt they were close enough for this.

"No," Daniel said simply. He looked out the window for a moment where the snow swirled and did a wild dance as the December wind tossed it about, then turned his head to look directly into Carrington's face. "I've loved Marian in one way or another for years. At first it was just admiration, and I tried to keep it at that. It's been very hard, Pastor."

"I'm sure it has," Carrington nodded, then he smiled. "But you've been faithful."

"But I'm still nervous."

Laughing outright, Carrington turned and walked over to his desk and picked up a black Bible. Returning to stand beside the door that led to the auditorium, he said, "Let's look at it this way. In twenty minutes or so, Dan, you'll be married. Now, the church may catch on fire, or one of the guests may have a heart attack, or perhaps a storm will lift the roof of the church off, but I'll guarantee you one thing—no matter *what* happens, in twenty or thirty minutes you will be married, and Marian will be Mrs. Marian Bradford. Now, try not to look so afraid. It's a bad example for the other prospective bridegrooms out there."

Daniel grinned abruptly, then moved over to stand beside the pastor. "All right. I'm quaking on the inside, but I'll put a good face on it."

The two men stood there until finally there was some sort of sign that Carrington seemed to understand. Murmuring, "It's time, Daniel," he stepped outside, and Daniel followed close on his heels. The two men walked into the sanctuary and came to stand in front of the pulpit, which stood on a low platform. Daniel looked over the congregation nervously and was surprised to see how many people were there. The family, of course, were up close—Sam, Rachel, and Jeanne—and a moment's regret struck him, for his sons Dake and Micah were still with Washington in New Jersey, across the Delaware. Matthew was in Europe. Daniel wasn't sure exactly where. His eyes ran along the visitors, and he saw Edward Ginn, his foreman at the foundry, with his entire family, his stocky form, black hair, and eyes that dominated his face. Doctor Claude Bates, his physician, was there, and Daniel saw a twinkle of humor in his eyes and hoped he didn't say anything. Bates had a thunderous voice. He was hard of hearing and somehow thought if he spoke loudly enough, he could understand people better. Bradford had heard one man say that Bates's voice was so loud and strident it made his hair hurt.

Across the room, halfway back, sat Mrs. Lettie White, the Bradfords' housekeeper, who was smiling placidly. She knew Daniel's heart, for he had been unable to keep it from this rather perceptive woman.

The organ music began to swell, and Dan straightened up almost as if he were a soldier at attention. A movement caught his eye, and there, down the aisle, came the woman he loved with all of his heart, escorted by her father, John Frazier. Her face seemed to fill Daniel's vision, and he thought suddenly, as he had thought many times, *I've never seen a more beautiful woman!* Her heart-shaped face was dominated by large, almond-shaped green eyes, and her auburn hair escaped the white veil she wore.

The dress itself he did not recognize. At first Marian had said that she wanted to simply get married in the pastor's home, but Daniel had been obstinate. "No," he had said, "we're going to have a church wedding. I want you to have everything, and I know a wedding is one thing that women long for."

He had insisted she buy a wedding dress, and now as he watched her come down the aisle smoothly with a slight smile on her broad lips, he felt she had chosen well. She wore a brocade gown in a delicate hue of violet with a low neckline edged in white lace. It had long sleeves that were decorated at the wrists by white embroidery and a large white lace ruffle, and a form-fitting bodice with insets of white lace that came to a point at the waist to meet the skirt. The overskirt was full and done with splashes of white, embroidered flowers hiding in the full folds of the violet material, and the petticoat was white with contrasting purple embroidered flowers. Marian's hair was swept back from her face and piled high on her head. A delicate lace veil encircled her hair and fell to the middle of her back.

Finally she stood beside him, and he heard Carrington's voice, which seemed to come from far away: "We are gathered together here this day to unite this man and this woman in holy matrimony. . . . Who gives this woman in marriage?"

As John Frazier gave Marian's hand to Bradford, the voice of the minister seemed to fade away, and Daniel suddenly saw Marian as he had seen her the first time. It had been years ago. He had been an indentured servant to Leo Rochester. Rochester had been an impossible man, Dan's bitter enemy, and had ground him into the dirt whenever possible. He had brought Marian Frazier to his plantation at Fairhope, in Virginia, and Daniel Bradford, taking one look at the woman from Boston, had known that for him she was like no other. He suddenly had a flashing memory of the first time he had seen her, when she had laughed down at him as he had helped her onto her horse—and today, even at the age of forty-four, she still possessed the beauty she had back then. She was one of those women who never seemed to grow old, or if she did, the aging process simply made her more attractive.

And now Daniel took her hand, and the ancient words were spoken: "With all my worldly goods I thee endow. . . . I take thee, Marian, as my lawful wedded wife, as long as we both shall live. . . ."

Her hand was warm and firm in his, and her fine eyes met his with an expression that he could not quite understand. He knew only that she loved him and had for years. Always, he had admired her for her faithfulness in staying absolutely true to Leo Rochester, though Leo was a dishonorable man no woman could really admire or look up to.

And then the words came, "You may kiss the bride. . . ." Daniel lifted the veil, and when Marian lifted her face to him, he put his lips on hers. They were soft and warm and willing, and when he drew back she whispered, "I love you, Daniel Bradford."

"I love you too, Marian."

She took his arm, and as they walked together down the aisle, Daniel thought, *This is forever. It will never change. . . !*

T   T   T

Daniel Bradford had not had a vacation for years. He had worked hard as an indentured servant until he had fulfilled his obligation to Leo Rochester, then had gone immediately to work as a blacksmith until finally he had formed a partnership with John Frazier at his foundry that had since prospered. Daniel's entire life had been active, not only in pursing a profession, but with the raising of his large family. Raising children with no wife had been difficult, and he had spent himself unsparingly in his devotion for them.

But now, for the first time since he could remember, there was nothing to do. He said as much to Marian. "I don't know what to do with myself." The two of them were standing inside the cottage nestled under a canopy of oaks that flanked Cape Cod. Daniel had rented the small house for a honeymoon from a friend, and now he looked around, saying almost plaintively, "I feel lost. No youngsters to look out for, no business, nothing to do but . . ."

Marian had been standing in the middle of the parlor looking around at the fine furniture. "Nothing to do but what?"

Instantly Daniel came over and put his arms around her. "Nothing to do but love you." He kissed her heartily and then said, "Mrs. Marian Bradford. How does that sound?"

Marian returned his smile and whispered, "I can't think of a better name on earth for a woman. Marian Bradford. Yes, I like it."

Releasing her, Daniel looked around and said, "This is a fine cottage." The cottage was a one-and-a-half-story clapboard structure that had been painted a brilliant white and trimmed with salmon and dark green. The windows were numerous, and many had no curtains so that the ocean view could be easily seen from each room. The rooms were small but tastefully furnished and decorated so as to appear more spacious. The walls were painted in delicate shades of yellows and greens, and the floor gave off a warmth with the glow of its waxed hardwood.

Each room had a brick fireplace with a pine mantel, painted pine cupboards, horsehair-covered furniture, and paintings on the walls depicting summer scenes on the beach.

Daniel stepped back from Marian, his eyes going over the room. "This has a warmth to it, doesn't it? It feels lived in. You know, some places just seem happy, and I think this is one of them." He sat down in a Morris chair, stretching his legs out in front of the fire that crackled and roared, sweeping the sparks up the chimney.

"It does feel good, doesn't it?"

Marian came over and sat down across from him on the sofa, and the two stared at each other. She was wearing a pale blue dress and her thick hair fell loosely around her shoulders. A peaceful sense of well-being filled her heart, and she felt suddenly like a traveler who had arrived at home port after a long and trying journey.

"I feel so strange," Daniel said. "For years I've had to bottle up my love for you, and now I don't have to do that anymore."

"I hope you never will do a thing like that. Bottled love isn't much good. It's like wine, I suppose. If you keep it in the bottle, what good is it?"

He laughed and stood up and came over to sit down beside her, putting his arm around her. They sat there watching the fire, and there was a peace and tranquillity that neither Daniel nor Marian had ever known. She had been bound to a brutal husband who gave her no love whatsoever. Daniel had been bound by his own strong Christian beliefs that had kept him from even speaking of his love, but now there was a relaxation in them that was soothing.

They sat for a long time, speaking quietly of the wedding and the family. Finally Daniel glanced out the bay window. "It's getting dark." He gave her a squeeze and said, "Are you going to cook supper, woman, or starve me to death?"

"Sir, I'm a dutiful wife, and I will do that which is right."

Rising at once, Marian went into the kitchen. She had no intention of cooking a big meal, but she had made preparations. She asked Daniel to fix her a fire in the big stone fireplace, which he did. "Now, you go read a book or something," she smiled, "while I fix our bridal supper."

Daniel left and went into the study. He searched among the books on the bookshelf and found a volume of Wesley's sermons. "Maybe there's one here on how to be a good husband," he grinned. Settling himself down by the fire, he read for a time, enjoying the sound of the crackling fire and the warmth that filled the room. Very soon, it seemed to him, Marian appeared and said, "The bridal supper's ready."

Rising from his chair, Daniel put the book down, then moved into the small dining room and pulled a chair out for Marian. Sitting down across the round oak table, he looked approvingly at the white table-cloth, the fine china that seemed to glow warmly under the flickering light of the lamp, and the silverware that glowed dully. "Our first sup-per together," he said quietly, then bowed his head and said, "Oh, Lord, we are grateful for this food, and we are grateful that you have given us to each other. May our lives be spent in love to each other, but most of all to you. In Jesus' name. Amen."

"Amen," Marian whispered, then she looked over and said, "Cold cuts tonight. I'll cook something better tomorrow."

"Why, this looks wonderful." Daniel studied the table and saw small platters of mutton and beef placed before him. China plates had been heaped with stilton, slipcoat, and cheddar cheese, a sliced loaf of wheaten bread, and a few seed cakes. A small bowl of butter and one of honey were placed toward the center of the table, and at the far end were bowls filled with brandied peaches and apricots. Fine cut crystal glasses held warmed apple cider to help take the chill out of the evening air.

The two ate hungrily, and finally, when they were finished, Daniel helped her clean the table, and they returned to the parlor, where he put another log on the fire and looked at it critically. "That wood is too green. It doesn't burn well," he said. "Tomorrow I'll find some dry limbs."

For a while the two sat on the sofa, and he read parts of Wesley's sermon, which was on the subject of the Second Coming of Christ, and they spoke for some time about this. "I've always longed for Jesus to come back," Daniel said once, "but to tell the truth, I had a secret wish that before He comes. . . ."

When Daniel paused, Marian smiled. "You wanted us to have each other? I've felt the same way, Daniel."

"I'm glad I'm not the only one." He returned her smile and said, "It's been a long day. Are you tired?"

Marian looked at him and nodded.

"I'll build the fire so it'll be warm in the morning." But instead of moving to the fireplace, he turned toward her. "I love you, Marian," he whispered and pulled her over to face him. The kiss was filled with longing and poignancy and sweetness for her. In contrast to Leo, Daniel was gentle, and there was a reverence in his embrace. Marian whis-pered, "I'll never let you go, Daniel."

"No, this was the way it was meant to be, Marian." As he looked back at her, she seemed like a child, simple contentment on her face, and he held her tightly, and they knew they had somehow come home.

T   T   T

The camp of the Continental Army was a bitter, frozen wasteland with nothing but hastily constructed huts that provided only a minimum of protection against the icy wind. New Jersey was a cold place, Micah discovered, and the people did not seem to be much warmer. He was sitting outside the small hut he and the squad had built for themselves, and Keturah was watching him carefully with her large eyes.

Dake was speaking about the New Jersey people, and there was bitterness in his voice. "They call themselves patriots!" he spat on the snow, then shook his head vigorously. "They're not patriots! They're nothing but Tories!"

"Not all of them," Micah insisted.

"All I've seen are! The general was expecting our people to rise up over here! Instead of that, what do we get? Nothing good!"

Micah knew this was true. He thought about the talk that had gone around, how that the army would increase when they got to New Jersey, with men from this colony rushing to join up. *If they rushed*, he thought ruefully, *it was in the other direction.* There had been almost no recruits. Now he poked the fire with a stick, watched it blaze up, and reached over and laid another stick on the top. "It hasn't been like we thought. I know the general's disappointed."

Keturah listened as the two men talked. Her small tent was thirty yards away. To her it was a place of sanctuary. She knew that the safety and security itself lay in Micah and Dake. She had not been troubled after Zeke Maitland had tried to put his hands on her, and Micah had marched up to him and without a word flattened him with a tremendous blow right between the eyes. It had swelled the man's eyes shut so badly he could not see for a few days. Micah had gone to him later and said, "I'm sorry I had to hit you, but you'll have to understand. This young woman's under my protection."

Zeke had peered at him between the slits and whined, "Why didn't you just say so instead of bustin' my head?"

"You don't listen good, Zeke," Micah had replied. "Sorry about that."

Micah's protection had filled Keturah with gratitude. She had never had a protector, and now as she looked across the flickering fire she felt again the stirring of admiration for Micah Bradford.

Dake had stopped speaking, and his eyes fell on the girl's face. *She's a right pretty little thing, but she's dead gone on Micah, and he's too dumb to know it. He sees her as just a child, which is a fool mistake.* He had tried to talk with Micah about this, and Micah had only scoffed at him.

Finally the fire began to die down, and Micah said, "I'll go get some more firewood, if that Pennsylvania bunch hasn't gotten it all."

"I'll go with you, Micah." Keturah came to her feet at once and followed him as he moved away from the fire. Dake was watching and shook his head, his lips drawn tight, but he knew Micah, for all his mildness, was a stubborn man. "He just doesn't hear what he doesn't want to hear," Dake muttered, then he rose up, went inside the tent, and rolled up in his blankets.

Micah and Keturah gathered broken fragments of limbs, such as they could find. They had no ax, so they had to drag some back. When they came back to the fire, he dropped his load and said, "You'd better go to bed, Keturah."

"Not now." She began to feed sticks to the fire and sat down and watched it as it started to blaze up. Looking up at him, her eyes seemed very large. They were startling eyes, so blue that they seemed to dominate her face. "I always hate to go to bed."

"You're afraid?"

"No, not afraid. I'm just afraid I'll miss something."

Micah laughed and came over to stand beside her. "You're not going to miss much out here. It's the same every night."

"I know."

Keturah continued to feed the fire, and he sat down beside her, adding a chunk or two himself. "I always did like fires, outside or inside. Something cheerful about it." He looked around at the miserable camp and shook his head. "We need something cheerful out here."

Keturah sat there and listened as he spoke. As always, she could not hear enough of his talk, and finally, after he grew silent, she turned to him and asked, "Don't you like me, Micah?"

"Why, of course, I like you, Keturah." Surprise marked Micah's voice, and he turned to face her, wondering what was going on in her mind. She was a strange person to him. Her life had been so different, but now he said, "What do you mean by that?"

"You never try to touch me, or kiss me, or anything like that. So I thought you didn't like me."

Carefully Micah thought how to answer her. He did not want to hurt her feelings. He stared into the dancing flames for a while, then finally said, "First of all, I haven't because I'm a Christian."

"I knew you were religious," Keturah said, then reached over and added more wood to the fire.

"Well, it's more than that. You see, I've given my life to Christ, and it wouldn't be right for me to . . ." He hesitated for a moment, then continued, "to be romantic toward you. You're a lot younger than I am—just a child, really."

"I know girls my age already married."

Micah could not argue this and said, "Have you ever thought about God? Have you ever listened to sermons or read the Bible?"

"No, not really."

"Would you mind if I told you a few things about the Lord?"

"I guess not." Keturah sat there while he went on quoting Scripture. She was not really listening to him. She was watching his strong face as the firelight reflected on it, thinking about what a good man he was, the best she had ever known.

Finally he said, "Do you understand this? How you need to turn to Jesus?"

"Not really."

A feeling of despair came to Micah. What could he do to make her understand? He said, "Well, it's late, and we're tired. We'll talk more about it another time, and we'll go to the service. The chaplain will preach, and you'll like it."

"All right. If you say so, Micah."

Keturah rose and walked back to her tent. She did not undress but wrapped herself in her blankets, and when she put her head down, she closed her eyes and thought about Micah, about how strong his hands were, and how handsome he was. She drifted off to sleep thinking, *He'd be good to a woman, and that's what I want to be someday—his woman.*

8

PARENTS AREN'T
ALWAYS KIND

A LIGHT SNOW HAD FALLEN OVERNIGHT, leaving the streets of Boston lacquered with a sparkling carpet of white. Sarah Dennison stood at the window, brushing her hair, admiring the snowfall as the winter dawn was breaking. She had slept poorly the night before, and now as the first wagons and horses left their tracks in the crystalline, sparkling snow, she started when a knock sounded at her door. She turned to see her mother enter, and at once felt a cold chill rise in her heart. For as long as Sarah could remember, the words she most dreaded to hear from her parents were "Now, Sarah, it's time for us to have a little talk."

She had learned over the years to read her mother's face, and now she knew the dreaded words were about to be spoken.

"Before we go into breakfast," Mrs. Dennison said, "we need to have a little talk."

"What is it, Mother?"

Mrs. Dennison stood before her daughter stiffly. She was a tall woman, her posture erect and proud, much like one of the king's guards. She was wearing a heavily embroidered dark green dress made of the finest silk, with a white lace scarf around her shoulders. Her clothing was always in style, and although the English blockade had narrowed down her choices, still many French goods had arrived in Boston, and she had taken advantage of them. She eyed her daughter for a moment and then said, "Why don't we sit down?" Without waiting for an answer, she moved over to the brocade-covered settee and waited until Sarah joined her. She spoke patiently but firmly, as one would speak to a rebellious child or to a servant who needed a firm hand.

"Your father and I have been waiting for you to say something about your engagement."

"My engagement!" Sarah's eyes flew open, and a faint color suffused the fair skin around her neck and cheeks. "But . . . I'm not engaged!"

"Now, Sarah, we've been over this before. It's not that your father and I want to *force* you into anything, but you're not like your sisters. They grew up knowing they were to marry one day, and your father and I had to do practically nothing to see that they did."

Sarah did not speak, but she knew this was a misconception that her mother had devised in her own mind. Sarah had watched as Mrs. Dennison manipulated and maneuvered each of her unmarried daughters until they married suitably—and *suitably* meant according to Mr. and Mrs. Thomas Dennison's selection and approval of a financially sound husband. They had no intention of allowing any of their daughters to marry below their social station, thus tarnishing the family's name in Boston's elite social circles. Sarah knew, however, it would be useless to offer her opinions on the matter to her mother, and as her mother continued to speak, Sarah twisted her hands nervously in her lap.

For a time the older woman spoke of the necessity of marriage and the desirability of a suitable husband, and finally she said firmly, "Your father and I have announced your engagement, Sarah."

"Mother, you didn't!" Sarah gasped.

"Why, of course we did. If we waited on you to make up your mind to accept Mr. Potter, he might get away."

She took a deep breath and said as firmly as she could, "Mother, I do not love Mr. Potter! I can't think that you would expect me to marry a man I didn't love!"

"Posh! You've always been too backward in these matters, Sarah. I would suspect you of reading too many romances, but I know that could not be true. If *I* had waited for whatever these romancers call "love," why, your father and I would never have married! None of us are romantic in this family—least of all you, I should think."

Sarah had no desire to argue with her mother's reasoning, yet even as her mother spoke, Sarah knew in her heart that marriage was much more than an agreement—arranged by parents—between two people to live together and raise a family. She could not define all of her feelings, and would, indeed, be too embarrassed to try. She felt she was being shoved into some sort of cage and the door was being slammed shut. She could not face her mother for a moment. Never in all of her life had she seriously challenged any decision that had been made on her behalf. Now, however, a strength rose up inside her spirit and she shook her head and said, "I appreciate what you and Father have tried to do. But in this case, Mother, I beg you—please don't force me into this marriage. It would be against everything I feel."

"Feel? Why, that's ridiculous! Mr. Potter has wealthy holdings and a fine house. He needs help raising his infant son. You'll have a fine life with him, my dear. Now, let's hear no more about this silly talk of love. It's settled." Mrs. Dennison rose abruptly and moved toward the door. When she reached it, she turned and critically studied Sarah, who sat on the sofa, her head down. "Now, I know that young women have a certain amount of fear about marriage and questions. That's entirely natural, and we will talk about those things before you are married. Now, when you come down to breakfast, we'll begin to make plans for the wedding, and Mr. Potter will be calling on you, I'm sure, this afternoon."

Sarah's shoulders drooped as the door closed firmly, very much like the closing of a prison door. The heavy oak door did not clang, to be sure, but still, there was a sharp and harsh finality to it that rendered her unable to move. *Married to Mr. Potter!* Agitation swept over her and she rose and began to pace the floor. She had no resources, for all of her life she had been under the domination of her mother, until now it had come to the point where resistance was unthinkable. Walking over to the fireplace, Sarah stared down into the flames unthinking, surrounded by fears and doubt that rose up like a black mist. Her lips trembled, and she deliberately firmed them and dashed away the tears that sprang unbidden to her eyes. "I can't think of it!" she whispered, then turned and left the room, knowing that her life was slowly being forced down a path she despised and hated, yet could do nothing about it.

✠   ✠   ✠

For two days after her mother's "little talk" Sarah endured the constant attentions of Mr. Potter. He seemed to take it for granted that their marriage was a settled issue. There was certainly no blatant romanticism on his part. He had simply come to her and put his arm around her, hugging her roughly, saying, "Well, your parents have given their consent, so we will soon be married." He had kissed her, and she had hated the touch of his lips on hers and pulled back.

Potter had stared at her somewhat disconcerted, then he had laughed coarsely. "You're not used to a man. Well, I'll take care of that, Sarah!"

She thought often of those words in the two days that followed, and shuddered at the thought of being married to a man whose very presence repulsed her. She hated the touch of Potter's hands, and his lips, and his forceful kisses. She said little during this time, and on Sunday morning, she got up, dressed, and went to church. Her parents did not choose to go that day, so she had the coachman take her to the Methodist church. As he handed her down, he said, "I'll be waiting, ma'am."

"You needn't wait, James. I can walk home."

"Not in all this snow, surely."

"Well, then I will find a way. I wouldn't want you sitting out here all morning in the cold." Ignoring his protests, she smiled at him and said, "Go along, now," then turned and entered the church.

Finding a place toward the back, she sat down, and as always a peace came to her. She loved this church and would have chosen it for her own, but her parents would not hear of it. To be called a Methodist was the same as to be called a wide-eyed enthusiast. The Methodist movement begun by John and Charles Wesley was sweeping over England, and there were stories of wild excesses in their meetings. Some of these outbursts had attached themselves to George Whitefield's meetings, but when Sarah had attended one of Whitefield's outdoor services, she had seen nothing like that.

The church was cold, but Sarah did not mind. She had worn a dark blue woolen dress, a heavy brown woolen hooded cloak, and a fur muff, and she sat quietly with her hands inside her muff, praying and waiting upon the Lord. Waiting on the Lord was something she had learned over the years. She could not have described it, nor did she ever speak of it to others, but it had consisted merely of closing her eyes and asking God to fill her spirit. Sometimes she would sit like this, seeking God for an hour, not consciously praying—although she did that at times. But this waiting upon God was what she prized, for it was then that God seemed most real to her. She would not ask for anything, nor make any petitions, but simply lift her heart to God. He would respond with a sense of His presence that she found at no other time. It was not tied to a church, for her waiting on God often took place in her own room, or when she was walking. She had thought once that she might make a good Quaker, for she understood that this was part of their worship service—simply to come to church and wait until someone was moved by the Spirit.

The service began, and she sat there joining in the songs, her sweet voice melding with the others. Now as the pastor, Reverend Asa Carrington, finally stood up to preach, she felt the weight of his rather intent dark eyes upon her. She liked Reverend Carrington very much, more than any other preacher she had heard in Boston. As he began to speak, she had the uncanny sensation that he had singled her out. He had chosen for his text Romans 8:28: "And we know that all things work together for good to them that love God, to them who are called according to his purpose." It was a text that Sarah had memorized, and many times, when difficulties had arisen, had fallen back on for encouragement. Reverend Carrington quoted many Scriptures, showing how godly men and women had throughout history often endured terrible difficulties. "But then the Scriptures said that these things were not actually as terrible as they seemed, for they were working for good in their lives."

"All of us can see how, at times," Reverend Carrington said, "things are working for good. When we are blessed, when our children do well, when we prosper financially, it is easy for any man or woman to say, 'Well, all things are working together for good, just as God says.' But when tragedy strikes, when we lose our loved ones, when our health is threatened, when any one of the slings and arrows of outrageous fortune, as Shakespeare put it, strikes us, then we begin to cry out. How can this be for my good, oh, Lord? It is terrible. It is not what I want for my life."

Instantly Sarah thought of her own problem, and her mind left the preacher's words for a moment. *How could marrying Mr. Potter be for my good when I so dislike him? Oh, God, show me your way! If this is what I must do, if it is your will, then I will endure it!* She prayed for some time and then came back to the words of the preacher, who continued for some forty-five minutes quoting many Scriptures from both the Old and New Testaments.

Finally the sermon was over, and Sarah rose to leave the church. As she reached the end of the pew, she found a young woman standing there, who greeted her with a smile. "It's Miss Dennison, isn't it?"

"Why, yes!" Sarah said. The woman looked familiar. She was rather tall, with red hair and attractive green eyes, and she was well dressed, wearing a plum-colored velvet cloak with fur around the edges and carrying a large fur muff.

"I'm Rachel Bradford, Miss Dennison. Perhaps you've forgotten me, but I believe you know my brother Micah."

"Oh—why, yes I do, Miss Bradford."

"He spoke of you very highly, Miss Dennison." Rachel saw that the words brought a flush to the young woman's cheeks. There was something almost childlike about Sarah Dennison that Rachel rather liked. She hesitated for a moment, then said, "We're so glad to have you visit our church. I've noticed that you visit here very often."

"I admire the pastor very much. He truly explains the Word of God."

"Yes, he does." Rachel smiled. She hesitated for a moment, then said, "I'm rather at loose ends this afternoon and all alone at the house. My father, as you may know, has recently married and lives with his wife in her family's home so she can be near her father who is very ill. My brothers are gone, and my sister-in-law is visiting friends, too. I'm wondering, if you have nothing to do, would you care to come, and we could have a lunch together? Cold cuts, tea, and a sweet cake that I've just made."

"Why, I would like that very much," Sarah said. She was curious about the Bradford family. She had heard, as most people in Boston had, of the marriage of Daniel Bradford to the widow of Sir Leo Rochester. Not all of the remarks had been kind, but she had discounted those. "I would be happy to, if it is no trouble."

"Why, it's no trouble at all. I've been dreading spending the afternoon alone. Come now. We have a carriage here, Miss Dennison. Why not Rachel and Sarah?"

"Of course, that would be very nice."

Sarah got into the carriage with Rachel Bradford and actually said very little. Rachel, having sensed her shyness, did most of the talking, and when they arrived at the Bradford house, she said, "I left the fire in the kitchen. Suppose we just go there and see what we can find?"

"I'd like that very much indeed."

Rachel led the way down the long hall to the end of the house where the kitchen spread out across the back. A large fireplace occupied the entire right wall, and on the left stood a storage unit. Pale sunlight filtered down through the windows, and soon the two women were putting together a meal.

Going to the icebox, Rachel found one thick slice of leftover venison, two chicken legs, and a small slice of beef. She took these over to the fire to warm them slightly, then placed them on a small plate. Sarah cut the seed cake that Rachel had baked the day before, then went in search of some preserves in the storage room. While Sarah was in the storage room, Rachel began to make the tea and then set about getting the table prepared. She was just about finished when Sarah came out carrying a jar of preserves, a jar of brandied grapes, and some butter. Sarah placed these on the table, and they both sat down to eat.

Finally, when Sarah had eaten her second piece of the seed cake, she smiled and said, "It was so kind of you to ask me. Sunday afternoons are a little bit lonely. I love the services at church, but then the rest of the day, especially during winter, seems to be rather empty."

"Yes, I know what you mean. Do you read a great deal?"

"Not as much as I should, I'm sure."

The two women talked about the books they liked, and for some time they sat in the kitchen enjoying the warmth of the fire, drinking tea slowly, and discovering that they liked each other quite well. Sarah admired the beauty of Rachel Bradford, her forthrightness, and wished that she had more of that latter quality. Rachel, on the other hand, saw a sweetness and gentleness in her guest that she found very appealing.

For some time they talked about the revolution, then about family. Rachel found that Sarah was very much interested in her family, so she spoke of her father and his wedding with Marian Rochester. She mentioned her brother Matthew, not saying too much about him except that he was studying art on the Continent. She laughed as she described some of her brother Sam's rather wild inventions, and then described Dake's marriage to Jeanne Corbeau, and related how much she liked the young woman who was now living with them until Dake was out of the army. She, however, quickly discovered that Sarah was mostly interested in Micah, which Rachel really had suspected. That was the real reason she had maneuvered the young woman into her house.

"My brother Micah will be out of the army soon," she said, "unless he rejoins for the duration of the war."

"Is that what he wants to do?"

"Not really. I think he wants to be a minister." She saw the light of interest leap into Sarah Dennison's eyes and smiled. "You find that hard to believe?"

"Not at all. I don't know your brother very well, but he is very widely read in the Scriptures."

"He's always been interested in the things of God. Matthew, on the other hand, and my brother Sam are not so interested." She laughed and said, "I'm not as devoted as I should be myself, Sarah." She went on to speak of Micah's interests, and finally she said, "I've talked about myself and my family. Now, what about you, Sarah?"

Sarah Dennison then did something that she had never done in her life. She had no confidants, no close friends she could open her heart to, and the hospitality of Rachel Bradford had warmed her spirit. She suddenly blurted out, "I've had a very calm life, Rachel, but now I have a terrible problem."

Rachel hesitated, then said, "If you'd care to share it with me, perhaps we can pray about it." She was rewarded by a nervous smile and a look almost of relief that crossed Sarah's face. She sat there quietly and listened as Sarah poured out her heart about her impending marriage with Mr. Potter, and how she had no desire for it at all. Finally, she ended by saying, "When the pastor preached on all things working together for good in the service this morning, I wondered if God was speaking to me." She shook her head and said, "The problem is, my parents are totally in favor of this marriage and have practically arranged it." For the first time in her life, perhaps, a criticism then leaped to her lips. It was spoken before she knew what she was saying. "They've always dominated the lives of my sisters, and now they are dominating me, and I feel uncharitable toward them. And I'm ashamed of that."

Rachel had seen Mrs. Helen Dennison a few times, and she had sensed that the woman was capable of such action. She said finally, "Parents aren't always kind. They mean well, but they sometimes are slow to realize that when children grow up, they must make their own decisions."

Sarah looked at Rachel with astonishment. "Do you think that is what's happening to me?"

"I can't say, but from what you yourself have told me, I think it would be hasty of you to marry Mr. Potter. I'm no expert in romance or marriage, of course, but I know one thing. I would marry no man unless I loved him with my whole heart, and obviously you do not have this sort of feeling for Mr. Potter."

As Sarah sat there talking, unburdening her heart for the first time to a woman who was almost a stranger, she was possessed of two feelings. One, it was a relief to speak her heart. Secondly, she could not find it in her spirit to fight against her parents. Finally she rose and said, "It's been a delightful time for me. I have so few friends." She colored and said, "I don't know why I spoke so frankly, but you're a very good listener, Rachel."

Rachel rose and came and put her arm around the woman and kissed Sarah on the cheek. She saw that the gesture pleased the young woman. "We all need friends," she said, "and I feel that we will become fast friends, Sarah."

Sarah left the house with Rachel, who drove her home in the carriage. When she went inside her house, Helen Dennison met her and demanded to know where she had been.

"Just visiting with a friend. We had lunch together."

"What friend?" her mother demanded.

"Oh, a young woman you wouldn't know," Sarah said hastily, and then said, "My feet are rather cold. I think I'll go change clothes." She left at once, avoiding her mother's further questioning. When she was in her own room, she sat down and thought of the pleasant meeting. She was a sensitive young woman, especially to the things of the Lord, and she wondered, "Oh, Lord, did you send Rachel Bradford into my life to give me good counsel? If so, I thank you for it very much!"

☦   ☦   ☦

Rachel looked up from the spinning wheel and said to Katherine

Yancy, "I wonder who that can be? I'm not expecting anyone."

Leaving the room, Rachel moved toward the front door, but it opened, and she was delighted to see Micah, who came in shaking the snow from his hat and stomping his feet on the floor mat.

"Micah!" Rachel cried and ran to him. She embraced him, kissed him on the cheek, and then said, "Come into the parlor. Katherine is here."

"It's cold out there today," Micah said, taking off his great coat and hanging it carelessly on a peg, then added, "Not a long visit this time, Rachel. I'll have to leave tomorrow."

"Did you come bringing dispatches for the army?"

"Yes. It was a hard trip. I wore out a horse getting to Philadelphia."

The two entered the parlor, and Katherine Yancy smiled and rose to come and greet Micah. She was a brown-haired young woman of twenty-one, tall with gray-green eyes, and a mouth that was too wide for real beauty. Nevertheless, she was an attractive young woman, and Micah was glad to see her. He had always liked Katherine.

"The soldier's home from the war," Katherine said and smiled as Micah took her hand and kissed it. "Well," she said, "you've been taking lessons in how to romance women, I see."

"Not really, Katherine," Micah grinned. "And I'm not back from the war. There's not any war right now."

"What's happening with the army?" Rachel asked, then said, "But come on into the kitchen first. We'll fix you something to eat before we talk about the war. I know you're hungry."

Fifteen minutes later, Micah was shoveling battered eggs and slices of fried ham into his mouth, talking around it as he chewed and washed it down with draughts of tea.

"Nothing going on now," he remarked. "The British are waiting for spring, then they'll come boiling out of New York after us. The only reason they don't come now is that we've got the river between us."

"What's it like in camp? Are the men still getting enough to eat?"

"Not likely," Micah grimaced. He looked at the plate full of food and shook his head. "I haven't had a good meal like this since I was here before. It's bad, and it's getting worse." He continued to speak of the hardships that the army was enduring and said, as he often did, "It's General Washington who holds us all together. There wouldn't be an army if it weren't for him."

After Micah finished, Katherine rose and said, "I must go. It's good to see you home, Micah."

After she had left, Micah drummed his fingers on the table and stared at the door. "What's going on with Katherine?"

"You mean about Clive?"

"Yes. Is that on or off? I can't keep up with the romances in our family."

Katherine Yancy was in love with the Bradfords' cousin Clive Gordon, the son of Leslie and Lyna Lee Gordon. Leslie was an officer in the British army, and Clive had served in an unofficial capacity as a physician. He had fallen in love with Katherine Yancy, but politics separated the two.

"Do you think she'll ever marry him, Rachel?"

Rachel picked up a china cup, sipped the tea, then shook her head thoughtfully. "She's too wise to make a marriage that's so dangerous. This war has separated a lot of our people. It would be awful to live with a husband or a wife who felt differently about it."

"You don't think she'll ever have him, then?"

"She'll have God, that's for certain. She's a fine Christian."

"Yes, she is." Micah handled the cup, turning it around, staring at the blue trees and little tiny bridge on it. It had come from Japan in a small set that Daniel had bought years ago. It was very fragile, and his hands looked chapped and weather-beaten as he touched it gently. Looking up, he said, "What have you been doing?"

Micah's visit had caught Rachel by surprise, but as soon as she had had time to think, she felt certain that she would have to say something about Sarah. It disturbed her, and she hesitated so long that Micah looked at her curiously, his eyes narrowing. "What's the matter? Is something wrong?"

"Not with me or the family. Father and Marian are very happy."

"What is it, then?"

"You haven't heard about Sarah Dennison?"

Instantly Micah gave her his full attention. "What about her?" he demanded.

"She's going to marry a man named Potter."

"She can't! She doesn't love him!"

"How do you know that, Micah?"

"Because I met Potter, and I know Sarah."

Rachel considered her brother's face. He was a simple man at heart and not too difficult to read. She and the rest of the family had been aware that he had developed some sort of an interest in Sarah Dennison, but none of them were certain how serious he was. Now she determined to find out, and when Rachel Bradford made her mind up, she went straight at it.

"Do you care for Sarah, Micah? I mean, are you serious about her?"

The question took Micah off guard. "I don't know," he said. "I like her very much, but we haven't been acquainted very long. You don't know her at all, do you?"

"Well, as a matter of fact, I do." Rachel related the details of Sarah's visit, and she said quietly, "I can see why you would be attracted to her. She's not as beautiful as her sisters, but very pretty—a quiet beauty, I think. Somewhat like I always thought a lady poet would look, and," she added thoughtfully, "she's very devout."

"Yes, she is. I think that's what drew me to her. That and a sort of childish quality."

"She's not *childish*!" Rachel rebuked him instantly. "She's *childlike*. There's a big difference. Actually, she's well-read, and I've never seen better manners in a woman."

"I've got to talk to her." He thought about his last visit and then reached out and took Rachel's hand and squeezed it. "You'll have to ask her here. The last time I went there, her father practically ran me off with a shotgun."

Rachel squeezed his hand and smiled. "All right. When?"

"Right now."

"Right now? You mean today?"

"I don't have much time."

Rachel was an impulsive young woman. She was much more like Dake in that respect than she was like Micah. "All right," she said. "I'll send a note by Charles right now. I don't know how I'll say it."

"Just say that you need to see her. If she doesn't come here," Micah said, "I'll have to go there." He grinned abruptly. "It'd be awful to be shot by a distrustful father instead of by a lobsterback, but we've got to risk it."

⚑   ⚑   ⚑

Sarah entered the front door when Rachel opened it. "I got your note," she said rather anxiously. "It sounded urgent. Is anything wrong, Rachel?"

"No, of course not. Come in, Sarah. Let me take your coat." She busied herself with hanging up Sarah's coat, then said, "Come into the parlor."

Sarah followed. She had received a note from Rachel simply asking her to come at once. She did not get many invitations like this, and she had not mentioned it to her mother but had hurried over. Now as she entered the parlor, she stopped dead still, for Micah, who had been standing beside the fire, came forward at once, smiling and holding his hands out. Without thinking, she lifted her own and felt him take them and squeeze them. "You're looking so well, Sarah," Micah said. "Here, you must be cold. Warm yourself at the fire."

Confusion spread across Sarah's face at once, and she noted that Rachel had disappeared. She could not for the life of her think of anything to say that did not seem mundane, so she remained silent until Micah finally said, "I apologize for deceiving you. I asked Rachel to send you the note."

"Oh! Well, I was a little surprised." She studied him closely as he poked at the logs in the fire, admiring the simple planes of his face, strong and definite. He was a handsome man, strong in body, and yet at the same time thoughtful and rather introspective. He did have times, she had already discovered, when silence would come on him, and she saw in him some of the same qualities she felt to be in her own spirit.

Micah leaned the poker back and said, "Come and sit down, Sarah. I have to talk to you." He waited until she was seated in a chair, then drew his own up closer to face her. "Rachel told me you're engaged to Potter."

"Yes, that's true. I am," she said, then looked down.

"Why are you doing it, Sarah? You can't love that man."

Sarah had been over this so many times in her own mind that she was confused and weary. Lifting her head, she finally said, "I can't talk about it, Mr. Bradford."

"Mr. Bradford? Stop that! It's just Micah, and you're Sarah! Now, we haven't known each other very long, but I've known people for ten years that I don't feel as close to as I do to you."

His honesty touched Sarah, and she managed a smile. "I feel the same way," she admitted. "But about my . . . engagement. My parents have already announced it."

"Then they can unannounce it!"

"They'll never do that."

"They will if you refuse to marry the fellow."

For some time the two talked, Sarah arguing weakly, and Micah overriding each objection. Finally she said, "But the Scripture teaches us to be obedient to our parents."

"That's open to interpretation. Suppose your parents tell you to do something that's wrong? And it's not as if you were twelve years old. You're a grown woman, and your happiness will be destroyed if you do what your parents wish in this case. I don't want you to dishonor them, of course, but you have to obey God rather than men, even when men happen to be your parents."

Suddenly Micah rose and came over, put out his hands, and lifted her to her feet. She came with surprise in her eyes, and her lips parted as she started to protest, but she had no opportunity. Without warning,

Micah leaned down and kissed her. It was a quick kiss, and she was surprised at the strength of his lips. She had been kissed before, once or twice, but somehow this kiss was different. It seemed to bring her a sense of security. He was not demanding, and there was a cleanness and a strength in him that she knew she needed.

"Sarah." He took her hand then and held it in both of his. "You have a beautiful spirit, sweet and gentle. The man who gets you will be a king, for he'll be married to a queen."

Sarah flushed and knew that he saw the rosiness of her cheeks, but she could not drop her eyes. "No one ever said anything like that to me before."

"You should be told things like that every day, because they're true."

The fire crackled in the fireplace, and they stood there for a moment. Sarah knew then that she cared for this man, but she did not have the strength to go against her parents, and she hated herself for it. She said quickly, pulling her hand back, "I . . . I shouldn't be here, and I can't listen to this anymore."

"Sarah—"

"No, Micah. I can't do it. I just can't!" The last word was uttered with a sob, and she turned and left the room almost at a run. Micah did not go after her and stood there until he heard the door slam.

Immediately Rachel entered the room and said, "Is she gone already?"

"Yes. She's gone."

Rachel saw the strain on her brother's face. "It didn't go well, did it?"

"She won't stand up to her parents. I'm afraid for her, Rachel. She's a sweet young woman. She's going to ruin her life."

Rachel stood there for one moment, then came over and put her arms around her brother. She hugged him and thought, *He's never been this interested in a woman before. What a tragedy it would be if it didn't work out.*

9

GRACE HAS A SUITOR

GEORGE WASHINGTON HAD PULLED his ragged army into such order as he could, but he spent a considerable amount of time writing to General Charles Lee, begging him to bring his troops and join forces. Lee, however, had other plans in mind, for he had decided that he was better able to run the war than Washington.

The soldiers who had been enticed to stay with the Continental Army were dwindling in number, and even those few were constantly urged by the state militia to join their forces, where they would get higher pay.

The foreign allies, such as France, in whom Washington put such great hope, did not offer any support, and Washington wrote to a friend, "The drum beats for volunteers, but not a man turned out. I spoke as well as I could to them, but what could I say? They have done the best they could, brave fellows. The present is emphatically at a crisis which is to decry our destiny. We must hold together, or the cause is lost."

But it was General Lee who created the biggest problem for Washington. He knew that he had to have men, and though Congress agreed to raise an army of sixty thousand men enlisted for three years, or for the duration of the war, their efforts had failed miserably. Washington's own army had scarcely three thousand men, while Lee commanded a force that would have given him a striking power in the spring.

Washington had read the letter from Lee to his adjutant, Reed, and knew exactly what Lee's real intentions were. Others had tried to have Washington removed, but none was such a threat as General Charles Lee.

At this point, an event occurred that changed the course of history. General Lee crossed the Hudson with four thousand men on December the fourth. Such a reinforcement could have made the difference between the fortunes of the patriot cause and George Washington's standing, but Lee refused to release them. On December the eleventh, Lee started marching his men in the general direction of Washington. During the march, he stopped at a tavern, where he became rather drunk and decided to stay the night. The next morning, when he arose, he was shocked when his aide burst into his room and said, "Here, sir, are the British cavalry."

Indeed, the house was surrounded by twenty-five men and four officers, including Banastre Tarleton. And Lee, who had betrayed Washington, was now, perhaps, betrayed himself, for he was captured. He went outside in his underclothing, begging for mercy, and was rushed off by the dragoons to New Brunswick.

General Sullivan, upon hearing of Lee's capture, took command and moved his men toward Washington's camp. They arrived with fewer men, for some deserted along the way, but when Washington saw them his eyes brightened and he thought, *Now perhaps something can be done!*

🔔　　🔔　　🔔

Grace Gordon moved around the dining table, touching the china lightly, and when her brother David came in, he smiled. "This must be important company we're having tonight, sister."

Grace said quickly, "It's Mr. Morrison and his brother."

David Gordon sat down in a chair and tilted it back. "Is he one of your suitors?"

Grace reached out and pulled David by the lapel. "Put that chair down flat! You'll scar the floor!"

"You didn't answer my question."

Grace gave him a quick smile. "You ask too many questions." David, at sixteen, was indeed inquisitive. She looked at his crisply curled dark brown hair and square face and thought, *He knows more about me than I would like. He always was very quick.* "Come along," she said. "You can help me finish setting the table."

As Grace set the last crystal goblet in place, there was a knock at the door. At the same time Lyna Lee Gordon came down the stairs, saying, "I'll get it." She opened the door and found two men standing there. "How do you do, Mr. Morrison?" she said, smiling. "Won't you come in?"

Stephen Morrison was a lean man, almost to the point of thinness. He had brown hair, an oval face, and soulful brown eyes that reflected his inner moods. His features were rather delicate. Indeed, he was romantic looking—like a poet, which he aspired to be. He smiled and bowed to his hostess, saying, "May I present my brother, Mr. Jubal Morrison."

"I'm honored, ma'am."

Jubal Morrison was very little like his brother. He looked stronger and huskier, and there was a pugnacious quality in his face. However, his manners were good, and Lyna nodded to him, saying, "You're welcome, sir. I wish my husband were here, but he's in the field with General Howe."

"So I understand," Stephen said. He looked up suddenly, for Grace had come into the room. "Ah, Miss Grace," he said. He went over to her and bowed, taking her hand and kissing it as she curtsied, then turned to say with a sweep of his arm, "This is my brother. May I present Miss Grace Gordon."

"I am happy to make your acquaintance, Mr. Morrison," Grace said. Like her mother, she was struck by the physical differences in the two men. Of the two, she rather liked Stephen's appearance the best. She noted the rough hands of Jubal Morrison and the scar beside his left eye that gave him a definite squint. He was strong, however, and his smile was pleasant enough.

"Let us go in and have dinner at once," Lyna said. "Then later we can adjourn to the parlor."

The dining room was small but elegant. Two floor-length windows on one wall were draped with yellow damask curtains. The walls were pea green, with a green and yellow flowered wallpaper bordering the windows. Candles flickered in brass sconces on the walls, reflecting their light in the numerous mirrors, and on the far wall a fire crackled in the large fireplace, adding its glow and warmth to the room. A heavy oak dining table, covered with a white linen tablecloth, was set for dinner. A large mahogany sideboard behind the head chair was filled with an array of dishes, and an oak serving table was heaped with the main course for the evening meal. As Stephen looked around, he nodded with appreciation. "This is a nice house," he said.

"Merely rented, of course. We were fortunate to get it, weren't we, Mother?" Grace said.

"Yes, we were. It is nice."

The meal consisted of oyster soup, cold lobster, flummery, roast beef, plum pudding, artichokes with toasted cheese on top, a cheese plate with stilton, slipcoat, and sago cheeses, fresh white bread, lemon biscuits with cream cheese and spiced apples, and trifle with a frothy syllabub on top.

David, as always, complimented the cook. "A fine supper. You gentlemen must come more often. You have no idea how bad the food is when I have to eat alone." A mischievous light twinkled in his eyes, and he ducked his head when his mother said, "David, be quiet!"

"I doubt that you're serious, David," Stephen Morrison said. He turned to Grace. "I can't imagine this lady putting anything other than an exquisitely prepared meal on the table."

They talked for some time of New York, and finally after the meal, they adjourned to the parlor, which was not as elegant as the dining room, but tastefully furnished. "I understood General Howe's troops were in New York. Your husband is with them?"

"He's been sent on a mission to the south to examine the rebel lines," Lyna said.

Up to this point in the evening, Jubal had said little, but now he asked, "Do you have relatives who are allied with the patriots, Mrs. Gordon?"

"Yes, my brother, Daniel Bradford, and his family are in Boston."

"I know. I've met them several times."

"Indeed, sir? How did that come about?"

"I'm interested in a venture that involves a member of the family."

Lyna examined the young man more carefully. "That couldn't be with my nephew Dake. He's in with Washington's army. Would it be with Micah, his twin brother?"

"No, it's with Sam."

"Sam!" Grace exclaimed. "Why, he's only a child!"

"No he's not," David said. "He's sixteen years old—the same age as I am." He turned to Jubal Morrison and said, "Would it be impolite to inquire about the venture, or is it business?"

"It's not a happy subject," Stephen Morrison said abruptly, which drew a look of surprise from his hosts. He moved impatiently in his chair and said, "My brother and I disagree."

"We do indeed," Jubal Morrison said calmly. "Perhaps it wouldn't be polite to discuss it here at this time."

"I think they should know what is happening," Stephen insisted. He turned to look at Lyna and said, "My brother is not sympathetic to our problem here."

"*Our* problem, you say?" Jubal said. "I'm not sympathetic to tyranny." His eyes narrowed and he sat up straighter in his chair. "If anyone tried to impose these kinds of restrictions on Englishmen in England, there'd be a revolution. You can bet on that."

"It's not the same thing, Jubal." Stephen spoke slowly and quietly. There was a mildness about him that was not evident in his brother. They were very unalike. Jubal moved restlessly as his brother continued to lay out the reasons why the Colonies were wrong in trying to win independence from the Crown.

Finally Jubal shook his head. "We will never agree on this."

"I fear not," Stephen said. "My brother wants to take his part of the inheritance and throw his lot in with the Colonists."

Grace blinked with surprise. "But surely, Mr. Morrison, you don't think they can win."

"I certainly do," Jubal insisted. "I don't fancy allying myself with losing causes."

"Not only does he think they can win," Stephen interjected, "he wants to build a boat with which he can take on the British navy himself!"

"I never said that, Stephen," Jubal protested. "In any case, I think it's impolite to speak of these things." Then turning to Lyna, Jubal said, "You must find it hard yourself, Mrs. Gordon, to face up to the differences between you and Mr. Bradford's family."

Lyna nodded heavily. "Indeed, sir, it is hard. I love my brother and his family. We all do. My husband, I might add, is not all that sympathetic to the war either. He feels he will lose much through this revolution, but he is a soldier and must obey."

The discussion went on more politely after that, but after the two men had left, David said to Grace, "You like that fellow, don't you? Stephen Morrison."

"Yes, I do, David. Do you?"

"He's all right, I suppose. What does he do?"

"He's a businessman, but he's also a poet."

"Is that right? Has he published anything?"

"Yes. He has a book out. I'll show it to you."

Grace took her brother upstairs to show him the book of poetry, and David retired to his room for the night with the book in hand. The next morning he returned it to Grace with a sly grin on his face. "It must be good. I can't understand a word of it!"

"That's not the test of good poetry," Grace objected.

"Isn't it? I thought poets were like preachers. You know how preachers are. Their worst fear is that someone might understand what they're saying, and that would prove that they weren't *deep*."

"You're awful, David!" Grace reached out, took ahold of his shirt, and shook him.

He simply grinned in response. "Well, I know there's not any money in poetry. I hope he's a good businessman."

"He is, so I understand. He and Jubal inherited the estate equally, but since Stephen is older, he's been controlling the purse strings. Now it appears that Jubal is tired of that arrangement."

"Well, he'll lose it all if he goes and sinks his money into a ship. Nobody can go up against His Majesty's navy."

🔔   🔔   🔔

Stephen leaned back in his chair and listened as Grace played the clavichord. When she had finished and came to sit beside him, he said, "You play beautifully."

"Why, thank you, Stephen."

"I wish I could play that skillfully, but I have no musical ability, or very little."

He sat there studying Grace thoughtfully. He had visited the Gordon house almost every day since the dinner two weeks ago when he had brought his brother, Jubal. This evening he had shown up unexpectedly and found Grace alone, except for the servants. David had gone out earlier with his mother for a visit across town.

Stephen had just read a poem he was working on, Grace had exclaimed over it, and then he had insisted on her playing some music.

Rising, Stephen walked over to the window and peered out. "It's very cold out, but I always liked the cold."

"That's strange for someone who lives in South Carolina. Isn't it very hot there?"

"Hot and very humid. I like that, too." He laughed and said, "I suppose I'm easy to please." He walked back to the settee and sat down beside her again, then suddenly reached over and took her hand. This surprised her, for he had not done anything like this before. "I can't tell you, Grace, how much I've enjoyed my visits here. You're so pleasant to be with."

"Why, thank you, Stephen."

"And," he smiled, a light of humor in his eyes, "you like my poetry . . . or say you do."

"I do like it!" she protested. "Although I'm not an expert, it seems very good to me."

"Well, I'm glad I don't have to make a living writing poems. The plantations are going well in the Carolinas."

"Isn't there a lot of patriot sympathy there?"

"It's about equally divided. Half the people are loyalists, the other half are rebels."

"Isn't it dangerous owning property there? I mean, if the war should turn wrong, wouldn't you lose it?"

"I don't think that will happen."

The two sat talking quietly, and finally he rose to say, "It's very late. I must go." She stood up with him, and he faced her and said abruptly, "I can write love poems, but somehow I can't say what I want to say about you, Grace."

"Can't you, Stephen?"

"No. I don't know why it is. When I try to say how I feel, I suddenly find myself speechless." He grinned crookedly. "A poor show for a poet." He stood looking at her, admiring her dark honey hair and gray-green eyes. She was an attractive young woman with a quickness about her that he admired. "I'm not given to hasty decisions, but I must tell you that I admire you very much." He started to say more, then abruptly kissed her hand, and turned and left.

Grace stood quietly for a moment, then went and sat down before the fire. She tried to analyze her feelings. She had never had a serious romance, but there was something about this thin young man that she liked very much. She could not tell how her parents felt about him, and David's judgment was not very reliable.

"I wish he would write a love poem to me," she whispered. "That would be something to treasure."

She rose when she heard her mother and brother come in and went to the front entryway to greet them. Seeing her, David asked impudently, "Well, did he propose?"

"David, will you be serious!" Grace said with irritation. "No, he didn't propose, David."

"Think he's going to?"

For one moment Grace hesitated, then she said, "Yes, I think he will."

🕆   🕆   🕆

The following day, Lyna Lee Gordon kept thinking about what her daughter had said. A soon as Lyna's husband, Leslie, returned that day, she asked him what he thought about Grace and Stephen.

"Do you like the man?" Leslie asked.

"He seems very personable, and he's obviously a good man. What do you think?"

"Why, I don't know him," Leslie said. "I'd like to see him out on the field. You can really tell about a man's character when he's under fire."

"He's a poet, Leslie, not likely to be a soldier."

The two sat on the settee in the parlor, holding hands, and finally Leslie Gordon said, "Well, it looks like Clive's not making much progress with Katherine Yancy. I wouldn't be surprised if he remained a bachelor. What do you think about them, Lyna?"

Lyna did not answer. She had been worried about Clive and his romance with Katherine Yancy, for she knew her son loved the woman dearly.

Finally she sighed and returned to the subject of Grace and Stephen. "He seems to be a good man, and I wouldn't object."

"You know best," Leslie said. He turned and pulled her close, and the two sat before the fire, watching it burn low.

10

WASHINGTON MAKES A CHOICE

COLONEL LESLIE GORDON ATTEMPTED with all the strength he had to admire his commanding officer Sir William Howe. Now as the two of them walked along the frozen Delaware River, Gordon dredged up from his memory the exemplary military service that Howe had done England in the past—and the list was long.

Howe *was* a good officer in many respects, Gordon reflected, but he seemed to have been afflicted with some sort of lethargy ever since arriving to serve as commander of His Majesty's forces in America. Time and time again, since the disaster at Bunker Hill, British commanders had not been able to summon the will to send their men in against the Americans. *It could have all been over in New York*, Gordon thought as the two officers trudged over the frozen ground, the snow up to the top of their boots. *We could have ended this revolution if we had only forged ahead. Washington was helpless.* He glanced over at his commanding officer and silently willed for some sparks of action to come out of the man, but he had little hope. General Howe was staring across the river and shivered as the cold December wind howled and whistled across the barren shores of New Jersey. Gordon had heard the talk that Howe was looking forward to a comfortable winter in New York spent in the company of the wife of his commissary officer, Joshua Loring. The general seemed unaware that the opportunity to end the war quickly lay in his grasp, and now as he walked along the frozen shores, he began to speak rather cheerfully.

"I don't think we need to fret ourselves over the situation, Colonel Gordon." Howe pulled his collar up, reached into his inside pocket, and pulled out a silver snuff box. Opening the top, he attempted to pour some on the back of his hand. The wind blew most of it away, but he still managed to sniff a goodly portion of the snuff. He sneezed heartily, and his eyes watered with the strength of the tobacco and with the freezing cold. "General Charles Lee was the only general with the rebels that I had any confidence in, and now that he's been captured, they have no one left who can command an army."

"I would argue that, sir. To me, General Washington is a far more formidable adversary than Charles Lee ever was."

"Oh, you think so? Well, in any case, Washington's men have been frightfully reduced, as you well know. Our spies tell us that he has nothing left but an army of scarecrows who are wretchedly clothed and starving. And, of course, he has no source of supplies. Their pitiful little Congress sits in Philadelphia and argues while they let their army starve to death. Such a group of rabble doesn't deserve to be a free nation!"

"All very well, sir," Gordon argued, "but all we have to do is cross the river. We have enough troops and cannons to take the rebels, then this war will be over. Then we can all go back to England again."

Howe said placidly, "We'll establish a line of forts along the river to keep the rebels on the other side. That way we can hold New York, and in the spring we'll come out and take them." He grinned then, saying, "Washington's a fox hunter, but this time he'll be the fox and we'll bag him. Eh, Colonel?"

"I hope so, General."

The two men turned and walked back toward the house they had commandeered for the campaign. General Howe said airily, "I'll leave you in charge of establishing the forts. I will go back to New York. There's much to do there."

Knowing full well what that "much to do" meant, Leslie Gordon kept a straight face, saying, "Yes, sir! I'll see to it!" But as he turned to begin speaking with the officers under him, he was dissatisfied and discontented with the general's apathy. "All we have to do is cross the river and it's over," he muttered. "But if we wait, who knows what will happen?"

T T T

Colonel Johann Rall, the commander at Trenton, held Americans in contempt in general, and the soldiers in Washington's Continental Army especially so. He had been fighting a rather boring war up to this point at Trenton, and now that Christmas had come, he was heartily sick of the whole thing. Like General James Grant, in overall charge of the defenses of New York, Rall boasted of how ruthlessly he would deal with these American rebels; also that he could keep the peace in New Jersey with a corporal's guard.

Rall was leaning back in his chair now when a short, stubby subaltern came in, saying breathlessly, "Colonel Rall, the rebels have fired upon our men at the Trenton Ferry!"

Rall's pale face flushed. "Why are you telling me this? Why haven't you killed them all?"

"Sir, we tried, but they ran away. They're nothing but cowards."

Rall drank from the trencher in front of him, the fumes rising to his head. He said, "They won't be back tonight. It's too cold."

"Yes, sir," the subaltern said. "Oh, sir. There's a man outside to see you."

"Man? What sort of man?"

"A civilian. A farmer of some kind, I think."

"Well, send him in." Rall took another drink while the subaltern left and looked up only when a heavyset man with mild, blue eyes and blond hair came to stand before him.

The farmer pulled his hat off and nodded. "My name is Honeyman, Colonel Rall. John Honeyman."

"Well, what do you want, Honeyman?"

"I want to sue for pardon."

"Oh, pardon, is it?" This was not unusual, for after the British took over almost any ground, a certain number of people would come forward saying basically that they had been forced to keep their loyalties secret, that the patriots would tar and feather them if they had become known.

"So you've seen the light, have you, Honeyman?"

"Oh yes, sir! I want nothing to do with those rebels, but they would have burned me, I think, if I had stood up for the king."

"Very well, Honeyman. You shall have your pardon. What's your business?" Rall asked half curiously.

"Oh, I'm a butcher and a dealer in cattle."

The man's answer interested Rall, for the supplies for the troops were running low. "A dealer in cattle, you say? Did the rebels take all of your stock?"

Honeyman grinned broadly. "No, sir. I hid them before they had a chance. I've got plenty of fat cattle. Would Your Excellency be interested in buying some?"

"By Harry, yes!" Rall got up at once. Christmas was coming, and he could almost smell the rich beef roasting for the Christmas dinner. "Go along with my lieutenant here. Bring the cattle in the camp, Honeyman. I'll see that you're well paid for them."

"How many, Your Excellency?"

"All you can spare."

"Yes, sir! God save the King!"

"God save the King!" Rall waved his hand negligently and went back and poured himself another glass of beer as the farmer left.

Honeyman accompanied the lieutenant and soon had arranged to have a place set up close to the camp for slaughtering the cattle and making the cuts.

"This will do very well," Honeyman said.

"You'll need a pass," the lieutenant said. He scribbled out a few words on a sheet of paper, then gave it to the butcher. "If any man bothers you, Honeyman, just refer them to me."

"Thank you, Lieutenant." Honeyman watched as the lieutenant left, and a rather crafty light shown from his eyes as he moved back to his wagon and climbed aboard. He spoke to the horses, his eyes shifting around the British camp as he moved along. It was as if he were memorizing something that he would need to know for the future.

🔔   🔔   🔔

"Well, Dake, I'm back."

Dake Bradford glanced up to see his brother Micah, who had appeared suddenly. Dake was sitting at the front of the tent that was barely big enough for two men, and he got to his feet at once. "Glad to see you back. How are things at home?"

"Fine. Pa sends his love, and so does Sam, and the women." He looked around and asked, "Where's Keturah?"

"She's in her tent."

Something in Dake's tone caught at Micah. "What's she doing in her tent this time of day?"

"Been ailing for two days now. Some kind of fever."

"Did the surgeon come by?" Micah demanded.

"No, he wouldn't tend to a civilian, especially a woman. He thinks they're all camp followers."

"Well, what is it?" Micah demanded. "Is it serious?"

Dake shrugged his shoulders, then drew his coat closer around him. "How should I know? I'm not a doctor. It doesn't look good to me, though. Hope you brought something good that we can make soup out of. She can't eat this stuff we've been eating. I think it's some kind of mule meat, or even worse."

Micah took the bulky bag from his shoulders and said, "Fish around in there. I think you can find something to cook up for her. I'll go over and say hello."

126

As Dake began pawing eagerly through the supplies that Micah brought back from Boston, Micah moved quickly over to the tent. Reaching it, he leaned down and said, "Keturah?"

Her voice was shaky and weak as she answered. "Yes. Is it you, Micah?"

"Yes. Can I come in?"

"I reckon."

Micah stooped over and stepped inside the tent, which was no larger than the one he shared with Dake. Keturah was lying on the ground wrapped in blankets, and one look at her flushed face brought a start to Micah. He moved beside her, knelt down, reached out, and put his hand on her forehead. The skin was hot and dry to the touch, and he saw that her lips were dry and cracked. "How long have you been sick?"

"I been down about two days. I felt bad afore that, though." Keturah licked her lips and rolled her head weakly from side to side. "I'm proud you came back, Micah."

"I brought some food with me, and Dake's cooking up something. It'll be better than what you've had."

"Can I have a drink of water, please?"

"Of course." Micah saw the wooden canteen over to one side, and removing the lid, he helped Keturah to a sitting position. Her body felt far too hot to his touch for normal health, and as she sipped the water thirstily, he thought, *What a place to get sick! Now what am I going to do with her?*

"Is that enough?" he asked.

When she nodded without speaking, he lowered her back down and replaced the top on the canteen. "Sorry you're not feeling well," he said.

"I'll be all right." Keturah's voice was thin and reedy. Her eyes seemed sunk back into her head, and there were dark circles under them.

Even in the short time she had been sick, she seemed, to Micah, to have lost weight. He rocked back on his heels and sat there, wondering what he could do to help her before she got any worse. "I wish there was a hospital for you to go to, but we don't even have one set up yet," he said.

"They wouldn't take me nohow," Keturah said quietly. Her spirit seemed to be weak, and after a few moments, her eyes rolled up and the eyelids fell in a startling way.

"Keturah—? Are you all right?" Micah asked anxiously. She did not answer, and he saw that she had fallen into a deep, unhealthy sleep, more like a coma than anything else. He stared down at the sick girl for a long moment, then rose and left the tent. Finding Dake stirring up a broth in the single saucepan that the squad possessed, he said at once, "Dake, I'm worried about Keturah."

"She's not too good, is she? I don't know what it is, but I hope it's not cholera or somethin' like that."

"Maybe she'll feel better after she eats."

"I don't reckon so. She hasn't been able to keep anything down."

The two men sat there for a time, and Micah was startled to find out how concerned he was about the young woman. She had always seemed self-sufficient, but now she looked almost like a sick child as she lay on the thin mattress in her tent. Micah was usually good with sick people, but here in the camp there was nothing—no medicine, no proper bed, and not even proper food to help nourish her strength back. As the broth began to heat, Micah turned his mind back to the army. "What's going on here? I brought some dispatches back, but they're wondering at Congress if the army can hold together."

"I don't see how we can stick it out much longer," Dake replied wearily. "Men are just walkin' away—whole regiments sometimes. The general's about to lose his mind, I hear. But there's nothin' he can do about it. It looks like it's all up for the revolution. . . ."

🔔   🔔   🔔

"Who's that?" Henry Lincoln demanded. He was a tall, thin sergeant, and he looked quickly around at his squad. "Prime your muskets."

"Ahh, he ain't nothin' but a civilian, Sergeant," John Jones replied.

They were all watching a tall, heavy man who was walking along the road with a whip. He cracked the whip loudly as he strolled, and the squad had been curious about it. Now Sergeant Lincoln said, "Come on, maybe he'll be able to tell us something about the British positions."

The squad fanned out and made the capture of the man easily. He offered no quarrel or resistance but stared at them with wide, blue, guileless eyes.

"What's your name?"

"John Honeyman."

"What's your business, Honeyman?"

"I be a dealer in cattle."

"You been inside the British camp?"

"That I have."

"Well, then. You'll have to come with us."

As the butcher found himself surrounded by men with loaded muskets, he nodded slowly. "All right," he said. "Looks like you got the best of the argument."

Sergeant Lincoln tried to get some information out of the tall, bulky man, but Honeyman seemed to be rather ignorant. They put him in a boat, ferried him across the Delaware, and took him into the camp, where they sought out Washington's headquarters. Inside a tent, larger than most, Washington was sitting in his camp chair staring blankly at the wall of the tent. His thoughts were bitter. *What does it matter now?* he was thinking. *Ten days and it will be up with the army. Ten days at the most.* He thought about how he had begged for help from the Congress and had received none, and how the people all over the country seemed slack and spiritless and confused. The fervor that had exploded with Lexington and Concord had been dampened by the many defeats the army had suffered. As the general sat there, black despair falling on him, he barely lifted his head when Colonel Hamilton stuck his head inside the tent and said, "We've captured a civilian, sir. We thought you might like to ask him about the enemy's movement."

"Oh, what's his name?"

"John Honeyman, sir."

"Honeyman? Why, he's a spy for the British! Bring him in!" Washington's voice grew hard, but a strange light sparked in his blue-gray eyes, and he straightened up immediately.

"Here he is, sir." The man was dressed as a cattle drover. His features were mediocre and blunt.

"You're from Trenton, are you, Honeyman?"

"Yes, sir. I've been there a spell."

"All right, Colonel Hamilton," Washington said. "I'll question the man."

"Yes, sir."

As soon as Hamilton was out of the tent, Washington lowered his voice. "You have a report, Honeyman?"

A smile touched the big farmer's face. "Yes, I have, General."

Washington leaned forward eagerly. "I appreciate what you've done, John Honeyman. You know you could have been hanged if you had been caught."

"They're not thinking about spies, sir."

"What's it like over in the camp?"

"Well, sir, General Howe, he's going back to New York for winter quarters."

"Howe?" Washington stared at the man, and an idea, even at that moment, began to form in his mind. If Howe were gone, that would leave Trenton in the charge of a subordinate. "Are you sure, Honey-man?"

"He went off yesterday." Honeyman ran his hand through his thick blond hair and grinned slightly. "I reckon he's anxious to get back to Mrs. Loring."

"So, Howe is gone," Washington said.

"Clean away, sir. I don't reckon those fancy British soldiers like to fight much in the mud and the snow."

"Who's left at Trenton, Honeyman?"

"Well, there's a garrison there—them German soldiers. What do they call them?"

"Hessians?"

"Yes, sir. That's what they are."

"A big group? A large force, would you say?"

"Not too big, sir. I guess maybe a thousand, maybe twelve hun-dred."

Washington's mind began working quickly then. "Who's their com-manding officer?"

"Colonel Rall. He don't think much of you, sir."

"Good. I hope he thinks even less. The less he thinks of me, the less on guard he'll be."

"Well, he ain't on guard much anyway. To tell the truth, General, discipline ain't much over there with those fellas. Especially not with General Howe gone."

"Here, show me the layout of the military situation."

"Do the best I can, sir, though I ain't no soldier." Honeyman moved over to the map that Washington had unrolled and put flat on his camp table. Honeyman pointed out accurately the streets where the soldiers were billeted, the location of the cannon, and the outpost where the pickets made their walks. When he was finished, he said, "That's all I can remember, General."

Washington's craggy face lightened. He put his hand out and let it rest on the tall farmer's shoulder. "I don't know anyone who could've done better, Honeyman."

Honeyman's face flushed. "Thank you, sir."

"Now, is it safe for you in Trenton?"

"Well, maybe not for a time, sir. Them Hessians are tightened now."

"Very well. Stay out of Trenton."

"I'd just as soon."

George Washington put his hand out and grasped the hard hand of the spy. "You've done a good job. Take care of yourself, Mr. Honeyman. You are valuable to the Continental Army."

"Yes, sir."

Calling Hamilton inside, Washington said, "Colonel, I must tell you that John Honeyman is one of our most valuable spies. Please see that he is taken across the river and set free."

As soon as a mystified Hamilton led Honeyman from the tent, Washington paced back and forth. He clasped his big hands together behind his back, gripping harder than he knew until they cramped. Outside he could hear the sound of a lieutenant drilling troops, trying to instill some order on his little force, but his mind was not on the man's sharp commands.

"There's a chance here," he whispered. "Just a small chance. We've got to do something! People have to have something to hope for, and they've had nothing since Bunker Hill."

Moving to the front of the tent, he stepped outside and saw Alexander Hamilton. "Colonel Hamilton, will you ask General Knox and General Greene to come to my tent, please?"

"Yes, sir!"

Ten minutes later Washington faced the two men he trusted the most and said, "I've just had word that General Howe has left to go back to New York for winter quarters."

"Well, that's no surprise," Knox said, his fat face looking round and full. It was a constant source of wonder to everyone how Colonel Henry Knox could remain as fat as a beef in the spring in an army of starving men. He was watching his chief curiously now and said, "Are you thinking of some sort of drastic action, Your Excellency?"

"They have fewer than two thousand men, and the last thing they would expect from us would be an attack. Not on Christmas."

The generals stared at each other almost in unbelief. *He means to attack!* Greene thought with a sense of raw shock. Then he thought again, *That's the kind of thing he would do!*

Washington talked very rapidly to the two men. "Sullivan has brought in the men that were under General Lee, and General Gates came on the same day. He had only six hundred men."

"Will General Gates support you, sir?" Greene demanded.

Washington shook his head. "No, he's going back to Philadelphia. He has personal business to attend to."

Neither of the men had the least confidence in General Horatio Gates. "We'll do as well without him, sir," Greene said with contempt.

"Very well. We'll cross the river and march on Trenton from three sides at dawn, after Christmas day."

The audacity of it all struck Greene and Knox. They stood there staring down at the map, lifting their eyes from time to time, searching

Washington's face, trying to see some sign of doubt or fear, but there was none. When they left the tent, Knox said, "I think he'd storm heaven if the notion took him."

"Heaven might be as easy to storm as Trenton. Just getting across that river is going to be a monumental task. But we can do it, Henry, as long as he's with us!"

11

VICTORY AT TRENTON

COLONEL JOHANN RALL HAD NOTHING but contempt for the tiny army of George Washington that lay across the river. Furthermore, Colonel Rall was homesick for England. He resented being sent to America to fight in a war that he felt was beneath his dignity, and although he had rendered good service up to this point, when Christmas Day of 1776 arrived, Rall ignored all of the usual military precautions that had been his habit. There had been a series of small actions against his forces, and day after day patriot patrols had made themselves into nuisances. Dispatches were brought daily to the colonel outlining these minor skirmishes, but, sick of his task, he chose to ignore them.

The Hessians under the command of Colonel Rall were also homesick. Their morale had sunk to a dangerous low, and a long sea voyage had weakened them further. Just for a few of them to appear on the Trenton shore was to invite artillery fire from the Pennsylvania side, but Colonel Rall made light of the complaints and of their worries. Like General James Grant, Rall had no fears of an attack. When one of his officers asked his permission to fortify Trenton with trenches, he shouted at him, "Let them come! We'll want no trenches! We'll go after them with bayonets!"

Even on the day before Christmas, when a leading Tory had given Rall the word that a black slave had come with a message that the Americans were drawing several days' rations, which suggested a campaign, Rall had snarled. "This is idle prattle! It's all women's talk!"

Christmas Day came, and the only precaution the colonel made was to place two of his six field pieces in front of his headquarters. These were more ornamental than anything else, and then Rall marched his bandsmen about for a review. After this ceremony, Rall went hastily inside and began to warm his frosty bones with strong liquor. Indeed, the entire garrison proceeded to get roaring drunk on Christmas Day.

Finally the commanding officer was carried to bed dead drunk.

🔔　　　🔔　　　🔔

Across the river, General George Washington tightened his lips and proceeded with his plan to attack Trenton. As Washington walked the shores of the Delaware, he studied the dark icy flood where the sixty-foot Durham boats awaited. Ice had thickened from a skin on the river to a shell and had become soggy-pitted, and now the river was in full flood. Washington stared at the massive sheets of ice that went crashing down the river and closed his mind against the doubt that attempted to rise in him. He went over his plan again, as he had done for hours.

It was a good plan. He had the boats, he had the artillery, and he had the ammunition. It all now depended upon the men. He could afford no indecision now, and even if others failed, he must not. He had sent General Cadwallader to cross the Delaware below Trenton, and General Ewing to the north, but looking up the river, doubts assailed him as to the determination of these two officers. He could not be everywhere, and he had to depend upon what officers he had. Now as he stood there, a tall, rawboned shape, Washington scrubbed at his nose, signaled his servant for his horse, then mounted. As he moved along, he studied the men as he always did. In the pale, graying twilight their faces were indistinguishable. A number of his troops suffered from lack of warm clothing, but some of the ladies of Philadelphia had sent the army a few hundred discarded coats, some with flannel linings, and he smiled to see red flannel in the gray, dusky light.

Finally he came to where Colonel Glover, commander of the Marblehead fishermen, stood waiting. It had been Glover and his fishermen who had saved the army at New York, ferrying them across in boats silently under the very noses of the British. He saw that the colonel's cheeks were hollow and there were deep, dark circles under his eyes. "I never thought," Washington said with a slight smile, "that the fate of our country would depend upon fishermen, but so it seems, Colonel. All my hopes are with you."

Glover's New England face showed little emotion as a rule, but the words of Washington seemed to warm him. "That's kind of you to say, sir."

"Can it be done, Glover?"

The New Englander knew exactly what Washington meant. He looked at the ice, punching and growling in the churning dark waters of the Delaware, and then turned back. "It can be done, sir, although it will be hard."

"The guns and the horses, too? We must have artillery."

134

"It will be hard," Glover repeated.

Washington, with a sudden impulse, reached out his hand. Glover took it, and the two men stood there as if turned into statues. Understanding passed between the two, and Washington said, "You have only my thanks now, Colonel Glover, but one day I will hope that the entire country will recognize your loyal service."

Washington turned and walked away, leaving Glover to stare after him. Washington made his way along the sides of the river and joined Nathaniel Greene. The two men stood there watching as the men limped along on the way toward the boats. They did not look like trim fighting men, but they were tough. They had run away more than once, but these, at least, had come back. They had committed themselves to a new nation, a new freedom, and as Washington watched them his heart swelled with pride.

"They're good men, Nathaniel."

"Yes, sir. Very good men."

"They don't sing or make much noise, but there's a stiff pride in them," Washington murmured. He watched as they moved along, carrying their muskets. Their eyes were set straight ahead, and there was a determination in them that Washington admired.

"The boats are ready, Nathaniel."

"Yes, sir. Who goes first, the men or the guns?"

"We must have both. Load each boat with one gun, then the rest with men."

"Yes, sir."

Washington found his horse, remounted, and began to ride along the line. Greene had given the order, and the artillery men began to sweat as they loaded their awkward cannon onto the Durham boats. Knox suddenly appeared, his huge voice booming out in the pale twilight. He threatened and cajoled and then moved his fat body alongside his gunners, shoving and heaving at the cannon. A barge overturned and three horses slipped into the water, and General Sullivan suddenly appeared, saying, "Get them out! Get them out! We need those horses!"

Knox finally came to Washington. His clothes were filthy, and his coat split in the back. "I'm doing the best, sir, but this ice is the very devil. I've been trying to get powder and shot into each boat."

"Well, get them across, Henry! I fear the future of this war hangs on our success this night!"

Washington stared at the river. It was ugly, and the stout Durham boats that had once been used to haul iron from northern New Jersey to Pennsylvania were finally loaded. They were forty feet long, some sixty, and others eight feet wide, capable of hauling considerable weight. They could be poled from plankings laid along the gunwales. He watched carefully as the Marbleheaders took over and then looked apprehensively at the ice, which came grinding and buffing down the river. It crunched against the hulls, creaking and groaning, and the wind blew the boats, despite the efforts of the Marbleheaders. The boats were monstrous to handle, and the officers screamed over the howling of the wind. Knox, his voice a trumpet, boomed out, and men scrambled into the boats. The pole men pushed off, and Washington could scarcely see his pocketwatch as he peered at it. *They must all be across,* he thought, *before dawn.*

But there was no way to speed up the difficult crossing. The men shivered as they waited on the riverbanks, and Washington walked through their lines encouraging them. They squatted in a frigid silence, and he stopped again to look at his watch. It was nine o'clock, then ten, then eleven.

"Can we do it by midnight, Glover?"

"No, sir."

"When then?"

"I can't say."

Finally the boats were all ready, and Washington got into one of them; it mattered not which one. The wind seemed to scream, and the pole men clunked forward, stabbing at the river bottom, straining every muscle. Jagged pieces of ice came smashing against the sides of the boat, and Washington was shaken. Knox reached out and steadied him, saying, "Don't fall in, sir. That wouldn't be good for the cause."

"Thank you, General Knox." He looked at Knox's vast bulk and said suddenly, "Shift your rear over there, Knox, and trim the ship."

Knox stared at Washington wildly, then saw humor in the commander's eyes and began to laugh. The men in the boat who had heard him joined in the laughter.

⚜   ⚜   ⚜

Somehow they made the crossing and unloaded the boats, but it was steadily growing light, and Trenton was nine miles away. There was no hope now of a night surprise, even of one close to dawn.

And so the long march began. The men limped over the rough, frozen gutters of mud, groping for a footing, and some of them fell as they trudged along. They marched until they came to a crossroads village four miles from the river. Here Washington called his officers together as the men rested. They noticed some of the men were eating cold breakfasts from the three days' cooked rations they had brought.

Greene and Sullivan approached, and Washington said, "General

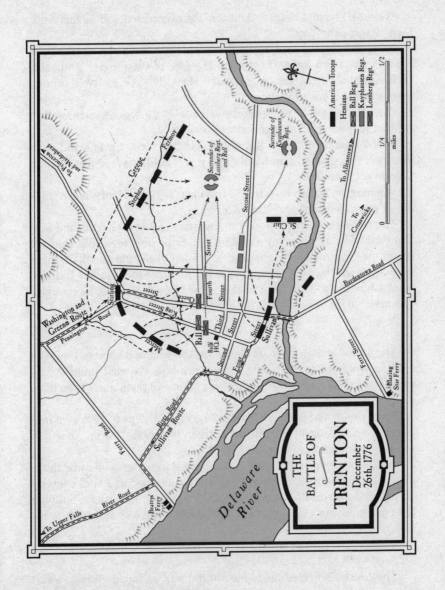

To Princeton
and Maidenhead

Greene

Fermoy

Stephen

Surrender of
Lossberg Regt. and Rall

Second Street

Surrender of
Knyphausen Regt.

To Allenstown

To Crosswicks

St. Clair

Street

Fourth Street

Washington and Greens Route

Street

Stirling

King Street

Queen Street

Third Street

Second Street

Pennington Road

Rall

Rall H.Q.

Street

Street

Sullivan

Burdentown Road

Mercer

Second Street

Forst Street

Ferri Street

Blazing Star Ferry

Ringo Road

Sullivan's Route

Ferry Road

Delaware River

River Road

To Upper Falls

Beatty's Ferry

American Troops

Hessians

Rall Regt.

Knyphausen Regt.

Lossberg Regt.

0   1/4   1/2
miles

THE
BATTLE OF
TRENTON
December
26th, 1776

Sullivan, I want you to take the crossroads there skirting the river and come in at the bottom of the town. You understand?"

"Yes, sir."

"Greene, you and Knox and most of the cannon will follow this road. I will accompany you."

"Yes, sir," Greene said. He pulled off his cap and scratched his bald head in the dawn light. He studied the face of Washington and said, "It'll be like a nutcracker." He grinned abruptly, saying, "We'll crunch them this time, Your Excellency!"

"I trust that will be so. Set your watches by mine, gentlemen, so that we hit the town as near together as possible."

"They'll be drunk, sir," Knox said. He had come up to stand with the other two generals, and, although it was cold, his face was sweaty. "We've got them now."

Washington nodded, saying, "I trust you're right, Henry. Now, command your men, and we'll move forward."

The resting men came slowly to their feet as Knox, Greene, and Sullivan moved out, shouting their orders. Sullivan's men followed off down the crossroads at right angles, while Greene got the main force moving down the road ahead that led to the little town called Trenton. As Washington rode in front of the column beside Greene, he thought, *This must not fail. If we fail here, it's all over. It must not fail!*

🔔   🔔   🔔

Micah had drawn his coat closer around him and shivered, for the chilling wind cut to the bone. "I don't see how the men stand it," he muttered to Dake, who was beside him. "Some of them don't even have proper footwear."

Dake shook his head. "We'll do it," he said. His lips were drawn into a tight line, and his eyes glittered with anticipation. "We've come this far. We're not going to turn back now."

As the two men spoke, they glanced up at a courier who came thundering along the road that right angled. He stopped and spoke loudly above the noise of the wind to General Washington. "General Sullivan is in position, sir," he said, "but his muskets are wet and useless for firing."

Washington spoke crisply. "Tell Sullivan to use the bayonets."

"Yes, sir!"

The courier wheeled his horse around and galloped away at a fast pace.

Micah trudged on along the frozen road. His feet were numb, and he could keep his eyes only half open, for the wind blew sharp particles of snow from the ground that stung his eyes. He was breathing hard, and glancing at Dake, he saw his brother was not. *He's in better shape than I am. I don't know how much longer I can keep this up.* He had seen several of the men drop out, unable to continue, and he now determined that he would not be one of those.

"There it is," Dake said suddenly. "That must be Trenton."

Looking up, Micah blinked his eyes and saw the scattered houses of Trenton ahead. They seemed to be silent, and he swept the scene where the ice glittered on picket fences, orchards, and some of the stone buildings. "Not much of a place," he said.

"No. Not more than a hundred houses, I'd judge," Dake said. "I don't see any force out there. Maybe this surprise will work after all."

"I hope so," Micah said grimly.

The two men moved on with the tattered troops. They had not gone another two hundred yards before there was a wild shout in German. *"Der feind, der feind! Heraus! Heraus!"*

"There they are!" Dake yelled as men began to tumble out of a stone building.

Instantly Greene began to call out commands. "Open fire!"

Micah leveled his musket and pulled the trigger but knew that he had missed. "They're too far away!" Dake muttered. "Come on! Greene's signaling a charge!"

Micah loaded his musket, then stumbled forward. A musket ball whistled past his ear. He thought he felt a slight cut there, and reaching up he found it was bloody. Ignoring it, he moved forward with the men, then formed a line with the others as Greene screamed out commands. They fired a second volume, a third, and then Dake yelled, "They're falling back!"

Washington, his face aglow with the light of battle, called out, "General Greene! Move the men in and wave the columns on!"

Micah ran forward as fast as he could. The boom of a gun sounded, and Dake shouted, "That's Sullivan! We're going to get 'em right in the pinchers!"

Ahead of them the Hessians were trying to form a line of defense. Micah could see them as he drew closer. He heard Knox yelling, "Give room for the artillery! Bring up the pieces!"

For a time the Hessian volleys kept the company pinned down. A musket ball suddenly struck the shoulder of Washington's horse. He came off easily as the animal fell, then mounted another that a lieutenant brought to him.

Washington was alive with the battle. He moved closer to Greene, and the two men heard musket fire and cannon fire over to their left.

"Who is that?" Greene asked.

"It must be Sullivan coming in hard."

"Yes, that'll be Colonel Stark and the Hampshire men," Greene nodded.

"Ready, sir. The guns are ready!" Knox, his eyes blazing, came to stand before Washington and Greene. He was fairly dancing with excitement. "Permission to fire, sir?"

"Permission granted," Washington said.

Micah watched as the artilleryman scurried back and gave the order to fire. The cannons, both men knew, were loaded with grape—small musket-size balls. When the guns exploded they saw a gaping hole appear in the line of Hessians. The rest of the German mercenaries wheeled and ran, making their escape.

By this time, Rall had been awakened by his aide. He had stumbled out into the early morning sunshine confused. He was a good soldier, however, and soon organized his men into a defense of sorts. It was hopeless, however, for he was surrounded. Rall raged up and down King and Queen Streets trying to rally the men, then suddenly Knox's cannon exploded, and Rall went down, his side chewed to bits by the fragments of grape.

The fall of their leader took all of the courage out of the Hessians. Many of them fled along the back ways seeking escape. Others threw down their muskets and raised their arms in surrender.

"I reckon it's all over," Micah said, lowering his musket. He found that his hands were trembling. He did not know whether it was from fear or excitement over the victory.

"I guess it is," Dake replied. He looked over at Washington and said, "It's about time His Excellency had a victory."

And a victory it certainly was. Washington stood almost as if paralyzed. He watched as Greene herded the captured Hessians together, and Knox and Hamilton approached him laughing. All around them the men were yelling with exultation. For the first time, the Americans had attacked in the open without benefit of breastworks or defense. They had charged in the face of enemy guns and had won over the finest trained troops that Britain had to offer. The enormity of it stunned Washington, and he had to pull himself out of his reverie as Greene came up, saying, "Eight hundred prisoners, sir. Probably four score of the enemy killed."

Washington's aide galloped up, and Washington demanded, "Our losses?"

"None killed. Four wounded. Captain William Washington and Lieutenant James Monroe were among them, sir."

"Your victory is complete, Your Excellency," Henry Knox beamed, and the other officers joined in.

"This will make a difference in the way our people see things," Greene said.

Washington could not speak for a moment; his throat was full, but always the soldier, he said, "We must get away. When word of this gets back to the British headquarters, they will send a relief column at once."

"Yes, sir! We'll take what supplies we can back across the river."

The crossing back was as difficult as getting over in the first place. The ice was even thicker, if anything, but a fresh victory was their prize, and the men were jubilant.

Micah was happy when he set foot on the ground again, and he went at once to where he had left Keturah. When he got there, he called out softly, "Keturah, are you awake?" Hearing no answer, he lifted the flap of the tent and saw that the girl was unconscious. Moving in, he bent forward and stared into her pale face. Touching her forehead, he shook his head. "Fever is higher," he said. "She's worse."

He sat down on the ground beside the sick young woman, all the joy of victory seeming to leave him. Then he began to pray and ask God to do a work in this young woman who had grown so attached to him.

12

A Very Sick Young Woman

THE VICTORY OF THE CONTINENTAL ARMY over the British at Trenton brought on something of an explosion—not only in America but in Europe also. General William Howe was stunned. He could not believe that three experienced and established regiments of British soldiers would lay down their arms in surrender to a ragged and undisciplined militia. Even James Grant, the British general who sneered at the patriots, admitted, "I did not think that all the rebels in America could have taken that brigade prisoner."

In New Jersey something happened that cheered the patriots. The loyalists in that area had identified themselves by hanging pieces of red cloth on their front doors. After the Battle of Trenton, however, the Tories immediately began ripping them down with all haste, and on the last day of 1776, the captured Germans were paraded through the streets of Philadelphia. The citizens could not help noting the contrast between the well-fed, warmly clad Germans and their own emaciated heroes. As the men filed by, many eyes filled with tears, and some of the congressmen watching determined to do better in winning support for their fledgling army.

On the last day of 1776, Congress all but made a military dictator out of George Washington. Without reservation, their decision gave him "full, ample, and complete powers to raise, in the most speedy and effectual manner, sixteen battalions of Continentals." It also bestowed upon Washington the power to displace and appoint all officers, which came as a great pleasure to Washington, who was sick to the heart over the ineffectual, politically minded generals who had been appointed by Congress.

The immediate pressure facing Washington was the calendar. After December the thirty-first, there would be no more service, no more regiments, for at that time the enlistments ran out. None of his commanders could give him any hope, and he sensed defeat in the air.

Finally he had the men called into ranks, and he began riding slowly past them. His voice carried over the cold air as he personally promised a ten-dollar bounty to every man who would enlist for six weeks. He finally wheeled his horse about and, riding in front of the regiment, addressed them:

"My brave fellows, you have done all that I asked you to do and more than can be reasonably expected. But your country is at stake, your lives, your houses, and all that you hold dear. You have worn yourselves out with fatigue and hardships, but we know not how to spare you. If you will consent to stay only one month longer, you will render that service to the cause of liberty and to your country, which you probably cannot do under any other circumstances. The present is emphatically the crisis that is to decide our destiny."

When Washington had finished saying all that he could for the cause of the revolution, there was a hesitation in the ranks. The wind blustered, and overhead the clouds moved across a gray sky as Washington stood with his eyes fastened upon the men. He knew a crucial moment hung in the balance as he waited. For a long moment no one moved, and Washington feared that all hope was lost. Then the officers stepped forward and began urging, "Who'll step forward? Who's for campaign?"

The drums rolled and finally one man said, "I will remain if you will."

Others began to move forward and to speak up. "We cannot go home under such circumstances." A few more stepped forward, then others followed, until nearly all who were fit for duty in the regiment had volunteered. General Greene inquired, "Your Excellency, should these men be enrolled?"

Washington shook his head emphatically. "No! Men who will volunteer in such a case as this need no enrollment to keep their duty."

On December the thirtieth the general wrote to the commander at Morristown, New Jersey:

> I have the pleasure to acquaint you that the Continental Regiments from the Eastern Governments have, to a man, agreed to stay six weeks beyond their term of enlistment, which was to have expired the last day of this month; because of this extraordinary mark of their attachment to their country, I have agreed

to give them a bounty of ten dollars per man besides their pay.

☩   ☩   ☩

Dake lifted the tent flap and stepped in to see Micah mopping Keturah's forehead with a damp cloth. "How is she?" he asked.

"No better. Worse, I think," Micah said. He looked up for a moment, then dipped the cloth into a pan of water, wrung it out, and began mopping again. "What about the men? Are they going home?"

Dake grinned broadly. "Going home? Not likely!" He squatted down beside Micah and gave a quick account of how Washington had given a fiery speech, appealing for the men to stay on for another six weeks. He looked over at Micah and said, "Your enlistment's up. It ends the last of the year. Are you going to sign up again?"

"I've been thinking about it," Micah said. "I'm worried about Keturah. She's very sick, and I don't know how to help her."

Chewing his lip thoughtfully, Dake shook his head. "An army camp is no place for a sick woman. She's likely to die. Lots of our men have."

"I know. If she stays here, she might not make it."

Dake knew his brother very well. He studied him carefully, then asked, "Are you thinking about taking her back to Boston?"

"I don't see any other way, Dake. She's not going to get any better around here, but I don't know how to get her back there."

"I think we can talk the officers out of some kind of a wagon. A lot of them are smashed up pretty badly, but we could put one together."

"What about horses?"

Dake grinned broadly. "We'll sneak up on the British and steal a couple of theirs."

Micah reached out and slapped Dake across the chest in a gesture of affection. "You rascal!" he said. "You'd do it, wouldn't you?"

"You take care of Keturah and I'll talk to the major. Since you're going back anyway, maybe we can get the general to give you some messages to take back. Hey, that's a good idea."

Micah blinked. "Yes, that's a good idea," he said. "I'm glad I thought of it."

"*You* thought of it?" Dake exclaimed when he saw Micah grinning at him. "All right. You're closer to the general than I am. Why don't *you* put it to him."

"I will. I'll do it right now."

Micah left the tent and went at once to headquarters. He found the officers celebrating the recruitment and hesitated to go forward. Colonel Knox saw him standing there and came over at once. "Well, Private Bradford, did you come to reenlist?"

"Actually I didn't, sir. I would like to, but, well, I have a problem. . . ." Micah explained the situation briefly to Knox and finally ended by saying, "She really is in poor condition, General."

"What do you propose to do with her?"

"I'd like to take her back to our home in Boston. My sister's there and could nurse the young woman back to health, I think."

Knox's round face broke into a smile. "And I suppose you want me to convince the general to do all of this?"

"Well, sir, I could take some dispatches back if that would help."

"Wait here," Knox said. "I'll go see what I can do."

Knox strolled over to where Washington was speaking to General Greene and quickly explained the situation. Glancing over at Bradford, Washington came across the frozen ground and said, "So, you're leaving us."

"Just for a while, General. I really feel responsible for this young woman."

"General Knox has told me your plan. I think that could be arranged. I do have some dispatches that need to go back, but you'll make slow time. I'll send the ones that don't matter as much."

Warmly Micah said, "Thank you so much, General. I hate to leave at a time like this. I know there will be more fighting."

"You might do more good for us back in Boston for a time. Get that foundry of your father's going. We need all the ordnance we can get. If he could start casting cannon, that would be a great relief. We wouldn't have to import so many from overseas."

"I'll talk to him, Your Excellency."

Washington nodded and said, "Godspeed to you, and I pray the young lady recovers."

Hurrying back to the tent, Micah said, "It worked, Dake. We'll be leaving right away with some dispatches."

"You might miss some good fighting," Dake said. "But I think it's the only choice you've got. Tell that sweet wife of mine that one of these days I'm going to get back to her."

"I'll tell her, Dake."

Two hours later, Micah stepped into the tent and leaned over, kneeling beside Keturah. Her eyes were open, and she said weakly, "Hello . . . Micah."

"Keturah, we're going to make a little trip." Putting his arms under her, he lifted her easily. He was shocked at how little she weighed. She was a small girl, small boned, and he could still feel the heat of the fever in her body. "I'm going to take you to my house in Boston. My sister will take care of you, and you'll get well again."

Keturah's mind was not clear, and she did not understand. "You're taking me to your house?"

"That's right."

"But . . . I ain't fit to go with your people."

"Don't talk like that!" Micah stepped up to the wagon where he had made a bed out of blankets, and Dake, who was inside the wagon, reached down and took Keturah from him. He laid her down and said, "Now, Miss Keturah, you behave yourself." He wrapped the blankets around her, then reached out and touched her cheek. "You'll see my wife, Jeanne. You tell her I said to take good care of you." Then leaping off the wagon, he slapped Micah and said, "Good-bye, brother. I'll put you in charge of Boston while I take care of all this business here."

"Be careful, Dake. Don't get yourself shot," Micah said. He climbed up in the wagon, waved at the soldiers who had gathered to watch them leave, then drove the horse out. He had already collected the oilskin packet from Washington's aide, and it was tucked safely inside his pocket. As he rode out of camp, he looked back and saw the tattered forms of the soldiers. Some of them waved, and he lifted his hat to them and said, "Godspeed!" loudly, then replaced it and slapped the reins. The horse cleared the camp, and soon he was alone on the road that ran beside the river. From time to time he looked back at the young woman, and once he stopped to rearrange the blankets around her. She stirred and put her hand out, and he took it. "You'll be all right, Keturah. Don't worry."

Keturah looked up, and her lips formed the words, "You'll take care of me?"

Micah squeezed the thin hand and said, "Yes, I'll take care of you, Keturah." He knelt beside her for a moment, feeling her hand tightly clinging to him, and saw the trust in her eyes. He whispered again, "I'll take care of you." Then he put the blanket over her, went back to the seat, and said, "Get up! We're going to Boston!"

PART THREE

—

A Winter at Morristown

January 1777

13

A Place for Keturah

THE DRIVING WIND DROVE MINUTE PARTICLES of snow directly into Micah's face, and the pain to his eyes was so intense that he shut them for a moment. The snow was almost as abrasive as small grains of sand, and for the past hour he had driven against such a forceful blast that he knew he could not go on for much longer. Turning stiffly in the seat he fell into a spasm of coughing, then controlling it, he looked down at the bundle on the bed of the wagon. The snow had filled the wagon bed so deeply that Keturah's form was almost obscured. Shaking his head in despair, he gasped, "Got to get out of this and find shelter before it's too late!" Turning back, he spoke to the horse, which picked up the pace a fraction, then immediately slowed it again. The poor animal was also feeling the punishment of the January storm. His eyes were nearly frozen shut, and he staggered from time to time under the freezing wind.

For half an hour longer Micah drove through the blinding storm, his hands numb with the cold, even inside his woolen mittens. Finally he stopped the horse, climbed into the back of the wagon, and began throwing the snow out with his hands. Leaning over, he pulled the blanket back and looked into Keturah's face. Her eyes fluttered, and she stared up at him and whispered, "What . . . what is it?"

"We'll be out of this pretty soon. Can you stand it a little longer?"

"Yes." Her answer was barely audible, and Micah knew she could not last much longer. Tucking the blanket carefully back over her, he clambered down stiffly and stumbled, not knowing when his numbed feet touched the ground.

"Shouldn't have tried it with this blizzard coming on," he muttered. Walking up to the horse's head, he grabbed the reins close to the animal's jaw and leaned forward. "Come on, Bob," he said, trying to encourage the gelding. Micah leaned against the biting wind, and the horse followed him reluctantly. As he stumbled forward, the wind seemed to pick up volume. The shrill sound was like a ghostly woman crying somewhere far off—a keening, whimpering that rose in a high-pitched crescendo from time to time.

For nearly an hour he staggered forward, his breath coming in short gasps and his legs trembling with fatigue. He had never been so tired, and he longed simply to bundle up in a blanket and wait the storm out. He knew full well, however, that blizzards were unmerciful, and to stop now would be fatal. He moved on, each step a herculean effort.

Finally, in the gathering gloom of darkness, Micah glimpsed a flickering point of light ahead. Hopeful that help was close by he whispered, "Come on, Bob, we can make it!" He quickened his pace, limping on his numbed feet, and the horse, as if sensing that shelter was near, moved with a brisker trot. A hundred yards later Micah's eyes brightened, and he said through stiff lips, "There it is, Bob. A place to stay for the night."

As he approached the homestead Micah saw that it was little more than a small cabin and a barn out in the back. A straggling fence surrounded it, now buried in smooth mounds of snow around the rails and on the posts. The house itself was covered with a rounded mound of snow, but out of the chimney rose a welcome sight of smoke, which was whipped away by the fierce wind.

Micah lifted his voice, "Hello in the house!" but knew that the feeble sound could not be heard by those inside. Stopping the horse in front of the fence, he stumbled back and climbed into the wagon bed, his movements slower all the time. He lifted the limp form, muttering hoarsely, "Shelter, Keturah. We'll be all right now."

He could do no more than drag her to the back of the wagon bed. Taking a deep breath that speared his lungs with a harsh coldness, he awkwardly descended, then moved around the wagon, stumbling toward the house. When he reached the door, he shifted Keturah's weight and banged on the door with one mittened fist. "Hello! Travelers here!" he called as loudly as he could. He stood there for a moment with the wind howling and screaming about him, almost in a diabolical shriek, and then the door opened. For a moment he was blinded by the light of the fire that leaped high in a fireplace at one end of the cabin. He was aware that a woman stood there, and he said hoarsely, "I'm sorry, ma'am, but I've got a sick girl here, and she needs to be in out of the weather."

At first, Micah thought the woman meant to refuse, because she hesitated. He said no more, and then the woman stepped back and said, "Come in the house."

Micah stepped inside holding Keturah. His eyebrows were frosted with snow, and the snow on his shoulders and cap fell off onto the puncheon floor. His eyes were gritty, but as they cleared he saw a man who had been standing back in the shadows, a slight man with a full reddish beard. He came forward now, saying, "Thee is welcome in our house."

"The girl. She is ill, you say?" the woman asked.

"Very sick. I'm trying to get her back to my home in Boston. My name is Micah Bradford."

"I am Ira Crenshaw. This is my wife, Mary," the man said. "Come, thee can put the young woman down in the bed over here." He stepped back and moved toward a bed that was fastened to the side of the cabin at a right angle. It had only one leg, the other points being held to the wall with pegs, but there was a corn-shuck mattress on it, with a wool blanket and a quilt, which the man pulled back.

Wearily, but with a sense of relief, Micah carefully put Keturah on the bed. He stripped off the wet, cold blanket and turned to the woman. "Perhaps I could dry this by the fire?"

"Let me do it." The woman took the blanket and pulled a chair in front of one side of the fire, where she draped the blanket, then moved back to stand over the young woman. "What is her illness, Mr. Bradford?"

"I don't know. I've been with General Washington's army." He hesitated, for one never knew whether the strangers met in passing were loyal to the Crown or to the patriot cause. He saw nothing in the woman's face, however, except a placid acceptance and a willingness to help. She was a small woman with a crown of brown hair neatly arranged around her head and a pair of level blue eyes.

"Does thee think it could be cholera?" the woman asked.

"I don't think so, ma'am." Micah shook his head. Turning toward Crenshaw, he said, "I'll have to see to my animal, sir."

Micah's knees were trembling from the ordeal, and suddenly he staggered. Crenshaw leaped forward, saying, "Come over by the fire, sir. Sit thee down. I'll see to thy horse shortly." He pulled a chair in front of the fire and maneuvered Micah into it. "I'll get thee something warm to drink, and my wife will fix thee a meal."

"I'd be most grateful to you," Micah said. The warmth of the fire had already begun to work on him, and he found himself growing drowsy. "I shouldn't have tried to make it in this storm, but I didn't think it'd be so bad."

"No night for anyone to be out," Crenshaw said, then he turned and moved over to put a kettle of water over the fire and busied himself with making a hot drink.

Micah tried to stay awake, but his chin slumped forward on his chest, and he simply went to sleep sitting up.

The woman, who had taken off Keturah's wet clothes and wrapped her in a woolen gown while the man made the tea, came over and looked at Micah. "He's played out, ain't he, Ira?"

"The Lord was with him, Mary. If he had missed this house, I doubt they'd have made it. There's no house for another ten miles, and as you say, he's played out. What about the young woman?"

"She's ailing pretty bad," Mary Crenshaw said. She glanced at the still figure and shook her head. "Needs a lot of care." She looked at the face of the man who was sleeping, noting the strong jaw and the lean features. "He must be a soldier," she observed. "I wonder if they be married?"

"He didn't say so."

"No, he didn't." Mrs. Crenshaw studied the still figure for a moment, then said, "I'll fix something, then I expect he'll sleep up in the attic room."

"I'd better see to the horse. No fit weather for an animal to be out."

Micah awoke as a voice said, "Wake up, Mr. Bradford. Take a bite to eat."

Micah smelled the aroma of bacon cooking, and his stomach contracted with hunger. Opening his eyes, he looked around in confusion for a moment and was relieved to see that Keturah was under the quilt and her wet dress was hanging beside the fire to dry. He got up and said sheepishly, "I guess I dropped off to sleep for a minute or two."

"For an hour. Thee was plum beat out," Crenshaw murmured. "Come, have some of this stew. It will make thee feel better."

Micah sat down and looked at the two, who shook their heads. "We've already eaten."

Micah looked at the bowl of stew sending up a delightful odor and said, "Thank you, Lord, for this good food, and for these dear people who have taken in strangers. In the name of Jesus I ask it."

He began to eat and saw a look of approval pass between his hosts. He tried not to gulp the food down, but he ate two bowls before he finally shook his head. "That's the best stew I've ever had, Mrs. Crenshaw."

"How far have you come, sir?"

"I don't know, Mr. Crenshaw. We left early this morning and we took a bad turn. I knew I was in trouble when that storm came up, but God was with us."

"You be a Christian man, I take it?"

"Why, yes I am. And I take it you're Quakers?"

"Yes we are."

"My commander, General Greene, is a Quaker." He thought for a moment and then added quickly, "Or was. I'm not sure if he had the blessings of your people when he became a soldier."

"We do believe in nonviolence," Ira said.

"So General Greene has told me. I think it's a grief to him that he has to go against the teachings. He's a very good and devout man."

For a few moments he sat there speaking, but weariness began to creep up on him.

"What is the young lady's name?" Mary asked.

"Keturah Burns."

A light of interest came to the eyes of Mrs. Crenshaw. "Keturah. That's a Bible name."

"Yes, I believe it is. That was the name of Abraham's second wife after Sarah died."

"You know your Bible, Mr. Bradford." Ira Crenshaw smiled briefly. "But what about the young woman? Does she have family?"

"No. That's the problem. Her mother was her only relative, but she died recently. I found Keturah almost destitute, then she got sick. I'm trying to get her back to Boston."

"What will thee do with her there?" Mrs. Crenshaw asked, concerned.

"Why, we have a home there, and my sister, Rachel, is very good with sick people, and so is my brother's wife, Jeanne Bradford. They'll nurse her back to health."

The explanation seemed to satisfy the pair, for Crenshaw said, "I'll pull the ladder down, and thee can sleep in the attic."

"That's kind of you, sir."

Micah stood, and when the man had placed a short ladder into the crevice in the ceiling, Micah started up, each step requiring all of his effort. He paused halfway and looked at Keturah, then turned to face his hosts. "I appreciate anything you can do for her," he said wearily.

Mrs. Crenshaw returned his glance and studied his face. "Thee is not too well thyself. I'll fix up a potion for thee to take, because, if I don't mistake, thee is coming down with whatever it is this young woman has."

For a moment Micah stared at her. He had felt his face growing flushed even back when he entered the cabin but merely thought it was the heat from the fire. Now, however, he felt exhausted and somehow knew that it was more than that.

"I'll be all right," Micah muttered, then climbed wearily up the ladder. Sitting on a corn-shuck mattress that was on the floor, he pulled his boots off and each seemed to weigh a ton. He saw his wet socks and slowly stripped them off. Finally he managed to remove his coat, but he had no strength left. He fell backward onto the mattress, and the rustling of the corn shucks was the last thing he heard. . . .

☫   ☫   ☫

Micah came down the ladder rather shakily, weak from the fever, which had been high for two days. This was now the third day that he and Keturah had been at the Crenshaw home. His fever had not been as severe as Keturah's but had been bad enough. He had suffered terrible chills along with the fever, and he knew it was only the care of the Quaker couple that had pulled him through.

"Well, thee's lookin' right pert," Mrs. Crenshaw greeted him.

"Thank you, ma'am," Micah smiled. She was standing in front of the fireplace, bending over the huge black pot and stirring a thick mixture that gave off a succulent aroma. She smiled at him, then rose and came over to study his face. "The Lord's done a work in thy body, I feel."

"Yes. I feel much better." He looked over quickly at the bed and saw Keturah sitting up. He went to stand over her and said, "Keturah, you're looking better."

"I feel a heap better," she said. "How are you, Micah? I been worried about you."

"Can't kill an old bird like me," he grinned. He studied her face, thinking how it had thinned down and now looked gaunt. Her eyes seemed enormous with her cheeks sunk in.

Turning to Mrs. Crenshaw, who called him to the table, Micah sat down and hungrily ate the griddle cakes she had made, pouring molasses over them and wolfing them down.

"Well, if your appetite's any sign, thee is well."

"I believe so." He looked out the window and saw Mr. Crenshaw coming back, driving a team and hauling a sled with wood piled high. "Storm's over," he remarked.

"Yes. A mite cold, but that never hurt a body."

After tending to the team, Crenshaw came into the house, sat down, and ate. Mrs. Crenshaw insisted that Keturah join them, which she did. She ate almost nothing, however, except to drink half a mug of milk. Then she went back to her bed as quickly as she could and fell sleep almost instantly.

"I think I'd better get her to Boston as soon as I can," Micah said, "since the weather's cleared up now."

"Thee is none too strong thyself," Ira Crenshaw observed. He rubbed his hands through his thick hair and said, "I think thee would be wise to stay around a bit—until you're both stronger."

"No, I think I'd better push on." Micah leaned back and studied his host. A smile turned the corners of his lips upward, and he said warmly, "I don't know what we would have done if it hadn't been for you and your wife."

"We did only what Christians should do," Ira remarked mildly, as if surprised it had been mentioned.

"Well, maybe so, but when I saw your light shining out of that blizzard, I was praying mighty hard for it to be someone who felt like that." After they talked for a while, Micah looked out the window and asked, "How far is it to the next town?"

"Not over ten miles."

"Then I think I'll push on. I'll go hitch up the horse."

"No, I'll do that. You get your things together. Mary, can thee fix something for them to take?"

"Does thee take me for a heathen, Ira Crenshaw!" the woman said indignantly. She proved her words, for in an hour she produced enough food to get them all the way back to Boston. Her husband loaded it into the wagon and came back, saying, "I fixed a bed in the back for Miss Burns."

"Thank you, Mr. Crenshaw." Micah reached out his hand and felt the hard grip of the other, then he turned to Mrs. Crenshaw and bowed. "I thank you, ma'am. Again, I won't forget you."

"Thee must take care of that child now. She's not over her sickness."

"I'll do that."

Micah went over to the bed and saw that Keturah was awake, but her face was still pale. When he lifted her up, she seemed to weigh nothing. "Time to go, Keturah." He carried her through the door, placed her into the wagon, and then pulled extra blankets over her. "All set? Are you all right?"

"Yes. I'm all right. Those were nice people, weren't they?"

"Fine Christian people. It won't be long now until we're in Boston—tomorrow at the latest, I think. We'll stay at an inn somewhere tonight."

⚓   ⚓   ⚓

"I think I'll have another biscuit or two, Jeanne."

Jeanne had been talking with Rachel across the supper table and looked over at Sam's empty plate. "What did you do with all those I gave you?"

"What do you think I did with them?" Sam shrugged eloquently. "I ate them."

"Well, there aren't any more."

"There is too! You have one right there." Sam reached over and adroitly plucked the biscuit off of Jeanne's plate and, ignoring her protests, broke it open and layered it with thick yellow butter. He dipped the spoon into a pewter pot and brought a dollop of blackberry preserves and spread it on top. "Thank you very much, Jeanne. You're always looking out for me." He grinned and then stuck half of the biscuit in his mouth.

Jeanne smiled helplessly at Rachel, saying, "Does he ever fill up? I think his stomach is bigger than all of him."

"He's never been full that I know of, and he's never refused biscuits and blackberry jam." She rose and went to stand at the window. "It's warming up a little, I think."

"I hope it's warming at the camp in Morristown. I worry about Dake and Micah. They must be almost frozen out there in the open like that," Jeanne said.

"Oh, they built some sort of shelter, I'm sure." Rachel stood for a moment studying the gray sky. It was late afternoon, and they had eaten an early supper. Now the sun cast pale shadows over Boston. Far off down the street she could see a wagon approaching but could not make out who it was. Turning back to the table, she sat down and poured herself a glass of milk. She sipped it, then said, her eyes coming alive with excitement, "Isn't it wonderful how the army's victories at Trenton and Princeton have changed things?"

She had spoken to Jeanne, but it was Sam who paused between bites of biscuits long enough to wave the spoon around, saying, "I'll say it is. Those Redcoats learned what it's like to fool with us, didn't they?"

The Battle of Trenton, which had been followed by the Battle of Princeton, had indeed turned the war around. The fighting at Princeton had lasted only thirty minutes. It was not technically a battle but rather a small skirmish. The British had lost one hundred men with two hundred taken as prisoners, while the Americans had suffered the loss of only forty.

Strategically, however, the effects of those two battles were enormous for the fledgling nation trying to emerge. Politically, the balance of power changed altogether. The British had been driven from New Jersey, at least from the eastern and central portions. But these victories had achieved more than military advantage, since the patriot cause—which had died down to almost nothing—now flamed anew, and the war continued. Somehow the brave actions of General George Washington and his Continentals had proven that America had a general as capable as any of the experienced officers in the service to the Crown, and an army that could stand up against the best troops Britain could send against them.

Jeanne listened as Sam spoke rather boastfully, then said, "It's awful what the British did to the civilians of Princeton."

"Yes, but they'll pay for it!" Rachel declared. "They already are. What they did was a grave mistake."

The British soldiers, frustrated by their recent defeats, had taken out their ire on the people of Princeton. They had destroyed the homes of the patriots, burning many of them, so that by the time they left, one resident declared that the town looked as if it had been devastated by an earthquake.

The Hessians, most of whom could not even speak English, were the chief culprits. They obviously could not look at a civilian and tell if he was a Tory or a patriot—neither did they care. Driven by the mercenary creed that any spoil belonged to them by right, they ruthlessly pillaged the entire town. They dressed their camp followers in the stolen clothing they had found in the homes of Princeton and sent them down the village streets. The indignity of their actions only further dampened any loyalist sentiment that remained in the town toward King George and the British cause. The razing of Princeton was the beginning of the barbaric English policy of striking out against civilians. It also added to the British mistreatment of American prisoners, which so incensed the Colonists that it united them with the cause even more passionately.

The three sat talking as Sam finished off the remains of the meal, then they all looked up at the sound of a wagon stopping outside. "I reckon that's someone come to visit," Sam remarked. "I'll see who it is."

Getting up from his seat, Sam walked out of the kitchen and down the central hallway to open the door. He stood silent with surprise for a moment, then he yelled, "Micah! It's you!"

Micah took the hard blow that young Sam delivered on his back and grinned. "Don't beat me to death. I've been sick." Then Jeanne and Rachel appeared, all smiles to welcome him. When they tried to pull him in, however, he said with some embarrassment, "Well, I'm not alone."

"Is Dake with you?" Jeanne demanded quickly, her eyes bright with anticipation as she looked out at the wagon.

"I'm afraid not. I wish he could've come."

"Who is it, Micah?" Rachel asked.

The three of them stared at Micah as he appeared at a loss for words. He shuffled his feet and slapped his mittened hands together awkwardly until Sam said, "Well, who is it? You didn't bring General Washington in that wagon, did you?"

"No. It's a friend of mine that got sick at camp. Needs some good nursing."

"Well, don't just stand there. Bring him in. Can he walk? Sam, go help Micah bring his friend in."

"Why, I don't need any help exactly." Micah flushed again and said, "It's a young girl named Keturah Burns."

Sam cocked his head to one side. "*How* young?" he demanded.

His meaning was clear, and Micah said, "Too young for what you're thinking. Anyway, she was taken sick, and I didn't think she'd make it in the camp, so I thought I'd bring her here to get some good nursing."

"Well, don't just stand there," Rachel said, smiling at Micah's obvious embarrassment. "Go bring her inside. We'll put her in the blue room. Come along, Jeanne. We'll get some blankets and get ready for our patient." Looking at Micah, she asked, "How old did you say she was?"

"She's sixteen."

Micah started for the door, moving quickly, but he stumbled.

"Wait a minute! What's wrong with you?" Jeanne asked. She pulled Micah around and studied his face. "Are you sick, Micah?"

"Just a touch of—"

"That's enough," Jeanne said. "Sam, you go bring the young lady in."

"Yes, and you get out of those wet clothes, Micah. When you get changed, come into the kitchen and we'll give you a good hot meal."

Sam ducked outside the door, his feet crunching over the snow. It was almost gone now, with only piles here and there in the corners of fences and at the eaves of the house. When he got to the wagon, he put his hands on the edge and peered over at the figure lying inside. He saw only a bundle, much like a cocoon. With the strength of youth he sprang inside the wagon in a swift, easy motion. Pulling the corner of the blanket down, he saw himself being watched by a pair of enormous light blue eyes that took him off guard. "Hello," he said. "I'm Sam Bradford. I'm supposed to take you up to your room."

For a long moment the young woman did not speak, and Sam was somewhat disconcerted. He was almost never taken off guard, but something about the gaze of the young woman made him stammer. "Well . . . got to pick you up now." He reached under her and heaved upward and was surprised. "Why, you don't weigh anything at all!" he exclaimed with astonishment. The blanket had fallen back from her hair, which was cut short but lay in curls about her face. He thought momentarily that she was rather good-looking but skinny and was immediately taken by the cleft in her chin.

"My room?" she said in a weak voice.

"Why, sure. We're going to put you in that room right up there. See that window?" Sam did not wait but walked to the back of the wagon. Without putting her down he leaped off, and in his overconfidence, he landed on a patch of snow. His feet went out from under him, but he kept his arms tight around the young woman. She landed right in the pit of his stomach, and it drove a large "oof" from him as his back hit the ground. He lay there for a moment mortified, his face reddening. The girl's face was only inches from his, and he muttered, "Are you all right?"

"Yes. Are you?"

"I'm not usually this clumsy," Sam said as he got to his feet. "It's this stupid snow! Come on, we'll get you out of this cold weather."

Carefully getting up with Keturah in his arms, he walked up to the door and slipped inside. Kicking the door shut with his foot, he went down the hallway. Keturah looked at the pictures on the wall and caught a glimpse of a cheerful fire burning in a large fireplace. The young man carried her as if she weighed nothing at all, and she studied his features, which were only a few inches from her face. He had, she saw, auburn hair, and his eyes were almost an electric blue, they were so bright. He was as tall as his brother Micah, she thought, but very strong.

When Sam reached the top of the stairs, he turned and went to a door that was standing open. Moving inside, he saw that Rachel had prepared a bed.

"Where do you want me to put her?"

"Right here in this chair, and then you can be about your business."

Sam deposited Keturah on the chair and stopped long enough to say, "Micah said your name, but I don't remember it."

"It's Keturah—Keturah Burns."

"Right pretty name," Sam said cheerfully, then turned and went down the stairs whistling.

"I know you must be exhausted after that hard trip," Rachel said. "Let's get you out of these clothes. I've got a fresh nightgown for you here, or do you feel like going downstairs and eating first?"

"I don't . . . think so."

Noting the paleness of the girl's cheeks, Rachel nodded. "Well, you get in bed, and I'll bring you up some broth. I'm sure you need something to eat."

Keturah was like a child in Rachel's hand. Her clothes were removed, she was dressed in a fresh, soft cotton nightgown, and she fell between the covers with a grateful sigh. Looking up at Rachel's face, she said, "You're Micah's sister."

"Yes. His only sister. Did you know Dake at the camp?"

"Oh yes. I know Dake."

"I'll have his wife, Jeanne, bring you some of that broth. You two can get acquainted. She's dying to hear anything about Dake, so you tell her something, even if you have to make it up."

Fear suddenly came to the girl's eyes, and she said, "Micah—will he be here?"

"Oh yes. His room is right down the hall. Now, you just rest, but don't go to sleep if you can help it until you get something to eat."

Rachel went downstairs and found Sam peppering Micah with questions about Keturah Burns.

"Be quiet and let Micah eat, Sam," Rachel said.

"Well, I never saw the like of it. Here we got soldiers going through all kinds of hard times, and there you come up with a pretty girl! I'd never thought it of a preacher!"

"Shut up, Sam!" Micah said, irritated by Sam's cheerful teasing. "She's had a hard time." He looked up and asked Rachel, "How is she?"

"She's nothing but skin and bones. How long has she been sick?"

"A couple of weeks, I think."

"I'll take her up some of this broth," Jeanne said. "Does she know Dake?"

"Yes, she does," Rachel answered. "Now, don't you pester her too much. She needs plenty of rest."

"I won't."

Rachel sat down and watched Micah eating the leftover mutton, saying, "Sam ate all the biscuits, but I have some bread I baked this morning." She got the bread and waited patiently as Micah ate. Finally he finished and said, "Dake's fine. I've been telling Jeanne about him. I hope he'll get to come home soon. Maybe he can be the courier now that I'm out of the army."

"You're not going back in?"

"Not right away. General Washington thought I ought to stay at the foundry awhile. He thinks Pa ought to start casting cannon. It might be a good thing, too. Not many guns are getting through the blockade now, and there aren't many places in this country where cannon can be cast." He looked up and said awkwardly, "I didn't mean to dump all my problems on you, but I felt sorry for Keturah."

"Tell me about her, Micah."

Rachel sat there listening as Micah explained how he had found the girl, and how Keturah had no place else to go since her mother had died. He did not know how much of himself he was revealing to his sister as he spoke. "I didn't know what else to do, Rachel. I think she would have died in that camp. Lots of strong men have. I wasn't too sure of myself when I got the fever on the way back."

"You did the right thing, Micah." Rachel rose, went over to him, and brushed his hair back gently. "You always were bringing stray cats in, but this is a little different."

Micah reached up, took her hand, and held it for a moment. "I guess it is, but I knew you and Jeanne would take good care of her."

"And what then?" Rachel asked. "Where will she go when she gets better?"

Her question disturbed Micah. He dropped her hand and clasped his own hands together. For a long moment he sat there, then he shook his head. "I don't know, Rachel. We'll have to think of something."

☙   ☙   ☙

For two days Keturah did little but sleep, although she was fed at regular intervals by either Rachel or Jeanne. Micah also grew stronger steadily and did not go out of the house a great deal.

Daniel Bradford came by the day after Micah's return and greeted his son warmly. He wanted to know all about the army and Dake. He listened quietly as Micah explained why he had brought Keturah Burns home.

"I didn't want to do it without your permission, Pa," Micah said quietly. Then a firmness came to his lips, followed by a smile. "But I know you would have done exactly the same thing."

"Well, I hope so, son." Dan had met the young woman, who had been almost speechless in his presence. "She's a quiet little thing, isn't she?"

"I think she's afraid she'll say the wrong thing." Micah stirred in his seat and rubbed the ear that had been nicked by the musket ball at the Battle of Trenton. It was almost healed now, but that little notch in his right ear would always be a reminder. Dake had said he had been ear-notched like a pig. "She's had a hard life," Micah went on, "and her manners are pretty bad." He looked up defensively and then spread his hands apart. "You're going to have to help us think of something to do with her, Pa. She's going to need someone who can help teach her some things."

"I think you're doing pretty well, Micah, but I'll help all I can. Maybe we can find a place for her here in Boston as a maid or something."

"I don't think that would work, Pa. She doesn't know *anything* about the life of a lady. Her mother, well, she wasn't much—just a camp follower, to be truthful. But now she's dead, so Keturah's all alone."

"It's hard to understand sometimes how God allows such hardship," Daniel Bradford said as he leaned back in his rocking chair. "But the older I get, the more I'm convinced of God's loving sovereignty."

"How's that, Pa?"

"I find myself thinking that everything happens for a purpose. *Everything*, I mean. Was it an accident that you were at the right place to save this girl's life? No, I believe it's because God had you coming along that exact road at just that exact moment. Suppose," he went on, "you'd been half an hour later, or had passed by half an hour sooner? You'd never have met this girl, and she would have been cruelly violated, and your life would never have touched hers. But you were there at that exact time, and you were man enough to protect her." His eyes glowed then, and he said, "I'm glad you did, son. I'm proud of you for that."

"Well, I . . . I guess maybe you're right, Pa—about God having a purpose in everything," Micah said to avoid his father's praise.

"And now she's here with all of us for some purpose," Daniel said. "We'll help her, Micah. Rachel and Jeanne say she's getting better. I'll go along home and talk to Marian. She'll help too, I'm sure."

Later that afternoon Keturah was sitting in a rocking chair, dressed in a pale blue robe that belonged to Rachel. She had tucked her feet up under her and was listening intently as Sam held up a musket and pointed out the different parts to it. "I thought I'd come in and entertain you a little bit, Keturah—show you my newest invention."

Now as Keturah listened, she understood little of what Sam was trying to explain. It had something to do with a better way of igniting powder, something about the frizzen and the pan. She enjoyed Sam's visits, for it meant she did not have to talk much. Sam took care of most of that!

Now he went on to explain, "You see? When I get this invention of mine fixed, I'm going to sell it to the army. Every gun will have Bradford's new device on there." His smile was infectious, and his auburn hair fell down over his forehead in a careless manner. "You want to see how it works?"

"Yes," Keturah said. She did not really care much about it, but somehow she had been afraid ever since she had come to stay at the Bradford house. She had never been in a private home like this before. All she knew was poverty and the cold army camps she and her mother had stayed in. Everything was so fine here, and obviously all the Bradfords were well educated. Keturah painfully knew that every time she opened her mouth she revealed her lack of education, and as a result they had found her to be a rather silent young girl. Rachel, she thought, understood her reluctance to speak but never pressured her.

With Sam, however, it was different. Sam bubbled over with information, and all he required was a single word of encouragement to keep him going. Keturah wrapped her arms around her knees and smiled at him. She had been eating well and was beginning to gain her strength back. Even in her brief stay here, she had begun to fill out a little bit, and now the paleness had left and color was beginning to come into her cheeks.

Sam noted this and said, "You're lookin' better, Keturah. You were pretty scrawny when they brought you in here."

"Was I, Sam?"

"Yep. Looked like a stripped chicken. Didn't weigh eighty pounds, I don't think. But you're lookin' better now," he added encouragingly. Then he turned to the muzzle and said, "Look. This is the way it works. . . ."

Sam, in his excitement, forgot that he had charged the musket with powder and a ball. He had intended to simply show her how, when the trigger was pulled, a flint would strike a spark into the pan, which would ignite the powder. This in turn would ignite the powder in the barrel, and the explosion would drive the ball out of the muzzle.

"You see how easy this pulls? Not like the old models," Sam said. "You just pull the trigger—"

Instantly, a tremendous roar filled the room as the musket exploded. The lamp sitting in front of the window shattered, as did the window itself, and Sam sat there with a look of shock etched on his features.

Keturah was suddenly amused at young Sam Bradford's expression of absolute astonishment, and she grinned broadly. "Works just fine, Sam."

"Well, it wasn't supposed to—"

The door burst open, and Micah almost fell inside, followed by Jeanne and Rachel. "What are you doing? What was that shot?"

"Well, I was just—"

"Why, you idiot!" Micah said. He leaped across the room and snatched the musket away from Sam, his face tight with anger. "Don't you know any better than to shoot a loaded gun in a house?"

"Oh no—Mother's lamp!" Rachel exclaimed. She dashed over to the shattered glass lamp and picked up a piece in each hand. Grief filled her face, and she said, "Sam, it was Mother's favorite lamp!"

Sam's face was pale, and for once he was not smiling. "I . . . I'm sorry, Rachel. It was just an accident."

"I'm tempted to beat your head in with the butt of this musket,"

Micah said fiercely. "Why, you could have killed somebody!" He looked over and asked, "Are you all right, Keturah?"

Keturah pulled the robe tighter about her chin and nodded. "It's all right. I'm not hurt." She saw Micah turn and begin berating Sam, who for once could not say a word. He stood there with his head down, staring at his feet.

Finally, Keturah made the longest speech she had made since coming to this house. "Please, Micah, don't be hard on him. He was just tryin' to be nice to me. He wanted to show me how his invention worked. It . . . it coulda happened to anyone."

Micah turned and faced her with surprise. He studied the pale face, noting that the color was beginning to come into her cheeks. There was an eloquence in her plea, and her lips were gentle and vulnerable as she added, "Please, don't say anythin' else to him."

Sam looked up quickly and studied Keturah's face, then he turned to Micah, who was looking intently at the girl also. "I didn't mean to do it, Micah. I'll put another window in, and I'll try to fix Ma's lamp."

"It's all right. We can put it back together," Rachel said, coming over to put her arm around Sam. She knew he was crushed by what he had done, and she added, "Lamps aren't like people, are they?"

"Well, come on, Sam," Micah said, somewhat mollified. "Let's get out of here. You'll need to patch that window. The wind's going to whistle through it."

"I'll fix it right away," Sam said, then turned and looked at Keturah. "I'm . . . I'm glad I didn't shoot you, Keturah." He turned and left, and as he walked down the stairs he was thinking, *I would have to act like an idiot in front of her!*

🔔   🔔   🔔

Sarah Dennison looked up at Rachel with pleasure. "Why, Rachel, how nice to see you. It was a good sermon, wasn't it?"

"Yes, it was." The two had met outside the church, and as they stood there discussing the sermon, Rachel suddenly said, "Have you heard about Micah?"

"He hasn't been hurt in the war, has he?"

Rachel noted the quick concern in Sarah Dennison's expression. "No," she said. "He's home. He caught a fever, but he's recovered now and is not going back to the army."

"What will he do, Rachel?"

"I think he'll go to work at the foundry with our father for a while." She went on then to explain that he had brought a young woman home, and how she and Jeanne were nursing her back to health. "I wish you'd come over and see us. Keturah's her name. She's a shy thing really and needs all the assurance she can get."

"I . . . I'm afraid I couldn't do that, Rachel."

"Why not?"

"My parents have forbidden me to ever come to your house again."

"I see." Rachel studied the young woman before her, but Sarah was unable to meet her gaze.

"I have to go now," Sarah said and turned away. As she walked rapidly toward her carriage, she was thinking, *I'm nothing but a coward*. She longed to see Micah Bradford, to talk to him, to explain again how she was being forced into the marriage with Mr. Potter, but she knew she would not go. As she settled down and the carriage pulled away from the church, she covered her face with her hands and tried to hold back the tears.

14

THE SPIDER CATCHER

MICAH COULD NOT HELP SMILING as Sam pulled him through the front door of the house. He had been sitting in the study reading when his younger brother had burst in, his eyes electric with excitement.

"Come on, Micah. You've got to come down to the shipyard!" he had exclaimed.

"What for?"

"You've got to come and see the new boat that Jubal and I are going to get rich with."

"It's too cold for that," Micah protested, though actually the sun had come out, and the bitter winter blasts had mitigated. Now as Sam tugged him by the arm toward the two horses that he had saddled, he said, "What number is this, Sam?"

Sam swung into the saddle and stared down at Micah. "What do you mean 'what number'?"

Easily Micah stepped into the stirrup, swung his leg over the horse, and grinned at Sam. "I mean," he said, a humorous light in his eyes, "what number of scheme for making you rich? A hundred and thirty-six, is it?"

Sam refused to be irritated. He simply tossed his head and pulled the mare's head around. "One of these days, Micah, you're going to be coming to me with your hat in your hand asking for a part of my business. Someday my inventions will catch on, and then you'll see!"

Micah simply laughed, for he was accustomed to Sam's rather bizarre schemes. Some of them had actually been rather dangerous, and most of them were foolish. Still, as he rode along listening to Sam chattering like a parrot about the new boat, Micah thought, *You know, we all might be wrong about Sam. He may come up with something someday that will make him rich. I wish he would. He's a fine brother.*

As they rode along through the streets of Boston down toward the harbor, Sam stopped talking about the boat long enough to say, "I wish Pa would let me join General Washington's army."

"Well, he won't, so you might as well make the best of it."

"I don't see why not!" Sam said rebelliously. He stuck his chin out in a defiant manner and swung in the saddle impatiently. That was the kind of young man he was—always ready for action *now*. Inaction bored him, and he longed to be in the fight for freedom that was sweeping the country. "I'm as old as Tad Mulhouse, and he's serving with General Washington."

"I thought this ship was going to help the country more than your serving in the army. Isn't that what you told me?"

For a moment Sam was quiet, and then he shrugged and grinned cheerfully. "Well, I guess that's right. When Jubal and I get our spider catcher going, we'll hurt the British plenty."

"I don't think you have to worry. The army's not going to be doing much this winter. Come next spring the British will come out, and then something will have to happen," Micah said. As they made their way toward the harbor he looked at the stores in the main part of Boston. Most of the windows, he noticed, were empty, for the revolution had put a halt to commercial sea traffic from England. The blockade had been effective in this way, and only the privateers brought in enough goods to keep the Colonies supplied with those items they could not manufacture for themselves. Actually there was a gloomy look about the city that depressed Micah, and he felt discouraged as he thought about the starving, poorly equipped, and poorly clad army that Washington commanded. England was the most powerful nation on the face of the earth, with the largest standing army, and at times like this, doubt assailed Micah, driving him to wonder how the revolution would turn out. He knew that Dake never had such thoughts—nor did Sam, of course—but Sam was an incorrigible optimist and had not seen the terrible suffering that he and Dake had seen firsthand in battle.

"There's the shipyard!" Sam exclaimed. "Come on, Micah!" He spurred his mare forward, and the two of them passed down to the shore, where Micah studied the vessels that were in various stages of completion. They passed by one where the bare ribs of a small ship were in place.

"It looks like a skeleton turned upside down," Micah said. But then forty yards down the beach he noted another vessel completely ribbed, and the plankers were putting the oakum between the joints. As they passed by the saw pit, Micah paused to watch two men cut a huge timber into planks. It was a primitive sort of affair. The timber itself was sixty feet long and at least a foot square. It had been sawed into a square shape, and now one man stood on top of it while another stood down in a pit. The man at the top tugged at the saw, which was approximately five feet in length and was held in a rectangular wooden framework. He lifted the saw up, the teeth cutting in, and the man at the bottom, when it was at its height, pulled it back down. As Micah watched, he saw the sawdust fall right in the unfortunate man's face who was in the pit. He grinned and winked at Sam, saying, "There's a job for you."

"Not me," Sam stated firmly. "I'm going to sail the ships, not build them."

"You've always been interested in ships, but I never thought you'd set out to be a sailor."

Sam had held many other ambitions, but Micah thought perhaps this might be the one that would last. As they moved along, they saw the workers carving ribs for a very large ship. "That's interesting, Sam. They have to find oak trees that already have a curve in them like the shape of the ribs, don't they?"

"That's right, and the best wood is white oak, black birch, or hickory," Sam said in a knowledgeable fashion. "Then they cut it down and season it. You see those fellows with the broad axes? After they get done squaring it out, they'll take an adze and finish the surface as smooth as a tavern wench's cheek!"

Despite himself, Micah laughed out loud. "What do you know about the cheeks of tavern wenches?"

"Just a figure of speech, Micah," Sam said airily, waving his hand. "Look, there's our ship, and there's Jubal right there."

The ship might have been called a boat much more readily, for it actually was long and open, and approximately thirty-five feet in length. It was turned right side up now, and as Micah dismounted he looked at it critically. "This is what's going to defeat the British navy?" he asked.

"You don't understand, Micah. Look, here's Jubal. He'll tell you about it. Jubal, you remember my brother Micah?"

"Yes, I'm pleased to see you again, sir," Jubal said, putting his hand out. When Micah took it and returned the greeting, he found his own hand clasped in a grip as powerful as his own. But Jubal was a powerful-looking man at least six feet tall with a deep chest and sinewy shoulders. He had pulled off his coat, even in the cold air, and the muscles beneath his light woolsey shirt moved as he waved his arm toward the ship. "Well, there she is, Mr. Bradford."

"Just Micah will do." He moved over to the prow of the ship and said, "I take it this is for the cannon."

"That's right," Jubal nodded eagerly. He had very sharp blue-gray eyes, and his rusty hair, slightly curly, blew in the breeze. He pointed out the structure of the cannon carriage and said, "You see, we mount the cannon right here in the prow. I'm intending to put at least an eight-pounder on here, maybe ten."

"Ten-pound cannons got a pretty good kick, Jubal," Micah observed. "What about the recoil?"

"Well, I've taken care of that. That's what this track is for." He laid his hand on a wooden track built of heavy timbers that inclined upward toward the rear of the boat. "When the gun is fired, it recoils back up here. It's stopped by these ropes."

Sam broke in eagerly. "So what we do is back the gun up, load it, and then push it forward. When it goes off, it kicks back up this ramp, and the ropes hold it tight. Oh, we're going to give the lobsterbacks a hard time!"

Micah exchanged an amused glance with Jubal and said, "You'll have to be careful about this young firebrand. He'll be attacking a hundred-gun ship of the line if you let him."

"I like his spirit. It reminds me of my own. We're both a little bit impetuous, I'm afraid. Well, let me show you. Here's where the rowers sit—twelve of them, six on each side. The oarsman steers here with the rudder."

"What about a sail?"

"We're going to set one in," Jubal said. "Just a simple sort of thing. Maybe a lateen sail. It doesn't take much skill to use one of those."

For over an hour Micah stayed and talked with the two would-be sailors. He was highly impressed with Jubal Morrison. He liked the young man's zeal, although he had little confidence that the scheme would get them rich. One shot from a frigate would easily destroy the little spider catcher.

"Why do they call them spider catchers?" he asked as he was preparing to leave.

"I don't know," Morrison shrugged. "That's what they call them, though." He suddenly turned his head to one side and said slyly, "You and I might be kinfolk someday."

Startled, Micah stared at the young man. "What do you mean by that, Jubal?"

"My brother, Stephen, is very taken with your cousin, Grace Gordon."

"Is that right?"

"Well, I don't know if it's *right* or not, but that's the way it is," Jubal grinned. "Every letter I get from him, all he talks about is how pretty she is, and how sweet, and all that. Fatal sign of a man in love. Here I'm wanting to talk business, and all he can talk about is how well she sings or the pretty dress she had on."

"He'd be getting a fine young woman," Micah said. Then he turned to the horse and said, "Sam, I've got to go to the foundry. You'd better come along. I think Pa has some work for you to do there."

"Aw, Micah, I want to stay here and help with the ship!"

"You do that on your own time," Jubal said quickly. He slapped Sam on the shoulder so heartily the young man staggered. Grinning, he said, "Get on with you now. I'll be here late. You come along, and perhaps we can figure out a way to set two masts in this thing."

"Yeah, a two-master!" Sam yelled. He jumped on his horse, kicked her with his heels, and jerking off his hat, went careening through the shipyard, startling the workers. More than one turned to look after him shouting a curse, but Sam merely shouted louder and drove the horse harder.

"That's some brother you have there, Micah," Jubal said, shaking his head.

"How dangerous is this thing going to be?" Micah asked suddenly. "I'd hate for anything to happen to him. It's taken all of us to keep him out of the army."

Jubal shrugged and bit his lip. He thought for a moment and then said, "Any time you board a ship it can be dangerous. We're not going after any men of war, of course. What we'll be after is a merchant ship, but some of them will be armed with small cannon. Of course, there'll be muskets and small arms. If we don't pretty well shake them up, we might have some trouble when we board. I can't guarantee anybody's safety, not even mine, of course."

"Well, we'll talk about it later. I think he'll be safer here than in the army." He put out his hand and said, "Look out for him, will you, Jubal?"

"Of course I'll do that. After all," he lifted one eyebrow quizzically, "we're almost cousins-in-law or something, aren't we?"

⚜   ⚜   ⚜

When Micah arrived at the foundry, he found the furnaces glowing and more men than he was accustomed to. When he came to the foreman, a tall, powerfully built man named Thaddeus Stephens, he said, "Thad, what's going on?"

Stephens nodded and shrugged his burly shoulders. "We put on some more men. We've got an order from Congress for ten thousand bayonets. Couldn't handle it with the small crew we had."

173

"Are they going to pay with Continental money?"

"What else? It's all they've got," Stephens said. "It'll probably break the firm, but you know your father. Anything for the army that will help, he'll do it."

Micah passed on down, watching the men grinding the bayonets on large grindstones, some of them shaping blanks out of red-hot steel, and wondered how much it would cost the business to furnish them to the army. As Thaddeus Stephens had said, however, not only his father but also John Frazier, his partner, was totally sympathetic to the revolution and had already given a great deal of the factory's output to the cause.

He made his way down the line of workers and turned up the stairs to where his father's office was located. When he entered the office, he found Albert Blevins, the manager, in some sort of heated argument with his father. Micah stepped in and watched, half amused, for he knew Blevins and his father had fierce arguments, but both had such a high respect for the other they always reconciled them.

"I'll tell you, sir, we can't go on like this! We'll be bankrupt!" Blevins was fifty-five, tall and lanky, with a rather cadaverous face. Now as he was pounding the table, on which were scattered various papers, his face flushed with his argument. "Look at these bills, sir! Do you think we can pay them with that trash they're calling money issued by the Congress? No, sir! We've got to cut back, and we've got to make the Congress pay in gold coins!"

"I wish we could, Albert," Daniel Bradford said. His face was serious, and he gave only a glance toward Micah, then added, "Where do you think the Congress is going to get any gold?"

"That's their business. Ours is staying out of bankruptcy court."

"We won't go bankrupt. God's in our cause, and he will undertake for us."

"All very well, but try telling that to our creditors!" Blevins snapped. He would have said more, but turning toward Micah, he suddenly began to shuffle his papers, muttering under his breath something about improvidence and wastefulness and men who don't know anything about business.

"Hello, Micah," Daniel said, coming over to greet his son. Clapping him on the shoulder, he said, "Albert and I are having one of our usual cheerful discussions."

"So I heard," Micah grinned. "You're pretty hard on him, Albert."

"Somebody needs to cut a cane to him. The way he throws money away is pathetic!" Blevins snapped. He gathered up his bills in both hands and stalked off to his own office, kicking the door shut with a resounding slam.

"I call him Happy Al," Daniel said with a grimace. He lowered his voice, and glancing toward Blevins' door, he said, "Albert's right, you know. The money situation is frightful."

"Will we be able to stay in business?"

"Well, God owns all the foundries in the world, and He owns this one. So, if it's His foundry, we'll be all right. I never heard of God going bankrupt, did you?"

"Not yet, Pa. Maybe I can take some of the load off you. I may go back in the army in the spring, but until then, whatever you want I'm ready."

"That's good to hear, son." Dan Bradford looked tired, and he rubbed his forehead. "I do need some help, especially on this business of forging cannons. The biggest thing you could do is to go to one of the other foundries and study their methods, then come back and tell me if it will be possible."

"Where would that be—Philadelphia?"

"There's one there, all right. Do you think you could do it?"

"I'll go next week, Pa. In the meanwhile, I'm going to pitch in here and give you a little rest."

"I could use it." This simple admission from Daniel Bradford was the equivalent of a cry of exhaustion from most men. Micah had already heard from Rachel and Sam how his father worked all day right alongside the workers, and then half the night, going home only when he was exhausted.

Bradford took a deep breath and looked around. "I'm going to start my little vacation right now. Come along."

"Where're we going?"

"We're going to the house. Marian's been nagging me to bring you home for supper. She wants to pamper you a little bit."

"So she's nagging *you*, and she's going to pamper *me*?"

Daniel laughed. "You'll find out about that one day. Come along."

The two left the foundry, and as they rode along toward the Frazier house, Micah asked, "How's Marian's father?"

"Oh, better some days, and worse on others," Daniel admitted with a frown.

John Frazier was a dear friend of his. He had been in bad health for two years, and now Daniel had to do all of the work. Frazier could help with the decision making, but he was so ill, even that was hard for him. When they reached the house and entered, Micah found himself embraced at once by Marian. She threw her arms around him and hugged him, crying out, "Why, you handsome thing! It's about time you came to see your stepmother."

Micah had always liked Marian Rochester. The dress she wore was made of a fine wool, with a moss green colored bodice and overskirt. Dark green ribbons decorated the neckline, the sleeves, and ran down the front. A simple white petticoat showed from underneath the overskirt that had two rows of the same dark green ribbon along the bottom edge. She was, he had always thought, one of the most beautiful women he had ever seen, and now looking at her, taking in her tall, trim figure, her dark auburn hair, and the green eyes that seemed to dominate her heart-shaped face, he said, "Ma, you're a good-looking woman."

"Go along with you now," Marian laughed. She colored, but she enjoyed his compliment. Taking his arm, she said, "You come into the sitting room, and I want to hear all about what you've been doing."

Micah followed her, and for the rest of the evening had, perhaps, one of the most pleasant times of his life. He was pampered, as his father had threatened, and enjoyed it thoroughly. He had been roughing it for so long he had forgotten what a pleasure a fine meal and a fine room was like. The dining room of the Frazier house was, indeed, the centerpiece. It was a large room with wall-to-wall dark green carpet, and the walls had a bold green and gold diamond-patterned wallpaper. Large French doors adorned the far end of the room, with white lace curtains that flowed to the floor and were held back by gold-colored bows. A verde and marble fireplace almost covered one wall of the room, and on the mantel sat various ormolu figurines and silver candleholders. Above the mantel was an elegant gilt-framed mirror, and a series of Chinese paintings and smaller mirrors decorated the walls. A large mahogany table was draped with the finest white tablecloth and was surrounded by ten Chippendale chairs covered in horsehair. A dark mahogany sideboard with a glossy marble top stood against the wall behind the head chair. An ornately carved and inlaid china cupboard displayed the finest cut-crystal goblets and English china. Silver candelabras around the room gave it a rosy glow, and side chairs covered in scarlet damask lined the walls.

The meal itself was outstanding. Roasted venison in a spiced wine sauce was the entree, along with a platter of roasted goose basted with butter. Small silver bowls containing savory bread sauce with tiny onions, spinach baked in cream and butter, and boiled potatoes in a sweet cream sauce surrounded the large silver candelabra in the center of the table. Fresh-baked buttered sponge biscuits were arranged on an ornately carved silver tray, and small plates of assorted cheeses sat near each place setting. When the table had been cleared of the main meal, a delicate peach flummery was served with dark roasted coffee.

After the meal was over, they had more coffee in the drawing room, where Micah stayed until late. He was very impressed at what a fine couple his father and Marian made. They were both good-looking people, and he could tell there was a happiness and a joy in them that had been lacking before. Marian had endured her marriage with Leo Rochester, but there certainly had been no joy in it. Now all that was womanly in her seemed to shine forth. When Micah was ready to go, he put on his hat and coat that his father handed him and turned to them. For a moment he was quiet, then he said, "I'm happy for the two of you. I can see God has given you to each other."

"Why, what a wonderful thing to say, Micah!" Marian exclaimed. She came over, kissed him, and said, "You must come back often. We've got to have the family over more."

"That's right, Micah," Daniel agreed. He hesitated, and a thought darkened his features. "I wish Matthew were here to be a part of it."

"How's he doing, Pa?"

"Still angry and confused, but he's mistaken about Abigail. He thinks she betrayed him, and she may have. But she's become a fine Christian young woman, Micah. I want you to spend some time with her. Maybe when Matthew comes home you can help convince him."

"All right. I'll do that. Good night."

As he rode home down the darkened streets, he deliberately went out of his way to pass the Dennison house. He pulled his gelding up to a halt and stared into the windows. There was a light in Sarah's window, and the temptation came to him to clamber up on top of the low roof below it as he had once done. But he shook his head, muttering, "That won't do," and continued on his way home.

☩   ☩   ☩

A tantalizing aroma of fresh bread filled the kitchen, and Keturah, who had come to sit in a cane-bottomed chair against the wall, watched as Jeanne moved around the kitchen. She was practically recovered from her sickness now, but Jeanne had insisted that she simply sit and watch. "You can help when you get your full strength back," she had said.

Looking around, Keturah admired the kitchen. She had never been in such a luxurious one in her life. Most of her experience with cooking had been outdoors on an open fire, or in a hovel with a smoky chimney, where she usually either burned the meat or had to eat it half raw. Now, looking around the kitchen, she thought, *They sure do have a nice place to cook here. Even I could cook in a place like this.* The kitchen was cheerful with bright yellow walls and small windows covered with white muslin curtains tied back with green ribbons to let the sunlight of the morning in.

Pine shelving surrounded the room, which held a multitude of brass and copper pots and bowls, and two long worktables were filled with utensils of all kinds. A large fireplace had a blazing fire going, and to one side of it sat a large oak settle.

Finally Jeanne came over and sat down, placing a cup of tea before the young woman. "Now," she said, "we can have our tea. Pa and Marian are coming over for supper tonight."

"That's your father-in-law and his new wife?"

"Yes. You'll like Marian. She's one of the sweetest women I've ever known."

"I reckon."

The girl toyed with the tea and shook her head. She said nothing for so long that Jeanne said, "What's the matter, Keturah? You look troubled. As a matter of fact, you haven't been happy for the last few days."

Keturah was wearing a wool dress that had belonged to Rachel. Jeanne had taken it in for her, and she looked rather fetching in it. The dress was a dusty mauve color with a scooped neck and long sleeves. A white linen scarf had been draped over her shoulders, wrapped around in front, and tied in the back into a small, delicate bow. Jeanne had helped Keturah with her hair, but there was a worried look in the girl's startling light blue eyes as she said, "I'm afraid she won't like me."

"Won't like you, Keturah? Why wouldn't she like you?"

"I ain't got fine manners. You know that, Miss Jeanne."

Jeanne Bradford suddenly knew exactly what the girl was going through. She herself had worried over what others would think of her when she first came to the Bradford house. Now she leaned forward and pressed Keturah's hand. "I know," she said quietly. "When I first came here, I was like a wild woods colt. I'd grown up out in the woods and had never even *seen* a tablecloth. I was scared to death at first. I knew Dake loved me, but I was afraid of his family."

"Is that right, Miss Jeanne?" Hope seemed to leap into Keturah's eyes, and she leaned forward, studying the young woman. She admired Jeanne greatly and wished she looked more like her. Jeanne Corbeau Bradford had shiny, curly black hair Keturah would have given one of her eyeteeth for, and she had a cleft in her chin, which Keturah had also and did not like. But she saw how attractive it made Jeanne Bradford, and now she said, "Do you really think I could learn me some manners?"

"Why, of course you could!"

"Would you help me, Miss Jeanne?"

"Yes, I will, and so will Rachel. And please just call me Jeanne."

"I thank you."

The two sat there for a long time, and after a while Jeanne was able to get Keturah to speak a little bit more freely. As the girl talked more, Jeanne saw that Keturah was terrified. No wonder—after the rough camp life the girl had endured! Now she looked over at the thin young woman and said, "We all want you to think of this as your home, Keturah, and us as your family." She hesitated for a moment and was about to speak again when she saw two large tears roll down the girl's cheek. Jeanne went over and put her arms around Keturah. "Now, I've always wanted a younger sister, and finally I've got one."

Keturah threw her arms around Jeanne and held to her tightly. "I ain't never had a family before." For a while she clung to Jeanne, then said shyly, "Do you think Mr. Micah will like me if I learn some manners?"

"I think he likes you now, and so does Sam. He's quite taken with you."

Keturah's eyes narrowed, and she said, "I'm gonna learn to be a lady, Jeanne. You watch and see!"

🏹   🏹   🏹

Micah encountered Abigail Howland at church the next Sunday. He met her outside as he was about to go in and went to her at once. "Why, Abigail. It's good to see you."

"Micah! I heard you were home." Abigail smiled at him. She was wearing a light wool dress in royal blue with a square neck, long sleeves, and a snug bodice decorated with a single green ribbon bow. She had light hazel eyes and a wealth of glossy brown hair, and a complexion that was the envy of every woman in Boston. Now she smiled at Micah, which she could tell had an effect on him. She had always been coquettish with men, but she was past all that now and merely inquired about Dake and the family.

Micah caught her up on the family news, leaving out any mention of Matthew.

"Well, we have a mutual friend now," Abigail said after an awkward pause.

"Oh, who's that?"

"I've become quite good friends with Sarah Dennison."

"Oh. Have you?" Micah asked, interested at once. "Have you known her long?"

"No. I only met her recently. She's a very sweet woman, isn't she?"

"I suppose so."

"Oh, you haven't noticed Sarah?" Abigail teased him. "Well, I think she'll probably be at church. She usually is."

But evidently Sarah had gone to the Episcopal church with her parents. They disapproved of the Methodists, thinking them wild-eyed enthusiasts.

After the service, Micah walked slowly home with Abigail. They talked more about the family, and Micah wondered whether to say anything about his brother Matthew. He knew that the two had been in love, but he also knew that Matthew felt Abigail had betrayed him. He did not know the ins and outs of it, but he thought to himself, *Matthew's crazy if he lets this woman get away from him.* His thoughts were interrupted as Abigail began to talk about Sarah.

"You know, she's actually very sad. That's rather strange for a woman who's about to be married."

"She doesn't love that big windbag!" Micah grumbled.

"Oh, you know Mr. Potter?"

"I know she'll be miserable if she marries him."

"I see. I've never met him." Abigail was an intuitive young woman, and as they walked along, she quickly discovered that Micah had a great interest in Sarah. Finally she said, "Have you called on her since you've been home?"

"No. Her parents made it clear that calls from me would not be welcome."

"I see."

They walked along until they got to Mrs. Denham's house, where Abigail and her mother lived. A thought came to her, and she smiled almost mischievously. "Do you know I'm supposed to meet Miss Dennison at the church? All the ladies are going to meet and knit socks for the soldiers."

Micah's eyes lighted up. "When is that, Abigail?"

"Tomorrow morning. She'll probably be walking from her house. It's not that far from the church. We're supposed to meet at nine." Abigail studied Micah and saw his mind working. *That ought to be hint enough,* she thought, then smiled and put her hand out. He took it, bowed, and kissed it.

"It's always a joy to be with you, Abigail." He hurried away, and Abigail smiled as she watched him go.

☫   ☫   ☫

Sarah Dennison had gathered up the yarn for knitting socks and stuffed it in a large bag. She left the house before her parents came down to breakfast, and she walked along the streets appreciating the mildness of the weather. *Perhaps the worst of the winter is gone,* she thought. But that brought to mind that spring was coming, and her parents had decided on a spring wedding—an early spring wedding. She had slept poorly all night, turning fitfully, and now as she walked along, a depression settled on her that she could not shake off.

"Hello, Sarah."

Sarah wheeled around and gasped as she saw Micah, who had suddenly appeared. He smiled at her crookedly and said, "I thought I'd walk you to church."

"How . . . how did you know I'd be here?"

"Oh, I know a lot of things about you. I spy on you to find out about them. Here, let me take your bag."

Sarah could not think for a moment, but Micah simply took over. Reaching out, he took her bag in his hand and stepped beside her. "Now, tell me what you've been doing."

Sarah managed to regain some composure. She stole a glance at him occasionally as they walked along, and she thought how fine looking he was. He was wearing a simple suit, but it looked very good on him. His wheat-colored hair escaped from under the corner edge of his tricorn, and when he looked at her, there was a warmth in his hazel eyes that pleased her.

"Are you home for long, Mr. Bradford?"

"I'm not Mr. Bradford. My father's Mr. Bradford. I'm Micah, and you're Sarah. I thought we had settled that." Micah was insistent, and reaching out with his free hand, he took her arm and guided her around an icy puddle. "Careful there. You might get your feet wet, and then you'd have to wear some of the socks you're knitting for the soldiers."

She laughed suddenly, and the smile made her look quite pretty. "You should see some of the socks I've made. I'm a terrible knitter. You could put a dog into some of them!"

It was the first cheerful sign he had seen in her, and he encouraged it as they moved along the street. As they approached the church, he said suddenly, "I have a favor to ask of you, Sarah."

"Yes, what is it, Micah?"

"Have you heard about the young woman that grew ill in the camp?"

"Oh, Rachel mentioned her. You mean the army camp?"

Micah nodded and told her some of the girl's suffering and illness. When he ended, he said, "She's getting better now, but she needs friends. I thought it would be nice if you would drop by and meet her. Maybe you could encourage her a little bit."

"What's her name?"

"Keturah Burns."

"How old is she?"

"She's sixteen. She's had a rough time." Micah hesitated, not knowing how much of the harsh realities to share with this cultured young woman. But he turned to her finally as they stopped in front of the church, saying quietly, "Her mother was a common woman, a camp follower, but she died. Keturah hasn't had any of life's advantages. Jeanne and Rachel are helping her, but it would be nice if she met someone outside the family. Would you go by and meet her?"

"Why, yes I will."

He reached out, took her hand, and kissed it. It brought a flush to her face, and he held it tightly when she tried to remove it. "Don't try to pull your hand away. I'm not through with it yet."

"Micah—people will see!"

"Good. Maybe Potter will hear about it and break your engagement for carrying on with broken-down soldiers."

"Don't joke about it! If my parents heard . . ."

Micah said suddenly, "I've told you this before. You're a grown woman. Your life is what God has given you. If you were twelve years old, or fourteen, or even sixteen, I wouldn't say this. Your parents, in that case, are to direct your life. But you're twenty years old, and it's time for you to think like a woman, not like a child."

As Micah spoke, something bore witness to the truth of his speech. When he kissed her hand again, whirled, and walked away after handing her package to her, she watched his tall, erect figure, and for a long moment thought about what he had said. Slowly she turned and went inside, and all morning long she was very quiet.

Abigail had seen Sarah outside talking with Micah and said with an impish light in her eyes, "Did you have a good walk to church?"

"Oh yes, I did."

"Did you see anybody interesting?"

Sarah's cheeks flushed, and she met Abigail's eyes. "You sent him, didn't you?"

"Yes, I did," Abigail confessed freely. "He's such a fine young man, isn't he?"

"But I'm engaged. My parents wouldn't like it."

Abigail did not feel qualified to give advice to this young woman. But she couldn't help noticing how unhappy Sarah was and now said, "Marriage lasts a long time. Make sure you marry a man you want to spend the rest of your life with. If he isn't your best friend and lover, you will be miserable the rest of your life."

This frank statement brought rich color to Sarah Dennison's face. She

182

dropped her head for a moment and could not speak, she was so confused. Then she looked up and met Abigail's eyes. "That's something I never forget," she whispered, then turned and began knitting very badly.

15

FAMILY DISAGREEMENTS

"SARAH, I DON'T KNOW WHAT'S THE MATTER with you! After all, it is *your* wedding—and you're taking absolutely *no* interest in any of the preparations! Why, you haven't even said a word about your wedding dress!"

Sarah Dennison sat beside her window looking out at the street below, wishing desperately that she could flee the scene she knew was coming. As soon as her mother had entered, one look at her expression told Sarah she was in for a stern lecture. Stiffening her back, she said in a plaintive voice, "Mother, I've told you before, I . . . I do not love Silas Potter! How can I make it any plainer?"

Helen Dennison moved across the room purposefully, coming to stand over her daughter. Her eyes narrowed, and anger crackled in her voice as she snapped, "I've never heard of such nonsense in all my life! You must realize that you simply can't let this opportunity slip by. After all, you are twenty years of age—this may be your last chance." Then she added the sentence that Sarah knew would follow. "Why, both of your sisters were married before they were your age."

Sarah had the impulse to leap up and scream, "I don't want to hear anything about my sisters! I'm *not* Mary, and I'm *not* Belinda!" However, ingrained submission over long years prevented such an outburst, so she bowed her head and remained silent, knowing that her mother was not finished with her sermon yet.

"I'm going to have Doctor Phillips take a look at you. It's not natural for a young woman to take so little interest in the most important thing that's ever going to happen to her."

"Please try to understand," Sarah whispered desperately, finally looking up to meet her mother's eyes. "I would rather be single all my life than be married to a man I don't love. Can't you see that? Doesn't that mean anything to you?"

"It means that you're immature and afraid to leave your parents' house—that's what it means to me." Helen Dennison felt herself a martyr. She had gone to great difficulty making all of the preliminary steps toward the wedding. It had been her desire to have a bigger and more ornate wedding than that of Julie Hampton, the daughter of John and Irene Hampton. She had said to her husband, "That wedding was absolutely vulgar! We're going to show Boston how a genteel wedding should be conducted." Now fully determined, she plunged ahead energetically. "It's beyond me how you can be so stubborn, Sarah! I wouldn't have thought it of you. You've always been such an obedient child."

Standing to her feet, Sarah clasped her hands together until they ached. "I have always tried to be obedient to you, Mother. You know that—and that's why you should be able to understand in this case I simply *can't* do as you and Father ask."

The argument went on for almost an hour, until finally Thomas Dennison stepped through the door, his eyes alert. "What's going on here, Helen?" he demanded.

"It's Sarah. She won't listen to reason."

"About her marriage? I thought that was all settled."

"It should be, but Sarah is being difficult."

Thomas Dennison was an easygoing man. He liked for his household matters as well as his business affairs to go smoothly. As long as they did, he was jovial, but when he was crossed, either at home or his office, he had a temper. It flared up now as he snapped, "Now, that's enough of this nonsense, Sarah! Silas Potter will make a good home for you! We've been over it a hundred times! Let's hear no more about it! Come along, Helen."

"Very well, Thomas." Turning to Sarah, Helen Dennison fired her parting shot. "There'll be a fitting at the dressmaker's tomorrow afternoon at two o'clock." For one moment she hesitated, studying the miserable expression on her daughter's face. Actually it was beyond the ability of this woman to understand her daughter's sensitivity. She herself was so firm in her way—*overbearing* many would call it—that she could not understand the gentleness in Sarah. She started to speak, then shook her head and left the room. When they were outside she said to her husband, "Do you think we're doing the right thing?"

Surprised at his wife's uncertainty, Thomas turned to her as they walked down the stairs. "You mean about Silas Potter? Why, of course we are! She hasn't had any other offers, has she?"

"No, but she's only twenty. She may find a man she likes better." But this was as far as Helen Dennison's "gentleness" could reach, and she bit her lip, then shook her head. "It's the right thing for her. Once she has a home and children she'll settle down, I'm sure. We must be firm about this, Thomas!"

"Of course, my dear. And I'm certain we'll handle it for her best interests. . . ."

As soon as her parents left the room, Sarah moved stiffly to stare blindly out her window. A light snow had fallen during the night, and a hard freeze had turned the bare limbs of the chestnut tree into a glistening work of art. Every limb was coated with ice that sparkled as it caught the sun. On the houses across the street were fresh new caps of crystalline, glittering snow. The scene had a fairyland quality, but Sarah's heart was burdened and she could not appreciate the beauty of it.

The ticking of the mantel clock tolled off the minutes with a regular cadence as Sarah stared at the street, unable to think clearly. She never even once thought of leaving home and beginning a new life. What could she do? Where would she go? She was not trained for anything except the arts of sewing, miniature painting, and other skills that every young woman was expected to master. She was accomplished in music, of course, but there was not a living in any of these. Nor did she have any relatives except her sisters, and she knew full well what would have been the result if she'd thrown herself on their mercy!

Finally, in desperation, she went to the cherrywood armoire, opened it, and pulled out a fine pelisse coat, her parents' Christmas gift. The coat was made out of dark blue velvet, had a fur lining, and was fur edged with a matching fur hat. She pulled the fur hat down over her ears, and as she pulled on her mittens, she gave voice to the thought that had been born in her. It had come almost out of a frantic desperation to escape from the house—away from her parents, actually, though she did not allow herself to think of that—and now as she pulled on her waterproof boots, she said aloud, "I'll go see that young woman who's staying at the Bradfords'. What was her name—I've forgotten it! No, I remember now. It was strange—Keturah, that was it."

Slipping out of the house by the side door to avoid her parents, Sarah walked rapidly down the brick walk, looking furtively over her shoulder at the window of her father's study, then ducked awkwardly under the bay window of the parlor. She saw no one, however, and reached the street without attracting attention. Turning to her right, she quickly made her way along the sidewalk.

The snow was light and fluffy, and her boots stirred tiny wispy puffs that rose as she continued her walk. Before she had gone no more than a few blocks, the cold numbed her lips, but it was refreshing to be out of the oppressive house. With an effort she put the scene she'd endured with her mother out of her mind and savored the bite of the few flakes that still fell on her cheeks with a burning kiss. Some of the tiny flakes touched her eyes, clinging to her thick lashes, and she blinked them to clear them away. Finally, she slowed her walk, took a deep breath, and tried to prepare something to say to the Bradfords. At the same time she wondered if word of her visit would get back to her parents. She had no close women friends—at least not that she could confide in—and could think of no other place to go.

By the time she reached the Bradford home, Sarah had regained some of her composure. Moving up the walk, she stepped onto the porch and tapped the heavy brass knocker. She heard light footsteps, and when the door opened, she saw Rachel standing there, surprise on her face.

"An uninvited guest, Rachel," Sarah blurted rather nervously.

"Why, Sarah, how delightful to have you! Come in out of the cold." Pulling her guest inside, Rachel hurried her to the parlor, where she took her coat and hat and waited until she had removed her overboots, all the time carrying on a light conversation.

As soon as she could, Sarah gave her reason for calling. "I've come to call on your guest, Miss Burns."

"Why, how thoughtful of you."

"Is she still ill, Rachel?"

"She's almost recovered. She's upstairs now, but you come along to the kitchen where Jeanne is. The two of you can keep company while I go get Keturah."

Leaving Sarah in the kitchen, where Jeanne looked up to welcome their guest with a warm smile, Rachel turned and went upstairs. Coming to Keturah's door, she knocked, then stepped inside at the sound of the girl's voice. "Keturah, you have a visitor."

"A visitor?" Keturah had been sitting cross-legged in a faded wicker chair with a book on her lap. She rose at once with a question in her eyes. "It can't be anybody to see me. I don't know folks here."

"Well, you soon will. Come along."

"Who is it, Rachel?"

"It's a young woman named Sarah Dennison."

"Oh, her!"

A sudden look of displeasure leaped into Keturah's eyes, and Rachel could not, for the life of her, understand why. "You don't know her, do you?"

"I know who she is. She's Micah's lady."

"Why, yes, she's a friend of Micah's—but then she's a friend of all of us. I'm sure you'll like her. She's actually very nice."

"I don't want to see her."

"Why, Keturah, I'm surprised at you!"

"You can be surprised all you want to be!" Keturah said stubbornly. She plopped back down in the chair and braced her back against the checkered cushion. "I ain't goin' down!"

For a moment an angry reply leaped to Rachel's lips, but studying the girl's face carefully, she began to inquire into the cause of her refusal. "If you don't know her, why do you dislike her so much?" She waited, but Keturah gave no reply. Her lips were set in a firm line, and she refused to meet Rachel's eyes.

Moving over to the girl, Rachel thought, *She's like a wild woods colt— she has no idea how to behave.* Then she remembered how warmly Keturah had spoken of Micah, and suddenly she understood the situation clearly. *Why, she's jealous of him! That's what it is! Jealous of Micah!* Aloud she said carefully, "I think you'll have to come down and meet her at least, Keturah."

"I ain't gonna do it!"

"Now, Keturah, you've been asking me and Jeanne to teach you better manners, and we've been doing the best we can, and this is a matter of good manners. In the first place, you have no reason for disliking Miss Dennison, and in the second place, even if you did, it would be very unkind and unmannerly to refuse to go meet her. All of us have to meet people we don't particularly like being with. That's part of being a lady."

Uncertainty overwhelmed Keturah, and she bit her lip. She gnawed on it for a moment and then slowly got to her feet. "Is it that way really, Rachel?"

"Why, of course." Rachel went over to stand beside the girl. Slipping her arm around her in a protective gesture, she said quietly, "You mustn't judge people before you meet them. You'll find most people better than you think." She looked at the girl, then said, "Let's fix your hair a little and then we'll go down."

For five minutes Rachel fussed over Keturah, noting, "Your hair's growing so fast! It'll be so beautiful when it gets long. Now, let me see how you look—oh, that's fine! Come along, now. . . ."

The two descended the stairs, and when they stepped inside the kitchen, Rachel said brightly, "Miss Dennison, this is our guest, Keturah Burns. Keturah, I'd like for you to meet Miss Sarah Dennison, a good friend of ours."

Sarah was uncertain, for she noted at once the look of unfriendliness in the young woman's eyes. "How do you do? I'm happy to know you, Miss Burns."

"Hello," Keturah muttered, dropping her eyes.

"Come and sit down," Jeanne said quickly, sensing the tension in Keturah. Pulling out a chair, she added, "Here, Keturah, have a seat. I'm fixing tea, and the sugar cookies are almost done. Don't they smell good?"

It was not a successful visit. Sarah sensed the antagonism in the young woman and was at a loss to account for it. She said very little—and Keturah spoke hardly at all—so it fell to Rachel and Jeanne to carry the conversation. After fifteen minutes, Sarah rose to say nervously, "I really must be going home."

"Why, you don't have to leave already, do you?" Rachel protested. But noting the unhappiness in Sarah's eyes, she said, "Well, come along, and I'll get your coat."

"It's been a . . . a pleasure to meet you, Miss Burns," Sarah said.

Keturah hesitated, then feeling the weight of Rachel's eyes on her, she nodded briefly. "I'm glad to have met you too, Miss Dennison." Prodded by a nudge from Jeanne's elbow, she added hastily, "You can come back and see us again."

"Of course."

As Rachel said good-bye to Sarah at the door, she said defensively, "You'll have to excuse Keturah's manners, Sarah. She really has none—but as Micah may have told you, she hasn't had any advantages."

"Of course. It was so kind of all of you to take her in."

"I'll tell Micah you called. He'll be very pleased."

Sarah gave her a startled look, then said nervously, "Y-yes, of course." Quickly she moved down the walk, her head bent and despair in every line of her figure.

She wanted to talk about something, I think, Rachel thought. *But she had no chance*. Hurrying back to the kitchen she found Jeanne alone. "Where's Keturah?"

"Back in her room. She shot out of here as soon as she could. What's wrong with her, Rachel? Why does she dislike Sarah so much?"

"It's Micah."

"Micah? What's wrong with Micah?" Jeanne asked with surprise.

"Nothing—but I'm afraid our guest is infatuated. She's very jealous of him."

Jeanne pushed her hair back from her forehead and thought for a moment, then nodded. "Yes, I can see that. She talks about him all the time—and now that I think on it, she's asked me more than once about Sarah. I suppose Micah talked about her a lot when he was in the camp. What do you think will come of it?"

Rachel shook her head. "I don't know, Jeanne. It's a bad situation."

"Does Micah know that she's infatuated with him?"

"I don't know. Men are so . . . so *dull* where women are concerned, aren't they?"

Jeanne smiled suddenly, a dimple appearing in her chin. "I don't know. I haven't had much experience with any men except Dake and Clive. They were both pretty thick, I thought."

The two young women laughed, but as Rachel left to go about her duties, a frown crossed her face. *There's going to be trouble over this,* she thought. Then she thought of Keturah and said, "I feel sorry for that girl. She has no notion of how to behave toward a man, and she's got her eye on Micah. You can almost feel it. . . !"

T T T

As Jubal Morrison strolled down the streets of New York, he noted the Dutch influence on the city and thought, *The Dutch really know how to build houses—at least to paint them pretty colors.* Indeed, contrasted with Boston, the streets of New York did seem colorful. The houses were made mostly of wood and were painted greens, blues, and bright yellows, with many of the windows and doors outlined in a startling white. Most of them were two stories, and red tiles sat like caps on the tops of many of them. The streets were better in New York than in Boston, paved with cobblestones that rang with the sound of the horses' hooves as they clipped along.

Making his way toward the business section at the tip of the island, Jubal noted that the British army was very much in evidence. Even with the freezing weather and the heavy snow on the ground, their presence could be seen everywhere. A troop of Redcoats marched by, their backs erect, rifles held at exactly the right angle, their red coats making a bloodlike splash against the white of the snow-covered streets. They moved with such unison that they appeared almost mechanical, their bearskin shakos making them look taller than they really were.

"They *look* better than the American troops," Jubal muttered. "But even with all of that spit and polish, those pretty red coats won't win any battles!" Thoughts of the surprise victories at Trenton and Princeton caused him to feel a warm pride, as it had all true patriots. It had brought a tremendous surge into the hearts of those who held the cause of American freedom dear. Though the victories were small and the Continental Army not very large, still it had brought General George Washington to a pinnacle in the hearts and minds of his countrymen.

"Wait until spring!" Jubal muttered as the troop marched out of sight around the corner, weaving with clocklike precision. "Wait until we get new men and equipment—then you'll see something. . . !"

191

Ten minutes later he entered the office that bore his name on the door, "Morrison Brothers," and looked around quickly, noting that Stephen was not there. Ralph Moore, the head clerk, rose to greet him. Moore was a tall, thin man of thirty-five with sharp features and bony fingers that he popped continually. He had a pair of alert blue eyes, and a thatch of cinnamon-colored hair that he parted down the middle. The hair matched his luxurious muttonchop whiskers.

"Why, Mr. Jubal!" he exclaimed, surprise in his sharp eyes. "I didn't expect to see you here."

"Hello, Ralph," Jubal nodded. "Is my brother here?"

"Why, no, sir, he's not. He was here earlier today, but he stepped out for a time."

"Do you know where he is?"

"I believe he went over to call on Miss Gordon."

Jubal shrugged and said, "Wind's blowing from that direction, is it?"

Moore combed his muttonchop whiskers with both hands. He caressed them lovingly, almost as if they were a person, and then fluffed them out, and his eyes gleamed as he admitted, "Why . . . yes, sir, I do believe something will come of that. He's been seeing Miss Gordon almost every day now. As a matter of fact, she herself was in yesterday. Most acceptable young lady, I must say."

"I'm sure she is," Jubal muttered absently. "I think I'll run over and see if I can find him there."

"You'll be most welcome to come back and see what we've been doing here in the office, Mr. Jubal." A touch of rebuke came in his voice, and he said, "I think you need to know what's going on. After all, it is *your* business—half of it, at least."

Jubal almost said, "Not for long!" but did not care to reveal his intentions to the clerk. He had never cared for Moore, although the man had always been civil enough. There was a certain air about the fellow he did not trust, although he could not put his finger on it. "Perhaps later. I'll be here for a few days."

"Certainly, Mr. Jubal. Anytime at all. I'm at your service."

"If I miss my brother, tell him I'll see him at the house later tonight."

Jubal left the office, stepped outside, then called for a cab. A short, fat man mounted on a hansom pulled his horse up and said, "Get in, sir. Where might I take you?"

Jubal gave the address, climbed inside the cab, and, as it moved along through the streets, ran over again in his mind the plan that he had come to New York to lay before his brother. It was not likely to be received with any great enthusiasm, for he well knew how Stephen was totally opposed to the revolution. "He'll just have to swallow it," Jubal muttered, looking with interest out the window at more of the British troops. He studied them, for he knew they were his enemy. He had grown enamored with America and was determined to be nothing less than an American citizen. Before this could happen, however, there had to *be* an America, and Jubal Morrison had made the decision that at any cost he would throw whatever weight he could to serve this fledgling country that was being birthed.

When the hansom pulled up in front of the Gordon house, Jubal stepped down and handed the man a shilling, nodding his thanks. Moving up the steps, he knocked on the door, then waited, stamping his feet to get the feeling back. Finally the door opened, and Lyna Lee Gordon stood there. "Why, Mr. Morrison," she exclaimed, "I didn't expect you! Come in."

Stepping inside, Jubal remarked, "I went to the office, but they told me my brother was here."

"He was here, but he and Grace have gone to do a little shopping." Seeing his hesitation, she said, "Come in by the fire. They won't be gone long." She led him into the parlor, a small room decorated in light browns and blues. Two floor-length windows covered with blue linen window shades adorned one wall, and a tall case clock stood like a soldier beside an oak bookcase that held leather-bound volumes on silk-lined shelves. Homemade samplers decorated the walls in dark wooden frames, and above the pewter and pine fireplace were paintings of the Gordon family. Small vases of flowers and brass candleholders holding blue candles flanked the mantelpiece, and a walnut mirror above the mantel reflected the dim light that filtered in through the windows. A mahogany sofa covered in brown moreen sat in front of the fireplace between two tapestry-covered armchairs, and Astral lamps decorated the rosewood tables on either side. It was a friendly, pleasant room and bore the evidence of much work on the part of the hostess.

Ten minutes later, Jubal was sitting before the crackling fire eating cheese on tiny bits of toast and drinking tea. While enjoying the refreshments, he furtively studied Lyna Lee Gordon, who was eagerly reading the letters that Jubal had brought from her brother, Daniel. *She's a beautiful woman,* he thought. Her hair was the color of dark honey, and she had gray-green eyes set in her oval face. He knew her to be forty-four and thought, *A lot of young women of twenty would like to have her complexion!*

Finally Lyna looked up and smiled. "I'm sorry to ignore you, Mr. Morrison, but I was so anxious to hear about Daniel."

"He's doing very well, Mrs. Gordon. I see a great deal of him through Sam."

Lyna held the letters for a moment, creasing them, and then put them down on the rosewood table beside her. "Have you ever met Katherine Yancy, Mr. Morrison?"

"Why, yes, I have encountered her once or twice at the Bradford house." He looked up and said, "Is she a good friend of yours?"

"She and my son Clive are . . . very good friends."

Instantly Jubal grasped the significance of what Lyna Gordon had said. "It must be difficult for them being on different sides in this war."

"Very difficult indeed." Lines of worry creased Lyna's smooth brow, and she bit her lip nervously. "I wish this war were over. Indeed, I wish it had never begun."

"I say amen to that, Mrs. Gordon!"

Lyna did not choose to pursue the subject. "You and your brother see the war differently, so you understand a little of how I feel with my brother on the patriot side."

"Yes, ma'am, I do, but I think—"

Jubal's voice stopped as the door slammed in the front, and he rose to his feet as Grace Gordon came in, followed by Jubal's brother, Stephen.

"Why, Jubal, I didn't expect you today." Stephen came over, and the two brothers shook hands. As they spoke for a moment together, Grace removed her coat and studied the two, thinking again how different they were. Stephen was thin and lean, whereas Jubal had heavy, square shoulders and looked very strong indeed. There was little fineness about Jubal. He was rough and durable, made for hard wear and hard work, whereas Stephen had more of the look of a scholar. Grace stood there thinking about how concerned Stephen was for his brother. The two of them had talked it over, and Stephen had finally said, "He's stubborn as a mule, Grace! He's got this crazy idea that the Americans are all heroes and the British are all villains, and once Jubal makes up his mind there's no changing him."

Jubal's voice interrupted Grace's thoughts. "I'll be in the office in the morning, if you'll be there, Stephen."

"Of course, but stay awhile, then we'll go home together."

The conversation continued pleasantly enough. Clive Gordon came in shortly afterward, and as Jubal expected, he was eager to speak with him alone. Clive asked several questions about his uncle and the members of the family, then finally asked diffidently, "I don't suppose you've encountered Miss Katherine Yancy?"

"As a matter of fact, I have," Jubal said. "You two are good friends, I understand."

"Well, yes we are."

"She spoke very highly of you, Mr. Gordon. She told me the whole story of how you rescued her father from the British prison ship—at some personal risk, I understand."

"Oh, there was no risk!" Clive protested, waving his hand in the air. He leaned forward and asked, "Was she well?"

"Very well. A most attractive young lady," Jubal said with a smile, seeing that Clive Gordon was obviously much in love with the young woman in question. "Will you be enlisting in the British army?" Jubal asked, remembering that Katherine had mentioned this was a possibility.

"No, I don't think so. But on the other hand, who knows what to do these days?" Clive shrugged his shoulders and shook his head. "It's a bad business, this revolution. My father says it will come to no good end for England, and I agree with him."

"So do I, but my brother does not."

"No, he doesn't. We've talked about it somewhat."

Jubal liked Clive Gordon very much, and as he and Stephen were on their way home he remarked, "Young Gordon is very much in love with that woman in Boston."

"He may as well forget her. She's a raging patriot! It would be terrible for both of them."

"What about you and Miss Grace Gordon?"

"Well, it comes as no surprise, I suppose. You must have seen how much I care for her."

"Does she return your affections?"

"I think she does. She's not given me any discouragement, and I'm hopeful, Jubal."

The two went home to the brownstone house that Morrison had purchased on first coming to New York. They said little that night about business, but the next morning after breakfast Jubal said abruptly, "Stephen, there's no point in our going to the office. I can say what I have to say better right here. I don't fancy talking in front of Ralph anyway."

Stephen had been rising to go get his coat. Now he settled back in his chair, a frown on his face. "I think I can guess what it is, Jubal, and I think you can guess what I'm going to say."

"We're going different ways on this thing. I'm sorry for it, but there it is."

Stephen Morrison shook his head in dismay. "Can't you see that this revolution is a lost cause? Why, Washington's troops are walking away by whole regiments now!"

"They'll come back as soon as spring comes. You'll see, Stephen!"

"Impossible! How could this group of ragamuffins beat the finest troops from the Continent?"

"They won at Bunker Hill, and they won at Trenton and at Princeton."

"Mere skirmishes!" Stephen protested. "When it comes to an open battle, which it must sooner or later, they'll run like rabbits! Then it'll all be over and we can get back to normal."

The argument continued for some time, but finally Jubal said, "There's no point in discussing it. I want the part of the inheritance that belongs to me. I have a use for it."

"You'll lose it all, Jubal!" he protested. "You're going to throw it into the cause of the patriots, aren't you? And when the cause collapses you won't have a penny!"

Jubal Morrison stood up and looked at his brother, whom he loved dearly. "Stephen," he said quietly, "let's not argue this. I've already made up my mind, so further talk is useless," he said, then turned and left.

For three days Stephen tried valiantly to make Jubal reconsider, but at the end of that time he saw the hopelessness of it. Not wanting to lose his brother, Stephen finally consented. It was a complicated business, but they divided the funds that were available.

"We can't divide everything. The land in Carolina is going to be valuable property," Stephen said, "and I refuse to sell it. I wish you'd go down there and take it over and run it. You'd be a rich man."

When all the business was finally done, Jubal stood at the door, his canvas bag in his hand.

"Good luck with Miss Grace," he smiled. Jubal had a real affection for his brother and was moved to add quietly, "I'm sorry we don't see alike on this, but we'll get over it. I can't afford to lose a brother like you!"

"Thank you, Jubal." Stephen took his brother's hand and shook his head. "You'll lose it all," he said regretfully. "Every penny of it."

Jubal could not answer. He hated the rift that had appeared between himself and his only brother but knew he could do nothing else. Then, as he turned to leave, he summoned up a smile. "Let me know when the wedding is. I'll come back for that."

"You'll be one of the first to hear." As Stephen watched the solid form of his brother disappear into the cab, a sense of loss swept over him. He turned and muttered aloud in a bitter tone, "This terrible war! Why did it have to come. . . ?"

16

"We're Too Far Apart. . . ."

THE DAWN OF 1777 APPEARED GLOOMY for the patriot cause throughout the Colonies. The recent victories at Trenton and Princeton had greatly encouraged those who struggled for freedom, but as Washington reviewed his scarecrow army, his scanty supplies, and the reluctance of Congress to provide an adequate war machine to defeat the British, he was skeptical about the chances of success.

In one sense the fight for independence was better off for a time. General Howe had abandoned New Jersey, and the inhabitants of that colony, having been treated cruelly by the Hessians and the Redcoats themselves, looked with more favor on the patriot cause. One of the British failings that constantly dogged their footsteps was their optimistic view that all the British army had to do was show up and loyalists would come rushing to the British colors by the thousands. The atrocities committed by Howe's army so angered the farmers and merchants of New Jersey that, whereas before they had refused to sell their goods to Washington for Continental dollars, they now began to do so with some frequency.

After his victories at Trenton and Princeton, Washington chose to quarter the army at Morristown. He did not intend to remain there long, but for the moment it seemed a wise strategic move. Morristown was perched on a rugged plateau in the Watchung Mountains. It could be approached from the east or the south only through narrow passes easily guarded. Moreover, it overlooked the plains of New Jersey between New York and Philadelphia and provided, in effect, a watchtower from which Washington could instantly spot any movement of British troops. Thus the only avenue of enemy approach ran through very rough country, potential death traps for European maneuvers, which demanded open plains for the movement of large bodies of troops.

But aside from his strong position, Washington felt helpless. The six-week men, whose enlistments ran out quickly, returned home. This time even Washington himself could not persuade them to stay. He waited impatiently for new units to replace them, but they did not come, so he set his men to making shelters from the winter snows that continued to buffet the army with freezing winds. Smallpox broke out, and Washington did what he could with his meager medical supplies, struggling with the almost impossible problems of camp sanitation. Knowing that idle time was not good for an army, in desperation he commanded that a fort be built. Since everyone in the entire army knew that Morristown would be abandoned at the earliest opportunity, the building of the fort was to them "make-do" work, and the soldiers did not throw themselves into it. It was christened by the men as "Fort Nonsense."

🔔　　　🔔　　　🔔

"Martha, my dear, you've come!"

Martha Washington had arrived at Morristown unannounced, and now as her husband opened his arms, she went into them. She was a small woman, and he was a large man; therefore, she always felt somewhat like a child when he embraced her. Looking up into his face, she ran her hand along his cheek. "You've been ill, and you didn't tell me, George!" she said accusingly.

"Oh, it was nothing." Washington had indeed been ill, and even now his usually ruddy cheeks were pasty. But he was a man of immense health, and as he pulled her into the house, he made light of her fears.

Once inside his quarters he began to inquire about Mount Vernon, asking first of all about his horses.

"How is Caesar?" he asked anxiously, mentioning his favorite stallion.

Martha shook her head in despair. "You ask about your horse before you ask about your children and grandchild?"

The long face of Washington showed a degree of embarrassment as he said, "I'm sorry. I wasn't thinking. How are the children?"

"All fine—but little Elizabeth, such a beautiful child she is!"

"Well, I'm not used to being a grandfather," Washington grinned ruefully. He had no children of his own, but Martha Custis had two, Elizabeth and Jack, when he had married her after her first husband died. For some time Washington fussed over Martha, placing several logs on the fire and seating her before the hearth. He listened as she sang the praises of the new arrival.

Knowing well his concern for the welfare of Mount Vernon, Martha spent at least half an hour giving him a review of everything she could think of. Finally, however, she said reproachfully, "You didn't even let me know you were ill, George."

Guilt came into Washington's gray eyes. "It came on me very suddenly. The first thing I knew the doctors were bleeding me, and for a while I thought I would die."

He grew restive under her accusations. She had always felt that he had not paid proper attention to the children, although he had done his best. Now, however, since he had become commander in chief, he'd had little time for anything except the army itself. He wanted to say, "Martha, you shouldn't be jealous of an army," but he knew full well that she would never understand. She was irritated about his asking about the horse before the family, which made him feel guilty. For a while they sat there making light talk. Outside could be heard the sound of voices as the troops lined up. He mentioned, "We're having them all inoculated for smallpox. I hope it helps."

Finally Martha relented, and she came to stand behind him, putting her hands on his shoulders. "This will be over soon, George, and then you can come home."

"I hope so."

His voice was tinged with futility and doubt, which was so unusual that Martha asked with surprise, "Why, things are going well, aren't they? I mean, after your victories at Trenton and Princeton—?"

"Things are going very badly, Martha." Washington reached up and covered her small hands with his large ones. He had always admired her fine, delicate hands. His own were awkward and seemed huge when they held hers. He stroked the tops of her hands for a moment and then said heavily, "The army is falling apart. Men are deserting constantly."

Confused, Martha asked, "But why would they do that?"

Rising to his feet, Washington moved restlessly to the small window, staring blindly at the bare limbs of the ash trees, which were black and shiny against the white snow. Lifting his eyes, he noted the tops of the maples woven together in a complicated fashion. For a long moment he was silent, then in a quick movement he turned to Martha, saying bitterly, "*Everything*, Martha. The men are sick. They have lice. There is no food or clothing. Some of the poor fellows are half naked."

"But you wrote that you had food."

"We did for a time, but it's all gone now." Despair touched his expression, and he ran his hand with a gesture of futility across his brow. "The hospitals—they're nothing but death houses. I'd rather die than go there, and so would most of the men."

Martha stood staring at him with consternation. This was nothing like she had anticipated. Now she whispered, "Is it all over, George? Have we lost?"

"No!" The answer was explosive, and the tall man drew himself up to his full height, a fire suddenly blazing in his eyes. "We will never lose! I'll take the men across the mountains into the Tennessee country. The British can never follow there!" He shook his head with dismay and said, "I've lost so many officers. I wish General Lee were back."

"I never liked that man," Martha said at once.

"He's the only European-trained general we have. He knows that style of fighting better than any man in our forces," Washington protested mildly.

Changing the subject, Martha said, "Did you know that General Gates has been promoted?"

"Yes, I heard that."

"I think that's an insult to you, George."

Washington shook his head. He knew that Martha had no idea of the infighting that went on in the Congress, and how much he'd had to show tact and guile in order to keep his forces together. He stood listening as she protested against the injustice of it all, until finally she said, "Don't you realize that General Gates is out to overthrow you? He wants to take your place as commander in chief."

Knowing that it was hopeless to explain the matter to her, Washington forced himself to smile. "I have more problems with my officers than I do with Gates."

"Whatever do you mean, George?"

"It's these so-called 'noblemen' coming over from France."

"But aren't they going to be a help?"

"Most of them are frauds, Martha," Washington stated bluntly. "We need the help of France very badly, but most of these men are mere adventurers. They've come not for the cause, but for their own selfish ends." He put his large hands together and squeezed them into a fist, then shook his head. "Most of them claim to be a cross between the Duke of Marlborough and Henry V—all military geniuses, but they are absolutely worthless as officers, or even as soldiers!"

"How did they get here?"

"They were given commissions either by Congress or by its agents abroad. Now they've descended on the camp like vultures, trying to take over the leadership." He tried to smile and said, "Knox nearly resigned recently because of one of them."

"Why, you can't do without General Knox! He's the best artillery-man in the country!"

"Of course he is, but a French officer named Coudray caught the eye of one of our agents in France. Somehow he had connections in court, and Silas Deane, our representative there, promised him a commission as a Major General." Washington's face turned sour and he pounded his fists into his hands. "And if you can imagine it, he promised the man that he could be the American chief of artillery."

"Oh no, George! What can you do?"

Washington's face suddenly broke into a smile. When he smiled there was a sly humor about him that most never saw. "Fortunately, he will *not* be chief of artillery. He rode his horse at a gallop onto a ferry in the Schuykill River—any fool would have known better!—and fortunately managed to drown himself."

Martha stared at her husband for a moment, then laughed reluctantly, trying to cover it. "You shouldn't make fun of him, George. After all, the man's dead."

"There would have been more dead if he had lived. Turning the army over to amateurs like that, no matter what their European reputation, will get men killed quicker than anything I can think of."

"Poor George. You have a time with your army and your Congress—and your wife," she finally added.

Running his hand over her neatly dressed hair, Washington put his arm around her and said, "Congress is difficult. Even John Adams talks about our soldiers waxing fat on society and doing nothing to earn their keep. I wish he would come to Morristown and see some of this waxing fat! But I can keep Congress happy. It's you I worry about."

"Never worry about that, George," Martha said quietly. She held her head up, and he kissed her tenderly.

"I'm glad you've come, Martha. I've needed you."

"I'm here, George. . . !"

☥   ☥   ☥

"What's it like, Jeanne—being married, I mean?"

Although she was accustomed to her youthful brother-in-law's frank questioning, Jeanne Bradford looked up with a startled expression in her violet eyes. She stared at young Sam, who was sitting with his stool tilted back, watching her curiously as she cooked. He had been talking for some time at great lengths about the spider catcher—the boat he and Jubal Morrison were building—and Jeanne had listened patiently, although she understood little of the technical side of it. Now the suddenness of his question caught her off guard. "What are you talking about, Sam?" she demanded.

"Don't stop cooking," Sam said as he waved his hand airily. "You can tell me what it's like to be married and cook at the same time. I'm starving to death."

"You're always starving to death!" Jeanne's voice had an asperity to it, but she continued working on the pease porridge she was preparing for supper. It was a simple dish, one they all liked, made by dumping a quart of green peas into a quart of water, along with some dried mint and a little fat. The mixture was boiled until tender, then pepper and a piece of butter rolled in flour was stirred in after two quarts of milk. As the porridge bubbled in the pot, Jeanne stirred it to gain time to think. "What do you mean, 'What's it like to be married?'"

Sam Bradford ran his hand through his auburn hair. His electric blue eyes danced with mischief as he watched his sister-in-law. Sam was seventeen, only two years younger than Jeanne, and since she had married his brother Dake and come to stay at the house, the two had become fast friends. He had discovered that Jeanne had a temper, and he loved to stir her up and shock her from time to time.

"Just tell me what it's like. Here I am seventeen years old," he said in a sprightly fashion. "Why, I might get married myself pretty soon."

"You're nothing but a baby!" Jeanne laughed.

"Oh, that's from Grandma Bradford, is it? How old are you—nineteen? And you were less than that when you and Dake got married." His voice changed, and he wheedled, "Come on. Make some of that pilgrim cake, won't you, Jeanne?"

Giving him a suspicious look, Jeanne said, "Don't you try to get around me, Sam Bradford!"

Sam came to his feet, walked over, and put his arm around her. He was a very strong young man, though not as tall as Dake and Micah. He reached out and put his finger in the cleft in her chin, and begged, "Oh, come on, sister. Do it for old Sam. I love that pilgrim cake!"

Unable to resist Sam's wiles, and knowing that he was getting the best of her, Jeanne shoved him away. "All right, you go sit down, and I'll make the cake."

"In the meanwhile, you can tell me about marriage. A young man has to have some idea about what it's like."

"You can ask your father or Dake."

"Dake's not here, and Pa's too caught up with his brand-new wife. So it'll have to be you."

"It wouldn't be fitting for a young woman to talk to a young man about such things."

Jeanne began pulling together the ingredients for the pilgrim cake.

She rubbed two spoonfuls of butter and sugar into a quart of flour, added cinnamon, then wet the dough with cold water. Moving over to the fireplace, she raked a spot in the hottest part of the hearth. Then she rolled out the dough into a cake an inch thick, floured it well on both sides, and put it in the hot ashes. She covered it with the ashes, then with live coals. It took her less than ten minutes to do this, for she had become a fine cook since coming to live with her husband's family.

"Now, let's eat the porridge, and maybe I can wait without starving until the pilgrim cake's ready," Sam said.

"Oh, all right," Jeanne said. She took two bowls down, put the pease porridge on the table, along with corn bread left over from the last meal, and looked at Sam. "I don't think you have enough grace in you to ask a blessing. You're wicked, Sam."

"Wicked? Why, I'm the best fellow I know. Just listen to this blessing." Sam bowed his head and said, "Thanks for the food, Lord. Amen."

Jeanne looked at him and sighed, shaking her head. "That's terrible! You ought to be ashamed of yourself, Sam Bradford!"

"For what?" Sam was shoving the porridge into his mouth, shifting it around to avoid burning his tongue, and mumbled, "It was a blessing, wasn't it? I don't aim to be a preacher, so I don't have to have the flowery kind they like so much. That'll be up to Micah. I expect he'll make a preacher someday."

"I expect he will, and he'll be a good one, too."

Sam ate two full bowls of the pease porridge and then looked longingly at the cake. "How much longer do you think it will be before that cake's ready?"

"Too long for me to waste time listening to your foolish talk. Now, you go on about your business, Sam."

But Sam reached over and poured himself another mug of milk and drank half of it noisily. "Not before you tell me about being married. Come on, Jeanne. After all, it's your sisterly duty."

Knowing well that Sam was teasing her, still Jeanne could not resist his wiles. Putting her hands in front of her, she thought back to the time when she'd lived with her father, just the two of them alone in the wilderness. There, in the deepest woods, she had known little of men, until Clive Gordon had suddenly appeared. She had found him very sick in the woods close to their house and brought him home. Her own father had been dying, and when she had discovered that Clive was a physician, she had felt that God had sent him to help her father. But her father had died, and she had grown fond of Clive Gordon.

Even as she thought of those days, Sam's bright eyes were studying her. "How did you decide to marry Dake instead of Clive? Flip a coin, or did you draw straws for them?"

"Don't be silly!"

"Well, how did you decide? I heard you say one time you really cared for that Englishman."

"I . . . I was fond of him."

Jeanne had thought herself in love with Clive, but now as she remembered how Dake had entered her life, the fights they had had, the arguments, and yet the warm feeling that had come over her when he had put his arms around her and kissed her, she struggled to put it into words.

"I just knew it was Dake—don't ask me how. Clive's a wonderful man, and I hope that he and Katherine get together. They love each other so much."

Sam listened as Jeanne spoke. She was a quiet girl and did not often fall into such lengthy monologues. She spoke of how Dake had courted her and the doubts that had come to her for so long, until finally Sam said, "That cake ought to be ready now."

"Oh, I forgot!" Getting up with alacrity, Jeanne went over to the hearth, removed the cake, and dusted the ashes off. Juggling it around to keep from burning her fingers, she took down a pewter plate from the cabinet. After she had set the cake on it, she came back to the table.

"We don't have to say grace again, do we?" Sam said innocently. "I think I just about ran out of blessings."

Again, Sam's audacity made Jeanne shake her head. "No, I think this one's still all right under your other blessing. Here, let me cut it for you."

"Don't need that."

Sam reached out, broke the cake in two, and pushed half of it toward Jeanne. The smell of the delicious cake filled the kitchen, and he took a bite, then immediately spit it out in his free hand. "Ow!" he complained. "That's hot!"

"Don't be such a pig. Let it cool off," Jeanne laughed.

"Never wait for things, Jeanne, old girl," Sam said. "Grab it while you can." He blew on the fragment, stuffed it in his mouth again, then rolled his eyes upward and closed them. "That's better than manna!" he exclaimed.

"How would you know? You've never had any manna."

"Couldn't be as good as this," Sam said. He juggled the food around in his mouth, reaching over once to get some honey, which he poured over the rest of the cake. Soon it was smeared over his lips and his fingers were sticky, but it did not trouble him. "Tell me some more about being married. Is Dake a good husband?"

"Yes, he is. I wish he were here now. I miss him so much."

The front door suddenly slammed, and Jeanne looked up and said, "Who can that be? I'm not expecting anyone."

"Maybe it's Micah."

Both of them looked toward the door, and then Jeanne let out a shrill cry, for it was not Micah but Dake who stood there.

"Dake!" Jeanne flew across the kitchen floor and threw herself into the arms of her husband. "Dake, you're home!"

"Sure am, wife!" Dake picked her clear up off the floor and kissed her thoroughly.

Sam rose at once and came over to stand beside the pair. "Now, Dake, that's what I've been asking Jeanne to tell me about—this kissing, and stuff, and marriage."

Dake set Jeanne back on the floor and stared at his brother. "Why, you young whelp!" he snapped. "I ought to take a strap to you!"

"That's what you ought to do! He's terrible!" Jeanne said as she reached up and stroked Dake's face. "You came home! Are you on leave?"

"Well, I didn't desert," Dake grinned. He put his arms around her tiny waist. "I would have deserted, but I was assigned to be the courier in place of Micah. Nothing going on anyway. No fighting."

"Sit down. You must be starved," Jeanne said.

Sam pulled his chair up and sat down and peppered Dake with questions about the army as Jeanne hastily prepared a meal. She served him the last of the pease porridge, some cold beef, and half of the pilgrim cake. Jeanne's eyes teared as she watched him eat hungrily. She knew he had not had the best of meals in the camp.

Dake shook his head as he ate. "I wish everybody at camp had a meal like this."

The three sat there talking until Rachel came in. She cried out and came to Dake, kissing him warmly, then saying, "Why didn't you tell us you were coming?"

"Didn't know myself," Dake grinned. "I was going crazy in that camp, and I finally went to Colonel Knox and asked him to let me come home on leave. The colonel's a good fellow. He gave me a few messages and told me to take some time off. Nothing's happening in the camp anyway until spring."

"How long can you stay?" Jeanne asked eagerly. Her eyes were bright, and she reached and put her hand out, which Dake covered at once with his own.

"Long enough to get acquainted with you again." Dake winked

across the table at Rachel and Sam, who laughed as they saw Jeanne's cheeks flame.

"Well, come on down to the docks. I want to show you our new boat," Sam said impetuously.

"I think not, Sam," Dake said, his gaze locked on Jeanne. "Tomorrow, maybe."

Rachel stood up and hauled Sam to his feet. "Come on, Sam. I've got some chores for you to do." When they were outside the kitchen, she said, "Leave them alone!"

"I wasn't bothering them!"

"They haven't been married all that long, and they've been separated for months. Dake doesn't want his brother around. He wants to see his wife."

Sam grinned roguishly at Rachel. "I was just asking Jeanne about what it's like to be married, but she wouldn't tell me much. I guess I'll ask Dake."

"No, you won't ask Dake—not now at least. You go chop some more wood." She watched as Sam, grumbling, put on his coat, then went outside. When she heard the sound of the ax splitting wood, Rachel put her hand on her cheek and smiled to herself and said, "They have to take every minute together. Life is so uncertain. I'll have to keep Sam as busy as I can, or else he'll pester them with more of his silly questions."

T   T   T

Katherine Yancy was always glad to see Jeanne, but she was somewhat surprised when the young woman dropped by unexpectedly for a visit.

"Why, Jeanne, how nice to see you! Come in."

Jeanne swept into the room, her eyes sparkling. "Dake's home, Katherine!" she announced.

"He is? How wonderful!"

"Yes, he came in yesterday afternoon! He can stay maybe as long as three weeks, or maybe a month, until he gets word from Colonel Knox."

Katherine smiled at the excitement in Jeanne Bradford's face. "Come in and tell me all about it. I'll make tea."

The two women sat in the parlor, and her parents, Amos and Susan, joined them. The four of them talked for a time, and it was Amos who said, "Dake is a fine young fellow. You've got a good husband, Jeanne."

"And he's got a fine wife," Susan Yancy smiled. She studied the face of the young woman, which was glowing with health and happiness. "I know what it's like to be separated from a husband. Pamper him as much as you can." Reaching over, she took Amos's hand and held it. They both were thinking of the time, not far gone, when he was imprisoned in a hulk, a British prison ship. It had been only the grace of God—and the help of young Clive Gordon—that had extricated him from a death sentence. His brother had died there, and Amos still showed signs of the atrocious treatment he had received on the prison ship. He had never completely regained his health, and a persistent cough plagued him till this day.

Katherine said quickly, "Yes, but you must share him with us. Can you come over for supper some night soon?"

"Of course, Katherine."

"Make it soon," Susan urged. Then she said, "Come along. Let the young women talk, Amos."

When the two left the room, Katherine sat quietly listening as Jeanne bubbled on about Dake. Katherine said so little that finally Jeanne halted and said, "I'm talking all about myself and Dake."

"Of course you are. What else would you talk about?"

Jeanne studied the face of Katherine Yancy, an attractive young woman of twenty-one. She had a wealth of dark brown hair and gray-green eyes set in a squarish face. There was a strength in her features, and her eyes crinkled when she laughed, which she was not doing right now. There was a sadness about her that was unusual.

"Have you heard from Clive?"

"Yes. I got a letter just yesterday from New York."

Despite herself, Jeanne asked, "How is it with you two, Katherine?"

"Not good, I'm afraid. You know the problems."

"Yes. It's terrible. My father-in-law and his sister, Lyna—they love each other so dearly, but Lyna's husband is in the British army, and Dake and Micah are with the American forces. It has split us right down the middle, but it'll be all right."

"I don't see how," Katherine murmured. She looked down at her hands for a time, then finally looked up and said quietly, "In his letter he said he loved me."

"And do you love him?"

"What good would it do if I did?"

A long silence fell over the room, so that only the ticking of the clock was audible. Finally, as Katherine looked up, there was pain in her fine eyes. "We're too far apart to be together."

Jeanne did not know what to say but gave what comfort she could. "Things change, Katherine. The war could be over soon."

"Yes it could, but it seems like it will never end."

Finally Jeanne rose to leave, and when she was alone, Katherine walked back into the drawing room. She removed the letter from a walnut box on the mantel and read again the line that said, "We are far apart, but one thing, Katherine, you must believe. I love you, and I always will. Nothing can ever change that!"

Katherine Yancy's eyes filled with tears as she folded the letter and put it back, then she moved away, her heart heavy with the thought that life was unfair. She shook her head and wiped her eyes quickly, her back straight. "God's still on His throne," she whispered. "That will never change!"

17

More Bradfords

ENGLAND HAD BEEN A REVELATION for Matthew Bradford. He had read everything he could about the native country of his forebears, but nothing had prepared him for what he found.

The only cities Matthew had ever seen were Boston and Philadelphia, with a brief visit to New York, but none of these compared to the grandeur of London. For weeks he had walked the streets, reveling in the history that met him at every corner. It sent a shiver up his spine to stand before Westminster Abbey, staring up at its twin spires. When he walked in and stood before the tombs of men such as Geoffrey Chaucer and Edmund Spenser, he had a sense of Englishness that simultaneously awed and thrilled him.

Matthew had found a comfortable place to live—a small suite of rooms close to the heart of the city. He was thankful that his real father, Leo Rochester, had seen to his financial needs before his death. Matthew was not accustomed to having money, but Leo had made more than ample provision for all his needs. It gave him a strange feeling even yet to know that when he saw a suit he liked, he did not need to plan ahead for a year on how to acquire the funds. He had learned to say with aplomb, "I'll take it," and had become quite the dandy. He was aware, of course, that the tailors and other tradesmen in London took advantage of him, but somehow that did not seem to matter.

One fine February morning he was strolling along at one of his favorite haunts, the British Museum, stopping to look at magnificent paintings he had never dreamed he would see firsthand back in America. He paused before a picture of a man standing with his hand on a marble bust. Matthew could not take his eyes off of it. The rich colors and the lights and shades as they blended seemed almost magical to him. "I would give *anything* to learn to paint like that!" he whispered to himself, then looked around self-consciously to be sure no one had heard him. He looked at the name of the artist, Rembrandt, shook his head in wonder, and moved on down, studying the paintings of Raphael, then some of the more modern painters such as Gilbert, Stuart, and Turner.

Finally he sat down before a massive picture by a late Renaissance painter he did not know—Tinteretto. The canvas was larger than life, and the colors and action almost seemed to make the canvas move. All was color and vigor and movement. Matthew sat there stunned into silence by the mastery of the artist, and finally, with something like despair, thought, *I'll never be able to paint. I'm just a dabbler. . . !* Somewhat discouraged, he rose and went outside, where the air was cold and a fresh snowfall had painted the city a glistening white. The effect would not last long, however, for over London rose a thick cloud of smoke as thousands of coal fires spiraled their waste into the air. It was so thick it fell in tiny flakes, and when Matthew rubbed his face as he walked down the street he discovered it was smeared with a dull gray color.

"A shame to spoil this fine snow," he muttered. "I suppose Boston will be like this one day, but it will never be as large as London."

Thinking of Boston brought a pang of homesickness, but he quickly put the thought aside. He stopped by a vendor selling hot chestnuts, paid his tuppence, then continued on down the street eating the delicious nuts he had learned to love. As he munched on them, he thought of how his stay in England had influenced him. He had come with great expectations, and with the inheritance from Leo Rochester, Matthew had enjoyed his new life of wealth immensely. Nevertheless, he had not been able to find a teacher who would take him on. Several well-known artists had looked at his paintings and shrugged their shoulders and recommended a lesser instructor. Their rejection had thoroughly discouraged Matthew, so that he had put away his paints and decided to spend all his time seeing London and the countryside. It was difficult during the winter, for the weather was cold and wet. The frigid winds seemed to go through him, and even now he shivered, drawing his wool overcoat closer about him and striking his hands together to stir the circulation.

An abrupt boom startled him, and he looked up to see the magnificent dome of St. Paul's Cathedral, where the famous Bow Bells were tolling the hour. The sound boomed on and on, and Matthew walked slowly by, studying the superb architecture of the great Sir Christopher Wren, wondering if anything in America would ever equal this.

Finally he turned toward the section where his rooms were located and found himself thinking of Abigail Howland. It was not unusual, although he had tried valiantly to block her out of his mind. Even now as he shook his head at the many vendors who offered him their wares, a picture of her formed in his mind. He saw her oval face, her bright hazel eyes, and remembered her full-figured beauty, and how warm and soft she had been in his embrace.

Angrily he shook his head, and with a gesture of violence he threw the remaining chestnuts aside.

All the way back to his rooms he struggled to forget Abigail. "She's no good. She betrayed me," he muttered, causing a young street sweeper to look up at him and say, "Ah! Clean your way, sir?"

Matthew shook his head curtly but tossed the boy a farthing. He could not help seeing the poverty etched in the lad's face, the thin cheeks, and the large sunken eyes. He was a compassionate man, this Matthew Bradford, sensitive to the needs of others, and carried a pocket full of change for just such occasions.

Finally he succeeded in driving any thoughts of Abigail out of his mind. By the time he reached his rooms and closed the door behind him, he was thinking of doing a painting of the boy—the street sweeper. "If I could just catch that sad look in his eyes and the hunger in his face, it might be something—not the sort of thing that would sell, of course." Removing his coat and hat, he tossed them carelessly aside, then as he moved to make a fire in the hearth, a knock sounded at the door.

Somewhat surprised, he went over to open it and found his landlady, Mrs. Neale, standing there with an envelope. "This came for you earlier today, sir."

"Thank you, Mrs. Neale."

"Will you be having supper tonight?"

"If you please."

Mrs. Neale was a round woman, well fed, with rosy cheeks and a pair of bright blue eyes. She was a widow, her husband having been killed in the Seven Years War, and she had been happy enough to find a boarder. "It'll be chops with a bit of fish."

"Sounds wonderful, Mrs. Neale. I won't be late."

When the door was closed he looked at the envelope and immediately recognized his father's handwriting. He felt a twinge of guilt, as he always did when he thought of Daniel Bradford. Sitting down on a horsehide chair and studying the outside of the envelope, Matthew pictured Daniel's face, the wheat-colored hair and eyebrows above the steady hazel eyes, and thought, *He never treated me any differently than his real sons.*

Opening the envelope, he began to read. His father had a strong, firm hand, and now Matthew carefully read the letter that had come so far across the sea.

3 January, 1777
Dear Son,

I trust this letter finds you in good health. I remember the winters in England seemed to be even worse than those here in Boston. My memory may be faulty, but I can well recall how Lyna Lee and I would shiver, it seemed, for six months out of the year. But, of course, memories play tricks on one, don't they. . . ?

Matthew read on about the news of the family. He was glad that Dake was safe, for he had been concerned about so many men dying of sickness in the Continental camp. He was amused with the story of Keturah and her infatuation with Micah, and a smile turned up the corners of his lips. "By George," he muttered, "I never thought Micah would get himself in such a predicament. Good enough for him!"

Reading on, he soaked up the news and found himself somewhat homesick. It was a strange feeling, for he had fled America to get away from the pressures there. Leo Rochester had begged him before his death to take his name and his title, and his father had urged him to do as he felt right. Daniel had said, "Don't worry about changing your name from Bradford to Rochester. The Rochesters are a fine family. Though Leo and I had our differences, you are his flesh and blood. A man wants a son to carry on his name, and Leo is past all that now. So do as you please."

Finally he came to the end of the letter and was surprised to read,

I have a favor to ask. If it is too much, do not let it trouble you, Matthew. You have heard me speak of my father's brother, Jacob. I met him only once, and I was a very small child. He was younger than my father and lived at that time in the lake country, far away from London. I thought of him many times over the years, and only recently have been able to find a trace of him. I have discovered that my uncle Jacob died quite some time ago, but he left a son. I have not been able to contact him by mail, and all I know is that his name is Lawrence and he lives in the Soho District. I know it's an imposition, but things are hard in America now, and we have such a small family. If you could possibly do so, I would ask you to make whatever effort you could to find your cousin and put me in contact with him.

> *Your loving father,*
> *Daniel Bradford*

Matthew studied the paper for a time and then said aloud, "Why, that's strange to have relatives that we've never seen. Of course, they're not blood relations of mine, but it means a great deal to Pa, so tomorrow I'll see if I can find Mr. Lawrence Bradford."

☖   ☖   ☖

By the time Matthew reached the section of London where his father had informed him he might find Lawrence Bradford, the sun was high in the sky. He had spent the morning painting and had managed to catch some of the essence of the young street sweeper he had seen the day before. As always, when he did a piece of work that he liked, it buoyed him up, and now he felt filled with a sense of satisfaction as he drove along in a hansom cab. He was thinking of the next phase of the painting when the coachman's head suddenly appeared around the corner—a red, round face with a pair of cheerful blue eyes. "Guv'ner, here we are in Soho."

Matthew Bradford looked out and saw a cluster of dingy houses, all leaning slightly to one side. A brick field dominated the scene, and pigs wandered among the broken windows in the miserable little gardens where nothing grew during this time of year. Stepping out, he avoided a puddle of oily water and saw that old tubs had been put out to catch the snow melting from the roofs. Despite the cold, some men and women were moving about, and dirty, ragged children stared at him with large eyes as he stood beside the cabby.

"Not exactly a garden spot, eh, guv'ner?"

"No it isn't," Matthew said shortly. "Do you suppose you could help me find a Mr. Lawrence Bradford?"

"Why, right you are, sir. You get in the cab. No sense getting your boots wet. Mine are soaked already."

The cabby, whose name was Samuel Bent, as Matthew had been informed, splashed his way through the puddles and approached a group of men slouching in front of a house, smoking pipes. Matthew climbed back in the cab and watched as Bent's arms waved in a windmill fashion. It seemed his speech organs were connected with his arms, and neither could work without the other.

Finally Bent came back and said, "Bradford's over across the way, guv'ner. Shall we go?"

"Yes, Samuel. I must find his family if possible."

Most of the afternoon was spent in moving from one wretched slum to another. Bent kept a cheerful countenance, but Matthew suspected that the fellow was always cheerful. *He'd probably be cheerful at his own funeral*, he thought as Bent came splashing back from the fifth stop. "Any luck, Samuel?"

"Well, sir, not as you might say exactly *luck*." There was a reluctance in the cabby's voice, and his cheerfulness had abated. He rubbed his whiskery cheeks and cocked his head to one side. "I did hear about the party you're looking for."

Eagerly Matthew said, "Is he here, Samuel?"

"Sir, I'm sorry to be the bearer of ill tidings, so to say, but Mr. Lawrence Bradford is no longer with us. Gone to be with the Lord."

Matthew felt a stab of disappointment. "My family will be sorry to hear it. We didn't know the gentleman, but he is a distant kin. Did he have any family?"

"His dear wife died some time ago, so I am informed, but he left two children. Both grown up by now."

"I would like to find them. Are they here?"

"Well, not to put too fine a point on it—no, sir."

"What does that mean?"

"It means, sir, that they're in Marshalsea."

"Marshalsea? What's that?"

"Well, as you might say, sir," Samuel Bent said reluctantly, "it's a debtor's prison."

"Oh, I see." Matthew thought for a moment, then made up his mind instantly. "Can you take me to this prison, Samuel?"

"Why . . . why, yes, sir. I can, guv'ner."

"All right. Let's go."

Somehow Matthew determined to fulfill his father's desire, and although Lawrence Bradford was dead, at least he could find out something about the man's destitute children.

After the better part of an hour, the hansom finally pulled to a stop, and Samuel said, "Here we are, sir. This is Marshalsea."

Matthew stepped out of the cab and looked at the oblong row of barrack-type buildings. The fog was rolling in, and the wispy tendrils, mixed with the chimney smoke that still fell in fragments, gave the place a mournful look. "Where do you suppose the head office is?"

"I'll find out, guv'ner." Bent disappeared but was back in a few moments. "The officials are right this way, if you'll follow me, guv'ner."

Matthew followed the cab driver through a narrow, twisting maze crowded with people. He had been informed by Samuel Bent that offenders against the revenue laws, or those who had incurred debts they were unable to pay, were closed up in a second prison enclosed inside the first.

He soon found himself standing before a rather tall young man with a cadaverous look.

"My name is Jones, sir."

"Mr. Jones, I would like to see two of your inmates, if I may."

"And their names might be?"

"I do not know their first names. Their last name is Bradford."

Jones ran his eye down the pages of a leather-bound book, rather the worse for wear, and said, "I have two Bradfords here. One Joel Bradford, age nineteen, and one Phoebe Bradford, age twenty. Miss Phoebe Bradford, of course, is not an inmate at Marshalsea. She is merely staying here with her brother."

"Would it be possible to see them?"

"Well, sir, I think it might for certain . . . uh, consideration."

Instantly Matthew reached into his pocket and came out with a gold sovereign. "Would this be sufficient, Mr. Jones?"

"Oh, thank you, sir! That should do very nicely. Come along. I'll escort you myself."

"Wait here for me, Samuel."

"Of course, guv'ner."

Matthew followed the cadaverous Mr. Jones down a twisting corridor, and he was sickened by the putrid smell. The flies swarmed around his face, and he tried ineffectually to brush them off. Finally, they reached some place in the interior of the prison, and Mr. Jones said, "A gentleman like yourself, sir, needs privacy. I'll bring the inmates to you here, if you'd care to wait in this room."

"Thank you, Mr. Jones."

Stepping inside the small room, which the turnkey had indicated, Matthew found himself wondering what it would be like to be incarcerated in such a horrible place. The room itself was bare except for a table and three chairs. There were no pictures, no decorations, nothing except the bare furniture. There was no window and the air was stale, so that Matthew felt almost as if he were buried alive.

It seemed to be a long wait, but finally the door opened, and the turnkey said, "Here they are, sir. Bradford and Bradford. Would you care for a refreshment?"

"No thank you. I will not be long."

"Knock on the door, sir, and we will be happy to show you out."

Matthew's eyes had become accustomed to the gloomy room illuminated only by a single candle on the table. He studied the two prisoners before him, both dressed in little more than rags. The young man was tall and at one time was probably strong, but now he was quite emaciated. He had fair hair, Matthew surmised, although it was difficult to tell with the grime of the prison so ground into it. However, he did have a pair of steady light blue eyes and a firm mouth.

The young woman, who was twenty according to the turnkey, studied him with a rather cautious look. She was not a tall girl and was better dressed than her brother, though the simple light blue dress revealed her abject poverty, for it was worn and patched. Her hair also was fair, and she had the same light blue eyes as her brother.

"My name is the same as yours," Matthew said. "I'm Matthew Bradford."

The announcement seemed to startle the young man. He blinked with surprise and looked at his sister and said, "I'm glad to know you, sir. My name is Joel, and this is my sister, Phoebe."

"Miss Bradford. Mr. Bradford." Matthew bowed and said, "I'm sorry to find you in such dire circumstances."

"We don't know you, do we, Mr. Bradford?" It was the young woman who spoke, and there was a clipped edge to her tone.

She's suspicious of everyone, Matthew thought rapidly. *Probably had very rough treatment.* Aloud he said, "No, Miss Bradford, we've not met, but I feel that we may be distant relations." He saw her eyes narrow slightly, and he went on hurriedly. "Your father's name was Lawrence, I believe."

"Yes, sir," Joel Bradford said. "That it was."

"What was your grandfather's name? Do you remember?"

"It was Jacob."

"Then we are related," Matthew said. He saw them staring at him and hastened to explain. "My father's name is Daniel Bradford. His father was named Matthew, and Matthew Bradford had a brother named Jacob. I believe it would stretch coincidence to think other than that we are from the same line."

Phoebe Bradford seemed to relax somewhat. "I've heard my father speak of his uncle Matthew. He didn't know him well, he said."

"No, I believe the brothers were never close. If I understand it correctly, your grandfather lived in the lake country."

"That's right, sir," Joel said quickly. "I've never been there myself, but our father used to tell us about that country many times."

"I was sorry to hear of your father's death. Is your mother living?"

"No, sir. She died at the same time. Both of them of influenza."

"I am indeed sorry."

"Thank you, Mr. Bradford," Phoebe said. She studied him carefully, then said, "How did you find us?"

"I've been in England for some months. I received a letter from my father yesterday asking me to find our relatives. I had no proper address, but a cab driver helped me considerably."

"It was considerate of you to call."

Matthew was suddenly at a loss as to what to do. He looked at the two and saw that they were watching expectantly, and finally he said, "I don't want to interfere with your private business."

"Private business!" Phoebe Bradford laughed almost harshly.

"There's no private business in Marshalsea. You may ask us anything you choose, Mr. Bradford."

"Of course. Well, I was wondering. This is a debtor's prison, so you've not committed any crime, have you?"

"Certainly not. A matter of some ten pounds." Joel Bradford's voice was bitter, and he shook his head. "A man loses his life and his liberty for ten pounds."

Matthew suddenly felt relieved. He had thought, perhaps, it might be hundreds of pounds. "You mean to tell me if you had ten pounds you could leave this place?"

Hope leaped into the eyes of both the young people. "Yes, sir," Joel said, "but it might as well be ten thousand pounds. I've been unable to get work, and I borrowed money, and the lender wouldn't give me time to pay."

"Well, I'm relieved to hear that it's so little a sum," Matthew said. "If you would accept help from one of your own name, I'd be glad to offer it."

"Oh, it's good of you, sir," Phoebe said.

Matthew saw the tears in the girl's eyes and dropped his own to keep from seeing her gratitude. "My father would take a cane to me," he said finally with a smile, "if I didn't do my best for you. He's very interested in reestablishing ties with the family." Then he added quickly, "I have the cash with me. What is necessary?"

Apparently very little was necessary, for money easily answered the problem. A scant twenty minutes later the trio left Marshalsea Prison, and Joel looked up to the sky, which was dull and gray, and said, "I've never been so glad to be out of a place in my life." He turned and put his hand out blindly. "Thank you, Mr. Bradford."

Matthew took his hand and felt its thinness. "Well, you must thank my father," he said quickly. "Now, what shall we do? I have a cab here. Do you have a place?"

"No, sir, we don't. But we can find a place with friends."

"I'd rather you came with me. I'm staying with a Mrs. Neale. She has other rooms, and they are very reasonable." He hesitated, then said, "Do you have other things?"

"Yes, we can go get them anytime, Mr. Bradford," Phoebe said quickly.

"Samuel, can you crowd us all into the cab?"

"Well, not to put too fine a point on it, guv'ner—yes, sir."

The three of them climbed inside the cab, the brother and sister sitting on one side facing Matthew. As the cab moved along, he studied their fine features. Both of them, he saw, would be handsome with the proper grooming. Now, however, he wondered, *Have I taken on too much?* Somehow he felt responsible for them. He thought about it until they drove up to a hovel where their things were stored with a friend, and when they were inside gathering them up, he thought, *I'll have to do the best I can for them, but I don't know for the life of me what that will be.*

🜨   🜨   🜨

"Oh, Mr. Bradford, how wonderful!"

Matthew smiled at Phoebe, who had tried on a new dress he had bought for her at a shop, and then glanced over at Joel, who was preening in a new brown suit. Joel turned to Matthew and said, "You sure you're not an angel, Mr. Bradford?"

"No, and I'm not Mr. Bradford. I've told you that," Matthew said. "Just Matthew is fine enough. You can call my father Mr. Bradford if you ever see him." At his words a sudden glance was exchanged between the two. It had been five days since Matthew had bought their release from Marshalsea. In that time he had cared for them almost as invalids. He had seen to it that they were well fed at Mrs. Neale's table, and had bought enough clothes to make them look respectable. Now as he studied Phoebe, who was wearing a very simple dress made of a lightweight fine wool in dark plum, a high neckline, long sleeves, and full skirt with black trim, he thought with a start, *Why, she's beautiful.* And her brother, he saw, was a handsome fellow. The two were hesitating, and finally he said, "What's the problem, Joel?"

"Well, sir, it's been bad here in England. That's how I wound up in Marshalsea," Joel said haltingly. "And the fact is, you've done so much for us, but we can't go on living on your charity."

"Not charify at all. Not among cousins."

"It is kind of you to say that," Phoebe said. "But Joel and I have talked it over, and we can't go on taking your generosity."

Matthew had already thought of this. Now he said, "Isn't there any work at all to be had?"

"None. Not unless one is a skilled tradesman, which I am not."

"And, of course, there's nothing for a woman. Nothing at all except—" She broke off quickly and dropped her eyes to the patterned figure of the carpet.

Matthew had written his father immediately, but the answer, he knew, would not come back for weeks. Now he studied the pair and said, "Do you have something on your mind, Joel?"

"Well, yes, we do." Joel looked up, and his eyes were bright with hope. "Would it be possible for us to go to America?"

Matthew was taken aback. "Go to America? Why, there's a war going on over there."

"Better a war than what's going on here!" Phoebe had spoken quickly, and she took her brother's arm, saying, "It's a new land. You don't know what it's like living here, begging your pardon, sir. I'd do anything! I could be a servant for your father, and you've told us about the foundry. Couldn't he use a strong young man there?"

Matthew scratched his head and thought quickly. "I can't commit myself to anything like this until I hear from my father. I ought to be getting a letter within a month or so, but the passage is slow enough as it is, and with a war on, the ships are even more unreliable."

The two seemed to wilt, and it was the young woman who said dully, "Yes, I understand that."

Matthew had a tender heart and said quickly, "Now, Phoebe, don't give up. I didn't say no. It's just not my decision to make."

"We appreciate all you've done for us, Matthew," Joel said, "but I've got to do *something*."

"I've come into a bit of money recently," Matthew said quickly. "Please think nothing of it. I can gladly afford to help you until we hear from my father." He held up his hand to wave off their protests. "I've made arrangements to go to France."

"To France?" Phoebe said, startled. "For good?"

"Oh no. Just to visit some art museums over there. In the meanwhile, I want you two to stay here in my rooms. I'll leave you money for your needs. You'll have no problems."

"How long will you be gone?" Joel asked.

"Perhaps four or five weeks. By that time I should have heard from my father, and we'll be able to make more plans."

"It's good of you to think of us."

Matthew nodded to Phoebe and smiled. "It's all in the family. Now let's talk to Mrs. Neale, and she'll fatten you up while I'm gone so that I won't recognize you when I get back. . . !"

18

Matthew Bradford Meets a Frenchman

THE BALLROOM AT VERSAILLES WAS LIKE nothing Matthew Bradford had ever seen before. As he entered the magnificent hall he caught his breath, startled by the opulence of the decor. The ballroom was a large oval-shaped room painted a brilliant white, with ornately carved pillars encircling the room. Cut-glass chandeliers hung from the ceiling all down the center of the room, and the light from the candles caught the crystal prisms, sending dancing rainbows flickering throughout the room and splashing onto the highly glossed white marble floor. Paintings of French scenery in gilded frames adorned the walls, and over a magnificent marble fireplace hung a massive portrait of King Louis XVI, flanked by several smaller portraits of late noblemen. Tables stood out from the walls, covered with the finest white damask, silver trays, dishes, and cut-crystal goblets, and laden with an array of food and drink arranged in elaborate designs.

As Matthew wandered around, he received curious looks from many of the occupants of the ballroom. They were dressed in the height of French fashion, the men wearing heavily woven silk suits, with overcoats that fell to just above the knees. The overcoats had turned-up cuffs and a large shawl-type collar. They were worn with only the top button buttoned, the ruffles on a white silk shirt showing around the neck and at the wrists. A waistcoat was made of the same material, but of a lighter color than the suit, and was heavily embroidered around the edges, worn buttoned from top to bottom. The breeches were somewhat loose and ended at the knees, with white silk stockings and black leather shoes finishing the outfit.

The women were even more excessive in their dress, and suddenly

Matthew felt conspicuously out of place. The ballroom floor flashed with swirling figures in reds, greens, yellows, and purples—all the colors of the rainbow—and Matthew was dazed by the sight.

"Ah, monsieur, you are an American."

Matthew turned quickly to meet the lively eyes of a woman. It was almost impossible to tell her age. She could have been anywhere between twenty and thirty. She wore a daring dress cut lower than Matthew would have thought possible, and he averted his eyes, his face flushing. "Yes, I am from America," he said.

"Ah, you speak French very well." The woman moved closer and he saw that her lips were unnaturally red. Her attractive figure was obvious enough, and there was a boldness in her eyes that Matthew had never encountered before. His time in France had been short, but when he had received an invitation from a gentleman named Beaumarchais to attend the ball at the palace, he had accepted at once. Now he stood awkwardly and struggled with his poor French.

"What is your name, monsieur?"

"Matthew Bradford."

"Ah, my name is Marie Duchamp."

"I am happy to know you, Mademoiselle Duchamp," Matthew bowed, feeling like a fool as he did so. The woman curtsied deeply, giving him an even more startling view of her décolleté. When she rose, she put her hand on his arm and said, "I must hear about the news from far-off America."

Matthew Bradford was not a ladies' man. He had heard that French women in the court of King Louis XVI were free with their favors, but he was totally unable to handle the situation. He found himself flattered, and when the woman pressed herself against him in a suggestive way his head swam. She was wearing a heady perfume that affected him like incense, and fifteen minutes later, he found himself alone with her in a secluded room with one wall covered by tall windows that reflected the night sky. Inanely he tried to carry on a conversation, but suddenly the woman reached up and pulled his head down. Her lips were soft, yet somehow demanding, leaving no doubt as to her intentions.

Despite himself, Matthew returned the embrace, and as he pressed her closely he felt her response. She kept her lips on his and locked her hands behind his neck, pulling him even closer.

Suddenly the sound of a door opening jarred Matthew's senses. He stepped back and swung around in time to see a heavyset man dressed in a crimson suit standing just inside the door.

"So, it is this, is it?" he demanded.

Matthew swallowed hard and glanced at the woman. Disdain filled her face rather than fear. She said, "Be off with you, Louis!"

But the man called Louis stepped up to Matthew and, without warning, slapped him in the face. "You trifle with me? I will see you dead! I will have satisfaction!"

Suddenly Matthew Bradford knew he had made a dreadful mistake. He was being challenged to a duel! Painfully aware of his incompetence with either a blade or a pistol, he was seized by the agonizing fear that this Frenchman was about to kill him.

"Monsieur . . . I didn't mean . . . that is to say . . ." Words failed him, and he saw the anger in the man's smallish eyes.

"My friend will call on you. What is your name?"

"Don't be a fool, Louis!" the woman intervened. "This man is an American! You will cause an incident!"

"I will cause his death!"

The three of them stood there, and Matthew had the ridiculous thought that it might make a good dramatic painting—the insulted husband, the sensuous wife, the innocent young American. In his mind, he could almost frame the picture as it would appear on the canvas. But then he thought, *I'll never have time to paint it. He'll kill me, and all of my paintings will go with me to the grave!*

He cleared his throat and said, "Monsieur, I must apologize. I was not aware that this lady—"

"I'm not interested in your talk! You will be a dead man before dawn!"

Even before Louis finished speaking these words, another person stepped into the room. At first Matthew thought he was a friend of Louis and drew no hope from the interruption, but then he heard the Frenchman say coldly, "You are insulting a guest of our nation, Duchamp!"

Matthew saw the surprise and shock wash over the face of the full-bodied man who had challenged him. Louis seemed to grow pale and stuttered as he said, "Oh, Marquis, I . . . I did not—" He cut the words off short, and the woman came over to take his arm. "Come away, you fool!" she whispered.

With his eyes fixed on the face of Duchamp, the tall man said, "If you crave satisfaction, I will be glad to oblige you. Shall my friend call on you?"

"Oh no—no indeed, Marquis! It was all a terrible mistake!" Louis spluttered. He turned to Matthew and said in a frightened voice, "May I ask your pardon, monsieur?"

Matthew could only swallow, for his voice was gone. He nodded slightly, and Duchamp turned and was pulled out of the room by his wife.

"I apologize for my countryman," the tall man said.

"I must say he had cause, but I was not aware—"

"I understand. Madame Duchamp is—how shall we say—too free with her favors. Her behavior is shameful, and I apologize once again."

"I must thank you, monsieur," Matthew said. He passed a hand in front of his eyes and found that it was trembling. He looked at it and said, "I would have been in poor shape. I'm no expert with weapons."

"Put it out of your mind, monsieur. You are a guest in our country."

"My name is Matthew Bradford."

"And I am the Marquis de Lafayette." He smiled slightly and said, "My full name is a mouthful. I was christened Marie Joseph Paul Yves Roch Gilbert du Motier de Lafayette."

Stunned by this list of names, Matthew could only bow and say, "I am happy to meet you, Marquis."

"You are lately arrived from America, I take it?"

"Yes. I have been in England for a short visit and came to your country only a few days ago."

He was studying the marquis as he said this and found him not at all handsome. His hair was red and his skin freckled. He had a long triangular nose and very light blue eyes. His features were tilted back from an uplifted chin to a sloping forehead, and he was, Matthew gauged, at least six feet tall. He knew nothing of French nobility, but somehow Matthew had the idea that this man was someone to reckon with.

"May I engage you for a time, monsieur?"

"Engage me?" Matthew stammered. "I don't understand."

"I am interested in your country. In the war. Are you sympathetic toward the revolution?"

Matthew somehow felt this could be a trap, but he could only be honest. "My family is sympathetic," he said. "My two brothers serve with General Washington, and my father operates a foundry that manufactures supplies for the American army." He did not know whether or not this would terminate his conversation, but he saw the light blue eyes of the marquis light up.

"Ah, excellent! I must hear more of this! I myself am totally in sympathy with your valiant cause, monsieur."

Matthew felt a sudden compunction and said hastily, "I'm afraid I am not committed to the revolution as much as my family is. I am not certain as to the wisdom of it. It seems difficult to think that the Colonies could ever win against a power such as Great Britain."

"Ah, but with a general like your George Washington. Hah!" The marquis's eyes glowed, and he waved his hands excitedly in the air. "You have never met him, I suppose?"

"Well, as a matter of fact, I have."

"You have met George Washington? Oh, monsieur! I must hear more but not here! Would you come to my home tomorrow and be my guest?"

"It would be my pleasure, Marquis."

"Where are you staying? My coach will call for you." The marquis fixed the location of Matthew's lodging in his mind and put his hand out impulsively. When Matthew gripped it he found it strong, and there was an excitement in the Frenchman that he did not understand.

"Tomorrow at my home we will talk about your war. . . ."

T   T   T

Matthew had been careful to inquire about the Marquis de Lafayette before his visit. He discovered that the young man was one of the wealthiest individuals in France. He was the son of the Marquis Gilbert de Lafayette, and his mother was Julie de la Rivere, the beautiful daughter of a wealthy and powerful Parisian family with close ties to King Louis XV. The father had died in battle, and Gilbert had become the marquis of the home in Chavaniac.

The innkeeper, who gave Matthew this information, rolled his eyes and said, "Ah, the marquis! He is such a man. You know him, monsieur?"

"I have been invited to visit his home."

"Well, you will find a gracious home indeed. The marquis was raised by his grandmother and two aunts. I fear it was not a cheerful childhood. His mother remained in Paris most of the time, but the young man has strong views."

"What sort of a man is he?" Matthew asked.

"My cousin is in charge of the wine cellars at the marquis's home. His name is Jean. You know how it is. Servants know a great deal. Jean tells me that after the death of his mother, the marquis inherited vast sums of money. No one knows how large, but tremendous holdings in Brittany and Touraine. However, he did not become a dissolute wastrel as many would have done. He instead became a master at fencing and riding and enlisted in the king's Musketeers. Ah, he longs to be a soldier, that Marquis de Lafayette!"

"Is he married?"

The innkeeper's eyes twinkled. "Yes. At sixteen he married a thirteen-year-old girl whose name was Adrienne de Noailles. His dowry was two hundred thousand livres! My cousin Jean was serving that night, and he said the two young people were put in a huge four-poster bed, and all the family and friends came in to tease them until the bride's father, horrified to see his daughter so openly upset, dismissed everyone."

"He's interested in the war, I understand?"

"Yes," the innkeeper nodded. "He thinks of nothing else. You will hear much about George Washington and the great cause of liberty that the Americans struggle for. Oh, you will find a friend at the home of the Marquis de Lafayette!"

🀆   🀆   🀆

His conversation with the innkeeper was on Matthew's mind as the carriage stopped. He stepped outside, taking in the large house and sweeping grounds, and caught his breath. It was a beautiful home, and when he met the marquis inside, he was greeted as warmly as an old friend.

"Come, my dear Monsieur Bradford. We must have refreshment." The marquis took his arm and walked with him into the drawing room, where he introduced him to the charming young woman who was his wife.

"We are delighted to have you," Madame de LaFayette greeted him, taking his hand and curtsying deeply. "My husband is so enamored of everything about America. He will talk you to death, I fear."

Matthew had difficulty following the French but managed to stammer, "It will be my pleasure, madame."

After a few minutes, Madame de Lafayette excused herself, and at once the marquis turned to say, "Now, tell me everything!"

Matthew found that the marquis meant exactly what he said. He wanted to know *everything* about America. For two hours the conversation went on, with the young nobleman leaning forward, his eyes gleaming. He prodded Matthew with numerous questions, interrupting him to ask various details. What did Washington look like? Did he ride well? How were the soldiers armed? How many cannon did the army have?

Finally Matthew threw up his hands. "You need my brother Dake, monsieur. He could answer all of these questions."

The marquis suddenly gave Matthew a searching glance. "Perhaps I may meet him."

The simple words caught Matthew off guard. "You mean—you're thinking of going to America?"

"I am determined to go." The marquis's thin face was set. His generous mouth was drawn into a tight line, and he nodded firmly. "I will join myself with the great struggle for freedom in your country."

"That's very noble of you, monsieur. I'm sure you will be most welcome to General Washington. When do you plan to go?"

"Ah, it is not as easy as this! The king refuses to let me go. The Comte de Vergennes has heard of my intentions."

"Who is he?"

"He is the head of our foreign department. The equivalent, perhaps, of England's prime minister. I was approached by Monsieur Silas Dean. You have heard of him?"

"Yes, I believe I have. My father mentioned he was sent to Europe to make contact with those sympathetic to the revolution."

"Exactly. When I met him I gathered a band of young nobles, and Monsieur Dean offered all of us a commission."

Suddenly Matthew remembered how his father had spoken of the unqualified foreigners who had flooded over to join the army, given commissions by this same Mr. Dean. Most of them were worse than useless, but he let none of this show in his face. He said quickly, "I'm sure you will be most welcome, monsieur. When do you think to go, then?"

"I've been ordered not to accept the commission, so I waited until after the birth of my daughter—you will see her before you leave, my friend. This will give me an opportunity to transfer from active duty to the reserve. Thus, I can be absent from France for some time without being charged with desertion. I have already sent an agent to Bordeaux to purchase a ship and to hire a crew. A friend of mine named deKalb will sail to the New World. We will both be made Major Generals!"

Matthew sat quietly listening as the marquis excitedly talked about the war. Matthew had never encountered an idealism on this level. Secretly he wondered if the young nobleman had any idea of the hardships and ugliness of war, but he felt it was not his place to bring up such things. Finally he left, after seeing the new daughter of the proud couple, but only after promising to meet again with the marquis the next day.

🏵   🏵   🏵

Three weeks had gone by since Matthew had met the Marquis de Lafayette. He had spent much of that time in the art galleries of Paris. As in England, he had been overwhelmed by the magnificence of all the great works of art he saw. He left the galleries each day depressed and once muttered, "I'll never be a painter! All I can do is smear paint on canvas."

Nevertheless, he continued painting and sought out a teacher—a huge man with muddy brown eyes named LeClark. LeClark was a household name in France, he discovered, one of the best of the teachers, and Matthew began his studies eagerly, despite his feelings of inadequacy. All day long he would stay at the art institute under the eye of the teacher, who gave him little encouragement. The evenings he either spent alone or met with the Marquis de Lafayette, where he talked not about art but about armies and swords and military maneuvers. Since Matthew knew practically nothing about military matters, it was mostly the marquis who carried on the conversation. The marquis seemed convinced that he would be leaving soon, and once he asked tentatively, "My dear Monsieur Bradford—pardon me, I would not offend you for the world—but do you not feel inclined to join the army yourself?"

It was a problem that Matthew had struggled with. He had not told the marquis anything about his personal life, but now he felt he owed him at least that much.

"I'm in a rather peculiar situation, monsieur. Only last year I discovered that the man I thought was my father, Daniel Bradford, indeed was not. He took my mother in when she was expecting a child, and he loved her—and me—all these years. My real father was an English nobleman, Sir Leo Rochester. Sir Leo died recently, and his last request was that I take his name and title and pursue a life of art in England."

The marquis stared at the young man. "I have never heard of such a thing before," he murmured. He was silent for a long time. "I do not know what I should do in such a case."

Matthew laughed shortly. "Nor do I. It is a very hard thing. My father encourages me to do what I feel is right. He says he will love me whether my name is Bradford or Rochester."

"Your father is a fine man, I would think. Not many fathers would do that."

"He's the finest man I've ever known, but still, there's a great deal to decide. I want to be an artist, and that's why I came to Europe. I'm studying now, but things aren't going well."

The Marquis de Lafayette sat there listening to the young man who, for the first time, had revealed some personal concerns that were troubling him. *He is a rather sad young man*, the marquis thought. *He does not know who he is really*. Finally he put his hand on Matthew's shoulder and said, "You have a difficult choice to make. I pray that God will help you make the right one."

The concern in the nobleman's voice encouraged Matthew. "You have been a great help to me, monsieur."

"Not at all. It is you who have been a help to me. I feel that I know your country much better. I look forward to meeting your family when

I get to America." He hesitated slightly, then said, "Will you be going home soon?"

Matthew could not answer. "I don't know," he said finally. "I have not been happy here, but I was unhappy in America."

They spoke no more of the matter that evening, but from that time Matthew grew more discontented. He walked the streets of Paris thinking of home and of his family and of Abigail Howland. He could not put her out of his mind, no matter how hard he tried.

Finally, on the fourth week of his stay, Monsieur LeClark detained him. "Monsieur Bradford, a word with you."

Matthew looked up quickly. He had been putting up his brushes, and now he closed the case and went over to stand before the burly painter. "Yes, monsieur?"

"You're wasting your time."

Matthew blinked with surprise at the blunt words of the instructor. "What does that mean, monsieur?"

"You are trying to be something you are not," LeClark shrugged. "You are trying to be a Rembrandt, or a Turner, or a someone else. You go around looking at the great paintings and you make copies of them. That is not the way art is—unless you want to be a copier instead of an artist. There's a market for that sort of stuff, I believe."

"No, that's not what I want!"

"Then I suggest you be what God made you to be and stop trying to be someone else."

Matthew swallowed hard. He looked into the eyes of the Frenchman and said, "I don't know if I have enough talent."

"You have some talent. How much I cannot say. You have not done what was in your heart. You have done what others have done. Go home. Paint what you see. Forget about selling. I have seen enough to know that, from time to time, you have this little spark of genius. Very small. Tiny! But I think it is there. Come back in a year, and we shall see."

Matthew walked out of the art institute, stunned by what he had heard. He did not go back the next day, nor the day after. He never went back again. He walked the streets, stayed in his room, and ate very little for days. But slowly a consciousness grew in him that what LeClark had said was true.

"I can't be somebody else," he finally said one night as he sat staring at the fire. It was long past midnight, but he had not been able to sleep. "If I can't be my own man, I'd be better off working in the foundry."

The next day he went back to the marquis's home and was welcomed cordially. The marquis stared at him after the greetings were over, and he said, "You seem to have something on your mind."

"You can tell that, monsieur?"

The marquis smiled. "It is not difficult. You look like there's a door in front of you, and you're determined to ram your way through it. What is this new determination I see in you?"

"I've decided to return home to America."

Immediately the marquis grasped his arm. "Wonderful! I have been hoping to hear that from you!"

"You have? Why, marquis?"

"This is no place for you. I do not know you as perhaps I shall in the future, my dear Bradford, but I know that you are a man who needs his own people. When will you go?"

"I must return to England first. The two relatives I told you about—I'll have to see to them. Maybe they'll want to return to America with me. In any case, my father has instructed me to give them what aid I can."

The Marquis de Lafayette took a deep breath. He nodded his head and said firmly, "We will meet in America." Then he looked out the window and was silent for a moment. When he spoke, his words were a whisper, but Matthew heard him say clearly, "I will serve General George Washington—or die in the attempt!"

PART FOUR

—

THE GATHERING OF EAGLES

Lafayette Joins Washington, Spring 1777

19

RETURN OF THE FIRSTBORN

A BITTER FEBRUARY WIND BIT AT Matthew Bradford's face as he made his way down the twisted street to the brownstone house where his rooms were located. As he leaned against the breeze, ignoring the stinging of tiny flakes of snow that fell intermittently, the thought of the Marquis de Lafayette was on his mind. The French nobleman was a puzzle to him, for he could not understand how a wealthy man could risk everything for a cause that was not his own. Matthew had hinted at this thought once to Lafayette, but the young nobleman had smiled gently and said, "The cause of liberty is not national. Every man is obliged to give of himself for the liberty of others."

As Matthew climbed the steps, he shook the thoughts of Lafayette out of his mind. He entered the house, removed his coat, shaking the light dust of snow from the garment, and wondered if he had done the right thing concerning his cousins. A letter had been forwarded to him in which his father had said, "Bring them at once. We must do what we can for them, Matthew."

Now as he ascended the stairs to the rooms his cousins were using, he stumbled slightly on numbed feet. When he reached the door, he hesitated for a moment. But it was time to act, and knocking, he heard a voice; then the door opened and Phoebe Bradford stood before him. He smiled and bowed slightly. "Good morning, Phoebe."

"Matthew, you're back!"

Phoebe was wearing the same dress he had bought for her before he left for France, and he thought again how good she looked in it. Stepping inside, he looked up at Joel, who came across the room at once, his eyes alight.

"How are you, Joel?" Matthew said.

"Very well. Very well indeed! Have you just arrived?"

"Just got off the boat an hour ago. It was a cold trip."

"Come over to the fire, Matthew," Phoebe urged. The two waited until their cousin stood before the fire, spreading his hands out, and then Phoebe said, "I'm glad to see you back."

"Did you have a good time? I mean, with your painting?" Joel asked.

"Not really." A grimace passed across Matthew's face, and there was an unhappiness in his eyes that his cousins did not miss. "How have you two been?" he asked quickly.

"I'm getting fat," Joel grinned. "Never eaten so well in my life! Mrs. Neale is a wonderful cook."

"Well, you won't be eating her cooking much longer," Matthew remarked. He turned from the fireplace, rubbing his hands together, adding, "I had to take passage when I could get it. We'll sail tomorrow on the *Endor*. She's an old merchant ship, and it will be a slow passage."

"I'm so excited to be going to America!" Phoebe exclaimed. She was a fine young woman with an air of grace about her in her movements. Now as she shook her head, she asked, "Are you certain it is all right with your father?"

"Yes, I received a letter from him in France. He's very excited about your coming," Matthew assured her. "We'll have to be quick to get ready, though. The *Endor* leaves at dawn."

"We're ready now," Joel responded. He shrugged his shoulders ruefully and said, "It doesn't take long to get our baggage together."

"We'll have to go out and get you some warmer clothes. It'll be cold in Boston when we arrive, and it's easier to buy clothes here."

"You've done so much for us already," Phoebe protested. "I don't feel right taking any more."

The two, however, had no choice. Matthew hurried them out, and after going to several shops, he purchased a wardrobe of sturdy clothing for both of them. That evening they ate their last meal with Mrs. Neale, who was sorry to see them go.

"You'll be leaving before breakfast, sir?" the landlady asked, sounding disappointed at their departure.

"Yes, Mrs. Neale, this is our last of your fine meals," Matthew said. "You've been a gracious hostess, and I appreciate all you've done for us."

"Think nothing of it, Mr. Bradford," she said.

Matthew slept in his own bed that night, and Mrs. Neale quickly prepared a spare room for Phoebe and Joel. He did not sleep well, however. He was still hearing the echo of his teacher: *"You are trying to be* someone else. *Until you learn how to paint what's inside of you, you will not be an artist.*" He tossed and turned restlessly, and as always, one of the last thoughts before he finally drifted off into a fitful sleep was of Abigail Howland. It angered him that he could not put her out of his mind, and he could not understand it.

"Why do I keep thinking of her?" he muttered, keeping his eyes tightly shut and trying to fall asleep. "She's nothing but a deceiver! I was warned about her—what kind of a woman she was—but I thought I knew better."

After a fitful night, he finally gave up in despair and rose in the darkness and quickly dressed. Looking at his watch, he saw that it was four o'clock, and moving down the hall, he tapped on the door of his cousins. "Time to be up," he said. "We don't want to miss the *Endor*." He found the two already dressed, and ten minutes later they were on the cold street, where Matthew was fortunate enough to hail a cab. The air was freezing, and Phoebe huddled in the carriage, anxiety lurking in her eyes. Joel, sensing that his sister was afraid, leaned over and took her hand, holding it tightly but saying nothing. Matthew observed this and thought, *It's a good thing they have each other. It's a new life they're going to. It would be hard to be alone.* Aloud he asked, "Have you ever been on a voyage?"

"No. Never," Joel answered.

"You might be seasick."

This, indeed, proved to be the case, at least for Joel. Two hours after they boarded the *Endor*, the captain guided her down the Thames. As soon as the ship left the mouth of the great river and began to dip and roll in the open water, Joel turned pale. Observing him, Matthew said hurriedly, "You'd better go to your cabin and lie down. It's not going to be pleasant."

"I . . . I think I will."

As soon as Joel had left, Phoebe, who did not seem to be affected by the motion of the ship, said in a worried tone, "I hope he'll be all right."

Matthew grinned faintly. "Seasickness has two phases, Phoebe. At first you're afraid you're going to die, then later on you're afraid you *won't.* He'll be all right. For some people it's over in a few hours. For others it's a matter of days."

Phoebe peered forward as the prow of the *Endor* punched a hole in the fog that rolled in long gray sheets across the water. Her thick eyelashes were damp with the moisture, and her lips were pulled together in a straight line.

Sensing her fear, Matthew put his hand on her shoulder. "Don't worry, Phoebe. You'll have a good life in America."

"Do you really think so, Matthew?"

"I'm sure of it. My father's the kindest man I know. He's very interested in you and your brother. I assure you; He'll see that you're well cared for."

Phoebe was quiet, for somehow the cloak of fog seemed to silence all the world surrounding them, so that only the slapping of the waves against the ship and the far-off calls of seamen speaking through trumpets came to them faintly in a ghostly fashion.

"Are you a Christian, Matthew?"

Taken off guard, Matthew turned quickly to look down at the girl. "Why do you ask, Phoebe?"

"Why, it's just that I'm a little bit afraid, and I don't know if I'm a Christian or not. I always envied those who were, though."

"You're going to the right place," Matthew said warmly. He was touched by the girl's vulnerability and longed to give her some reassurance. "I'm not much of a Christian myself. Oh, I belong to a church, but I'm not like my father or his wife, Marian. They just recently married, as I mentioned. Both of them are fine Christians."

For a time Matthew stood there on the rolling deck speaking to the young woman, and finally she said abruptly, "I believe that I was beginning to give up on God. Everything was so bad, and ever since we lost our parents, it seemed as if nothing would go right. Then when Joel and I went to jail, I didn't think I could stand it. He loves the outdoors so much. It was like seeing an animal caged up, and I began to doubt God." She bit her lower lip thoughtfully, gripping the rail as she stared down at the frothy water stirred by the prow of the *Endor*. "I even accused Him once of not caring about us."

"Did you, Phoebe?"

"Isn't that ridiculous?" she whispered softly. "Someone telling God what to do and what not to do! I'm not a Christian, but I believe that God cares for us even when things are bad. Don't you?"

"I think that's a good thing for you to believe." Matthew evaded her question, for he had not been at peace with God for years. Now he stood there thoughtfully as the dawn began to break, a thin gray line of light toward the east. The waves rolled in smooth billows, breaking into whitecaps, and as the captain of the *Endor* set more sail, Matthew thought about what Phoebe had said. She finally left him to go below deck and check on Joel. Matthew stood there staring out to sea for a long time.

As they rounded the coast and began to pass the white chalk cliffs of Dover, brisker winds pushed the sails forward. He calculated the days that the voyage would take but somehow found little joy in the trip itself. He was going home, but it did not feel like home anymore. He had fled from Boston to get away from the tumult in his heart over Abigail Howland's perfidious treatment. It had festered in him, tormenting him almost day and night, and now as the *Endor* pointed toward her destination far across the Atlantic, he wondered what would become of him. Would he become Sir Matthew Rochester, taking Leo's name and title? What would it be like if he stepped outside the immediacy of the Bradford family? And would he ever forget Abigail Howland? *That* was the burning question.

Finally, in despair he began to pace the deck of the ship, oblivious of the sails overhead that slapped with gusts of wind as the *Endor* dipped into the gray waters of the English Channel. For hours he walked, unhappy and disturbed, then finally whispered, "I ought to be grateful for this opportunity—but I'm not. What's *wrong* with me?" The thought tormented him, and he went below deck and sequestered himself in his cabin, but he could not escape the troubling questions that persistently plagued him.

☗ ☗ ☗

"Do you think we've done something to offend Matthew?"

Phoebe was standing at the prow of the *Endor*, her eyes fixed on the faint line of land that lay ahead. She drew the dark green cloak around her shoulders, for there was a biting cold in the air, even more pronounced, it seemed, in America than in England. She moved closer to Joel as if for reassurance. Looking up, she repeated her question. "Do you think we've angered him somehow?"

"I don't see how, but he has been difficult, hasn't he?"

"He's not a happy man. I don't understand him."

"I don't either. From what I can see he has plenty of money. He could even have a title if he decides to take it, but something's eating at his insides." Joel shrugged and said, "He's not angry at us though, Phoebe. He tries to be pleasant, but there's something bothering him."

The two stood there watching the land grow more pronounced, and finally Matthew came to join them. He was wearing a dark blue coat that came down to his knees and a pair of shiny black boots. "Well, there it is . . . Boston," he said as he leaned on the rail. "Are you glad to get here?"

"Oh yes!" Phoebe answered quickly. "I'm a little bit nervous, though." She bit her lip in a habitual nervous gesture, and her clear blue-gray eyes were troubled. "It seems such an imposition for your father."

Matthew laughed slightly. "Don't worry about that. This is all his idea, you know."

They stood there speaking softly as the crew guided the ship into the harbor, and when they were anchored, Joel said quickly, "I'll get the baggage, Matthew." He hurried to the cabins, and soon the three were stowed in a small boat with their baggage, being rowed to shore by a burly seaman. The two visitors took in the harbor, and it was Joel who asked, "Is this where they dumped the tea into the harbor . . . where the Boston Tea Party took place?"

"Yes, it is. My brother Dake was right in the middle of it."

"I suppose you worry about him a great deal," Phoebe asked, "being in the army in such dangerous times?"

"Yes I do, and my brother Micah, too. He's much calmer than Dake, but he was headed for the army when I left for England."

When the seaman pulled the small boat secure, Matthew was the first one out. Leaning over, he helped Phoebe step onto the dock, then took the baggage Joel handed up.

"We'll go right to my father's house," Matthew said. "I'm glad we didn't arrive in the middle of the night."

Ten minutes later they were in a carriage with their baggage stuffed overhead. Matthew observed that the two were growing more nervous as time went on. He had, however, done all he could to assure them of a sincere welcome and now sat silently looking out the window. When they pulled up in front of the Frazier house, he stepped out and helped with the unloading of the baggage. Then as the three of them stood amid the small pile of luggage, he said to the driver, "If you'll bring it in, there'll be an extra half crown." Upon receiving the man's eager nod, Matthew turned and smiled at his cousins, noting their anxious manner. "Come along. I hope Father's here, but he's probably at the foundry." He pulled his watch out and mentioned, "Almost eleven o'clock. Yes, he'll be there."

Phoebe moved reluctantly up the steps. She was intimidated by the size and grandeur of the house to which Matthew Bradford had brought them. It was a rather ornate three-story house made of dark red brick with a set of wide steps. It had a formal entrance set off by rusticated stone and Flemish-bond brickwork with pediment at the eaves. The windows were six across each level, and the frames were painted a brilliant white. The tall gabled roof was covered with black shingles, and a tall chimney flanked each end of the house. A separate wing to the right of the main house housed the kitchen area.

Matthew knocked on the door and at once was met by a servant who said, "Why, Mr. Matthew, you've come home!"

"Yes I have, Martha. I don't suppose Father's home?"

"Why no, sir. He's done gone down to the foundry, but Miss Marian, she's here."

At that moment Marian appeared on the stairs. A look of surprise mixed with gladness spread across her face as she greeted the party. "Why, Matthew, you're back!" she said. "We didn't expect you so soon!" She came forward, and Phoebe and Joel studied the woman, who reached up and pulled Matthew down for a hearty kiss on the cheek. She was a beautiful woman, they saw, somewhere in her mid-forties. She was tall, with dark auburn hair and green eyes. She turned to them then, and the kindness in her smile quickened their feeling of welcome.

"These are my cousins, Joel and Phoebe Bradford, and this is my stepmother, Mrs. Marian Bradford."

"I'm so glad to meet you both!" Marian advanced and took the hand of each of them. "Why, your hands are cold. Come into the parlor. Daniel's not here, but I'll send someone for him at once. He'll be so glad to see you!"

"I didn't know exactly when we'd get here, Marian," Matthew said. "You know how these voyages are." They all moved into the parlor, and for a time he and Marian spoke, giving the two visitors a chance to warm themselves by the fireplace. As they rubbed their hands before the fire, Phoebe and Joel looked at their surroundings in astonishment. The parlor was more ornate than any room they had ever been in. It was a large room, carpeted with a brilliant crimson, green, and gold-painted floor cloth. The walls were dark green with a gilded papier-mâché border around the windows and doors. The two took in the fine Queen Anne chairs with crimson silk damask covers, the green-japanned corner cupboard decorated in shades of gilt and red standing in the far corner of the room, which contained delicate china vases and silver boxes of all kinds. A small, lightly constructed harpsichord was positioned below a Biblical tapestry depicting the Passover and the death of the Firstborn woven in wools, silks, and metallic threads. Pictures in rich wood frames covered the walls, and Chinese artifacts could be found in all corners of the room.

Marian turned her attention from Matthew. She had seen how nervous the two were, and with her usual tact, she had given them time to get their bearings, but now she turned to say, "We're so glad to have you come all the way from England to be a part of the family here."

Marian Bradford's sincere words were like a soothing balm on the spirits of these two young people who had already suffered so much loss. Unaccustomed to kindness, they had experienced some serious doubts about the difficulties of becoming a part of a wealthy family.

Both of them felt awkward and insecure, but the warmth of Marian Bradford won them instantly. It was Phoebe who said, almost in a whisper, "I feel so strange, but Joel and I are so grateful to your husband, and to you, ma'am."

"I want to find work right away," Joel spoke up. "Matthew here has been so kind to us, but you know a man likes to make his own way. There was no work at all in England, but I'm hoping I can find work here."

"I'm sure that will not be a problem," Marian said. "Daniel and I have already discussed it. He'll be wanting to speak with you, Joel, about going to work at the foundry."

"Oh, that'll be fine, Mrs. Bradford!"

"And you, Phoebe, would you care to work here? We always need more help with this big old house. My father's practically an invalid. Caring for him takes most of my time and I don't have a maid just now. Perhaps you'd like to be my maid?"

"Oh, ma'am, I don't know much about that, but I can learn," Phoebe said eagerly.

"That's fine. Come along and I'll show you to your quarters. You'll both be staying here."

🔔   🔔   🔔

By the time Daniel Bradford arrived from the foundry, he found that most of the decisions had already been made. After embracing Matthew with a long hug, he turned and greeted the young man and the young woman. He then looked slyly at Marian and said, "I see I'm not going to be bothered with making a lot of decisions."

Marian's eyes glinted with humor. "I didn't think you'd mind, Daniel. That nice room out in the carriage house will do nicely for Joel, and I've given Phoebe the maid's room on the third floor."

"I don't know much about foundry work, Mr. Bradford," Joel spoke up, "but I'm strong, and I learn very quickly."

"I'm sure you'll do fine, Joel," Daniel said, then turning to Marian, he grinned. "Now, have you got anything to eat, wife?"

"Do I have anything to eat?" Marian said with mock indignation. "What a question to ask! How many times have I failed to have something for you to eat?"

"Never once. Let's rejoice and keep it that way!" Daniel smiled. He went over to stand beside her, and as the three watched, he slipped his arm around her and said fondly, "A wife fit for Daniel Bradford. Isn't she beautiful?"

Phoebe was pleased at Bradford's open admiration of his wife, and she saw that Joel was, too. *He loves her so much. You can just see it!* she thought, and then she saw the light in Marian's eyes and found it pleasing. *And she loves him, too.* It was a comforting thought that they would be living in a household where there was love as well as plenty.

♦ ♦ ♦

"I like our English cousins very well, don't you, Matthew?"

"Yes, sir, I do." Matthew looked across toward his father and nodded his agreement. "They seem to be very happy in their new home." The two of them were sitting alone in Daniel's office. A fire crackled on the hearth, sending cheerful warmth throughout the office. Outside, the snow was falling lightly, swirling in small cyclones of motion. Matthew had stopped by at his father's request and had mentioned their relations had settled in to their new jobs. It had been two weeks now, and Matthew had seen very little of them. He himself had been busy settling into his quarters at a boardinghouse near the Bradford home, where he set up his own private art studio.

"How is young Joel working out in the foundry?"

"Very well. He's very strong and very quick," Daniel said, then rose and went over to the fire, where he stood looking down at the dancing flames for a moment.

Matthew watched him in silence. There was a strength about his father that had always fascinated Matthew. He knew that his own frame, which was not so strong, came from his real father, Leo Rochester. With a pang he thought, *Dake and Micah, they're like Pa.* But he said nothing of all this. "How is Phoebe working out as a maid?"

"Marian says she's doing fine. She doesn't know much, of course. She's had few advantages in life. Both she and her brother have had a hard time, but I feel very good about their coming here." He turned and clasped his hands behind him, putting his hazel eyes on Matthew. "It was kind of you to take the trouble to bring them."

"It was little enough to do, Pa."

"I feel better having them here. We Bradfords are a small enough family. Now we're two stronger." He hesitated, then said, "We haven't seen much of you, Matthew. I'd hoped that you'd come to the house more often."

Matthew shifted restlessly, and for a moment he could not meet his father's eyes. He had been to the house only once since his arrival in Boston, and he hadn't stayed at the old home with Rachel and Sam. He had visited there, of course, but he had taken rooms in the center of the city and had spent most of his time alone. "I'm sorry, sir," he said. "I'll try to come by more often."

Seeing the disturbance in Matthew, Daniel moved away from the fire and took a seat. Picking up a pen, he toyed with it idly for a moment, then said, "Would you like to tell me how your painting lessons went?"

"Not as well as I'd like."

"What was the matter? Couldn't you find a good teacher?"

"I think the teacher couldn't find a good pupil," Matthew said, his lips showing a slight bitterness. "Oh, I don't mean to complain, Pa, but the best teacher that I finally found over there told me that . . ." He hesitated for a moment, then shrugged. "He said that I wasn't painting from within myself."

"What does that mean, Matthew?"

"It means that I'm just copying what other men do. He said that true art has to reflect what's in a man's own heart."

"I think it's that way with any kind of work, isn't it?" Daniel murmured. He knew little about art, but somehow the principle seemed to ring true. "After all, the Bible says, 'As a man thinketh in his heart, so is he.' I have no gift for art, but I think I see what the man meant."

"Oh, I have no doubt he was right. It's much easier to try to imitate than it is to come out with something from your own genius—not that I have any genius."

"Don't be too quick to say that!" Daniel rebuked the young man. "You're young yet. Tell me more about it. I'm interested in you more than you'll ever know."

A warm feeling flooded through Matthew. He lifted his eyes and smiled. "Thank you, Pa. I know that's true. Not many men would be willing to have their son give up the family name."

"Have you decided to do that?"

A heavy sigh escaped Matthew, and he shook his head. "I can't seem to make up my mind. I simply don't know what's the right thing to do." He wanted to speak of the uncertainty that had torn him since he had left, but he could not. Nor could he speak of his troubled feelings toward Abigail Howland. He had not seen her since he had returned, but he found himself looking for her on the street. Now he merely spoke of his time in London and how he had found his destitute cousins. Finally he said, "I met a man whom you'll be seeing here in America, I think."

"Who is that, Matthew?"

"A French nobleman. His name is Lafayette." He related his meeting with the marquis and saw that Daniel Bradford was tremendously interested. "It would have quite a good effect, I'd think, to have a man like that enlist in the army."

"Yes, indeed," Daniel agreed. "There have been some from Europe who were no asset to our cause, but this young man sounds different. He's only twenty, you say?"

"Just that, I think. He has a wife and child. I don't see how he can leave them to come over to a strange country on such a dangerous endeavor, but I'm very impressed with him. I think General Washington will be, too. "

The two men sat there for some time, and finally, when Matthew rose to leave, Daniel said, "Don't forget you'll be coming to dinner. Will tonight be too soon?"

"No, not at all. I'll look forward to it."

"Good. We'll have the whole crew here—you, Sam, Rachel, Micah, Dake, and Jeanne—and our new family members."

"And Keturah?"

"Yes, of course. I've grown quite fond of that young lady."

🏹   🏹   🏹

Rachel Bradford had become closer to Abigail than to any of her more long-standing friends. It had become her custom to stop by Mrs. Esther Denham's house, where Abigail and her mother stayed, once or twice a week. Now, as she sat in the small parlor, the two spoke for a while of the war, and the news was not encouraging.

"I don't see how the army can go on long from what Dake says," Rachel murmured. The two were working on a quilt, and their needles flashed in the bright sunlight that flooded through the window. The weather had mitigated so that most of the snow was melted off, and now the brilliant light from the sun flooded the small parlor. A fire crackled on the hearth, and there was a warmth about the small room that pleased Rachel. "This is a nice house," she interrupted herself. "It's so fortunate that Mrs. Denham had a place to come to after her home burned in New York."

"Yes. It was providential," Abigail nodded. She looked around the room quickly, then shrugged. "I don't know what my mother and I would have done if it hadn't been for her gracious hospitality."

Rachel had been waiting for Abigail to mention Matthew, but she never had, even though he had been home for two weeks. Now, taking a deep breath, Rachel looked down at the needle as she sewed and said quietly, "You never asked about Matthew. You know he's home, don't you?"

"Yes, I've heard."

Surprised at the brevity of Abigail's reply, Rachel looked up. "Is something wrong?"

"No, not really." Abigail Howland made a pretty picture as she sat sewing the colorful squares that composed the quilt. She was wearing a dress that fit her full figure snugly. The dress was made of a light green wool, and two small jade earrings caught the light and twinkled as she moved her head slightly. She said no more for such a long time that the silence seemed to thicken in the room. A tall grandfather clock tolled off the time with a rhythmical gong.

"I can't fool you, can I, Rachel?" Abigail suddenly smiled ruefully and put her needle down. She clasped her hands together and stretched her back and seemed to be trying to think of a way to say what was in her heart. "I think about him all the time, Rachel. I love him very much." There was such simplicity and dignity in Abigail's voice and demeanor that Rachel felt a touch of compassion.

"He'll come around."

"I don't think he will. You know him better than I do, but I think once Matthew makes up his mind, he's difficult to change."

"Yes, he always was that way. He's more sensitive than Dake," Rachel said slowly. "Of course, when we were growing up, we had no idea that he was Leo's son, but we always knew that Matthew was different. Maybe it was just the fact that he was artistic, and the rest of us weren't particularly. But he was always, more or less, set off."

"He is different from the rest of you. Sometimes I wish he were more like his brothers, but he's who he is."

For a time Rachel studied the young woman across from her, thinking of her brother's checkered history. She herself no longer thought of the wayward past that Abigail Howland had known, but others in Boston were not so kind. There were still knowing glances and whispered gossip about the life that she had led several years earlier. Now, however, seeing the peace in Abigail's eyes, Rachel said suddenly, "My father always says it's nice to take whatever comes in life." A dimple appeared in her right cheek, and her eyes reflected the humor that lay in her. " 'Whatever is to be will be—even if it never happens,' he'd always say. I don't know what that means. But I do know that he believes very strongly that God has more to do with what happens to us than most people think."

"Your father has a great deal of wisdom, but somehow I can't see that God has much to do with this. I hurt Matthew very deeply when I agreed with Sir Leo to betray him," Abigail said.

Rachel had heard the whole story of how Leo had hired Abigail to entice Matthew to fall in love with her, and then to convince him to take the Rochester name. Somehow the scheme had gone awry, for Abigail had found God and then had made an open confession to Matthew. Instead of forgiving her, however, he had been filled with bitterness and had fled to England to get away from her.

"He'll come around," Rachel said again.

"I don't think so," Abigail said, a sadness weighing her heart. "It would be a difficult thing for a man to forgive. It would be different," she said, "if he were a Christian. But he's not found the Lord yet."

"Why don't you go see him? Go to him?" Rachel urged.

"I couldn't do that."

"Why not?"

"He has to find his own way, Rachel. No one can help him."

The two women were silent for a long time, and Abigail thought of her last meeting with Matthew. His eyes had blazed with anger, and there had been bitterness in every line of his body as he had accused her of deceiving him. Since she had done exactly that, she had no defense, and now a great sense of loss swept through her. She loved him no matter what he thought of her, and she knew somehow that she always would.

🏹　　　🏹　　　🏹

The Methodist Church was packed for the Sunday service, and Matthew Bradford was stirred by old memories as he sat in the pew. He had been practically raised in this church, but now as he listened to the minister speak, he found it difficult to keep his mind on the sermon. He had come at the urging of Dake and Jeanne and now sat beside Sam as the service came to an end.

Sam, at once, as soon as the last amen was said, grabbed Matthew's arm, saying, "Come on down to the harbor. We can look at the spider catcher."

Matthew grinned at this younger brother of his. "You're not going to enlist me for a wild, harebrained scheme like that."

"What's harebrained about it?" Sam protested loudly. "All we have to do is find a fat merchant ship loaded with goods, point the cannon at her, and threaten to blow her out of the water if she doesn't surrender."

"What if she has a cannon?"

"Then we'll get bigger ones."

As they walked out of the church, Matthew was amused by Sam's brash schemes and somehow felt that this new idea might really amount to something. He was startled and forgot Sam immediately when he came face-to-face with Abigail Howland.

"Hello, Matthew." Abigail's face was pale. She was wearing a smoky gray-colored wool dress with long sleeves and a slightly square neckline. It had white ruching edging the wrists and neckline and running down the front of the form-fitting bodice. The dress cinched tightly at the waist, then billowed into a full skirt. She had been watching Matthew in church, sitting slightly behind him so that he could not see her, but she had studied his face and decided to speak to him.

"Hello . . . Abigail." Matthew's voice was strained, and it seemed to be an effort for him to use her name. "How have you been?" he asked coolly.

"Very well."

Matthew could not think of another thing to say. He studied Abigail's face and, as always, was struck by the richness of her beauty. He knew no other woman so beautiful and half hated himself for being drawn to her.

The two stood there for a moment, and Abigail thought, just for an instant, that Matthew intended to speak. She wanted to burst out, to tell him again how sorry she was that she had betrayed him. But people were pressing on, and with a slight nod of his head, he whirled and shoved his way through the crowd. Abigail watched him go, and a voice within her tolled like a funeral bell. . . .

He will never forgive you—never!

20

A Royal Volunteer

OCCASIONALLY THE WORD "UNIQUE" may be applied to an extraordinary individual—not often, of course, for most human beings are, more or less, put into the same mold as their fellows. However, the young Marquis de Lafayette, more than any other man of France, deserved such a description. In almost every instance, he refused to conform to what was expected of a young French nobleman. Reared by his grandmother and a pair of dour aunts, he developed a love for battle and military prowess. Upon his marriage at the age of sixteen, he purchased a captain's commission in the Noailles Dragoons, which had been named for the father of his own father-in-law. It was his dream to become a man of military fame, but since there was no war in France, his life quickly became a boring round of parades and military reviews.

Lafayette differed from other French noblemen in that he refused to take a mistress. It was rumored that, at the court of young King Louis XVI, he was tempted to choose a mistress for himself, but resisting this, he remained faithful to his young wife, who was indeed the love of his life.

Lafayette became an avid listener to any news from America. He delighted in the interesting descriptions of George Washington and his Continental Army. Finally, here was a chance to give more than lip service to what he desired most of all—military glory. "I am persuaded that the human race was created to be free and that I was born to serve that cause."

He sought out Silas Dean of Connecticut, who had come to France on a secret mission to enlist French aid for the American cause, and was offered, along with Jean de Kalb, a commission in the American army. However, the foreign minister of France, Comte Devergennes, did not believe that France was quite ready for another war with England, so he ordered Lafayette and the others to reject the commissions. Lafayette was not deterred by the foreign minister's orders and was determined to leave France and fight in the American Revolution. At the birth of his daughter, Henrietta, he found a way. Sending an agent to Bordeaux to purchase a ship and hire a crew, Lafayette determined to sail to the New World and join the forces of General George Washington.

Soon Lafayette and his friends boarded *La Victoire* in Bordeaux, bound for the New World. He was intercepted by a courier from King Louis, bearing an order for the young men to report for a tour in Italy under his father-in-law, the Duc de Noailles. It would seem that the young marquis's father-in-law had triumphed, but once again nineteen-year-old Lafayette carved out his own destiny.

"We will not return to France. We will go to America and fight for the freedom of our brothers in that country!" he declared. Marquis de Lafayette stared defiantly into the face of Jean de Kalb. The two men were standing in the master cabin of *La Victoire*, and Lafayette held in his hand the king's order commanding their return to duty in Italy.

Jean de Kalb, a sturdy, middle-aged soldier of experience and renown, shook his head. "You know," he said quietly, "what could happen, my dear friend."

"I care not."

"Then I also care not." De Kalb smiled enthusiastically, his dark brown eyes lit up. "Let us go find our place beside those who fight for freedom."

"Good! Come, we will give the orders." Lafayette strode out of the cabin and, finding Captain DeSpain, said, "Weigh anchor, Captain. We go to America."

Captain DeSpain, a small man with jet black hair and eyes to match, studied the young nobleman. "Are you certain, monsieur?" He had heard of the king's command and knew what Lafayette would give up if he followed his bold course of action.

"Yes, set your sails, Captain."

🔔   🔔   🔔

For fifty-nine days *La Victoire* battered its way across the Atlantic's contrary winds. Neither Lafayette nor de Kalb enjoyed the necessity of traveling by ship, but they amused themselves by exercising daily with foils and broad swords, and reading books on military strategy and tactics. Finally on June 15, 1777, *La Victoire*'s captain cast anchor near Charleston, South Carolina. Lafayette went ashore at once, accompanied by de Kalb, and as they made their way inland, they were astonished at the magnificent vegetation that adorned the lowland south swamp forest. Huge, towering pines of astonishing height and enormous oaks spread their great limbs high overhead, almost shutting out the sun.

"Look at the waterfowls!" Lafayette exclaimed to de Kalb, waving his hands in a windmill of excitement: "Every size and color!"

"Yes, and those strange-looking beasts sunning themselves there," de Kalb said, looking nervously at what appeared at first to be a group of logs but actually were alligators. "I would not like to have one of those fellows take a bite out of me."

The small company continued their journey until finally they reached Charleston, where they were instantly lionized. The patriots of that colony were astounded that a man of Lafayette's stature would cross the ocean at his own expense to fight for liberty. The streets were lined as Lafayette and de Kalb were led down through the center of the city and given the welcome of heroes. Lafayette was delighted to find many who spoke French well. Many of the settlers were Huguenots who had settled in America to escape religious persecution.

At once a series of receptions and reviews surrounded the Europeans, but Lafayette soon tired of this, as well as the roving eyes of the pretty girls who swarmed around him.

"We've got to get away from all this. I didn't come to America to attend parties."

"I agree. Let's go at once to our destination. We will have to buy wagons and horses for our men."

On June 22, Lafayette, having bought wagons and horses for his sixteen officers, left Charleston. Though the sea voyage had been dismal and dangerous, the trip to Philadelphia was a miserable ordeal. Day after day the small party struggled over the treacherous roads and endured the primitive inns that were scattered over far distances. Sometimes drenching cloudbursts fell upon them like a torrent, and at other times the scorching sun beat down upon them with a fierce intensity. At times the wagons broke down, or the horses had to be pulled from great seas of mud, but although Lafayette's men became discouraged, the young commander reveled in the new adventure. He loved plants and animals and kept a detailed record of the different flora and fauna that they encountered along the way. Lafayette wrote back to his young wife, "The United States is the most marvelous land on earth!"

A marvelous land it might have been, but when the party reached Philadelphia they received a cool welcome. They were splendid in their dress uniforms, and bearing their commissions, they descended upon Congress. Instead of being welcomed with open arms, Lafayette was told that Silas Dean had exceeded his authority and that Congress did not have the money to pay even its own army. Therefore, their services would not be required. Lafayette was politely urged to return to France, but he replied in a letter, "After the sacrifices that I have made in this cause, I have the right to ask two favors at your hands: The one is, to serve without pay, at my own expense; and the other, that I be allowed to serve at first as a volunteer in the ranks."

The members of the Continental Congress were stunned at his generous proposal. They were accustomed to foreigners crossing the Atlantic with their hands out and expecting to be royally paid for their services—which often proved sadly inadequate.

"Let General Washington decide about this man," John Adams said, and so a letter was dispatched to Washington. The general agreed at once to confer with Lafayette, and a meeting was arranged.

🔔　　　🔔　　　🔔

"I'm not sure, Your Excellency, that this meeting with the young Frenchman is at all to our advantage."

Washington brushed the dust off of his epaulet and looked up with surprise at Henry Knox. The huge captain of artillery was eating an apple and looking somewhat worried.

"He hasn't come to take command of the artillery as that other fellow did, Henry," Washington observed mildly.

"Oh, I know that, General. But, still, these foreign fellows haven't proved any worthwhile service to us."

Alexander Hamilton, who was copying orders for Washington, looked up from his desk. The three men were in a low-ceilinged room that served as a command post for the commander in chief. "I am not sure I agree with you, Henry. After all, this man isn't a penniless volunteer and certainly not a fortune hunter. He has a fortune of his own in France."

"That may be, Colonel Hamilton," Knox grunted. He ate the last bite of the apple and stared regretfully at the core, then tossed it toward a box in the corner.

Washington listened as the two men argued the merits and liabilities of the foreign officers who had come at the bidding of Silas Dean. He, more or less, agreed with Knox that most of them could not serve effectively as a private, much less as a lieutenant general in the Continental Army. He was tired now, and the lines drew his eyes closer together. He sat at the desk loosely, every muscle lax, it seemed, and stared down at his big hands as his two officers continued to argue their cases. They were interrupted by a knock at the door, and Nathaniel Greene stepped inside to say, "Your Excellency, the Marquis de Lafayette is here."

Instantly Washington rose from his chair, saying, "Show the marquis in." As Greene disappeared, he looked at the two across from him who had also risen and said, "We will show courtesy to our guest no matter what the outcome." As soon as he finished his words, he turned to face the young man who had entered, escorted by Greene.

"May I present His Excellency the Commander in Chief of the Continental Army, General George Washington. General Washington, the Marquis de Lafayette."

"Excellency!" Lafayette's fine eyes glowed, and he rushed across the room, ignoring protocol. Putting out his hand he grasped Washington's firmly, saying in French, "I cannot tell you how wonderful it is to be here, my dear General."

Washington was taken aback by the exuberance of the young Frenchman. He caught a smirk on Henry Knox's face but had no time to rebuke him. Somehow the general liked the young man who had entered and returned the greeting in English. "I speak French so abominably, my dear Marquis, you must humor me by speaking in English."

"*Certainement*—I mean certainly, Your Excellency."

Washington introduced the marquis to Knox and Hamilton and then said, "We must have refreshments, Knox. See what you can provide."

Knox began scurrying around, light on his feet for such a bulky man, and soon the four were enjoying the refreshments, which were rather spare.

"I apologize for the scarcity of our fare, but there is little luxury here, Marquis."

"It is nothing." Lafayette beamed as he began to speak with excitement of his pleasure at being here.

Finally Alexander Hamilton said, "Your experience would be invaluable to our cause, Marquis."

Lafayette said quietly, but with intensity, "I am here to learn, sir—not to preach or teach."

That one remark won the hearts of all three of the general's staff instantly. A sense of relief seemed to fill the room, and Knox himself went over and put his good hand forward to shake that of the marquis. He would have made two of the young nobleman, and his eyes were bright as he said, "I welcome you, my dear Marquis, into the Continental Army."

Washington was pleased with the young man. He did not know it at that instant, but before long a father and son relationship would develop between the commanding officer and Lafayette—the one had never had children of his own, and the other had never known a father. As Washington examined Lafayette—who spoke so enthusiastically of the cause when many of Washington's own people were discouraged and fearful—he said to himself, "If I had a hundred young officers like this one, the revolution would be safe."

𝕿   𝕿   𝕿

"Well, you're quite a seamstress, I believe, Keturah."

Keturah looked up startled from her needlework at Matthew Bradford, who had suddenly materialized in the smaller of the two parlors. With a reluctant smile she shook her head. "No, sir, I reckon not. Look what a mess I've made of this."

Matthew took the dainty cloth that was, indeed, even to his unpracticed eyes, not exactly quality work. He said quickly, "Well, you're just learning. It's always that way when we begin to learn something."

"I won't never be able to sew like your sister or like Jeanne."

"Of course you will," Matthew said. He sat down across from the young woman and stretched his legs out in front of him, studying her carefully. Her dark brown hair was beginning to grow out. It curled over her neck, and he admired the thick dark lashes and the arched eyebrows. Ever since he had met the young woman, he had felt a certain pity for her. Perhaps it was because he knew himself to be, in some ways, not a member of the family—not completely. He realized this was not the fault of his father or his brothers or sister, but something that was within him. Having heard Keturah's story, he thought how alone she was in the world, and he determined to make her feel at home.

"I felt the same way when I began trying to paint, Keturah," he said quietly. "You can't believe the messes that I made!" He laughed softly at the thought and shook his head in mock despair. "Sometimes I painted a dog that looked like a horse. I remember Rachel said that one time."

"I can't believe Rachel would say a thing like that."

"She was trying to be kind. I painted our dog, and it looked so much like a horse that she made a natural mistake and told me I was very good at painting horses."

Keturah's full lips curved upward in a smile. "Did it make you mad?"

"Well, yes it did. At first I wanted to paddle her, and then I wanted to quit painting. But I kept on."

Keturah looked up at a painting on the wall across from where she was sitting. "You do so good," she murmured. "I don't see how anybody can do a thing like that."

The picture she referred to was one Matthew had done the year before. It was a simple enough seascape done at the Boston harbor. The

sun glinted on the water, and Matthew remembered how much difficulty he had had in painting the precise shadings of light on the canvas.
The sea was that shade between blue and green, so hard to come by for
a painter, and overhead a slate gray sky was ruffled with white clouds
scudding across it. The ships with their tall masts filled the harbor, and
he said now, "I'm not very good at ships. I hope Sam doesn't see some
of the mistakes I made."

"Oh, it's right pretty, Mr. Bradford," Keturah argued.

For some time Matthew sat there quietly, watching the girl try to
sew, and noticed that she kept jabbing her fingers in a painful fashion.
Finally Keturah looked up and said sadly, "I don't think I'll ever be able
to learn this. I don't know anything about being a lady."

"It takes time, Keturah."

"No, you have to be born in a place like this. We never had anythin'
good. Not like this."

"I'll tell you what. I can't teach you to sew, but I would like to paint
your picture."

"Me?"

Amused at the girl's astonishment, Matthew spoke his thoughts
aloud. "You have beautiful coloring, Keturah. Your hair is such a rich
auburn. It might be hard to catch, but I think I can do it. What do you
say?"

Keturah sat there dumbfounded. Only wealthy people had their
likenesses painted, and she was, in truth, somewhat awed by Matthew
Bradford. "Why, it would pleasure me a heap!"

"Come along, then. We'll have a sitting right now."

Twenty minutes later Matthew was standing before an easel in the
large parlor. It was too cold to do an outside painting, but he had arranged Keturah sitting on a dark wine colored couch, and was now lay-
ing out the painting with swift strokes of a charcoal.

"But I can't wear this old dress to get pictured!" Keturah protested.

"That won't matter today," Matthew assured her. "We'll get Rachel
to find a suitable dress. I think something, perhaps, in dark blue. If she
doesn't have a dress, maybe Jeanne will."

Keturah sat quietly, still somewhat amazed that anyone would want
to paint her picture. She studied Matthew Bradford as he worked, admiring him greatly. He was not strong and powerful like Micah, but
there was a grace in his slender frame, and his face had an aristocratic
look that she admired.

"What's going on here?"

"Painting a picture, Sam. Can't you see?" Matthew said.

Sam advanced into the room and stood behind Matthew, watching as his brother laid the colors on. "Well, that doesn't look like anything to me," he announced. "Are you sure you're painting Keturah and not some wild beast you saw?"

"Sam, you have my permission to leave!"

Keturah found Sam amusing and could not refrain from smiling. "You go along, Sam. I'm getting my picture done."

"I'd better stay and supervise. This brother of mine might paint you with cross-eyes."

For a time Matthew endured Sam's suggestions, most of them ridiculous, albeit amusing, and finally he turned to say with exasperation, "All right, Keturah. We're not going to get any work done with this fellow here."

"Good," Sam said cheerfully. "When you get it painted I'll hang it in my room."

"You will not!" Keturah snapped.

"No, it'll be too good for that. What are you up to, Sam?"

"Going down to fire my cannon on my ship."

"Are you going to blow the windows out of it like you did in the bedroom?" Matthew had heard of Sam's misadventure with a musket and grinned at Sam's discomfiture. "Watch out for this fellow, Keturah. Don't have anything to do with him. He's going to blow up the whole house one of these days."

"That's all you know, Matthew," Sam retorted. He turned to Keturah and said, "Come along, Keturah."

"You mean go with you to the ship?"

"Sure. Get a good warm coat on. It's still cold out there."

🔔   🔔   🔔

An hour later Sam and Keturah were standing on board the vessel, with Jubal Morrison instructing Keturah on the use of the cannon. He had taken off his hat when she had arrived with Sam and greeted her warmly, saying, "One of you two is in bad company, and I suspect it's you, Miss Burns."

"I've come to show Keturah how the cannon works," Sam said.

"Sam decided he's to be the chief of gunnery on our ship." Jubal was wearing a dark brown serge, double-breasted great coat with a triple cape collar, turned up at the cuffs, and it came down past his knees.

He looked roughly handsome to Keturah, and she smiled shyly at him. "I bet Sam will do well at it, Mr. Morrison."

Jubal shook his head in mock despair. "He'll probably blow up the whole ship—but we'll see."

Sam and Keturah spent a pleasant afternoon as the two men, anxious

254

to show off the virtues of the spider catcher, explained the simple craft. Keturah listened intently and said finally, "I think you two are so smart to build a ship like this. Will you really be able to sail it out and fight the English ships?"

"Well, not a very big English ship," Jubal smiled. He had a squarish face, and his rusty hair caught the bright gleams of sunlight that turned the waters of the harbor red. "But we'll catch a prize or two, I don't doubt."

Keturah spent most of the afternoon with Sam, and the next day Jubal asked about Keturah and listened as Sam explained some of her background.

"You're kind of sweet on her, aren't you, Sam?"

A flush touched Sam Bradford's face, and he stared indignantly at his partner. "No I'm not!" he announced defiantly.

"Wouldn't be surprised if you were. She's a mighty pretty girl."

Sam chewed his lower lip thoughtfully and his bright eyes were troubled. "She's in love with Micah."

Jubal Morrison considered his young friend's face. Sam was like a younger brother to him, and he saw how the wind blew. *He admires the young woman, and she's got a pretty bad case of infatuation on his brother.* Grinning rashly he said, "I may take her away from him."

Sam's jaw dropped, and he could think of nothing to say for a moment—a rare moment indeed for young Sam Bradford. He usually had something to say about every occasion, but now he could only stare at Jubal, struck dumb by the young seaman's bland, confident expression.

"I don't think you ought to do that," he finally muttered.

"Why, I understood your brother was pretty well interested in a young lady in town."

"He is."

"Well, where does that leave Keturah? Kind of out in the cold, I'd say."

Sam ordinarily had to be ordered directly home, either by Jubal or by written command of his father, but somehow the moment was uncomfortable. He muttered, "Guess I'd better get home," turned, and left without another word.

Watching his young friend plod away, Jubal ran his fingers through his rusty hair and shook his head. "It's awful to be young." He himself was only twenty-six but felt ancient compared to the seventeen-year-old Sam Bradford. He thought back to the time when he had fallen madly in love with the daughter of the local Presbyterian minister and grinned abruptly. "Love is no fun—not all it's cracked up to be." But as he turned, he added with a cheerful air, "But it'd be a sorry world without it!"

21

At the Ball

LAWRENCE OLIVER WAS AN OVERBEARING YOUNG man of twenty-four years. The arrogance he displayed came in part from the fact that his father was one of the prominent powers of government in Boston, and young Oliver was not averse to recounting at every opportunity how one day he would take his father's place. He had come to dinner at the invitation of Rachel Bradford, and now as he looked around the table with satisfaction, he spoke of how things were going to change soon. He had a high-pitched, rather unpleasant voice and a habit of emphasizing at least one word in every statement. Oliver was dressed in the latest fashion, which consisted of a double-breasted coat of a striped black and gray material worn buttoned to the top and cut away in the front, a white silk shirt with ruffles at the neck and at the wrists, and a solid gray waistcoat. Tight-fitting white breeches ended just below the knees where white silk stockings with black embroidery at the ankles were tucked into black leather shoes with silver buckles.

"As soon as we get this business of revolution out of the way," Oliver proclaimed, "we'll see things humming here in Boston! Why, I've got enough ideas to make this city the queen of the Colonies."

Dake Bradford, sitting next to Jeanne across from Oliver, abruptly put his fork down and laid a hard glance on the visitor. "There's a little matter of winning a war first," he said, his voice flinty and his eyes even more so as he studied Oliver.

"Oh, we don't need to trouble ourselves with *that*," Oliver said airily. As he waved his hand, a large diamond on his finger caught the glow of the lamps and threw off fragments of light. "I know you're optimistic that this thing will succeed, Dake, but you *must* see by now that there's no hope."

Micah, seated next to Jeanne, lifted his own glance to the visitor. "I'd not be too quick to say that, Lawrence."

"Why surely, Micah, a bright fellow like you *must* see that there's no chance," Oliver snapped. Leaning forward, he said urgently, "We *need* England. What we need to do is come to terms on a few of the details, and this stupid war will be over and we can get back to business as usual."

Rachel was seated next to young Oliver with Keturah across from her. She turned to eye the young man, started to speak, then shrugged and held her peace. She could not imagine for the life of her why she had invited Oliver to come, except that he had driven her nearly out of her mind with his attentions. It had been flattering enough for a time, for Lawrence was the most eligible bachelor in Boston. He came from a good family of great wealth and was quite good-looking. He was no more than middle height and had a fine head of brown hair that he paid inordinate attention to. Studying him, Rachel thought, *I don't know what he thinks about me. He's chased after me enough, but he's done that with other young women.* She listened as Oliver dominated the conversation, until finally he turned to her.

"I'm looking forward to the ball tomorrow night, Rachel. I'll call for you at seven."

Rachel was surprised, for it was the first time he had mentioned the ball. "I'm not sure I want to go, Lawrence."

"Not want to go!" Lawrence stared at her in amazement. "Why, of *course* you want to go! Everybody will be there—and my parents particularly want you to come. . . ." He spoke persuasively and was not to be denied.

Sam, slouching in his seat next to Keturah, had said little enough during the meal. Now he glanced at Keturah and was somewhat shocked as she suddenly picked up her bowl of soup and slurped it noisily. He wanted to reach out and stop her, but it was too late.

Almost everyone turned at the unexpected sound, and Oliver, leaning around to peer at the young woman, snickered loudly. "Well, that's *one* way of eating soup, I must say!"

Keturah had been thinking little of her table manners. She had been watching Micah, for the most part, listening with half an ear to Lawrence Oliver. Now suddenly, feeling the eyes of everyone on her, her face flamed. She hastily set the soup bowl on the table, and seeing that the wealthy young guest was laughing at her openly, she rose from the table and almost ran out of the dining room. Sam muttered his apologies, jumped up, and followed her.

"Noisy little beggar, isn't she?" Oliver laughed. "I never heard anyone eat so loudly."

Micah's brow clouded, and he wanted nothing so much as to rise and toss the arrogant young man out the bay window. However, catching a warning look from Jeanne and Rachel, he settled back with a frown and said no more.

After the meal the talk died down, and even Oliver became aware of the tension in the room. He made his excuses early, saying to Rachel as she escorted him to the door, "I didn't mean to offend your young guest, but she was amusing, wasn't she?"

"I don't think so, Lawrence."

Oliver blinked with surprise, then glanced sharply at Rachel. Her eyes were fixed on his and a disapproving set tightened her lips. Quickly he muttered, "Well, I'll pick you up tomorrow." He left quickly, and Rachel turned to go back toward the kitchen. She was met by Dake, who demanded, "What in the world do you see in that fellow? It was all I could do to keep from punching his head!"

"He's not very pleasant, is he?"

"Pleasant! Why, he's a boor!"

By then Micah had come in, his face a thundercloud as he said, "I've never seen such a pompous fellow! You're not really going to the ball with him!"

"I believe I will," Rachel said. She forced herself to smile, saying, "I haven't had any other offers, and I do want to go. Are you going, Micah?"

"I . . . I suppose I might drop in for a while." His answer was evasive, and Rachel studied him carefully, then shrugged and turned to ascend the stairway. She knocked on Keturah's door, and when a muffled voice said, "Come in," she entered and found Sam sprawled on a horsehide chair, running his hand through his hair in a nervous fashion.

At once he said, "I'd like to shoot that Lawrence Oliver! What do you see in him anyway? You're not interested in him, are you, sister?"

"No, of course not. He's just pestered me into going out with him a few times." Looking over at Keturah, Rachel saw that the girl's eyes were swollen and that she was trying to conceal the tears she had shed. "Don't mind him, Keturah," she said, crossing the room to stand beside the girl. She sat down and put her arm around Keturah and gave her a squeeze. "He just doesn't know any better."

"I don't even know how to eat!" Keturah wailed. She suddenly threw her arms around Rachel and began to sob. Rachel held her tightly, as a mother would a hurting child, then she nodded slightly to Sam and framed the words silently, "Leave us alone."

"Well," Sam said quickly, "I'll see you later, Keturah."

As soon as the door closed, Keturah pulled away from Rachel, rubbing her eyes with the back of her hand. "I don't rightly know what's the matter with me," she finally said, drawing back. She sought for a handkerchief, and not finding one, Rachel produced one.

"Here—you can keep this one. Are you feeling better?"

"I feel terrible. I made such a mess of everything!"

"Well, it wasn't the smartest thing you ever did, but you're learning so quickly, Keturah."

"I'm nothing but a country bumpkin!"

"You mustn't talk like that! Your manners need some polish, but most of us need that."

"Not *you*."

"Why, of course *me*," Rachel smiled, patting the girl's shoulder. "Now, I want you to do something." With a light of mischief in her eyes she said, "I want you to go to the ball tomorrow with me and Lawrence."

"With him? I wouldn't go to . . . to a dog's funeral with him!"

"He's a pompous young man, and I just love to punch pins into proud fellows like that," Rachel said. Her eyes glinted with the sharp humor that lay in her, and she urged, "If you want to get even with him, this is the way to do it."

Instantly Keturah's eyes flew open. "Get even with him?" she demanded. "How can I do that?"

"Well, I can't think of anything that he would dislike more than having you tagging along; therefore, you ought to do it."

Instantly Keturah's lips grew firm, and a light glinted in her cerulean blue eyes. She reached up and ran her hand over her dark brown hair, which was now almost to her shoulders. "I'll do it!" she vowed. "And I'll get some of my own back on him!"

"Good! Now, we'll find you a dress. Either Jeanne or I will have one—or perhaps Marian will be able to help out." She stood there talking for a while and then left, but she went at once to find Micah. She found him sitting in the study reading a book of sermons and said instantly, "Micah, I want you to take Keturah to the ball."

"What are you talking about?" Micah looked up, shock sweeping across his face. "I can't do that."

"Certainly you can. What's to keep you from it?"

Micah stammered and put the book down. Getting to his feet he stared at Rachel suspiciously. "What's this all about?"

"She needs to get out more and meet people. She gets lonely here."

Micah fumbled with the book and Rachel saw that he was trying to find a way out. She began to persuade him, and although he was reluctant, he finally said, "Oh, I suppose I could take her."

"Why didn't you ask Sarah to go?"

"Her parents wouldn't let her go anywhere with me."

"Well, in any case, she'll be there," Rachel said. "Everybody will be. It'll be a good chance for you to see her."

Micah brightened and said, "All right, Rachel, I'll do it!" He rubbed his chin thoughtfully and said, "I wonder if she'll behave herself—Keturah, I mean."

"Don't worry, she'll do fine," Rachel said firmly. "Now I'm going to find her a dress to wear. . . ."

🏵   🏵   🏵

Noah Pierce was a tall, thin individual with a pair of light gray eyes that some said could see through the door to a bank vault. He had a shock of prematurely gray hair, and the remains of at least one previous meal evidenced itself on his waistcoat. He spent little of his money—which was considerable—on clothing, and now was wearing an old-fashioned outfit much the worse for wear. He had on a dark gray wool overcoat with braid trim, a stand-up collar, and large turned-up cuffs with patches over the elbows. He wore a white cotton shirt tied into a small bow under his chin, a light green waistcoat with braid trim, and a pair of black breeches that were very tight-fitting and ended just below the knees, with two mismatched buttons holding the breeches in place.

"Well now, if I understand you correctly, Mr. Bradford, you're considering taking the name of Rochester."

"Yes I am, Mr. Pierce. What would it involve?"

Matthew had appeared at Pierce's office unexpectedly. He had been going over and over in his mind the decision that lay before him and finally had come to the lawyer to at least find out the legal problems.

Pierce made a pyramid of his fingers and tapped them together. They were long fingers, abnormally so, and he stared at them for a moment with admiration, then lifted his eyes to face Matthew. "Well, there's very little to it, sir. We'll have to write a document and take it to the court. What do you know about the other heirs of Sir Leo Rochester? Will there be problems there?"

"I'm not sure, Mr. Pierce."

"If I understand you correctly, Daniel Bradford is not your real father."

"No, he's not."

Pierce regarded the young man's face and considered the answer, which was short and terse. He looked at the paper before him and studied it for a moment, then said, "It might help if you would explain the situation to me, Mr. Bradford."

Matthew cleared his throat and said with some hesitation, "My mother was pregnant before she was married. Daniel Bradford married her and gave her his name, and I was born several months later. Nobody except my mother and Daniel actually knew who my father was. I certainly didn't. Only recently did the truth come out."

"How does Mr. Bradford feel about your changing your name?"

"He's put the matter in my hands. He's a very fine man, Mr. Pierce."

"Yes, I know him well. We've done business together. Not every man would look at it like that."

"I'm not certain I want to do it," Matthew blurted out. He sat in the chair, twisting nervously, pulling at his clothing, and finally shook his head. "Sir Leo wanted it—wanted his name to go on, I mean. He had no other sons, so I feel some obligation to him."

"A very admirable sentiment. It would also be a very profitable thing." Then Pierce grinned abruptly and said, "Men would practically commit murder to be called Sir anybody."

"I don't really care about that, Mr. Pierce, but I'm wondering what's the right thing to do."

"I don't think there is any *right* thing to do," Pierce observed. He leaned back in his chair, locked his hands together, squeezed them gently, then let the silence fall over the room. He studied the face of Matthew Bradford, thinking how different this young man was from his brothers and from his father. There was a slenderness about him, none of the muscular strength of the other Bradford men. He was, somehow, more fragile looking than they, and now as he looked at the young fellow, he said abruptly, "I think either way you would benefit, but on the other hand it might be painful."

"How do you mean that, sir?"

"No matter what your father says, when you take another name, you, in effect, assume a different identity. You'll be known by everybody not as the son of Daniel Bradford, but as the son of Sir Leo Rochester. I'm sure you are aware of our effective system of gossip in this city and know that the minute this becomes public everybody will know exactly what happened. It will be very difficult for you, I would think."

"I hadn't thought of that."

"Well, it's not insurmountable, but it will be somewhat unpleasant. More so, perhaps, for your family than for you. But, on the other hand," Pierce shrugged, "there are advantages. Certainly, from what I understand, Sir Leo's estate in Virginia is an excellent piece of property. He's already left you well cared for financially, but you would have all of his assets—something to be considered."

Matthew stared outside the window as he sat nervously in the chair. After a long silence he suddenly turned and said, "I will have to have a little time, Mr. Pierce—and I think I'll have to go see Leo's family."

"They'll be your family, too, if you pursue this matter. I don't think," Pierce smiled frostily, "that they'll be too happy to see you."

Looking up quickly, Matthew understood the man at once. "No, I suppose not—but I mean them no harm."

"They won't know that. You haven't met them, have you?"

"Yes I have, briefly. I made a visit there with Sir Leo. I'm not sure they knew at the time that I was his son."

"Nor the heir," Pierce said wryly. "Well, Mr. Bradford, my advice is that you go and see the family, think about it, talk to your father—then come back. If you decide to pursue this course, it will be relatively simple. I'll be glad to help you through the legal morasses that men often drown in."

Matthew rose and put out his hand, which was taken by Pierce. He left the office and wandered the streets of Boston for some time, troubled by the thought of changing his name. It bothered him, for there was something so final about it. "Sir Matthew Rochester. . . ." He spoke the name aloud unconsciously, and a ragged street sweeper turned to look at him. He had lost most of his front teeth, and they made a black gap as he grinned broadly.

"Wot's that, sir? You speak to me?"

"No," Matthew muttered, embarrassed, then hurried on down the street. When he arrived at his old home, he found Micah in the library and stared at him for a moment. "Have you got time for a cup of tea?"

Surprised, Micah looked up. "Why sure, Matthew. That sounds good."

Ten minutes later the two young men were sitting in the parlor sipping their India tea. Micah saw at once that Matthew was troubled and spoke lightly of other things until finally Matthew said abruptly, "Something's bothering me."

"I thought there might be."

Instantly Matthew grinned. "You always did have an insight into what went on in my mind. I wonder why."

"Oh, I don't think I have any more insight than anyone else, but obviously you've been troubled ever since you got back from England. Would you care to tell me about it?"

Matthew sipped the tea, stared at the blue figures on the cup, then shook his head. "I'm trying to decide whether or not to change my name—to become Matthew Rochester."

"Why does that trouble you?"

Surprised, Matthew stared at Micah. "Wouldn't it trouble you? How would you like to be Micah Rochester?"

Taken by surprise, Micah leaned back and twirled the cup around on his strong fingers. "I hadn't thought of it," he admitted. "I suppose it does make a difference if you choose to take the name of Rochester. Not to me," he added hastily, "nor to any in the family."

"Pa says it's up to me," Matthew muttered. He shifted nervously, then shook his head, doubt clouding his eyes. "I'm going to have to decide something very soon."

"Whatever you do won't change the way any of us feels about you. I hope you believe that, Matthew."

"That's good to hear, and I know you mean it." He sat there for a time listening as Micah spoke slowly, thinking, *He's a good man. Got more sense than I have, and more than Dake. He's the smartest of all of us. I suppose it's fitting that he'd be the preacher. Dake's too hot-tempered, and I'm not fit for an office like that.* Finally he ended the conversation by saying abruptly, "I'll be leaving soon for Virginia. I must go see Leo's family there. Well, my family too, I suppose." Troubled thoughts passed through his mind, and he finally left after a brief farewell, leaving Micah to stare after him with a thoughtful gaze.

🛡   🛡   🛡

"Now, *that* is what I call a pretty dress!"

Rachel had just helped Keturah into a dress that she had gotten from Marian. The two women were much the same size, and very little alteration was necessary. It was an azure blue gown of a lightweight velvet material with a low-cut square neckline edged with white lace. The elbow-length funnel sleeves had long, elegant lace ruffles that fell almost to the wrists, and the bodice was white, with small lace insets and delicate blue ribbon bows all the way to the waist. The overskirt was free from any decoration, but the petticoat was very full and layered with white lace edged with delicate embroidery.

Keturah looked in the mirror and said, "Do you really think it looks good? On me, I mean?"

"You look beautiful, Keturah!"

"Really?" Keturah hesitated for a moment, swallowed hard, then turned to face Rachel. "Do . . . do you think Micah will like it?"

"I'm sure he will," Rachel said, wondering if she had the heart to tell her of the dangers of infatuation. She had tried before, but now seeing the sparkle in Keturah's light blue eyes, she decided to make one more attempt.

"Keturah," she said slowly, "I want to tell you something."

"Have I done somethin' wrong again?"

"Why, we've all done something wrong, I suppose," Rachel smiled, "but it's what *might* happen that I'm concerned about."

"What is it?"

"I am afraid you may have become too fond of Micah."

Instantly Keturah's eyes flew to meet those of Rachel Bradford's. "What's wrong with liking Micah?"

The question made Rachel uncomfortable. She had great difficulty sometimes talking to Keturah. The things that other young women had learned through a lifetime of trial and error growing up in society, Keturah had missed. There was a primitive quality in her that sometimes was very attractive, but at other times led to embarrassing situations. Keturah had seen the rough side of life firsthand with her eyes fully open, and at times she said things so blatantly unladylike that Rachel often flushed and did not know how to correct her. Now she said carefully, "I've talked to you about this before, Keturah, but it's not unusual for young women to admire an older man too much. I did the same myself a few years ago. It's a wonder I didn't make a fool out of myself when I was not much younger than you."

Keturah stared at Rachel Bradford. She had learned to love the young woman very much, and now she whispered, "You don't think I ought to like him?"

"Why, of course I think you should like Micah! He's a fine young man, and there would be something wrong if you didn't like him. But what I'm saying is . . . well, don't expect too much out of Micah."

Keturah was not quite sure of Rachel's meaning. She stared wide eyed at the young woman and listened as Rachel stumbled, and finally she said, "I don't rightly understand all of what you're saying, Rachel."

Rachel saw that the simplicity of the girl was a great handicap, and now she said only, "Just be careful."

All afternoon Keturah thought about the ball. She had built it up in her mind as a time when she would be close to Micah Bradford. She thought back to the time when she had looked into his eyes and had said simply, "I'll be your woman, Micah." She knew it had embarrassed him, but nothing in her heart had changed. Never in her life had she met anyone with the kindness of this young man who had saved her from dishonor and, perhaps, even from death when she was sick. She was a single-minded girl, simple in almost every way. Yet there were complexities in her deeper than anyone knew. Deep down she longed for security, for someone to love—and someone to love her. Love she had not known, and since coming to the Bradford household, she had discovered a whole world that she had never comprehended, never even dreamed about. She had been almost shocked to see the affection between Daniel Bradford and his wife, Marian, and almost as much between Dake and Jeanne.

"If Jeanne can love Dake, I don't see why I can't love Micah," she said. She was troubled by what Rachel had said, but determined that she would make Micah proud of her at the ball.

🔔   🔔   🔔

When the time came for the group to leave for the ball, Keturah found herself almost trembling. She was wearing the blue dress, and when Micah came up and smiled at her, saying, "Why, you look very nice, Keturah," she could do no more than nod and give him a grateful smile. He was wearing a dark green suit of fine wool with an overcoat that came below his knees, had a small turned-down collar, small turned-back cuffs, and it was worn open to reveal a dark green waistcoat, buttoned from top to bottom, with embroidered edges and the ruffles of a white silk shirt at the neck and wrists. The breeches were loose-fitting and ended just below the knees, held in place with buckles, and a pair of white silk stockings and black leather shoes finished his look. She thought, *He'll be the handsomest fellow there.*

Lawrence Oliver arrived in his family's ornate carriage—and was deflated when Rachel said sweetly, "Keturah is going with us, Lawrence. Isn't that nice?"

"Why . . . I didn't . . ."

Oliver's face was such a mixture of chagrin and disgust that Rachel giggled aloud. "I knew you'd be pleased. And you can have all the dances with her you please. You don't mind, do you, Micah?"

Aware of Oliver's discomfort, Micah saw the mischief lurking in his sister's eyes and understood at once what she was up to. "Why, certainly not." He winked at Keturah, adding, "It'll be an education for you, Keturah."

Keturah, nervous as she was, took a keen pleasure in puncturing the pompous manner of the young man. When they entered the large carriage, instead of sitting down with Micah across from Rachel and Oliver, she plunked herself firmly down between them and asked Oliver on the way, "You got a plug of tobaccer on you? I left mine to home."

As soon as the trio entered the ballroom, Marian came over to them at once, complimenting the women on their dresses. "You're just in time," she said. "The music's just starting."

Keturah looked around at the ballroom and was stunned. It was a large oval room with floor-length windows on three walls. Dark blue drapes covered each window, were swagged to each side and held in place with gold-colored bows, and the material flowed down onto the floor in large folds. The floors were made of polished white marble with swirls of gold running through it, and the walls were painted the brightest white she had ever seen and were covered with numerous Oriental paintings. The white palladian, coffered ceiling had gilded edges around each panel, and the room was richly gilded in architectural detail around each window, door, and around the chimney piece. Four large crystal chandeliers hung from the ceiling down the center of the room, and silver candlesticks had been placed on all the tables and in sconces between the windows to help light the large room. The fireplace was made of white marble with gilded detail, had a long mantel with Chinese vases and silver boxes placed along the edge, and above it on the wall hung a large Rococo oval mirror. Mahogany chairs covered with dark blue and gold silk damask lined three of the walls, and small mahogany card tables were placed along the walls and between some of the chairs. Six long mahogany tables, covered with the finest white cloths, lined one of the walls and were heavily covered with silver plates with an assortment of cheeses, platters of meats, trays of breads, and bowls of fruits and desserts. Cut-crystal glasses sparkled like diamonds in the candlelight.

She had never danced at a ball such as this, but both Jeanne and Rachel had instructed her, and even Sam had danced with her. She had found it fun with Sam, but now as Micah came and said, "I believe this is our dance, Keturah," she suddenly felt fear. *I'm so clumsy. What if I fall down?* She almost panicked, but then when she began to move with the rhythm of the music, Keturah found that she could at least keep her feet. She noted that Lawrence Oliver had practically dragged Rachel away, and she called out, "Don't fergit, Lawrence—we'll have them dances together."

As they moved to the sound of the music, Micah cocked his head to one side, saying, "You and Rachel are treating Oliver pretty badly, but he deserves it."

"They look very good together, don't they, Sam?" Marian said, watching the couple.

"They look okay."

Surprised at Sam's surly tone, Marian turned to look at him. She studied the tense quality of his face and decided to ask no more questions. "Well, I'm afraid you're going to have to dance with an old woman, Sam."

This cheered Sam up considerably, for he had admired Marian for a long time. The two moved out onto the floor, and finally Sam said abruptly, "Micah doesn't treat Keturah right."

"Why, I'm surprised to hear you say that, Sam!"

"Well, I don't mean he's unkind to her or anything like that! But he just sort of—well, he *ignores* her."

"I'm sure it's unintentional," Marian said quietly. "Micah has beautiful manners."

"Well, I got beautiful manners, too!" Sam said pugnaciously.

Marian laughed aloud. "Yes you do, Sam. A little bit rough and crude, but you're a very fine young man."

Perhaps Marian should have taken more of a hint from this, but she thought little about it. Sam, however, after dancing with Marian, retired to the refreshment table and stood watching as Keturah danced across the floor with Micah.

Sarah Dennison entered the ballroom half an hour after the Bradfords, and Mrs. Dennison was displeased. She turned to her husband, saying, "It's a shame that Mr. Potter can't be here, Thomas."

"A man with a case of measles can't go to a ball, Helen," her husband replied shortly. The note from Potter saying that he was ill had come only that morning, and despite Sarah's plea to remain home, her parents had insisted that she attend with them. Now they moved to the line of chairs, where Sarah sat down, a forlorn expression on her face.

Sam was watching Micah and Keturah dance. He saw Micah look up, a startled expression on his face. Following the direction of his brother's gaze, he saw that he was staring at Sarah Dennison, who was sitting in a line of chairs. To Sam's surprise, Micah simply walked away, left Keturah standing alone, and headed straight for Sarah Dennison.

"Why, look at what he's doing, Marian! He needs a larruping!" Sam growled. He saw that Keturah was deeply hurt by what had happened and started to move toward her, but then he settled back on his heels, his mouth settling into a firm line. "I can't go running to her every time he acts like she's not there! Let her hurt a little bit. It'll do her good."

Keturah *was* hurt. She stood in the middle of the floor watching Micah, who had, without the briefest word of apology, turned and left her alone. She was aware that others on the floor were staring at her, and her face grew warm. *I ain't fit for a place like this, but he shouldn't have left me!* She turned and made her way through the dancers and was leaving when Sam caught up with her.

"Wait a minute! Where you going?"

"Home! I won't stay here!"

"Aw, come on, Keturah. Let's me and you dance."

"I don't want to!" she snapped.

"Well, I do," Sam growled. "Come on, now. You can't go running away like a whipped puppy!"

"Leave me alone, Sam!"

Sam, however, took her arm firmly and guided her back to the floor. "I'm not as good a dancer as Micah," he said, "but I don't want you to go home."

Keturah looked up into Sam's face. He was not as tall as Micah or Dake, but there was a strength in him, and his bright blue eyes matched her own. "You don't really want to dance with me."

"I wouldn't have asked you if I didn't. Come on, now."

Across the room, Micah was totally unaware of the deep hurt and embarrassment he had caused. He had gone straight to Sarah, who had looked up at him, and as he spoke, saying, "Hello, Sarah," he noticed unhappiness in her eyes. "Come along. It's time to be foolish," he said.

Sarah rose and gave an agonizing look toward her parents. They were watching her, she saw, but she turned and let Micah escort her to the floor. As they began to dance she said nothing for a time, but she was very conscious of her parents' anger. "You shouldn't have done this, Micah. You know my parents won't like it."

"Do you like it?" Micah demanded. "That's all I care about."

Sarah did like it, indeed. As Micah guided her through the figures of the dance, she realized she would have been perfectly happy if it were not for her parents' displeasure. She pushed the thought of them out of her mind for a moment, and as the two danced to the sound of the sprightly music, Sarah found that they danced very well together.

Micah said, "I usually don't like to dance, but I enjoy dancing with you."

"You're a very good dancer," she said, looking up into his eyes.

"Sarah," Micah said abruptly, "have you made up your mind to get rid of that fellow Potter?"

He had no sooner spoken when suddenly Thomas Dennison appeared at their side and said abruptly, "Mr. Bradford, a word with you. . . !"

Micah was shocked and stopped abruptly. Sarah's hand was in his, and he said, "Yes, sir, but is this the place?"

"This place is as good as any!" Thomas Dennison was not a particularly tactful man, and he knew that others were watching, but he cared not a whit what others thought. "I have tried to be a gentleman about this, but you have not, sir."

"I'm sorry you should think that, Mr. Dennison."

"What else am I to think? I've done everything but run you off with a pistol! Man, have you no sensitivity at all?"

"I think I do," Micah said. He was angered now and did not care that the eager ears of many were listening. "I'm sorry if I've offended you, but—"

"It seems that nothing but a public spectacle will satisfy you, Bradford, and, therefore, I'm going to make this public. Come along, Sarah."

"Father—" Sarah tried to protest, but her father's strong hand closed on her arm as she felt herself pulled from the floor. She was humiliated and bit her lip to hide her emotion. The music came to a halt, and Thomas Dennison, his face flushed with anger, said, "Ladies and gentlemen—" He waited until every dancer had stopped and even the musicians were watching, then he announced in a clear voice, "I wish to announce the engagement of my daughter to Mr. Silas Potter."

There were the usual sounds that accompanied such announcements, but Micah heard none of them. He was angry and shaken to the core. He tried to meet Sarah's eyes, but she refused to look at him. Without a word, he turned and walked out of the ballroom.

Sam was standing beside Keturah and knew instantly the battle raging in his brother. "Keturah," he said, "you wait right here. I need to speak to Micah." He turned and left the room quickly. When he exited from the building, he called out at once, "Micah!"

Micah, who was almost blinded by disappointment mixed with anger, turned, saying roughly, "What do you want, Sam?"

"I want you to behave like a man!"

Micah stared at Sam, baffled. He was still seething over Dennison's actions and shook his head. "I don't know what you're talking about!" he said angrily.

"You're treating Keturah as if she didn't even exist! You're supposed to be a preacher, or going to be, and here you're acting like some kind of a mad dog! What's the matter with you anyhow?"

"Shut up, Sam!"

"I won't shut up! And what's more, I want you to know that if you don't straighten up and act better toward Keturah, I'm going to whip you!"

Micah blinked with surprise and then shook his head. "Sam, get out of my way!" He reached out and shoved Sam just to move him aside. He was caught completely off guard when Sam drove a looping overhead blow that caught him square in the mouth. Sam was strong and quick, and the blow had driven Micah backward. He struggled to keep his feet, but before he did so Sam was on him, his arms flailing like windmills.

Micah went down flat on his back, and then anger ran through him like a flame. Roaring, he jumped to his feet and swung at Sam, catching him high on the head. It hurt his knuckles, and he thought he had broken a finger. The pain was so sharp he lowered his hands, and instantly Sam pummeled him.

The two scuffled and blows were thrown quickly. Sam was much lighter than Micah and not nearly so strong, but he was faster. Micah felt his face swelling from the blows that hit him, and then he caught Sam with a hard blow in the stomach. Sam doubled up and almost went to the ground.

"Stop it, you fools!"

Micah and Sam both turned, out of breath, their faces bleeding, to find their father standing beside them. His face was a thunderstorm, and he said angrily, "I'm ashamed of both of you! Brawling in the street! Now, go home!"

"Pa," Sam said through swollen lips, "he's not treating Keturah right."

"So you're going to fight with him out here? That's going to make him better? Get home, Sam! And, Micah, you're a grown man! I shouldn't have to speak to you like this, but I think it's time for you to go, too!"

Micah looked up at his father, shame filling his face, which was bleeding. "You're right, Pa," he said. "I don't know what's the matter with me. I just—" He looked up and saw that the Dennisons had come outside, along with many others. Sarah was standing beside her father, and he could not read the expression on her face. He did hear Mrs. Dennison say, "Look at that, Sarah! That's the kind of man he is! Brawling like a dog in the street with his own brother!"

Micah Bradford looked around and saw the displeasure on every face, even Rachel's, who had always been supportive. Without a word he turned and walked away, wondering why it had all started and what a fool he had made of himself in front of everyone. He hung his head in shame as he walked home, thinking of the disgrace he had caused his family.

22

A MIDNIGHT VISIT

CAREFULLY MATTHEW LAID THE FINAL LINES of paint on the canvas held firmly in the easel in front of him. April had come now, and the bright yellow sunlight streamed through the window. Matthew remembered that it had been cold, with snow on the ground, when he had started Keturah's portrait, but now the singing of the birds outside the window and the mild, warm breeze that blew through from the outside made the large room pleasant. Stepping back, he cocked his head to one side and studied the effect of his last strokes.

"Not quite right," he murmured. "Hold it just for a moment, Keturah."

Keturah had been a good model. She had the ability to hold a pose for long periods of time. Now, although she had not moved for nearly thirty minutes, she still remained absolutely motionless. Only her eyes moved as she studied Matthew's face. She had grown fond of Matthew Bradford, for although he had built a wall around himself that she could not penetrate or understand, she knew there was a goodness and a fineness in him that had been missing from most men she had known from her earlier days. She admired the fine contours of his jaw and the rather aristocratic set of his features and thought of his past relationship with Abigail Howland. She had heard the whole story, of course, from Rachel and Jeanne, and it grieved her to think of it. She had a tender heart, though it was hidden under a rough exterior. All of her early years, being reared among the roughest of circumstances, had not scarred her. It had made her cautious of men, of course; otherwise she would not have survived. Still, she thought, *I wish Matthew wouldn't be so hard against Abigail. I don't guess she was a good woman, but she is now. I wonder why he can't see that?*

Matthew carefully traced a line with a fine brush and heard the door slam behind him. He smeared the line and turned to say with irritation,

"Sam, you wild bull! Don't you know how to come into a room?"

"Sure I do," Sam said carelessly. He moved over and stood beside his brother and stared at the picture critically. "Not bad," he admitted.

"Can I see, Matthew?" Keturah asked.

"You might as well. It's all finished except for this last line that this buffalo made me mar." He carefully redid the line as Keturah came and stood beside him. Her eyes grew wide, for he had not let her see the painting for some time.

"I don't look like that!" she declared.

"Yes you do," Sam nodded. "Just like that."

Matthew had decided to have Keturah seated on the wine-colored couch, and she wore a light green dress that had belonged to Rachel. Her hair was long enough now to comb back, and he had managed to bring out the rich dark colors of it, and the curls framed her face in a charming fashion. He also had caught the thick dark lashes, the slightly turned-up nose, and despite Keturah's protest had put the cleft in the chin. Now she looked at it and said, "It's so good, but I wish you'd left out the canyon in my chin."

"It makes you look firm," Sam asserted. He grinned at her and said, "It'll look good on the wall in my room."

Keturah could not grow angry at Sam Bradford. He had been close to her ever since he had first carried her into the house, falling on his backside as he stepped out of the wagon, which she often teased him about. Now she said firmly, "No, it's not yours!" Turning to Matthew she asked quickly, "What will you do with it, Matthew?"

"Well, I could sell it for a lot of money," Matthew grinned, "or I could give it to you."

"Please, Matthew, let me have it! I promise I'll keep it all my life!"

Matthew appeared to consider the proposition. The girl made a fetching picture as she stood before him, but, of course, he had intended for her to have the portrait all the time. Now he said, "All right. It's yours."

"Oh, Matthew!" Keturah threw herself forward and hugged Matthew tightly, pinioning his arms to his sides. "Thank you so much!"

Matthew winked at Sam and said, "You've got to learn to express your feelings more freely, Keturah." He teased her gently like this, and when she released him, he said, "Don't be afraid to just let yourself go."

A rich flush appeared in Keturah's cheeks, for she knew she had been forward. Shooting a glance at Sam, who was grinning broadly, she snapped, "Don't you be laughing! If you could paint a picture like that I'd hug you, too!"

"Well, I let you shoot my cannon, didn't I? I didn't get any hug for that."

Matthew began to pack his paints and brushes together as the two argued loudly. Finally he said, "Don't move the painting today, Keturah. It won't be dry for twenty-four hours." He left the room, and as soon as he was gone, Keturah went and stood before the painting. She was silent for a long time.

Finally Sam asked, "What are you thinking about?"

"I was just thinkin', Sam. I ain't never had my likeness made before. Probably won't ever have it again."

"Sure you will."

"No, I don't think so." She cocked her head to one side and studied the painting carefully. "Do you really think that looks like me, Sam?"

"Spittin' image," Sam nodded cheerfully. "Just look in the mirror and you'll see. You look a lot better than you did when I hauled you in here. You looked like a sick chicken then."

Keturah thought of the weeks she had spent in the Bradford household, and her heart grew warm. It had been a time of kindness and warmth and happiness for her, such as she had never known. Never had she dreamed that there could be such a kind family as the Bradfords, for she had known nothing like it in her brief lifetime. Now something came to her mind and a shadow crossed her face.

Seeing the frown, Sam asked, "What's the matter?"

"It's . . . it's about you and Micah, Sam."

"What about us?"

"You shouldn't have fought with him."

"I ought to have busted him up worse than I did," Sam stated bluntly. With all his good humor Sam had an explosive temper, and as he thought back to the night of the ball when he had fought with Micah, his lips tightened into a firm line and he shook his head adamantly. "I may whip him again before it's over with! He didn't have any call to treat you like that!"

Keturah hesitated. She had a deep affection for Sam but felt herself in love with Micah Bradford. Finally she said softly, "Sam, you don't know what you're talking about."

"Why don't I know? He was wrong, Keturah."

"I reckon maybe he was a little bit, but you don't know what it's like to be without a family, Sam. I never had nobody except Ma, and most of the time I didn't have much of her."

It was the most revealing thing Keturah had ever said about her past. Sam, of course, had heard from Micah that Keturah's mother had been a common woman, and that she had known nothing of love, or care, or consideration. Now he studied her face and saw a gentleness in her lips and a thoughtfulness in her eyes. It gave him pause, and finally he said, "I've got a good family. I've always known that."

Keturah dropped her head for a moment, then finally turned and walked to the window, saying nothing. She stood staring out, and Sam, surprised by the suddenness of her movement, walked over to stand behind her. "Did it bother you that Micah and I had a fight?"

"Yes it did."

"Why, we've fought before. I never won one, of course, but some of these days I will."

Turning to the young man, Keturah suddenly put her hand on his arm. "Please don't fight with him anymore—especially not over me. I . . . I don't know how to tell you, Sam, what it's meant to be here in your house with your family. I couldn't stand it if I was the cause of bringing trouble."

Usually Sam Bradford was a voluble young man, but something about the young woman's soft words struck him and he held his tongue. He looked into her eyes for a moment, then said, "Why, you couldn't break up our family. Micah and I have had our differences before. So have Dake and I, and Matthew. I've even had fights with Rachel. Some pretty hot ones. She's got a temper, you know. Not like me."

At that statement Keturah smiled. "Not like you, Sam? You were like a cannon going off when you went for Micah. You've got a *terrible* temper!"

"I do?" Sam seemed genuinely surprised. "I never knew that." He shook his head and a thoughtful look passed across his face. "I'll have to watch it, I guess."

"I never had a family, so maybe I see it a little clearer than you do. But, Sam, don't ever forget to be kind, even when your brothers, or your sister, hurt you."

Sam stared at Keturah. He was conscious of her hand on his arm gripping it tightly. She was very serious about this, he saw. He had become very fond of this young woman, and suddenly he leaned forward impulsively and kissed her on the cheek. Surprise flared in her eyes and he grinned rashly. "Now you're a member of the family, so I reckon I can give you a kiss once in a while." She was staring at him so oddly that it flustered him. "Well," he muttered, "I reckon you're right about Micah. I'll make it right with him." He turned to leave and stopped to give a glance at the picture. "It looks just like you," he said. "I still think you ought to let me keep it in my room."

He turned and left quickly, leaving Keturah to stare after him. She moved over to look at the picture once again, studied it carefully, then shook her head in wonder at how skillfully Matthew had taken a little paint and a piece of canvas and had put it all together so that she looked out at herself. "Ain't that a wonder now," she breathed.

🜚   🜚   🜚

Micah stood awkwardly before his stepmother, meeting her eyes with some difficulty. He had come by to talk with his father about a new idea he had for the foundry, and Marian had greeted him, saying, "Daniel's with my father. They have this time every morning."

"Well, I'll see him later at the factory," Micah shrugged, then turned to leave.

"Just a minute, Micah." Marian Bradford had been thinking a lot about Micah. She and Daniel had talked about the situation concerning Keturah Burns and Sarah Dennison, and now she said bluntly, "Micah, I've always thought you were the most level-headed of all of your brothers, but you're behaving very badly."

Instantly Micah flushed, for he knew exactly what Marian spoke of. "You're talking about the fight I had with Sam? Well—"

"I'm talking about the way you behave toward Keturah, and of course your behavior at the ball was inexcusable. To walk off and leave her standing alone! I can't believe you did that, Micah."

Micah shook his head. He had no defense and had been embarrassed ever since the night of the ball. He started to speak, but at that moment his father came in, and Micah said, "Hello, Pa."

"I'm glad you came by, Micah. I've been wanting to talk to you. I was embarrassed and humiliated by the way you acted at the ball."

"Dear, I've already spoken to Micah about that," Marian said.

Very rarely did Daniel Bradford manifest any anger toward his sons, and this was especially true of his behavior toward Micah. Dake had sometimes given him a hard time, and Sam, with his pranks and mischievous tricks, sometimes drove him to distraction—but Micah had always been the steady one among the brothers. Daniel said so now. "I wouldn't have been surprised if one of your brothers had done a thing like that, but I thought you were more mature, son."

"Well, I guess I'm not," Micah mumbled. He hated to displease these two. He had always admired his father and, of course, felt a great respect for his stepmother. Now he said, "I don't know what to tell you. I just made a mistake."

"Have you told Keturah that?" Marian demanded.

"Why no, I haven't."

"Then you should at once. I felt so sorry for her. After all, she hasn't had many advantages."

"I'd hate to think," Daniel broke in, "that she'd get her ideas about our family from your behavior, Micah. Now, I'll say no more about it, but I'm disappointed in you."

Micah left the house in as low a mood as he had known for years. Ever since the night of the ball and the fracas over his treatment of Keturah, and his brawl with Sam, he had been miserable. A fine sensitivity ran through him, and he did not need anyone to tell him he had behaved badly. Walking along the street, he made up his mind abruptly. *I've got to apologize to Keturah—should have done it already. . . .*

Instead of going to the foundry he turned and went home, where he encountered Sam almost immediately. His younger brother had evidently seen him coming and headed him off by stepping around the house.

"Micah, I've got to talk to you."

Micah turned and faced Sam, saying, "Before you say anything else, I'm sorry, Sam, that I hit you. I shouldn't have done that. You were exactly right to bust me. I deserved it."

Sam had been pumping himself up all morning for his meeting with Micah. Now he was somewhat taken aback. "Well," he muttered, "it looks like you stole my thunder. I was gonna tell you the same thing. I got so mad I wasn't thinking, but I shouldn't have hit you, Micah. I'm right sorry about that."

Micah summoned a grin. "When a man makes a fool out of himself, he deserves to get his face punched."

"Well, to tell the truth—I thought you were a real idiot!"

"That's putting it kindly, but it's not the first time."

"It's the first time I ever heard of you behaving like this." Sam was roughly dressed, for he had been working on the plumbing system that fed hot water into the bathroom. Their house was one of the few in Boston that boasted such a thing, and it was Sam's invention. He stood there now, grease on his hands and a smear on his cheek, studying his brother. "You've always been the one I went to when I was in a jam. I never thought about you doing anything wrong. Kind of caught me off guard, I reckon."

His brother's words warmed Micah, but he shook his head. "Well, I appreciate that, but I've been wrong lots of times, and I'm headed right now to tell Keturah I'm sorry. Do you know where she is?"

"She's probably still in the study. Matthew finished her picture, and she won't leave it alone. Just sits there staring at it."

"Well, I'll go right now."

Micah entered the house and went at once to the small study where he, indeed, found Keturah seated, looking at her portrait. "That's a nice picture," Micah said as he entered. Keturah came to her feet and faced him. There was a wariness about her, and a vulnerability, he noted at once. *I've hurt her pretty bad*, Micah thought and tried to find the words that would somehow express his feelings.

"Keturah, I don't know what came over me at the ball, to walk away and leave you like that. I just came to tell you I'm sorry."

"Oh, that's all right." Keturah was taken aback by Micah's words. She was breathing more rapidly than usual, and her eyes were alight and a smile came to her lips. "You don't have to apologize."

"Why, of course I do," Micah said firmly. He came forward and put out his hand. "Will you forgive me?"

Keturah put her hand out and Micah's big hand closed around it. It was a strong, powerful hand, and she found herself looking into his eyes, thinking of how her life now was so good and it was all his doing. Gratitude was rich and strong and full in her, and she squeezed his hand, whispering, "You've been powerful good to me, Micah."

Micah was very conscious of the girl's large eyes. She had startling blue eyes, widely spaced, overshadowed by thick dark lashes, and he remembered how pitiful she had been when he had first found her. Now he released her hand quickly, too quickly almost, and said, "Well, if you forgive me, I feel much better."

"It wasn't nothin'."

Relieved that he had made his peace with Keturah, Micah turned and studied the picture. "It doesn't do you justice. You're prettier than that."

Flustered and almost shocked by his words, Keturah turned to Micah, saying, "No, that ain't so."

"It is to me. You've become a very attractive young lady. I won't be surprised when we have to start ordering young men away from here who are coming to court you."

Keturah wanted to say, "I don't want anyone to court me. I just want you," but she knew that would be wrong. Finally she said, "Maybe you'd like to have the picture. Sam wants it, but if you want it, Matthew gave it to me."

Micah shook his head. "It's too valuable for that. You keep it, Keturah. One day there'll be a young man come along wanting to marry you, and he's the man that ought to have this."

A fleeting look of disappointment touched the large, expressive eyes of Keturah Burns. She said nothing for so long a time that Micah finally said, "Well, it's a beautiful painting. I know you'll treasure it always." He said a few more pleasant things and then turned and left the room.

"I wish you wanted it," Keturah whispered. Somehow the joy in the painting had left her. She had planned to give it to Micah, and he had refused her gift. She went to the window and stared out, and suddenly tears came to her eyes. "He didn't want it," she whispered, and although the sunshine outside was bright and cheerful, there was little joy in her heart.

☙ ☙ ☙

For several days Micah went about his work at the foundry in a mechanical fashion. He visited his father's house once for supper and found Matthew there as well. It was a good evening, but after they left the house together, Matthew said, "You hardly said a dozen words, Micah. What's wrong with you?"

"Why, nothing, I don't suppose. Just don't have much to say."

Matthew was, of course, well aware of the situation, and he reached out and grabbed Micah's arm. "You're walking around like a man in a daze," he said almost accusingly. "Are you in love with Sarah Dennison?"

Shocked by the tenor of Matthew's tone, Micah said sharply, "I know she doesn't need to marry Silas Potter!"

"That's not what I asked you. If you're not in love with her, what do you care who she marries?"

Stung by Matthew's words, Micah lifted his eyebrows and said more sharply than he intended, "I don't think you're anyone to be giving advice to the lovelorn! Not after the way you've treated Abigail!"

Anger flared in Matthew's eyes, and he said abruptly, "That's none of your business!"

"Of course it's my business. You're my brother, aren't you? Besides, if you're telling *me* what to do about women, I suppose I can do the same."

For a long moment Matthew stared at Micah, then shook his head. "You're changing. You were always so calm and quiet and reasonable—but now you're as touchy as a man without skin! What's the matter with you?"

"I don't know, Matthew." Micah tried to laugh but then frowned, his eyes hooded. "It seems I can't do anything right anymore."

The two walked along the sidewalk slowly, neither of them speaking much. When they finally separated, Matthew headed toward his rooms in the center of town, and he said quietly, "No offense. My own life is a mess, but I don't like to see you unhappy."

Micah continued to walk along. It was late now, and the shadows were falling. Instead of going home, he walked down to the harbor, where, for a long time, he sat watching the sun sink into the horizon. It burned the water for a time into a crimson mass of color outlining the tall high-masted ships that lined the harbor. The smell of the sea was rich and sharp and tangy, and overhead the gulls were crying in their hoarse voices. They swooped down on his head, but he waved them away and continued to walk along the beach.

Finally the moon came up, and he was startled when he looked at his pocket watch. "Past midnight," he said. Dissatisfied with himself, and unhappy, Micah started back toward home. He thought of how he had fallen into ill favor with all of his family. "It seems like I've been bawled out by everybody," he murmured, "and not that I don't deserve it. I've been behaving like an idiot!"

The moon was a silver globe in the sky with tiny pockmarks. A thought came to him, *I read somewhere that some people believe that the moon causes lovesickness. That's why people are called loonies. They don't behave like normal people. I guess I must be a loony then. I've certainly behaved like one.*

Abruptly he changed his direction as a new thought came to him. He was a thoughtful young man, but suddenly the impulse came strong to see Sarah. He knew she would be in bed by this time, but he set his jaw and hurried along the dark streets of Boston until he reached the Dennison house. All the windows were dark, and he made his way quietly along the edge of the property.

"I'll probably get shot," he muttered as he ascended the low roof that stretched under Sarah's window. The sound of his feet on the shakes seemed to be loud, and he fully expected a window to fly open and Mr. Dennison to challenge him with a gun.

Nothing happened, however, as he stealthily crept to Sarah's window. Taking a deep breath, he tapped gently on the windowpane. No sound. Again he tapped. Finally, after the third or fourth time, he tapped loudly and whispered, "Sarah!" Instantly he heard someone, then peering in, he saw Sarah coming through the darkness. The moon illuminated her face, and as she was drawing a robe about her, tying it at the waist, she came to the window.

"Micah, you shouldn't be here!"

Sarah's face was troubled, but somehow Micah was aware of the gentleness that always attracted him—had drawn him as no other woman ever had. She was unsmiling and the silver moonlight seemed to warm her cheeks and light her eyes with the brightness. He had not intended to say it, but suddenly he exclaimed, "Sarah, you're so beautiful!"

The words were softly whispered but with an intensity that seemed to strike Sarah with the force of a blow. She was not accustomed to being told she was beautiful. Micah's bulky form was outlined against the moon, and she whispered, "No, I'm not beautiful."

"Can I come in?"

"No you can't come in! Have you lost your mind?"

"I think I have, Sarah." Micah stood there stubbornly and said, "Look, it's going to be a little awkward if someone passes along and sees me standing here talking to you in your window."

"It'll be worse if they come to my room and find you!" Sarah exclaimed. "Micah, go away!"

"I won't do it. Let me in."

Seeing the stubbornness in Micah's lips, Sarah was dumbfounded. She had remembered how he had come to her window once before, had kissed her and held her tightly in his arms. She had thought about that every day since it happened. She felt afraid, for she did not know how to handle the situation, but finally when she saw he was determined, she took a deep breath and said, "All right, but only for a moment."

Stepping inside, Micah looked down at Sarah. Her hair was down, and she brushed a lock of it back from her forehead as she stood looking up at him.

"What do you want, Micah?"

"I had to see you."

"You shouldn't have come like this."

"There's no other place for us to meet. Sarah," he said, "I don't know what's wrong with me. I'm acting like a crazy man."

"You certainly are!"

"Well, if you think that, you agree with everyone else. Every member of my family has ripped me up one side and down the other for the way I behaved at the ball."

"You were very rude to Keturah."

"I didn't even think about her. When I saw you sitting there, it was like everything else was blocked out." Micah shook his head in wonder. "I never behaved like that before. I've always been so methodical, but somehow ever since I met you, there's been something wrong with the way I think and the way I act."

The moonlight flooded the room, and Sarah studied Micah's strong face. His straw-colored hair was almost silver in the light of the moon, and a certain puzzlement lurked in his hazel eyes, revealing an uncertainty that was not his nature. As always, he spoke slowly in a gentle drawl, but his voice was troubled and a nervousness marked his manner.

Suddenly Micah reached out and put his hands on Sarah's shoulders. Her flesh was warm and soft, and he could smell the scent of lilacs in her hair. She stirred him deeply, and he said huskily, "Sarah, I'm in love with you."

"You mustn't be!" Sarah was hardly able to speak. The touch of his hands stirred her, and she wanted to pull back, but at the same time wanted to move closer. His closeness caused her to tremble, and it frightened her. When he pulled her forward, putting his arms around her, she made one attempt to break away, but it was a halfhearted move. His hands left her shoulders and pressed against her back, drawing her into his arms. Her lips were half parted, and as she looked up, she saw he was going to kiss her. She had one impulse to pull away, to turn her head, but then his lips were on hers, firm and demanding. She found herself being drawn into his embrace and his caress with a willingness that shocked her. Her lips suddenly had their own pressure and her arms went up around his neck. For this one moment all of her fears and anxieties fled. She was only conscious of the strength in his arms as he held her tight. She clung to him with an abandon she had never known in her entire life. Time suddenly ceased to exist, and she knew that this man truly loved her.

"Sarah," Micah whispered when he lifted his head, "do you feel like I do? Do you care for me at all?"

"I . . . I can't say."

"You know if you love me."

"It's not that simple. Turn me loose, Micah."

"I won't!" Holding her closer, Micah said, "I've never kissed a woman like this before. I've never felt what I feel for you, and I never will. You can't marry Potter."

At the sound of the word "Potter" something seemed to break within Sarah. All her fears came back to her and she thought of her parents, and suddenly, placing her hand against Micah's chest, she said, "Please—you have to go now!"

"But Sarah—"

"Quickly! I can't talk to you anymore!"

Micah stood there helplessly in the warm moonlight. He saw that Sarah was not far from tears. He also saw the fear in her, and he said quietly, "Never take counsel of your fears, Sarah," but he understood that more talk was hopeless. He stepped back up to the window and crawled outside. He cast one look at her and saw that she had turned her back and that her shoulders were shaking. He started to speak again and finally said, "Don't ruin your life, and my life—and Potter's life. You love me. Nothing else matters." Then he descended to the ground, being as quiet as possible.

All the way home he thought of the sensation that had gone through him when he had held her tight and kissed her. "She must love me," he whispered. "A woman couldn't kiss a man like that unless she did love him."

As soon as Micah left, Sarah moved unsteadily to the bed and sat down. She was trembling, shocked with the emotions that his embrace and his caress had stirred in her. Confusion came as she thought of the problems that loving him had brought. She slept no more that night, and the next morning, when it was time to go down, she had a wild impulse to simply leave the house, go to Micah, and never return. She could not do this, however, and finally, with circles under her eyes, she dressed woodenly and descended the stairs to try to pick up the strands of her life.

23

A Bitter Truth

IN ONE SENSE THE RULE OF THE Hanoverian kings was for England its most terrible tragedy. George I hated England thoroughly and refused even to learn to speak English. He was a dull German gentleman who preferred the company of wags and buffoons to any of his wiser English advisers. Lord Chesterfield, the noted statesman and orator, said of George, "England was too big for him."

George II was no improvement. Again Chesterfield summed up this second of the Hanoverian line by stating flatly, "Avarice, meanest of passions, was his ruling one, and I never knew him deviate into any generous action." Short and stout, with puffy features, George II was honest and brave, and at sixty he personally led the English in a victory over the French at Dettingen. This was the last time a sovereign of England would ever lead troops into battle.

But he was a miser and, for some reason never quite explained, had an undying hatred for his son, the Prince of Wales, Frederick Lewis. His mother had the same feelings for her son and declared frankly, "Fred is a nauseous beast, and he cares for nobody but his nauseous little self."

The Prince of Wales produced one son named George, who would grow up to rule the most powerful nation on the face of the earth. George III would be forced into leading his nation into an unpopular war against Englishmen who happened to be living in America.

George's education was a disaster. He himself appeared to be a rather virtuous young man, and over and over again his mother would tell him, "George, be a king!" These words were instilled in George, and he determined to be a patriot king, which to him meant only an unshakable faith in the divine right of kings. This doctrine had served some English kings well, but sometime between the death of Elizabeth I and the rise of her successor, the English had lost their taste for despots with unlimited power.

Nevertheless, George did his best. He ruled a nation of some ten million people, taught by the aristocracy whose self-indulgence included drink, gambling, racing, and dancing, unequaled anywhere in Europe. The consumption of gin rose to eleven million gallons a year under George's reign, and crime escalated so that it was unsafe for a woman to walk the streets.

George was a rather handsome man during his younger years—tall, well built, with dignified gray eyes, and he was determined to show the realm and his mother that he could indeed be a king. He fell in love with Lady Sarah Lennox, who produced child after child, and George eventually found himself the proud and happy father of fourteen healthy children.

The American Revolution proved to be the most difficult element in English government. Lord North, the prime minister since 1770, tried time and time again to explain to his king the difficulties of winning such a war, but since North himself did not understand the situation completely, he made several errors in judgment that actually helped bring on the war.

One cold morning, King George III sat across the table from Lord North and demanded, "Why is it that we cannot defeat the Americans? We have thousands of soldiers with the finest arms. The rebels are nothing but a bunch of ragtags, and yet this Washington has defeated British troops in open battle."

Lord North was not a handsome man, nor a particularly wise one. He would have liked nothing better than to resign, but this the king forbade. Now the prime minister sighed heavily and began again, he knew not how many times, to explain the difficulties. "Your Majesty, this war in America is not like any other war our nation has ever engaged in."

"And why is that?" George demanded. "We have beaten the Americans at Long Island, but they escaped to Manhattan. We beat them at Manhattan. They escaped to White Plains. We drove them out of New York, and they survived, winning a battle at Princeton. I do not understand it."

"It is difficult, Your Majesty. What we are facing is different from any war in Europe. On this continent we know how to fight wars. It is very simple, Sire. When we go to war with a country," North went on patiently, "we besiege towns, we fight battles, pawns are exchanged. We have negotiations. This goes on until finally one side or the other is declared to be a winner and carries off some portion of the nation it has defeated."

"Why are you telling me all this?"

"I am trying to explain that the war in America is different, Your Majesty. In our kind of wars we are civilized. Indians are not here to scalp people, riflemen do not deliberately aim at officers. Civilians do not rush out from their homes with their muskets in their hands to take part in the battle by shooting soldiers from behind stone walls and trees." North settled back in his chair, his pudgy face worried and his eyes cloudy with doubt. "In Europe, when we capture the enemy's major city and drive his forces from the field, he has sense enough to admit that he is defeated and to make peace."

"Then why cannot these stubborn fools in America see that? Why, having lost, do they go on fighting?"

"I cannot answer. They are madmen, I suppose. Colonials have lost the sense of England." North hesitated, then touched on a rather difficult subject, somewhat embarrassing. "Sire, I must mention that our generals have asked for another two hundred thousand troops."

The king's face flushed deeply. "Each bulletin says, 'I am winning the war. Now send me more troops. Send me more men. Send me more equipment.' And we have France and Spain waiting in the wings. We've had to devote sixteen ships of the line to deal with the problem of American privateers."

"All that is true, Your Majesty, regrettably. But the real problem is here at home." Receiving a disbelieving glance from the king, North went on quickly. "The national debt is higher than it has ever been in our history, and I fear the land tax will have to be raised to four shillings on the pound."

"Impossible! We cannot do it!"

"Then we cannot continue the war!" North said, spreading his hands wide. He was a good financial manager despite his other shortcomings. He knew all the signs of trouble; indeed, he faced them every day of his life. There were rising insurance rates due to the privateers, with taxes escalating daily. For a time he attempted to speak to the tall man across from him, but George shook his head stubbornly.

"I am not going to give up to a group of barbarians in America, and I'm not going to back down on Parliament! Let them complain about the taxes! Let them stand as Englishmen and all will be well!"

"You are going to have difficulty, Your Majesty, with France."

"With France?"

"Yes, Sire. I have mentioned this before, but our agents are well aware that France is supplying the Americans with war supplies."

"Then why do we not put a stop to it?"

"How?" Lord North spread his hands apart. "Would you have us declare war? We cannot afford a war with France right now." He set out again to try to get the simple facts into the head of the King of England. This seemed to be a very difficult task, but he was very patient. "You are aware of Beaumarchais, Your Majesty?"

"The playwright?"

"He has written a very clever play called *The Barber of Seville*, a satire on the aristocracy, Sire. It is not his play writing that disturbs us. He has led the life of a cheap adventurer, but he is a shrewd man and sympathetic to the revolution in America."

"How could a playwright be such a problem?"

"He has set up an import-export firm known as Hortalez and Company to supply the Americans. Our agents tell me that he has received a million livres as a loan from the French, the same from the Spanish, and has raised a private fortune. This company has bought equipment from the French arsenals—such as muskets that were being replaced in the army—and sent them to America."

George stared at his prime minister with disbelief. "I cannot believe it, but I insist we push forward. This is my final word on the subject."

"Yes, Your Majesty." Lord North rose heavily and, bowing, turned and left the room. *He is a fool even though he be King of England* was his thought. Already his mind was reaching out to the months, perhaps years, that lay before England. He saw his country being bled dry by the expense of such a war, and in his heart of hearts was convinced that there could be no victory for the British Empire in America.

Somehow the war seemed very far away to Sam Bradford. He found himself preoccupied and was not even aware that his behavior had changed. To his family, he was a different young man. Ever since Keturah had arrived at the Bradford house, he had been interested in her. As she had improved in appearance, he had found himself more and more preoccupied with this young woman.

At his father's insistence, Sam continued his studies of Latin and Greek and the classics, an endeavor he considered totally useless and kept him from the work he did think worthwhile—the spider catcher, which was now practically complete. Even though the end of his project was finally at hand, he had lost his early burst of enthusiasm.

"What's the matter with you, Sam? You act like you're going around in a fog!" Rachel demanded.

Sam had been moodily eating leftover corn bread soaked in buttermilk. His appetite, seemingly, was never affected by anything, and now he slurped noisily at the mixture without answering.

Rachel examined her younger brother carefully. "It's unnatural for you to be so quiet. Are you sick?"

"No, I'm not sick! I feel good," Sam muttered. He scraped the bottom of the mug with his spoon and looked at the last piece of corn bread. "Perhaps I'd better have that," he said. "No sense wasting it." Picking it up, he crumbled it into the mug, doused it liberally with buttermilk, and began eating again.

Rachel hesitated. She was an astute young woman with keen insight into most of her family. Sam, up until recently, had been simple enough in some ways. His schemes had been complicated, but he had been a cheerful, happy-go-lucky young man. For the past few weeks, however, he had been abnormally quiet, and Rachel felt she knew his problem. But she had no answer for him and finally left Sam alone in the kitchen.

Sam finished the corn bread and buttermilk, rummaged through the cabinet until he found a jar of preserved pears, and sat down, fishing them out and eating them steadily. As he ate he thought of Keturah and Micah, and by the time he had eaten three of the pears, he had made up his mind. Putting the remaining pears back in the cabinet, he turned and walked away, pausing only to wipe his hands and mouth on a dish towel, then went at once to the foundry. He found Micah working with a piece of white-hot iron, beating it into shape, and waited until Micah dipped it, sizzling, into a bucket of water.

"Micah, I have to talk to you."

Micah turned suddenly, for he had not heard Sam approach. He was wearing a leather apron over his working clothes, and his throat was hot and dry with the work.

"All right. Let's go get something to drink."

"No, I want to talk to you right now."

Startled by Sam's determination and the set of his jaw, Micah hesitated. *What's he got on his mind? He looks like he's prepared to run through an oak door if he has to.* "All right, Sam," he said, "let's go outside." The two moved outside until they got under the shade of an apple tree, and Sam said as soon as they stopped, "Micah, I've got to know what you're going to do about Keturah."

"Why, I've already apologized to her."

"I know that!" Sam snapped. "You think that solves all the problems? I want to know what you're going to *do* about her!"

Micah stared at his younger brother, puzzled and somewhat alarmed, and yet at the same time he was aware that there was some truth in what Sam was hinting at. He squeezed his hands together and stared down at the ground for a moment. A colony of ants were trundling some sort of food across the ground, all of them tugging and pushing, and he studied them for a long moment before he finally looked up and said quietly, "Say it all, Sam. What's on your mind?"

"Well, she's in love with you, Micah," Sam burst out. "Don't you know that?"

Shifting his feet uncomfortably, Micah raised his hand and ran it through his hair nervously. In truth he had suspected Keturah's feelings toward him. It would have been impossible for an astute man not to have noticed the looks Keturah gave him, and besides, she had already offered herself back in Pennsylvania, when they had stood together on the banks of the Delaware River. He remembered now how she had looked up at him and said, "I'll be your woman, Micah." Somehow Micah had managed to put this out of his mind, but now it came back to him, and suddenly he remembered how Keturah watched him constantly. He remembered too how she had held on to his hand when he had apologized. Now desperation came to him, and he said, "She's not in love with me. She's just infatuated."

"And you think she knows the difference? What's the matter with you, Micah? She's just a kid!"

"Well, I can't help it, Sam. What would you have me do?"

Sam Bradford was not a particularly deep thinker. He was, however, quick enough with his wits to see an answer when it was before his face. He straightened up and caught his brother's eye, then said, "The honorable thing is for you to go to her and tell her you don't love her."

"Why, I can't do that, Sam! It would hurt her!"

Sam Bradford shook his head in disgust. "When you've got to bob a dog's tail, Micah, what do you do? Cut off an inch today, then another inch the next day, and another inch the day after that? You think that's bein' kind to the dog?"

"That's ridiculous, Sam! That has nothing to do with what we're talking about!"

"For a smart man you're pretty stupid, Micah! You're hurting Keturah every day. You don't love her. She thinks you do, and sooner or later she's going to have to find out about it. You're in love with Sarah Dennison, aren't you?"

Micah bit his lower lip, then nodded slowly. "Yes I am."

"Then the only honorable thing for a man to do is to tell Keturah that you don't love her."

The inexorable logic of Sam's words struck Micah with the force of a blow from a fist. Suddenly it was all crystal clear, and he knew what he had to do. Slowly he said, "You're right, Sam. I should have seen it myself."

"You'll do it, then?"

"Yes, I'll do it, but I'd rather die a thousand deaths! I feel like such a fool."

"Feel like what you want to, but you owe it to her. Do it right now!"

"I've never seen you so adamant about anything, Sam." A thought suddenly brushed against Micah's mind, and the corners of his eyes drew down as he studied Sam carefully. "Do you have a vested interest in this?"

"What does that mean?"

"How do *you* feel about Keturah?"

Sam blushed. He had fair skin and hated it when he did so, but his voice was strong as he said, "I think a lot of her, but that doesn't matter. She's in love with you. She's gonna take about as bad a bump as a girl can get, so go on and get it over with. . . !"

✠ ✠ ✠

Keturah was out in the garden putting up stakes for beans. The sun was hot on her back, and she had put on her oldest clothing to do the work. She was alone and enjoyed the sound of the bees humming and the birds singing in the trees beside the garden. Work was a pleasure for her—this sort of work anyway—and she hummed a tune as she worked.

"Keturah. . . ."

Turning quickly, Keturah saw Micah, who had come around the corner of the house. She brightened up and started to smile, but then she saw the serious expression on his face and the trouble in his eyes.

"What's the matter, Micah? Is something wrong?"

Coming to stand before the young woman, Micah planted his feet and put his hands behind his back, clasping them together so tightly they ached. He had practiced his speech all the way to the house, and no matter how he put it, it still sounded unkind, and he dreaded what he had to do. Still, he knew that Sam was right.

"Keturah, I've got to talk to you."

"Yes, Micah?"

"I think you ought to know," he said slowly, "I'm in love with Sarah Dennison. I have been, I think, for a long time. She's the woman I love and want to marry." He saw the light die in her eyes, and her lips began to tremble. Desperately he tried to ease her hurt and disappointment, when he knew that was impossible. "I know you . . . think a lot of me, Keturah, and I'm glad of it. But what you feel is gratitude. I was able to do you a service, and I'm so glad I did come along when you needed somebody."

Keturah was riveted to the spot. She fought back the tears that came,

291

and slowly the earth seemed to settle back into place. Quietly she said, "I'm glad you told me, Micah."

Keturah took a deep breath, knowing she had to conceal the hurt that was in her. She also was aware that it would not pass away quickly but would take much time. This was the first man who had ever been kind to her, but she was convinced she felt more than gratitude. Still, Micah had said it plainly, and she could say no more. Finally she swallowed hard and said again, "I'm glad you told me about Miss Dennison."

"Keturah, you mustn't let this hurt you too much."

"All right."

Micah fidgeted, not knowing what else to say. "Anything I can do for you I always will. I hope you know that."

"What about Miss Dennison?"

Micah was suddenly embarrassed. "Well, she's in a bad predicament."

"How's that? You love her, don't you? Does she love you?"

"I think she does."

Curiosity came to Keturah Burns. "Well, what's wrong, then? Why don't you two marry up?"

"She's afraid of offending her parents. They won't give their permission."

Impatience flared in Keturah's eyes. "That's dumb!" she exclaimed. "If she loved you, she'd go with you anyway."

"Well, she feels an obligation to her parents. She's always been an obedient girl. . . ."

"Why don't you do something about it?"

Taken aback by the abruptness of Keturah's question, Micah blinked with surprise. "What do you mean, do something about it? What can I do?"

"Why, go take her. Run off with her!"

"Why, Keturah, I can't kidnap her!"

"*Why* can't you? You love her, don't you? I don't see why you can't kidnap her."

For Keturah this was the complete answer. If the two loved each other, they should let nothing stop them from being together. That had been her life. She had seen little of love, and much of the rougher side of life, but she remembered that there was a gentleness in Sarah Dennison, and she knew there was honor in the man who stood before her. Now she faced him, her chin protruding in a defiant manner. "That's what you have to do, Micah. You have to kidnap her. I'll help you if you want me to."

Micah did not know whether to laugh or cry. He stood there staring at the young woman before him and knew that it was the sort of daring thing she would do. Then another thought came to him, *It's the sort of thing Dake would do, too.* Aloud he said, "Why, I could get put in prison for that, kidnapping someone."

"How old is Miss Dennison?"

"She's twenty-one years old."

"Then she's old enough to go with a man. You're not afraid of her pa, are you?"

"No, I'm not afraid of him. I just don't want to hurt her."

"You're going to hurt her more if you let her die an old maid or marry some man she doesn't love." Micah's face changed, and Keturah saw it. "What'd I say?"

"That's just it, Keturah. They're going to make her marry a man named Potter. He's got a pile of money, and her parents are determined she must have him."

"Well then, that settles it! At least I think it does. Don't you think so, Micah?"

Micah Bradford stood in the shade of the tree, totally unconscious of the mockingbird over in the hedge that was screaming angrily at a scrawny tomcat that was creeping along toward her nest. She waited until he got near, rose in the air with a flash of white wings, and came down like a comet. Striking the tom until he fled, she beat her wings triumphantly and flew back to the nest.

Micah saw none of this, however, but was staring into Keturah's clear blue eyes. A slow smile came to him then. He was slow-moving and slow thinking and slow to make decisions, but now he suddenly reached out and took Keturah by the shoulders. "I think you've got more sense than I ever had!" He held her for a moment, then whirled and ran away.

Watching him go, Keturah felt tears gather in her eyes. "Well," she murmured softly, "I ain't gonna get him." She turned and began driving the stakes into the ground with a rock. She was a hearty young girl and had endured much, but she knew that this blow would not pass away easily. It was the first love of her life, and although Micah had called it gratitude, she knew she had looked at him as a woman looks at a man and she would not forget Micah Bradford quickly.

Ten minutes later she heard her named called and looked up to see Sam, who was coming toward her. He looked slightly pale and troubled, and quickly she tried to erase the grief that was in her face. Sam came to stand before her, and she waited for him to speak. He finally said, "Are you all right, Keturah?"

For some reason Keturah understood immediately what had happened. "Did you have a talk with Micah?"

"Who, me?"

"Yes, you!" Keturah studied the youthful face before her. Sam was too guileless to put on an act, and she immediately understood what he had done. "You did go to him and talk to him, didn't you?"

"Well, I guess maybe I did." Sam shuffled his feet, looked over his shoulder at nothing, and then finally brought his eyes back to meet hers. "I saw you were hurting, Keturah, and—well, I knew how he felt about Sarah, so I told him he had better tell you."

"That was right nice of you, Sam."

Sam studied her carefully, saw the grief in her clear eyes. "I fell off a barn once. Landed on my back," he said. "Knocked all the air out of me. I couldn't do anything for a while. Couldn't move, couldn't breathe, couldn't talk. I got up and walked around and still couldn't do any of those things. It looks to me like that's kind of the way you are, Keturah. Does it hurt that bad?"

"Bad enough." Tears suddenly flooded Keturah's eyes, and without warning she leaned forward and Sam put his arms around her as she fell against his chest. "Yes, it does, Sam. It hurts so bad I can't hardly stand it!"

Sam held her tightly, shocked at the pressure of her youthful body pressed against him. He felt the shaking of her shoulders and patted at her back ineffectually. He had never seen her cry before and knew that it took a lot to do that. Finally the sobs began to subside, and she straightened up and stepped back.

"Well," Keturah said, pulling a handkerchief from her pocket and wiping her tears away, "I guess I'm nothing but a crybaby."

"I wouldn't say that," Sam said, then hesitated. He wanted to help her but knew that a hurting heart would take time to heal. "I'll tell you what," he said. "Let's me and you go down and try out the cannon on the spider catcher. I'll let you shoot off a charge."

"You reckon that'll fix a broken heart, Sam?"

Sam stared at her and saw that she was trying to make a joke. He stepped forward and put his arm around her shoulder and said, "Sure, never known it to fail. Come on now. Let's go."

As the two of them left the garden, Rachel stood at the window watching them and thought, *I wonder what those two are up to now?*

✠   ✠   ✠

Abigail Howland saw at once that Sarah Dennison was terribly disturbed. She had been on her way to the store to buy some meal when

294

she had encountered the young woman walking almost blindly along
the street. One quick look at her assured her that something was troubling Sarah, and she said at once, "What's wrong, Sarah? Are you ill?"

"No. I'm not ill."

"Come along," Abigail commanded imperially. She had a strong
way about her when she chose, and she led Sarah to a bench beside one
of the large houses. It was vacant and no one was in sight, so she said,
"Sit down. Tell me what's wrong."

"Oh, Abigail, I don't know what to think! I don't know what to do!"
She began to relate the incident of Micah's visit to her room, and as she
poured it out, she finally said, "I'm so miserable! I just don't know what
to do!"

Abigail Howland reached over and took Sarah's hand. "I'm not a
wise woman, but I know you'd better find the will of God in this matter.
You can make a mistake about some things, but if you make a mistake
about the man you marry there's no turning back."

"But how can I know God's will?"

"I know it's difficult at times," Abigail said quietly. "It would be
wonderful if God would just speak from heaven or send us a letter. But
He doesn't do that, does He?"

"I've heard of people who spoke of knowing the will of God, but I've
never known how they did it. Do you know the will of God, Abigail,
for your own life?"

"No. Not always. I haven't been a Christian very long, you must
remember. I think if you talk to Rachel she might give you more advice.
Better than I could."

"No. I can't talk to Rachel. She's too close to Micah."

"Sometimes," Abigail said quietly, "I think we know the will of God
simply because the door opens."

"Not always. The door's open for me to marry Mr. Potter, but I can't
believe that's God's will. I don't love him."

"Then if you know that's not God's will," Abigail said quickly,
"that's one step. The next step is very simple. Do you love Micah?"

Sarah bowed her head and closed her eyes. She was silent for a long
time and finally nodded silently. "Yes," she whispered so quietly that
Abigail had to lean forward. "I love him with all my heart. I'm such a
coward, though. I can't go against my parents!"

Abigail had learned to pray short prayers, and now she did. *Oh, God,
help me to give this woman the right advice.* Aloud she began to speak from
her own limited knowledge of the Scriptures on how an individual can
find the will of God. She had a quick, retentive mind and knew many
Scriptures by heart and quoted them one after another. Finally she said

with sorrow tingeing her voice, "I've missed God most of my life and have lived immorally. You know that. But I've given myself to Him now, and I know He has forgiven me and cleansed me. But I know this one thing now. If Matthew ever said he loved me, I'd leave everything I have and go with him. He doesn't love me, but I'll always love him. And now you have a man who loves you, and you say you love him. That to me is the will of God. You remember the story of Ruth and Naomi?"

"Yes, of course."

"Do you remember what she said?"

"She said, 'Entreat me not to leave thee or to return from following after thee. . . . ' I can't remember the rest."

Abigail took Sarah's hand and quoted the old words softly. "For whither thou goest, I will go; and where thou lodgest, I will lodge: thy people shall be my people, and thy God my God: Where thou diest, will I die, and there will I be buried." She hesitated and Abigail saw that Sarah was weeping. "I think that's your answer. If you love Micah, leave everything and go with him. I know this is hard for you. You've always been an obedient, dutiful daughter, but your parents are not greater than God."

Sarah Dennison sat there for a moment trying to keep the tears back. The strain had been terrible for her, and now she clasped at Abigail's hands tightly. Even as she did, a resolve began to form in her heart. It came first as a gentle nudge, just something she knew she must do, then as the enormity of it flooded her heart, fear came also. She looked up and said, "I . . . I want to marry Micah, but I'm afraid."

"God has not given us the spirit of fear, but of power, love, and a sound mind." As Abigail quoted the words she saw a flicker of hope in Sarah's face. She put her arm around her friend and said, "God never gives fear, Sarah. If you obey God, then He will allow nothing evil to happen to you."

"All right!"

Suddenly Sarah Dennison felt a touch of something she had never felt before. She could not define it, but she knew with certainty that her life had come to a moment of decision. She would either choose the man she loved—or she would refuse him and go the way her parents directed and be miserable the rest of her life. Even as fear attempted to rise in her again, she put it down firmly. Her lips were trembling, but she turned with brimming eyes to Abigail and said, "I believe God sent you, Abigail."

"You'll marry Micah?"

"If he asks me, I will!"

⚜   ⚜   ⚜

Abigail was happy, for after she left Sarah she knew somehow that a victory had been won. Her own life was not as she had hoped it to be. She had an ailing mother and no future and a past that people pointed at, but still she was filled with quiet joy as she moved along the street. Finally a thought came to her—one that she rejected instantly. It came back again, so she examined it. It had come to her that perhaps she ought to go to Matthew and once again ask his forgiveness. She had already done so, but she knew she had lost him and he had lost the love he once had for her. She continued to think about the matter for the rest of the afternoon, and finally, when it was almost dusk, she moved resolutely toward Matthew's boardinghouse. She had never called on him here, and when a small lady with sharp brown eyes opened the door, she said, "I'm looking for Mr. Matthew Bradford."

"Come in, ma'am. I'll tell him you're here."

As Abigail stepped inside, she suddenly realized what she was doing. Matthew had already rejected her, fled America, and sailed to Europe to shake off her presence, and here she was again.

Matthew suddenly stepped in through a pair of double doors and stopped abruptly, as if he had run into a wall. His face grew pale, and he bowed jerkily, saying, "Abigail, I'm surprised to see you."

"Matthew, could I speak with you for a moment?"

For just an instant Abigail thought he meant to refuse her, but then he seemed to shrug and said, "The parlor's over here. I think we can be alone there." He stepped toward a door, moved back, and allowed her to pass. It was a small parlor with blue wallpaper and well-worn horsehide furniture. "Will you sit down?" he said.

"No. I won't take much of your time."

Matthew was studying Abigail carefully. He was disgusted with himself, for he could not control the feelings that rose up in him. He had loved her for a long time, until he had found out about her agreement with Leo Rochester to use him. Now, even as he saw that she had changed, he hardened his heart and said, "What is it?"

"I know this is hard for you, Matthew. It's . . . it's hard for me, too. But I had to try one more time." She stood before him, her oval face pale, her eyes open wide. She was wearing a simple dress, unlike the ornate dresses she had worn at one time. She was a beautiful woman who had the power to stir him at any time, even though now she was not trying to do so. Yet Matthew felt himself drawn toward her.

"Well, what is it?" he said, deliberately making his voice sharp.

"I came to tell you one more time that I was wrong to agree with your father to betray you. I have no excuse, but I want to tell you one more thing."

"And that is?" Matthew was stirred by her honest words. There was such an innocence in her face, yet still he had been so badly hurt by her behavior he could not allow himself to lower his guard.

"I just wanted to say how much I love you, Matthew. That's all."

Matthew Bradford was a sensitive man. He had loved this woman with his whole heart at one time, and now as she stood before him, he knew there was still something in him for her that he would never feel for any other woman. He remembered the touch of her lips under his, and how she had melted against him. Night after night he had thought of her in this way, and now as she said the simple words of love, a powerful longing surged through him and he almost stepped forward to take her in his arms, but he could not. A stubborn willfulness that had grown over the months stopped him, and he said bitterly, "It's very easy for you, isn't it?" He began to pace the floor like a caged animal. "I must have been very easy for you to deceive, but then you've had a lot of practice, haven't you? You've always known how to handle men!"

Abigail did not move. She kept her back straight and her eyes fixed on Matthew as he paced back and forth. All that he said was true, but each word entered her like a sword, and she knew great bitterness and despair.

Finally he came to her and took her by both arms and shook her, anger in his voice. "How could you have treated me so, Abigail?" Then despite himself he put his arms around her and pressed his lips against hers. It was not a kiss of love, but one to show his disdain. He hurt Abigail and was glad of it. And when he stepped back, he said, "I'll never trust you, Abigail—or any other woman ever again!"

Whirling, Matthew left the room, and Abigail reached up and touched her lips with trembling fingers. He had hurt her, not only her flesh but her spirit. Blindly she made her way out of the house, and as she moved away, the thought came as if it were carved in solid marble, *I'll never have the man I love—never!*

24

A TIME TO LOVE

DUSK HAD GATHERED OVER BOSTON, and as Micah moved with resolution down the street toward the Dennison home his jaw was clenched tight. He had gone to his room after his talk with Keturah, fallen on his knees, and prayed for guidance as he had never prayed before. All day long he had prayed and sought God, and now as he moved along with long strides, there was a firmness and a determination etched in every line of his body.

Reaching the Dennison house, he walked up the steps without hesitation. A brass door knocker was there, and he firmly grasped it and banged three times as hard as he could. He stood waiting, and when the door opened he saw the maid whose name he had forgotten. "I'm here to see Miss Dennison and her parents," he announced firmly.

The maid stared at him almost with fear. Along with all the other servants, she knew secrets of the Dennisons, and had said once to the cook, "Miss Sarah is going to have to make up her mind about that young Bradford gentleman. She's in love with him. No doubt about it."

"Yes, sir. Come in, Mr. Bradford. I'll announce you."

Stepping inside, Micah waited, and a calmness seemed to fall upon him. The decision was made—at least as far as he was concerned. Now it would be up to Sarah. He heard a slight sound and turned to see Sarah had appeared at the end of the hallway. She stood there shocked, but then something seemed to move across her face and she came toward him.

When she got to him, she reached her hands out and Micah took them. He kissed them and said huskily, "Sarah, I had to come."

"I'm glad you did, Micah."

"You are?" Micah stared at her with shock. He saw something in her face, in her expression, that he had never seen before. Her clear eyes had always had something furtive in them, as if she were fearfully waiting for someone to correct her. But now she had lost that. Her smile was relaxed as she said, "Yes, I'm glad that you're here."

At that moment Mrs. Dennison stepped into the foyer. She took one look at Bradford and said instantly, "Mr. Bradford, you've been asked not to come to this house!"

"I think you'd better call your husband, Mrs. Dennison," Micah said. He settled back on his heels and realized that he was still holding Sarah's hand. He smiled easily and held on to one of her hands with both of his. "I think we have some talking to do."

Mrs. Helen Dennison was not accustomed to being crossed. An imperious answer rose, but the stern set in Micah Bradford's eyes gave her pause. She turned to Sarah and said instead, "Sarah, you will go to your room, please. I will deal with this."

"No, Mother. You will not."

Helen Dennison stared blankly at her daughter. For the first time in twenty-one years this young woman had refused to obey a command. Unable to speak for a moment, anger swept over her and then Mrs. Dennison said, "Very well. I will call your father."

"I think that would be best, Mother."

As her mother left the room, walking rapidly down the hall and turning into the library, Sarah turned and put her other hand on Micah's. "Are you ready to be crucified?" she asked. "I think Papa will be ready to shoot you."

"Let him fire away! You're worth it, Sarah!"

"Do you really think so, Micah?"

"Yes. Are you ready to face them and tell them you're marrying me?"

"Yes, I am."

Micah stared at her. "What's happened to you? I've never seen you like this."

Sarah would have answered, but at that moment her parents stepped out into the hall. Mr. Thomas Dennison led the way, with his wife right behind. "Sir," he said, "get out of my house!"

"I will be most happy to, but I don't want to go behind your back. Sarah has agreed to be my wife, and I would like for us to maintain a good relationship."

"She will not marry you! I've told you that! She's engaged to Silas Potter!"

"Papa, it pains me to do this," Sarah said quietly. She removed her hands from Micah's grip and went over to her father. She stood before him and met his eyes evenly. "I've always obeyed you, but it would be wrong for me to marry a man I did not love. I haven't been able to make you understand this. I love Micah, and I'm going to marry him."

"He has nothing!"

"That's true, Sarah," Micah spoke up. "I love you, but I have no money and no prospects for making very much in the future." He lifted his eyes and spoke firmly, locking gazes with Mr. Dennison. "I'm going to be a minister of the gospel, a poor one probably. I'm not a good catch if a life of leisure is what you want for Sarah. Nevertheless, I love your daughter with all my heart, and she will never know anything but love from me."

Micah's words seemed to stun Thomas Dennison. He exchanged a nervous glance with his wife, who, for once in her life, was willing to let her husband handle the problem. Clearing his throat, Dennison said, "Well, sir, what do you expect me to say to that?"

"I expect you to invite me in and get to know me better. I expect you to show love for your daughter, whose life would be ruined if she married a man she didn't love. That is what I would expect from a gentleman and a loving father, and a loving mother."

Surprisingly, it was Helen Dennison who spoke first. She watched her husband change color several times, it seemed, and then said, "Come into the drawing room, Mr. Bradford."

Sarah said, "Mother, we will be glad to come into the drawing room, but Micah will be your son-in-law. You can receive him as such or you can refuse to speak to him, in which case you will never see me until you do. Whichever you do, he will be my husband."

The words seemed to strike against both Helen and Thomas Dennison. Perhaps it was the shock of being challenged. Certainly the pride that was in their daughter, her eyes flashing, impressed both of them.

Mrs. Dennison could not speak for a moment, then finally she said, "Come in, then, and let us talk about it, Sarah." She hesitated and then forced herself to say, "And you too, Micah."

Sarah knew with a burst of joy that the battle was won! When her mother used Micah's given name for the first time, she sensed the victory. Going back to Micah, she took his arm and said, "Come along. I want you to get to know my parents. They're going to love you, Micah."

Half an hour later Micah and Sarah stepped outside of the Dennison house and the door closed behind them. They walked down the street arm in arm, and Micah said, "It wasn't as bad as I expected. They still don't like me much."

"You don't know what a victory it is. My parents have never changed their minds about *anything*," Sarah said with wonder. She stopped and turned toward him. "Give them time," she pleaded. "They will never love you as much as I do, but I could tell they respect you."

Micah Bradford was unaware of his surroundings. He looked into the eyes of Sarah Dennison and saw his whole world there. "It's going to be difficult. There's a war on, and I may have to serve in the army. And after the war I'll have to be educated for the ministry. And even then there will be no money, or very little."

Sarah reached up and put her hands on his cheeks. She held them there, and a quiet joy filled her heart. "You know, that doesn't matter, because I have the one thing I want."

"What's that?"

"A man who loves me." Sarah pulled his head down, and her lips were soft under his. She held him for a moment, and then pushed him back abruptly, and a sudden humor danced in her eyes. "Do you know what we're going to have, Micah?"

"What, Sarah?"

"We're going to have—ten children! Five boys and five girls."

Micah Bradford reached out, picked her up, and swung her around, uncaring of who saw. Putting her down again, he said, "Yes, ten's just about the right number for a poor preacher. Come along, now, and we'll try to think of some names. How about Melchizedek for the first boy?"

"No, I like Mephibosheth better!"

The two walked down the street and Sarah's laughter was soft. She held Micah's hand tightly, for she knew she had found the man whom God had given her.